PENGUIN BOOKS

SECRETS

D1053858

Secrets

LESLEY PEARSE

PENGUIN BOOKS

PENGUIN BOOKS

Published by the Penguin Group

Penguin Books Ltd, 80 Strand, London WC2R ORL, England

Penguin Group (USA) Inc., 375 Hudson Street, New York, New York 10014, USA

Penguin Group (Canada), 10 Alcorn Avenue, Toronto, Ontario, Canada M4V 3B2
(a division of Pearson Penguin Canada Inc.)

Penguin Ireland, 25 St Stephen's Green, Dublin 2, Ireland
(a division of Penguin Books Ltd)

Penguin Group (Australia), 250 Camberwell Road, Camberwell, Victoria 3124, Australia
(a division of Pearson Australia Group Pty Ltd)

Penguin Books India Pvt Ltd, 11 Community Centre, Panchsheel Park, New Delhi – 110 017, India

Penguin Group (NZ), cnr Airborne and Rosedale Roads, Albany, Auckland 1310, New Zealand
(a division of Pearson New Zealand Ltd)

Penguin Books (South Africa) (Pty) Ltd, 24 Sturdee Avenue, Rosebank 2196, South Africa

Penguin Books Ltd, Registered Offices: 80 Strand, London WC2R ORL, England

www.penguin.com

Published by Michael Joseph 2004
Published in Penguin Books 2005

13

Copyright © Lesley Pearse, 2004
All rights reserved

The moral right of the author has been asserted

Typeset by Rowland Phototypesetting Ltd, Bury St Edmunds, Suffolk
Printed in England by Clays Ltd, St Ives plc

ISBN-13: 978–0–141–01696–2

To my father, Geoffrey Arthur Sargent, who died in 1980, too soon to see me become a published writer. I chose to set *Secrets* in Rye because it was his home town and he loved it.

Also to my uncle, Bert Sargent, who remained living in Rye until his death in 2002. Some of my best childhood memories were of holidays spent there with him, my aunt Dorothy and my cousins.

I read too many books in my research to name them all, but the most noteworthy ones were: *Fighter Boys* by Patrick Bishop; *The London Blitz, a Fireman's Tale* by Cyril Demarne OBE; and *London at War* by Philip Ziegler. And extra special thanks to Geoffrey Wellum DSO, for his inspiring book *First Light*, his story of his time as a fighter pilot in the Battle of Britain. A big thank-you to William Third for digging out information on Hastings and Winchelsea. You were always a dear friend, now you qualify as a researcher too.

Part I

Chapter One

Adele had a stitch from running by the time she reached Euston Road. She was late for collecting Pamela, her eight-year-old sister, from her piano lesson on the other side of the busy main road. Aside from the darkness and the usual six o'clock heavy traffic, crossing the road was made even more hazardous by the lumps of blackened ice in the gutters from a fall of snow a few days previously.

Adele Talbot was twelve – small, thin, pale-faced and waif-like in a worn adult tweed coat many sizes too large for her, woollen socks fallen to her ankles and a knitted pixie hood covering her straggly brown hair. Yet despite her still tender years, there was an adult expression of anxiety in her wide, greenish-brown eyes as she hopped from foot to foot impatiently watching for a break in the traffic. Her father was supposed to have collected Pamela on his way home from work but he forgot, and Adele was frightened that her little sister might have got tired of waiting for him and set off for home on her own.

Poised on the kerb, panting from her run, she suddenly spotted Pamela through the traffic. There was no mistaking her – the street lights picked up her long blonde hair and her vivid red coat. To Adele's dismay she wasn't just waiting either, but hovering on the kerb, as if intending to cross on her own.

'Stay there!' Adele yelled out, waving her arms frantically. 'Wait for me.'

Several more buses came past in close succession, preventing Adele from seeing what her sister was doing, and suddenly there was an ominous squeal of brakes.

Heart in mouth, Adele darted out between a bus and a lorry. As she reached the centre of the road her worst fears were realized: her little sister was lying crumpled on the ground between a car and a taxi.

Adele screamed. All the traffic stopped abruptly, steam rising like smoke from the bonnets of cars. Pedestrians halted, gasping in shocked horror; everyone was looking at the small mound in the road.

'Pamela!' Adele yelled out as she ran to her, terror, disbelief and absolute horror enveloping her. The taxi driver, a big man with a fat belly, had got out of his cab and was now staring down at the child between his front wheels. 'She just ran out!' he exclaimed, looking round wildly for assistance. 'I couldn't help it.'

People were already crowding around and Adele had to push and shove to get through them. 'Don't touch her, luv,' someone said warningly as she finally got right into the circle and crouched down beside her sister.

'She's my little sister,' Adele gasped, tears streaming down her wind-whipped cheeks. 'She's supposed to wait until she's met. Will she be all right?'

Yet even as Adele asked the question, she sensed that Pamela was already dead. Her blue eyes were open wide, her expression startled, but there was no movement or sound, not even a grimace of pain.

Adele heard someone say an ambulance had been called and a man stepped forward, felt Pamela's pulse and removed his coat to place it over her. But he shook his head as he did so. That, and the stricken faces of everyone gathered round, confirmed her fears.

She wanted to scream, to pummel the taxi driver responsible. Yet at the same time she couldn't believe Pamela's life was over. Everyone had loved her, she was so bright and funny, and she was too young to die.

Leaning over her sister, Adele smoothed Pamela's hair

back from her face and sobbed out her shock and heartbreak.

A woman in a fur hat took hold of her round her waist and drew her away. 'Where do you live, sweetheart?' she asked, holding her tightly against her chest and making a comforting rocking movement. 'Are your mum and dad at home?'

Adele didn't know how she replied, all she was aware of in that moment was the rasp of the woman's coat against her cheek, and the feeling she was going to be sick.

But she must have answered her questions before she broke free to vomit by the kerb, for later, after the arrival of the ambulance and the police, she heard the same woman informing them that the sister of the child who had been run over was Adele Talbot and she lived at 47 Charlton Street.

Yet in the time until the police and the ambulance arrived, Adele wasn't aware of the faces of those around her, what they said to her, or even the biting cold wind. She felt only her own anguish, saw only the golden glow of street lights picking out Pamela's blonde hair fluttering in the wind on the black, wet road, and heard only the noise of car horns honking impatiently.

Euston belonged to her and Pamela. Maybe to others it was the dirty and dangerous hub of London which people were forced to pass through on their way to other safer and more attractive parts of the city, but to Adele it had always felt as harmless as a park. Charlton Street was right between Euston and St Pancras, and the railway stations were like her personal theatres, the passengers characters in a drama. She was always taking Pamela into them, particularly when it was cold or wet, and she would make up stories about the people they saw there to entertain her. A woman in a fur coat, tripping alongside a porter carrying her big suitcases, was a countess. A young couple kissing passionately were eloping. Sometimes they saw children travelling alone with a label pinned to their coat, and Adele would make up some fantastic adventure story involving wicked stepmothers, castles in Scotland and treasure chests full of money.

At home there was always an atmosphere. Their mother would sit for hours in sullen silence, barely acknowledging her children or her husband's presence. She had always been the same, so Adele just accepted it, but had learned to read the danger signs which preceded the eruptions of wild rage and got herself and Pamela out of there as quickly as possible. These rages could be terrifying, for their mother would fling anything that came to hand, scream abuse and more often than not lash out at Adele.

Adele tried to convince herself that the reason the full force of her mother's anger was always directed at her, rather than Pamela, was just because she was the elder. But deep down she knew it was because Mum hated her for some reason.

Pamela had sensed it too, and she had always tried to make up for it. If she got any money from their mother she always shared it with Adele. When she got her new red coat for Christmas she'd been embarrassed because Adele hadn't got one too. In her little way she'd done her best to make amends. With her sunny smile, her generosity and sense of fun, Pamela had made Adele's life bearable.

Now, as she stood there crying helplessly, wanting an adult to put their arms around her and reassure her Pamela wasn't dead, merely unconscious, Adele was all too aware that if her sister was really gone for good, then she might as well be dead too.

A burly young policeman took Adele's hand as Pamela was lifted into the ambulance. As they laid her on the stretcher, they put the blanket right over her face; unspoken confirmation that she was really dead.

'I'm so sorry,' the policeman said gently, then bent down so his face was on her level. 'I'm PC Mitchell,' he went on. 'Me and the Sergeant will take you home in a minute, we have to tell your mum and dad about the accident, and get you to tell us exactly what happened.'

It was only then that Adele became afraid for herself. From the moment she'd heard the squeal of car brakes, her mind had been centred entirely on Pamela. All her thoughts and emotions were single-track, nothing else existed but her sister's little body on the ground and what they were to each other. But at the mention of her parents, Adele was suddenly terrified.

'I c-c-can't go home,' she blurted out, clutching the policeman's hand in fear. 'They'll say it was my fault.'

'Of course they won't,' PC Mitchell said disbelievingly, and rubbed her cold hand in his two big ones. 'Accidents like this can happen to anyone, you're only a kid yourself.'

'If I'd just been a bit quicker,' she sobbed out. His big kindly face full of concern for her was only a further reminder of how little her parents cared for her. 'I ran all the way, but she was already by the road when I got up here.'

'Your mum and dad will understand,' he said, and patted her shoulder.

The ambulance drove off then, and the crowd began to disperse. Only the taxi driver was left talking to the two policemen as Adele waited. Everything went back to normal so quickly, cars now driving over the very spot where Pamela had lain just minutes before, the onlookers fading away to go to the pub, catch a bus or buy the evening paper. For them it was just an incident, a sad one maybe, but they would have forgotten it before they even reached their homes.

Adele had been aware right from when she was very small that Euston was a place of huge inequality. The stations, those vast and magnificent buildings, presided over the neighbourhood like towering cathedrals, employing hundreds of people. Those wealthy enough to travel relied on the labours of the poor to make their journeys comfortable and enjoyable.

The railway workers lived in the mean, dirty streets around the station. A porter might know the times of every single train, each stop and halt from London to Edinburgh, and he would strain his back and arms each day carrying heavy luggage. Yet he would never visit any of those places whose names tripped off his tongue so effortlessly. If he managed to take his wife and children for a day at the seaside he'd consider himself fortunate. Likewise, the maid who changed the beds in the smart hotels where the travellers stayed probably had no sheets on her own bed, let alone an indoor lavatory or a real bath.

Adele had so often watched the rich collide with the poor around here. An elegant lady in a fox fur buying flowers from a ragged old soldier with only one leg. A gentleman in a gleaming car signalling impatiently for the dwarf who sold newspapers to bring him one. Adele knew the dwarf lived in an archway under the railway. She had seen the old soldier doff his cap and smile at his customers even though he was frozen with the cold and tottering on his crutches. When the business people left their offices to go home to the leafy suburbs, out came the poor to clean up after them.

Yet Adele had always vowed to Pamela that there was something better in store for them. She had spun her stories of them living in a posh part of London, and how one day they'd visit all those destinations they saw on boards in the stations. But now, as she waited to go home, without her sister, all those dreams and ambitions were gone for good.

The taxi driver got into his cab, and for a moment he looked at Adele as if wanting to say something to her. But maybe he was too shaken himself to speak, and he drove off as the two policemen came back to her.

'It's time to go now,' PC Mitchell said. Then, taking her hand firmly in his, he led her off towards the police car.

Adele had never been in a car before, but just that was a

further painful reminder of Pamela. Her favourite game had been to put two chairs one behind the other to make an imaginary car in which she was always the driver, and Adele the passenger who decided where to go.

The Talbots had three small rooms on the top floor of a terraced house in Charlton Street. The Mannings lived beneath them with their four children, the Pattersons and their three children on the ground floor.

As in most of the streets in the area, the front door opened straight on to the pavement, but unlike most of the others the house was occupied by only three families and had the luxury of a shared bathroom and inside lavatory.

The front door was shut because it was so cold, and Adele put her hand through the letter box and pulled out the key. She looked back at the policemen before she used it. The younger one, who had said he was taking her home and introduced himself as PC Mitchell, was blowing on his fingers to warm them. The older one, whom Mitchell had called Sarge, was standing further back from the house, looking up. They both looked apprehensive, and that made Adele even more frightened.

As they mounted the stairs to the top flat, Adele saw the building as the policemen must and felt ashamed. It was so dirty and smelly, bare wood on the stairs and the distemper on the walls so old it had no real colour. As always there was a great deal of noise, the Mannings' baby yelling blue murder and the other children shouting over the top of it.

The door to the top flat was flung open before they reached it, presumably because her parents had heard the sound of men's feet on the stairs. Adele's mother, Rose, looked down at them, her face contorting when she saw the uniformed men and Adele. 'Where's Pammy?' she burst out. 'Don't tell me something's happened to her?'

Adele had always thought of her mother as beautiful, even when she was miserable and nasty. Yet in that moment, with the light from the living room behind her, she saw her as she really was. Not a golden-haired beauty with an hour-glass figure, but a tired, worn woman of thirty, with a sagging body, muddy complexion and bedraggled hair. The pinafore she wore over her skirt and jumper was stained and torn, and her slippers, brown checked ones, had holes in the toes.

'Can we come in, Mrs Talbot?' the sergeant asked her. 'You see, there's been an accident.'

Rose let out a terrible shriek, taking Adele by surprise. Her mouth just dropped open and out came the noise like a runaway train.

All at once Dad was there too in the doorway, demanding to know what was going on, and all the while Adele and the policemen were still standing on the stairs, and down below people were opening doors to see what was going on.

'She's dead, isn't she?' her mother screamed, her eyes closing up till they were just two slits. 'Who did it? How did it happen?'

The policemen almost pushed their way into the flat then, PC Mitchell nudging Adele in ahead of him. The room was both kitchen and living room. It smelled of frying and the washing drying round the fire, and the table was laid for tea. The sergeant made Rose sit down in an armchair and he gently began to explain what had happened.

'But where was Adele? She was supposed to collect her,' Rose interrupted, looking daggers at her elder daughter. 'Why did she let Pammy run across the road?'

Adele had expected to be blamed, purely because she always was, whatever went wrong. Yet a small part of her had clung to the hope that with something as awful as this, the usual system would be bypassed.

'I ran all the way to get her, but she was already trying to cross Euston Road when I got there,' Adele said frantically, tears running down her face. 'I called out for her to stop, but I don't think she saw or heard me.'

'And she was hit by a car?' Rose asked, looking up at the sergeant, her eyes begging to be told this wasn't so. 'And she was killed? My beautiful Pammy is dead?'

The sergeant nodded, looking to Jim Talbot for help. But he was slumped in his chair, his hands over his face.

'Mr Talbot.' The sergeant touched him on the shoulder. 'We are so sorry. An ambulance arrived within minutes, but it was too late.'

Adele watched her dad take his hands from his face. He looked towards her and for a brief moment she thought he was going to beckon to her to come to him for comfort. But instead his face contorted into a scowl. 'Too late,' he roared out, and pointed his finger at her. 'You were too late to collect Pammy, and now she's dead because you were too bloody idle to get a move on.'

'Come on!' the sergeant said reprovingly. 'It wasn't Adele's fault, she wasn't to know Pamela would try to cross the road alone. It was an accident. Don't blame her, she's only a child herself, and she's in shock.'

Adele remained standing by the door, too stunned and stricken even to find a seat. She felt she had no business to be there, like a neighbour who'd come in to borrow some sugar and wouldn't leave.

This feeling grew even stronger as the two policemen tried to comfort her parents, calling them Rose and Jim as if they had known them a long time. PC Mitchell made a pot of tea and poured it; the sergeant picked up a photo of Pamela from the mantelpiece and remarked what a pretty girl she was. Her father cuddled her mother to him and both policemen tutted in sympathy as they were told how clever Pamela was.

But no one turned to Adele, not after the sergeant had given her a cup of tea. It was as though she'd become invisible to everyone.

Maybe she only stood there for five or ten minutes, but it

seemed like for ever. It felt as though she was watching a play and was hidden from the actors' view by the spotlights. She could see, hear and feel their shock and grief, but they were completely oblivious to her pain.

She so much wanted someone to hold her in their arms, to tell her it was not her fault and that Pamela had been told dozens of times that she was never to cross Euston Road alone.

After a bit Adele sat down on a small stool by the door and put her head on her knees. The adults all had their backs to her, and even though she knew this was mostly because of how the chairs were arranged, it felt deliberate. While Adele could agree wholeheartedly with everything that was said about her sister, how she was liked by everyone, top of the class, a sunny little girl who had special qualities, it seemed to her that her parents were pointing out that her elder sister was just the opposite, and it was unjust that she should be the one they were left with.

The talking and crying went on and on, round and round. Rose would get hysterical, then calm herself to relate yet another instance when Pamela was extra special, then Jim would butt in with his views. And in between her parents' voices there were the two policemen's calm, measured tones. Young and inexperienced as Adele was, she could sense their skill at dealing with grief, maintaining just the right amount of interest, care and sympathy, yet gradually trying to bring the couple to the point where they would accept their daughter was dead.

While she was touched they had enough compassion to do this, a small part of her very much wished she dared point out to them that Jim Talbot's favourite words to both his daughters had always been 'Shut up, can't you.' That he was the one who was supposed to collect Pamela, and forgot. She also wondered if the policemen would be as sympathetic to Rose if they knew she was mostly too morose to get out of bed in the mornings. Adele had always given Pamela her breakfast and taken her to school.

'Would you like us to take you to see Pamela?' the sergeant asked some time later. Rose was still crying helplessly, but not in the hysterical way she had been earlier. 'She has to be formally identified, and it might help you to see that she died instantly and that there are no visible injuries.'

Adele had remained silently on her stool all this time, lost in her misery, but when she heard that question she came to with a jolt. 'Can I come too?' she asked impulsively.

All four adult faces turned to her. Both policemen looked merely surprised, they had clearly forgotten she was still in the room. But her parents looked affronted at Adele's request.

'Why, you little ghoul,' her mother exploded, getting up as if to strike her. 'It isn't a freak show. Our baby is dead because of you.'

'Now, now, Rose,' the sergeant said, moving between mother and daughter. 'Adele didn't mean it like that, I'm sure. She's upset too.'

Sergeant Mike Cotton wished he was anywhere but 47 Charlton Street. In twenty-odd years of police service he'd been called hundreds of times to inform next of kin of a death, and it was always a painful duty. Yet when it was a child's death it was a hideous task, for there were no words that could soothe the pain, nothing that could justify a healthy child being cut down without warning. But this was one of the worst cases he'd known, for the moment Rose Talbot opened the door, and Adele didn't rush into her arms, he knew there was something badly wrong within the family.

All the time he was explaining how the accident happened, he had been very aware of Adele still standing by the door. He so much wanted to call her over, sit her on his knee and comfort her, but that should have been the father's job. Just as it should have been him who went to collect his small daughter on a dark, cold January night. Euston Road was not the sort of area any young girl should be out in alone. Every kind of scum hung around there – beggars, prostitutes and their pimps, men looking for a woman, thieves watching out for anyone to rob.

Mike had to admit that the Talbots were a slight cut above most of their neighbours in this street. He knew families of eight or ten crowded into one room, where survival depended on the mother being wily and strong enough to wrench some money for food from her husband's hands before he spent his wages in the pub. He knew others that rooted about in filth like animals, and some where the mother turned the kids out into the streets at night while she earned money to feed them lying on her back.

The Talbots' flat might be shabby but it was clean and warm, and an evening meal was prepared. Jim Talbot was still in work too, despite the financial depression which was slowly strangling the country.

Mike thought that Rose Talbot was almost certainly from middle-class stock: she spoke correct English even if it was peppered with London slang, and she had a refined manner. He had noted that despite his shocking news, she had still quickly removed her pinafore and run her fingers through her untidy hair, as if ashamed of being caught unprepared for visitors. Her skirt and jumper were clearly from a market stall, yet the subdued shade of blue enhanced her lovely eyes and gave her a surprisingly stylish air.

Jim, in contrast, was from the bottom of the social scale. Although tall and slender, he had that give-away stoop and awkwardness which always seemed to go with products of London slums. His London accent had a kind of nasal whine to it, and with his bad teeth, thinning sandy hair and washed-out blue eyes, he looked prematurely middle-aged, even though he was just thirty-two. He wasn't the brightest of men either, for when Mike had asked him how secure his job was, he didn't appear to understand the question. Why would an attractive and well-bred woman like Rose marry a man like Jim?

Yet if the parents were ill matched, there was an even greater disparity between how they felt about their two children. There were several photographs of Pamela on display on the sideboard, and one of her paintings pinned on the wall, but there was nothing of Adele. Mike had noticed that Pamela had been wearing a good warm coat, she had mittens on her hands, and she was prettily plump. Adele, in contrast, was very thin and pasty-faced and her coat was an old adult hand-me-down. The coat wasn't necessarily hers, it could be that she had grabbed her mother's to run out in. But he didn't think so, for looking at Adele now under a bright light, she seemed malnourished. Her stringy, mousy hair had no shine to it, and her navy blue school gym slip, like the coat, was far too big for her.

Her appearance meant little in an area where there were hundreds of girls of a similar age even more shabbily dressed and ill fed. Yet Mike was pretty certain that all their mothers, even those who were drunken sluts, would be unable to ignore a child so obviously in need of a little comfort and tenderness.

The girl had just witnessed something even the most hardened policeman would want to weep over, so surely Rose, however traumatized, could manage to put her own emotions on hold long enough to reach out for her elder child?

Adele felt a sense of relief when her parents finally left with the policemen, ordering her to bed. But the moment she went into the icy-cold bedroom and saw the bed she had always shared with Pamela, she began to cry again. She was never again going to feel her sister's warm little body snuggled up tight against her, gone were the whispered night-time conversations, the giggling and all the little confidences. She'd lost the only person she could always count on for affection.

She couldn't really remember anything before Pamela was born. The farthest back her mind could stretch was to a pram, too big for her to push, and the cot, with a baby in it which she had thought much better than a doll. They had lived somewhere else then, a basement flat she thought, but she could remember moving into this place, because Pamela was just beginning to walk and she had to watch she didn't try to go down the stairs.

Dozens of memories came flooding back as she lay scrunched up in a ball, shivering and crying. Of pushing Pamela on the swings, drawing pictures for her, telling her stories and teaching her to skip out on the road.

She had always known Mum and Dad liked Pamela more than her. They laughed when she said wrong words, they let her into bed with them, she got larger helpings of food. Pamela hardly ever got secondhand clothes and shoes, and Adele never had new.

Pamela's piano lessons were the only thing Adele had ever felt jealous about. She'd accepted all the other unfairness because Pamela was the baby of the family, and she loved her too. But the piano was different – Pamela had never shown the slightest interest in playing any instrument. She said she wanted to dance, to ride a horse and swim, but didn't care about music. Adele did, and although she'd never dared ask outright for lessons, she'd hinted about them hundreds of times.

Adele knew only too well that England was in the grip of something called a 'Slump'. Every week the queues of men looking for work grew longer and longer. Adele had seen a soup kitchen open in King's Cross, families down the street being turned out of their homes because they couldn't pay the rent. Her father might still be in work, but she knew he too might lose his job at any time, so of course she didn't really expect a luxury like piano lessons.

Then out of the blue her mother announced that Pamela was to go to Mrs Belling in Cartwright Gardens for lessons every Thursday afternoon.

Adele knew this was to spite her, for what other reason was there when Pamela didn't want to go? Only a couple of weeks ago she'd told Adele she really hated the lessons and that Mrs Belling had said it was pointless teaching her when she didn't have a piano at home to practise on. Now she was dead because of it.

Adele heard her parents come back later. She could hear their voices, if not what they were saying, and her mother's alternated between a kind of sobbing sorrow and a whine of bitterness. Her father's was more constant, an angry rasp, now and then punctuated by a thump on the table with his fist.

Adele guessed they were drinking, and that was even more worrying, for it usually made them argue. She wanted to get up and go to the lavatory, but she didn't dare for it meant going through the living room.

She wondered if she would be expected to go to school in the morning. Most children she knew were kept home when there was a death in their family, but then her mother wasn't like other girls' mothers.

Sometimes Adele felt proud of the differences, for in many respects Rose Talbot was superior. She looked after her appearance, she didn't shout or swear out in the street like so many of their neighbours. She kept the flat clean and tidy, and there was always a hot dinner every night, not bread and dripping like so many other children round here got.

But Adele would've preferred mess if it made her mother happy and affectionate, the way other mothers were. She rarely laughed, she didn't even chatter, she never wanted to go out anywhere, not even to Regent's Park in the summer. It was as though she chose to be miserable because it was a good way to spoil things for everyone else.

Eventually Adele knew she'd have to go to the lavatory, or she'd wet the bed. She opened the door very quietly, hoping against hope she could just slip out down the stairs without being noticed.

'What do you want?' Rose snapped at her.

Adele explained and went straight out of the front door before anything further could be said.

With just her nightdress and bare feet, it was freezing on the stairs. The lavatory smelled bad again and it made her heave. Mum was always moaning about Mrs Manning never taking a turn to clean it, in fact she thought she should do it twice as often as she had twice as many children. In the last row about it, Mrs Manning threatened to knock Mum's block off. She said she was a stuck-up cow who thought her own shit didn't stink.

As she got back into the flat again, Adele hesitated. Her parents were sitting either side of the fire in the armchairs, both with a drink in their hands, and they looked so sad she felt she had to say something.

'I'm really sorry I couldn't get up there quicker,' she blurted out. 'I did run all the way.'

Her father looked round first. 'It couldn't be 'elped,' he said sadly.

For one brief second Adele thought they'd both come round, but she was badly mistaken. Without any warning an empty beer bottle came hurtling at her, catching her on the forehead, then falling to the floor and smashing on the lino. 'Get out of my sight, you little bastard,' her mother screamed. 'I never wanted you, and now you've killed my baby.'

Chapter Two

'I don't want her at the funeral,' Rose Talbot snapped at her husband.

Alarmed, Jim looked up from cleaning his shoes. He had anticipated Rose might start shouting at him for cleaning them on the table, so he'd put newspaper down first. But he hadn't for one moment expected that with less than two hours to go to the funeral, she would find something further to be difficult about.

'Why?' Jim asked nervously. 'Because she's too young?' Rose had been making him very nervous ever since Pamela's death. Her grief he understood – most days he wished he could die too and be rid of this terrible ache inside him. Having to wait two weeks for a coroner's report before the funeral had made it even worse, stringing out the misery, but he didn't understand why she was being so savage to Adele.

'If you want to tell everyone else it's because she's too young, do so,' Rose retorted, flouncing away across the living room. 'But it's not the reason. I just don't want her there.'

'Now look here,' Jim began, thinking he must be tough and stop all this before it got out of hand. 'Pammy was her sister, she ought to be there. People will talk.'

Rose turned and gave him a long, cold stare. 'Let them. I don't care,' she said defiantly.

Jim did what he always did when Rose was being difficult, let it go, and finished polishing his shoes till they shone like glass. Maybe he ought to be tougher, but he was very aware that Rose didn't love him as he loved her, and he was afraid to go against her.

'If that's what you want,' he said weakly after a couple of seconds' thought.

Rose stormed off into their bedroom, afraid that if she stayed near Jim another minute she'd blurt out how she felt about him too. She pulled the curlers out of her hair angrily, and as she picked up her hair brush and moved to the mirror, what she saw made her feel even more angry.

Everything about her sagged, both her face and body. She supposed she was still attractive in most people's eyes, but in her own she was like an overblown rose, the petals on the point of falling.

Putting her hands on either side of her face, she pulled the skin back tighter. Instantly her jaw was firmer and the lines around her mouth disappeared, evoking memories of how she had once looked. She had been a head-turner, with her perfect figure, pouting lips, beautiful blonde hair and skin like porcelain, and if she'd made a good marriage to a wealthy man, maybe she'd still look that way now.

But fate had conspired against her all the way down the line. All the suitable young men went off to war when she was just thirteen, and of the few that came back, most were spoken for, or else damaged the way her father was.

Thirty wasn't so very old, but there was no way of changing her life now, any more than there was of arresting her fading beauty.

She had married Jim in desperation because she was pregnant with Adele. She saw him as a temporary refuge, believing that after the baby was born something better would turn up. But instead she'd landed herself in a trap.

It was bitter irony that Pamela's arrival four years later had changed her view of her marriage for a while. The last thing she'd wanted was to be burdened with another child. Yet she had loved her from the first moment she held her in her arms.

In one of those soppy romances she used to read so avidly

as a girl, she ought to have come to love Jim truly too, but that didn't happen. She just became resigned to being stuck with him. Yet while she could look at Pamela, so much like herself, she still had a trace of optimism there was something good around the next corner.

But without Pamela there would be nothing. She was back to where she'd started with Adele, the very cause of her blighted life, and Jim of course, a man she couldn't love or even respect.

Adele was sitting on her bed trying to darn her only half-decent pair of socks when Rose came into the room.

Her immediate reaction was to say how nice her mother looked. But she bit it back, afraid it wasn't appropriate to compliment anyone dressed for a funeral. But black suited her mother, and the way her blonde hair was curling round the little black netted hat was very pretty.

'Is it time to go already?' Adele asked instead. 'I was just finishing darning this sock. I've only got to put it on.'

'You needn't bother, you aren't going,' her mother replied sharply. 'Funerals are no place for children.'

Adele felt a surge of relief. In the two weeks since Pamela died she had thought of the funeral with absolute dread. Pamela had always been scared of graveyards, and Adele knew she'd feel spooked watching as her coffin was lowered into the ground.

'Is there anything you'd like me to do while you and Daddy are gone?' she asked. She knew there wasn't to be any kind of tea afterwards, as neither her mother nor father had any relatives coming. But Adele thought it possible they might bring back a few neighbours.

A slap across her face startled more than hurt her. 'What did I say?' she asked in puzzlement.

'You don't bloody well care, do you?' Rose shouted. 'You little bitch!'

'I do care. I loved her just as much as you,' Adele retorted indignantly, and began to cry.

'No one loved her like I did.' Her mother pushed her face right up to Adele's and her eyes were as icy as the weather outside. 'No one! I wish to God it was you who was killed. You've been a thorn in my side since the moment you were born.'

Adele could only think her mother must have gone mad to say such a terrible thing. Yet however scared she felt, she couldn't let it pass without fighting back. 'So why have me then?' she retorted.

'God knows I tried hard enough to get rid of you,' her mother snarled, her lips curling back like a dog's about to bite. 'I should've left you on someone's doorstep.'

The door burst open and Jim came in. 'What's going on?' he asked.

'Just a few home truths,' Rose said as she flounced out of the room. Jim followed her.

Adele sat on her bed in deep shock for quite some time. She wanted to believe that her mother was just suffering from some kind of sickness through losing Pamela, and that she hadn't really meant it. Yet people didn't say things like that, even when they were hurting themselves, not unless it was true.

Adele was still sitting like a statue when she heard her parents leave for the funeral. They didn't say goodbye, just left without a word as if she was nothing. Adele's room was at the back of the house, so she couldn't see the street. She waited until they'd gone down the stairs, then went into her parents' bedroom, pulled the closed curtains back just a crack and saw the hearse waiting down below.

No one in Charlton Street had a car, so when one stopped in the street it was quite an event, and all the boys rushed to look at it. Adults would discuss who it might belong to and the purpose of the visit.

Hearses, however, created a different kind of reaction, and today's was typical. The neighbours who were going to the funeral were gathered in a little group, looking almost unrecognizable in tidy black clothes.

Further down the street women watched from their doorsteps. Men passing by took off their hats. Any children not at school had either been taken indoors or if still outside were being made to stand still in respect.

While it was reassuring to think her sister was afforded the same degree of respect as an adult, it was unbearable for Adele to think of Pamela lying inside the shiny coffin. She had been such a show-off, so chatty and lively. There was hardly a house in the street that she hadn't been into at some time – she was nosy, funny and so lovable that even the crustiest of old people were charmed by her.

Yet there weren't very many flowers. The neighbours had got together to buy a wreath, Adele had seen it when it was brought round earlier. It was only a small one because no one had much money to spare, and as in January flowers were hard to come by, it was mainly evergreens. The one from the teachers at Pamela's school was bigger, like a yellow cushion, and there was a very nice bouquet from Mrs Belling, the piano teacher.

The wreath from Mum and Dad was small too, but at least it had pink roses. It was very pretty and Adele felt Pamela would have approved.

As she watched, she saw her parents move to stand behind the hearse, and Mr and Mrs Patterson from the ground-floor flat beckoned to the other neighbours to fall in behind them.

Then the hearse slowly pulled away and crept on up the street to the church, everyone walking behind it with their heads held down.

Now there was nothing more to see, Adele could only think again of the nasty things said earlier, and she began to cry again. Had her mother really thought of leaving her on a doorstep? Surely all mothers loved their babies?

Two months later, in March, Adele trudged wearily home from school. Every single day since Pamela died had been misery, but today when they played netball, Miss Swift, her teacher, had asked her in front of the whole class how she got the marks on the backs of her legs.

Adele had said the first thing that came into her head, that she didn't know. Miss Swift said that was ridiculous, but her knowing look suggested she knew exactly how the marks were made.

The truth was that Rose had hit her with the poker the previous Saturday morning. She had picked it up as Adele was kneeling laying the fire, and struck her because she'd spilled ashes on the rug. At the time, Adele was hardly able to walk. But by Monday morning it was bearable and fortunately her gym slip was long enough to hide the weals. But she hadn't thought about stripping off to her knickers for netball.

Maybe if Miss Swift had asked her about the marks when Adele was on her own, she might have been able to tell the truth, but she couldn't with all the other girls listening. Lots of them lived in Charlton Street too, and Adele didn't want them all rushing home and telling their mothers that Rose Talbot was going crazy.

Adele knew that was no exaggeration because her father had said it dozens of times recently. Rose hadn't only hit her, she'd hit Jim too when she was drinking. And she was drinking all the time now, and everything was falling apart. She didn't cook meals, buy food, clean the flat or do the washing. She was never there when Adele went home for dinner, and when she got home from school in the afternoon she was usually sleeping off the drink.

Adele did the cleaning, and her father usually sent her for

fish and chips when he got in from work. If he complained about there being no dinner, her mother would either start crying or get nasty, and quite often she'd run on out again down to the pub and Jim would have to go after her to bring her home.

It was all so horrible. Adele had grown up with her mother's black, silent moods – they were as much a part of her life as going to school or taking the washing to the laundry room at the public baths. But Rose was no longer silent, she screamed, shouted and swore, often threw things too, and Jim was getting just as bad.

He had always been such a quiet man, in fact her mother's favourite insult had been to call him feeble. But now Rose kept goading him, saying he was stupid and common, and he'd become almost as vicious as her. Just a couple of nights ago he'd lashed out at her with a flat iron.

Adele knew very well that her father was a bit slow, he could only read the simplest of words, and he had to have things explained very carefully before he understood. But he could add up well enough, and he was getting really angry at the amount of money Rose was spending on drink. Adele had heard him telling her mother that he'd had a cut in pay because his boss hadn't got enough building work coming in. He kept saying too that he might be thrown out of work completely, but even that threat didn't make any difference.

As Adele got in the front door Mrs Patterson opened her door and it was clear by the way she scowled and put her hands on her hips that she was angry.

'Your mum's been at it again,' she blurted out. 'I can't stand much more of this, however sorry I am about your sister.'

Mrs Patterson was a nice woman. She had three children of her own but she'd always made a fuss of both Adele and Pamela, and in the past she'd often had them in for tea if their mother had to go somewhere. She was a tiny, wiry woman with jet-back hair plaited round her head like a crown. Adele and Pamela used to wonder how long her hair was when she let it loose. Pamela was sure it went right down to her feet.

'Been at what?' Adele asked.

'Screaming down the stairs at Ida Manning,' Mrs Patterson rolled her eyes towards the flat upstairs. 'Accused her of stealing a bag of groceries she left in the hall. Your mum's never been near a grocery shop, the only shop she goes to is the off licence.'

'I'm sorry,' Adele said weakly. She knew Mrs Patterson must be at the end of her tether to complain to her. She was always so kind normally. But Adele didn't dare linger talking about it as her mother would skin her alive if she caught her discussing her with the neighbours.

'Sorry's not good enough any more. That's all I get from your dad too,' Mrs Patterson said, wiggling a finger at Adele. 'This house is full of kids. We don't want no drunks shouting the odds. We've all tried to help her since Pamela went, but all we get is the brush-off.'

'I can't do anything,' Adele said, and began to cry. She felt she couldn't stand any of it any longer. She dreaded coming home.

'There now, don't cry,' Mrs Patterson said, the previous harshness of her tone softening. She came over to Adele and patted her shoulder. 'You're a good girl, you don't deserve this. But you must talk to yer dad. If he don't put a stop to it soon, you'll all be thrown out.'

Adele was alone in the living room when her father came in from work later that same evening. 'Where is she?' he asked.

'She went out, about half an hour ago,' Adele said, and began to cry again. Her mother was lying down in the bedroom when she got in from school, so she'd left her in peace for a while. Later she'd taken her in a cup of tea, and

26

got slapped round the face when she asked what was for tea. 'There isn't anything to eat, but maybe she's gone to get something,' she added.

Dad sighed deeply and sank down on to a chair, still with his coat on. 'I dunno what to do any more,' he said helplessly. 'You don't 'elp neither, always upsetting 'er.'

'I don't do or say anything to her,' Adele retorted indignantly. 'It's all her.'

She was so hungry she felt sick with it, and there wasn't even a piece of bread in the cupboard. While she was well used to her father blaming her for everything, this time she wasn't going to accept it.

Angrily she launched into telling him what Mrs Patterson had said. 'Can't you do something, Dad?' she begged him.

She expected a clout round the ear, but to her surprise Jim just looked sorrowful. 'She don't take no notice of anything I say,' he replied, shaking his head slowly. 'It's like I'm the cause of 'er troubles.'

Adele was struck by the depth of hurt and sadness in his voice. He had never been like fathers in books, he didn't rule the house, and mostly he skulked about like a lodger. He didn't talk much, seldom showed his feelings, and Adele knew very little about him because most of the time he totally ignored her. Yet from what she knew of other fathers, Jim Talbot wasn't a bad one. He might be rough and slow-witted, but he didn't drink much or gamble and he went to work every day.

But Pamela's death, and the huge hole in the family she'd left behind, had made Adele notice her father more. She didn't want to agree with some of the nastier things her mother said about him, even if most of them were true. It wasn't his fault after all that he couldn't deal with even the simplest problems. He was in fact like a big, strong child, and as such she felt a bond of sympathy with him because she knew what it was like to be constantly ridiculed.

'How can you be the cause of her troubles?' she asked.

'I dunno,' he shrugged. 'I've always done whatever she wanted. But she's deeper than the Thames. I dunno what goes on inside 'er 'ead.'

When Rose finally came home around nine, Adele was in bed. She and her father had only a bag of chips between them for their tea, as Jim didn't have any more money. Adele was still very hungry, and she knew her father must be too. Going to bed was a way of forgetting about it, and avoiding the fight when her mother came home.

The expected row began the minute Rose got through the door. Jim said something about a bag of chips not being enough for a man who'd worked a ten-hour day. Then all at once they were at it, hammer and tongs, Dad f'ing and blinding and Mum sneering because he had to resort to that.

It all washed over Adele for some time; mostly it was all stuff she'd heard dozens of times before. Rose saying that she was meant for better things than living in Euston and Jim throwing back that he did his best for her.

Then suddenly Adele heard Jim say something which made her prick up her ears. 'You'd have ended up in the fuckin' workhouse if it weren't for me.'

Adele sat up in shocked surprise.

'Why else would I have married you?' Rose screamed back at him. 'Do you think I would have let someone like you near me if I wasn't desperate?'

Adele gasped at her mother's cruelty.

'But I loved you,' Jim replied, his voice cracking with hurt.

'How can you love someone you don't know?' Rose retorted. 'You never let me tell you how it was, you just wanted to own me.'

'I did the right thing by you,' Jim said indignantly, and now it sounded as if he was crying. 'You needed a man beside you with a baby on the way.'

'Call yourself a man?' Rose snorted with derision. 'I

wouldn't have looked twice at you if I hadn't been pregnant, and you always knew that. Don't make out you cared about the kid either, all you wanted was to get into bed with me.'

There was a sharp crack and Adele knew he'd hit Rose.

'You fuckin' bitch,' he yelled at her. 'If it was down to you Adele would be a bastard and in some foundling home.'

Adele was so horrified she pulled the pillow over her head so she couldn't hear any more.

She knew that babies grew in a woman's stomach, and that their husbands put them there. But if Adele hadn't been put there by Jim, it surely followed that her mother had been a prostitute!

Adele had grown up familiar with the word 'prostitute', or its more commonly used version of 'prozzie', because there were so many around King's Cross and Euston. Yet it wasn't until she was about ten that she discovered exactly what they did. An older girl at school explained that they got money for letting men do the act to them that made babies. She said men were mad about making babies, but as their wives didn't want lots and lots of them, they went to prostitutes instead.

Adele had always been concerned as to where all the babies were kept as she never saw any of those women pushing prams. Now it seemed from what her dad had said that they went to the Foundling Home. But he had married Mum to prevent Adele going there too.

Adele wasn't sure whether she should consider herself lucky she escaped that fate, or not. As her mother claimed she'd spoiled her life, maybe she had liked being a prostitute?

It seemed her parents had gone into the bedroom now, because although they were still shouting, she couldn't make out what they were saying. But she could hear the Mannings downstairs banging on their ceiling with a broom handle because they were making so much noise.

Then all at once there was an almighty crash from the kitchen. It sounded as though one of them had knocked all the saucepans off the shelf at once. Above it Mum was screaming at the top of her lungs.

Instinctively Adele jumped out of bed and ran into the living room. But instead of finding Jim hitting Rose as she expected, Jim was cowering in the bedroom doorway, with blood running down his face. The saucepans were clearly Rose's doing – they were all over the floor with some plates too, and she had the carving knife in her hand.

Adele immediately knew that this was very different from the usual fights. She could see Jim's fear and feel the real menace in the air. Rose was still yelling like a madwoman, quivering with rage, and she was poised to stab Jim again.

'Stop it!' Adele shouted.

Rose wheeled round at the sound of her voice, and her face was utterly terrifying. Her eyes were almost popping out of her head, her mouth was all slack like a panting dog's, and she was a strange purple colour.

'Stop it?' she shouted back, lifting the knife right up in her hand as if to stab anyone who came near her. 'I haven't even started yet.'

'Someone will get the police,' Adele pleaded fearfully. 'We'll get thrown out of here.' She wondered if she dared run for the door and get out.

'Do you think that bothers me?' Rose snarled at her with bared teeth and flaring nostrils. 'I hate this place, I hate London, and I hate both of you.'

Adele had seen her mother angry hundreds of times, and usually it ended suddenly with her slumping down on to a chair sobbing her heart out. But she was different this time, she looked savage, almost as if she were possessed by some evil spirit. Adele was stricken with terror, instinct telling her that she was really dangerous.

'You killed my Pammy,' Rose yelled out, spitting with rage, her mouth all contorted. She lurched towards Adele in a curious ape-like manner with her shoulder hunched, the carving knife poised for a frenzied attack. 'She was the only thing I loved and you killed her.'

Adele was frozen with terror. Her mind said she must run, if not downstairs at least back to her bedroom, but all she could see was the glinting of the knife and her mother's bared teeth, and she wet herself with fright.

'You filthy little bitch!' Rose shrieked, and catching hold of Adele's hair with one hand, she raised the knife to plunge it down on her.

'No, Rose!' Jim shouted, and grabbed her wrist from behind.

'Get off,' Rose screamed, but Jim was shaking her wrist so violently that the knife was wobbling in her hand, less than an inch from Adele's cheek, and Rose still had a firm grip of the child's hair.

Adele thought she was going to die any minute. She couldn't get away, her mother's breath was hot and rancid and her eyes were wild and rolling. She screamed out and at the same time tried to push Rose away. She felt the knife touch her cheek, then clatter to the floor.

Jim was wrestling with Rose, desperately trying to drag her away from Adele, and as he pulled her back, a clump of Adele's hair came out by the roots.

'For fuck's sake get out!' Jim yelled, pinioning Rose's arms behind her back.

Adele tried to move but she was pressed up against the wall, and suddenly a violent blow from her mother's knee caught her in the stomach. As Jim finally managed to restrain Rose, Adele fell to the floor doubled up with pain.

'You messed up my life,' she heard her mother screaming at her as if from a distance. 'If it wasn't for you I could have had a good life. Your father was a lying bastard, and I've had to live with your ugly face for twelve years, every day a reminder of him.'

Jim was still trying to haul Rose away from Adele when the front door burst open and in came Stan Manning and Alf Patterson, his two neighbours.

'She's gone fucking mad,' Jim shouted, trying to hold on to Rose who was bucking against him, spitting and yelling abuse. 'She was going to kill the kid. Help me, then one of you get a doctor.'

Chapter Three

Alf Patterson stayed only long enough to help Jim and Stan restrain Rose. They forced her on to a chair, tied her wrists together behind her back with a scarf, and secured her to the chair with a leather strap. Then Alf ran up the street to the doctor's.

He was short and stocky, with a beer gut and thinning hair at thirty-three, but Alf was a happy man. He loved his job on the railway, he had a decent home and the best wife and kids any man could ask for.

He and Annie had moved into number 47 as newly-weds, some eight years ago, and the Talbots took the top flat soon afterwards. The two couples had never been what Alf would call friends. The two men bought each other a drink if they saw one another in the pub, and Rose had the occasional cup of tea with Annie, but that was all – the only common ground between them was their kids. Alf's eldest, Tommy, was just a year younger than Pamela, and Adele would take both children to school. She'd done this right from when they started at the infants', when she was still at the juniors' next door.

Annie had always found Rose puzzling. She could be snooty or nasty one day, then as nice as pie the next, especially when she wanted something. If it hadn't been for Adele, for whom she had a soft spot, she wouldn't have bothered with her mother at all. But when Pamela was killed Annie's best efforts to comfort and help were rebuffed. She worried about Rose's drinking, she said she suspected Adele was being ill treated, and begged Alf to have a word with Jim. Alf thought his wife was over-reacting, and that it would all blow over.

But in the light of what he'd just seen, Annie was right to be concerned. Rose Talbot was mad and dangerous.

Reaching the corner of the street where Dr Biggs lived, Alf banged loudly on the door. It was opened a few seconds later by the doctor, ready for bed in his pyjamas and a red dressing-gown.

He was a small, balding man, known as much for his jovial manner as his medical skills. 'Sorry to disturb you, Doc,' Alf panted out. 'It's Rose Talbot upstairs to me. She's gone mad. She attacked Jim and then set about her kid with a knife. Me and Jim had to tie her up she was so crazy.'

It took Dr Biggs a moment or two to place who Alf Patterson was talking about. Then he remembered the Talbots were the parents of the child who was run over a while back. 'Hold on, I'll be with you immediately,' he said. 'Just let me put some clothes on and get my bag.'

'Any idea what set Mrs Talbot off?' the doctor asked as they hurried back up the street just a few minutes later. He knew Alf and Annie Patterson well, as he had delivered all three of their children and before the younger two arrived, Annie used to clean his surgery for him.

'Dunno,' Alf said. 'Of course, she's been in a state since the little girl got run over. We've 'eard a lot of rows. But Jim ain't said nothin' else was up.'

Dr Biggs barely knew the Talbots, but he had called on Rose just after the funeral to see how she was coping with the tragedy. Rose had kept him at the door and said she was fine. She didn't look fine, she looked completely washed out with dark circles under her eyes. He said as much, and suggested she call in to see him at the surgery, but she never came. He could hardly make a nuisance of himself by calling again uninvited.

Quite a crowd had gathered outside number 47, all of them looking up at the light in the top-floor window and listening to the shrieks coming from inside the room.

'Go home, all of you,' Dr Biggs said firmly. 'There's nothing to see.'

'It's what we 'eard which bothers us, Doc,' one of the men retorted. 'Sounds like she needs locking up.'

Dr Biggs didn't reply, but went on in, nodding briefly at Annie Patterson who was standing anxiously at the bottom of the stairs with another woman. The noise from the top flat was much louder inside the house, and along with the shouting was the sound of something being dragged or scraped over the floor.

'You stay here with your wife,' Biggs said to Alf. 'I'll call you if I need any further help.'

The scene which met Dr Biggs's eyes as he walked into the top flat was very alarming. Rose was bound by a leather strap to a chair, her eyes almost popping out of her head. She was rocking and scraping the chair on the floor, shrieking abuse at her husband as she struggled desperately to get free. Jim Talbot was trying vainly to pacify her, and he had blood pouring down his face.

Another man the doctor didn't know, but who presumably was another neighbour, was kneeling down beside the daughter, wiping blood from her face. The girl was wearing a nightdress, and at a glance the doctor could see it was wet with urine and splattered with blood. The whole living-room floor was littered with pots, pans and broken china.

Dr Biggs knew immediately that this was not an ordinary domestic incident. Rose wasn't going to calm down over a cup of tea and a chat. In fact he suspected both her husband and daughter would be at risk if she stayed here. The only course of action open to him was to sedate the woman immediately and get her admitted into a mental asylum before she could do any further damage to others, or herself.

'Now, what's all this about, Mrs Talbot?' he asked soothingly as he approached her.

'Fuck you,' she screamed at him, baring her teeth like a savage dog and rocking the chair even more violently, despite her husband's efforts to hold her still. 'Get out of here, the lot of you!'

A string of obscenities followed, her voice so shrill and deranged that the doctor winced.

'Why's she gone like this?' Jim asked pitifully. 'I never did anything to 'er.'

'The death of your daughter appears to have brought on a nervous collapse,' Dr Biggs said briskly, opening his bag and bringing out a phial of sedative and a hypodermic syringe. 'Was she behaving oddly before tonight?' he asked as he prepared it.

Jim nodded. 'She's bin strange fer weeks now. Couldn't say nothing right to 'er. She's been drinking and carrying on.'

If Jim had been intending to add anything further to this, Rose cut him short. 'You fucking bastard, slimy no-good worm,' she yelled at the top of her lungs. 'I wouldn't be like this if it wasn't for you.'

'Now, now, Mrs Talbot,' Dr Biggs said calmly, the prepared syringe in his hand. 'You are just overwrought, and I'm going to give you something to calm you down.' He looked towards the neighbour who had got up from tending to the girl and was standing there looking horrified. 'If you would help Jim to hold her steady.'

Rose bucked and writhed in her chair with the strength of half a dozen men, but Jim and Stan managed to keep her still enough for the injection.

'It will only be a few moments before it begins to take effect,' the doctor said as he withdrew the needle from her arm. 'I shall have to go out in a moment and make a quick phone call for a hospital place, but first I will see to the child.'

'Bastard!' Rose spat at him. 'You'd better not be sending me to the madhouse! It's her that made me like this!'

Within less than a minute Rose stopped struggling, and her shrieks died down to mere croaks, and the doctor moved over to kneel by the girl to examine her. She was conscious, seemingly just too stunned to speak, and her face had been cut, presumably by the same knife used on her father. But it was not a deep cut, little more than a bad scratch. When he asked her if she had any other injuries, she put one hand on her belly.

'Help me move her to the bedroom,' he said to Jim, who was intently watching his wife as her head began to droop down on to her chest.

'No point in doin' that,' he retorted. 'She can't stay 'ere if her mother's going to a hospital.'

'I need to examine her,' Dr Biggs said curtly. He assumed Jim thought a child of her age couldn't stay in the flat alone while he went to the hospital with his wife. 'And there'll be no need for you to accompany your wife. Provided your daughter's injuries don't require treatment, she can stay here with you.'

'She ain't my daughter,' Jim said, his tone as cold as if he were talking about a stray dog. 'And injured or not, I want 'er out of 'ere tonight.'

Dr Biggs prided himself on being unshockable, but he was astounded by that remark. 'We'll talk about that later,' he said curtly. 'But meanwhile I have no intention of examining a child on a cold, hard floor. So I'd be grateful if you'd help me with her. Once I've done that I can phone for help for your wife.'

Once he had the girl in her bedroom she told him her name and that her mother had gone for her with a knife and kicked her in the stomach. The doctor lifted her nightdress and saw a red mark which bore this out, and he also noticed several other old bruises on her body and legs which suggested she'd been beaten before. Although she was in shock, there were no bones broken and the facial scratch didn't require stitching, so she didn't need to go to hospital.

'I've got to go and make a phone call about your mum,' he explained as he helped her off with her wet nightdress and covered her up with a blanket. 'But you just stay here and I'll be back to see you in a little while.'

Rose Talbot was so heavily sedated that she offered no resistance at all when the two ambulance men carried her down to their ambulance on a stretcher. Dr Biggs had only just got back to number 47 from making the telephone call when they arrived, so he'd had no time yet to dress Jim Talbot's facial wound, or speak to either him or Adele again. Once the ambulance had driven away he went back into the house and saw Annie Patterson waiting in the hallway looking anxious.

'Will she be all right?' she asked. 'Is there anything I can do to help Jim or Adele?'

'Mrs Talbot will probably be in hospital for some little while,' the doctor said cautiously. He knew Annie Patterson was a good woman, not given to idle gossip, but even so he couldn't bring himself to tell her Rose Talbot was bound for the mental asylum. 'However, there does seem to be a further problem upstairs, and it's possible Adele won't be able to stay there. Would you be prepared to put her up for the night if necessary?'

'Of course,' Annie said without any hesitation. 'The poor love, a young girl like that shouldn't have to see and hear such things. You bring her on down if you need to, it'll only be on the couch, I'm afraid, and she'd better bring some blankets with her. But she's more than welcome.'

'You're a good woman,' Dr Biggs said with a smile. 'She'll be in need of a little mothering, I suspect she hasn't had much of that lately.'

*

Up in the top flat Jim was now alone, sitting at the kitchen table staring into space, seemingly oblivious to the pots and crockery on the floor. He didn't even look up when Dr Biggs came in.

'Right, let's look at your injuries, Jim,' the doctor said, keeping his tone jovial. He put some hot water from the kettle into a basin and taking some swabs from his bag, he cleaned up the man's cheek. 'Only a flesh wound, I'm glad to say, it doesn't need stitches,' he announced after a few minutes. He put a dressing on and used some sticking plaster to keep it in place, then sat down at the table and looked sternly at Jim.

'Now, suppose you explain to me what's been going on?'

'Nothin' much to tell,' Jim said, his tone sullen. 'Rose ain't bin right since our Pammy was killed. It got worse every day, what wif the drinkin' an' all. You saw what she were like, gone right off 'er rocker.'

'The death of a child is enough to send any mother off the rails,' Dr Biggs said reproachfully. 'You should've called me long before it got to this stage.'

'I can't afford doctors,' Jim said. 'I've 'ad to take a cut in wages. Besides, Rose wouldn't 'ave let you near 'er.'

'Why was she blaming Adele?' the doctor asked.

'Well, she's the one what done it. If she'd got a move on to pick our Pammy up, she wouldn't 'ave been run over.'

'You cannot blame a road accident on another child,' Dr Biggs exclaimed in horror. 'Adele will probably always feel it was her fault anyway, accidents do that to people, but the blame should not come from her mother and father.'

'I told you, she ain't my kid,' Jim said petulantly. 'Now mine's dead thanks to her. And her mum's gone barmy. You should'a heard what she were blaming me for! I can't take any more of it. I done me best all these years fer Rose and the kid, and that's all the thanks I get. So I don't want nothin' more to do with either of 'em. So you can get that kid out of 'ere right now.'

Biggs was appalled by the man's callous attitude towards Adele, but at the same time he guessed Rose must have been taunting Jim, perhaps ever since his own child was killed. The man was in shock, by tomorrow he might see things differently, and as Adele was in the next room, possibly listening to all this, the best solution was to take up Annie Patterson's offer for tonight.

'I will take Adele away for now,' Dr Biggs said pointedly. 'Not because of your feelings, Mr Talbot, but because she is suffering from shock and needs some tender care. I shall be back to talk to you tomorrow. I hope by then you will have calmed down and remembered that by marrying Rose, you have a legal and moral responsibility for her child.'

'I've got to go to work tomorrow,' Jim said.

'Then I'll come at seven in the evening,' Dr Biggs said sharply. 'I suggest before then, you spend some time thinking about the child's needs, rather than your own.'

Annie Patterson showed all the compassion for Adele that Jim Talbot lacked when the doctor took her downstairs. 'You poor dear,' she said, giving the girl a hug. 'I'm sorry we haven't got a proper spare bed, but a little thing like you should be all right on the couch.'

The only clean nightdress Dr Biggs had been able to find had clearly belonged to the dead sister. It barely reached Adele's knees and with a blanket around her shoulders and strapping on her face she looked pitiful.

'This is very kind of you, Annie,' he said, putting down a blanket and pillow. 'It is only a temporary measure. I'll talk to Mr Talbot tomorrow evening when he's calmer.'

Adele hadn't said a word, not to ask about her mother, or herself. Biggs hoped this was because she hadn't really taken in what had happened upstairs.

But that hope was dashed as he was about to leave, when suddenly Adele became agitated. 'I can't stay with Dad, ever again,' she blurted out. 'He doesn't like me. Neither does Mum.'

'That's nonsense,' Annie Patterson said briskly. 'Your mum's ill and your dad doesn't know whether he's coming or going.'

Adele looked from the neighbour to the doctor helplessly. She couldn't really believe that her mother had tried to kill her. Or that she'd really said all those terrible things.

Yet young as she was, she knew she'd come face to face with her mother's real feelings for her tonight. It was something like spilling a bottle of milk, you could mop it up, but you couldn't put it back in the bottle.

She knew now with complete certainty that the many slaps, nastiness and cruel words in the past were all symptoms of her mother's simmering hatred for her. Tonight it had just boiled over.

She didn't see how she could have spoiled her mother's life by just being born, but she doubted there was anything she could do or say that would ever make her mother feel differently about her. Likewise, she sensed that neither the doctor nor Mrs Patterson was in the mood for any further discussion tonight. So there was nothing for it but to do what they wanted, to lie down on the couch and go to sleep. To do or say anything further would only set them against her too.

'I'm sorry to be a nuisance,' she said weakly, looking from one adult to the other. 'I'll do whatever you say.'

'There's a good girl.' Mrs Patterson smiled and smoothed her cheek affectionately. 'Everything will look differently in the morning, you'll see. And you can have a lie-in as it's Saturday.'

An hour later Adele was still awake, despite the cocoa Mrs Patterson had made her, and the hot water bottle on her sore stomach. There was moonlight coming in through the window by the sink and glinting down on to the backs of the chairs at the table. The couch she was lying on was more of a padded bench really, covered in brown, cracked imitation leather and very hard. It was behind the table and used as extra seating.

The Pattersons' flat was the biggest in the house but a bit dark. The kitchen and the front bedroom where Mr and Mrs Patterson and their one-year-old baby Lily slept had big double doors between them. Then there was a passageway from the kitchen down to the room four-year-old Michael and seven-year-old Tommy shared, and a further door to the back yard.

What was going to become of her now? She'd heard what her father said to the doctor, and she was pretty certain he meant it. As far as she knew, orphanages were for young children and babies, she'd never heard of anyone of twelve being put in one. But she couldn't get a job and keep herself until she was fourteen.

She must have gone to sleep eventually for she woke with a start to hear Mrs Patterson putting the kettle on.

'Sorry to wake you, lovey,' she said cheerily. 'Did you sleep all right?' She came over to the couch and smoothed Adele's hair back from her forehead.

The woman's black hair was loose now, and it was so long it reached her waist. She was wearing a dressing-gown that was so threadbare it looked ready to fall apart.

'Yes, thank you,' Adele replied. Her stomach still ached a bit, and her face felt sore, but apart from that she was all right.

'My Alf's going off to work now,' Mrs Patterson said. 'You snuggle down for a bit longer and I'll make you a cup of tea after I've given Lily her bottle. We'll have a little chat then too.'

Adele stayed where she was for a very long time, pretending to sleep while she watched and listened to the Pattersons. She saw how Mrs Patterson kissed her husband goodbye and gave him his sandwiches. How she fed baby Lily and then bathed her in the kitchen sink. Lily's wet nappy stank, but it was nice to hear her gurgling and splashing in the water. Then Michael and Tommy got up, and their mother made them toast and a cup of tea.

There was a cosiness about the family's routine that Adele had never experienced herself. Mrs Patterson patted her children's heads and bottoms affectionately, she even kissed their cheeks for no real reason, and she answered the boys' questions in a quiet, calm manner. Adele was used to her mother snarling at her.

'How about a cup of tea now?' Mrs Patterson asked when the boys had gone off to their room to get dressed. Baby Lily was put on the floor to play with some wooden blocks, and she shuffled about on her bottom.

Adele got up cautiously, very aware that Pamela's night-dress was far too short, and she hadn't thought to bring any clothes down with her.

Mrs Patterson must have read her thoughts. 'We'll go up later and get you some things. I heard your dad leave for work earlier. That's a good sign, at least he isn't brooding.'

'I don't think he'll change his mind about me,' Adele said, assuming Mrs Patterson meant that he wasn't brooding about her. 'You see, he isn't my dad, Mum said so last night.'

Mrs Patterson put her hands on her hips and made a stern face. 'She said a great many daft things by all accounts, but she couldn't help it, love. She was beside herself.'

'It must be true, Dad said it too, to the doctor,' Adele said in a small voice, hanging her head with the shame of it. 'Mum's been saying lots of nasty things like that lately. She said she tried to get rid of me and it was the only reason she married Dad. She even wanted to kill me last night.'

Mrs Patterson fell silent, and Adele knew it was because she didn't know what to say.

'I suppose I'll have to go to an orphanage, won't I?' Adele said after watching the older woman busying herself making the tea for a few minutes. 'There isn't anywhere else.'

All at once she found herself enveloped in a warm hug. 'You poor love,' Mrs Patterson exclaimed, clutching her to her plump chest which smelled of baby and toast. 'This is an awful business, but maybe after your mum's had a rest in hospital things will get better.'

Adele liked the hug, it made her feel safe and wanted, something she hadn't really felt before. Yet all the same she thought she must warn this kind woman just how Rose Talbot felt about her elder daughter.

'I don't think she'll want me, not even when she's better,' she began. It took her some time to explain just how bad things had been since Pamela's death, and that even before that, her mother had been indifferent towards her. 'So you see,' she finished up, 'there's no point in me hoping that when she's better everything will be all right.'

It seemed an interminable day to Adele. Mrs Patterson decided it wasn't a good idea to go back to the flat to get some clothes, so she gave Adele a sort of overall of hers to wear. It was red and white check and nearly as broad as it was long, but with a belt tied round, it didn't look much different to a dressing-gown. Adele tried to take her mind off what was likely to happen to her by helping around the flat, but her aching stomach kept reminding her. When she caught a glimpse of herself in Mrs Patterson's bedroom mirror she began to cry again, for her eye was going black and the scar on her cheek looked horrible.

Finally it was seven o'clock and Dr Biggs arrived, but Jim still hadn't come home.

'He'll have gone to the pub,' Adele admitted.

Dr Biggs sighed and looked at Mrs Patterson who had the kind of look that said 'I expected as much.' She beckoned for the doctor to come into the front bedroom with her, pointedly closing the door behind them.

'Our dad goes down the pub too,' Tommy said, looking up from drawing moustaches on people in an old magazine.

Adele had known the Patterson boys from birth and liked them a great deal, even if they were funny-looking with pale faces, sticking-up black hair and scabby knees. As she had always taken Tommy to school with Pamela, she knew him best – he was cheeky, noisy and sometimes a bit rough, but lovable too. He had done his best to make her laugh today; even his remark about his dad going to the pub was intended to make her feel better. But Adele couldn't really respond, she was straining her ears to hear what Mrs Patterson and the doctor were talking about.

Meanwhile both adults were doing their best to keep their voices down.

'I'll have to make a report to the authorities,' the doctor said sadly. 'I suspect Jim's got no intention of taking care of Adele, and we can't let it go on and on. Is there any other family? Grandparents, aunts or uncles?'

'Jim's got a sister somewhere up north,' Annie replied. 'But he never sees her. If Rose's got any family they've never been here.'

'No parents?' the doctor asked.

'I don't think so,' Mrs Patterson replied. 'She grew up in Sussex, by the sea, that's all I know.'

'I'll ask Jim when I get hold of him,' the doctor said. 'If her parents are still alive, maybe they'll help out.'

'I hope so. It grieves me to think of that sweet girl going to an orphanage,' Annie Patterson said, and her voice had a kind of break in it as though she was crying.

'I'll write a note for Jim, and Adele can leave it upstairs for him while she gets some clothes.'

'I doubt he can even read,' Annie said scornfully. 'He's not the full shilling, you know.'

'I know,' Dr Biggs agreed. His wife had informed him of that last night. She heard all the gossip in the neighbourhood. According to what she'd been told, Jim's family, the Talbots, had been a notorious family in Somers Town back in the early 1900s, the boys all villains and thugs, the girls tarts, and the parents even worse. Jim was the youngest of eight, and generally known to be backward. He joined up in 1917 when he was eighteen, and it was assumed he must have been killed in France, as at least three of his brothers had been, for he didn't return. His parents and the two younger sisters who were still living at home died in the flu epidemic of 1919.

Everyone was astounded when Jim Talbot suddenly turned up again in Somers Town four years later. Not only because he had survived the war which had taken so many of the young men in the area, but he came back with a pretty, well-bred wife and a four-year-old daughter too. They were even more astounded when he managed to hold down a job at a wood yard, and they discovered that his wife wasn't a slut as his mother and sisters had been.

In the light of what Dr Biggs had heard the previous night, it seemed likely that Rose Talbot only married Jim as a last resort, because she was carrying another man's child. He thought that years of living with a man she didn't love, in considerably reduced circumstances compared to what she was used to, had caused a huge resentment towards Adele to grow.

Dr Biggs couldn't find very much sympathy for Rose, who had no right to blame an innocent child for her mistakes or misfortune. But he did feel a little for Jim, for he had been up against it from birth. No doubt he'd consulted his workmates today, and they'd all encouraged him to reject Adele. Perhaps he also thought of it as a way of showing Rose he was tired of being her provider and doormat.

'I'll write a note anyway,' he said. 'But I'll come round again in the morning and try to catch Jim.'

Adele walked up the stairs very reluctantly, the note from Dr Biggs in her hand. She was scared of going into the flat, it was only going to make her think about her mother with the knife again. As her dad hadn't come back to speak to Dr Biggs it was clear he didn't care what happened to her. She wished it was she, not Pamela, who was dead.

As she opened the door of the flat and turned on the light, Adele felt sick. The saucepans and broken plates were still on the floor, and there was a bloodstain on the tablecloth, along with the knife. It smelled nasty too, of drink, cigarettes, her dad's sweat and socks. She wanted to run right out and never come back again, but she steeled herself to go into her bedroom and collect her things.

She didn't have much to collect, just her best Sunday skirt and jumper, one clean vest, school blouse, knickers and pair of socks, her shoes and gym slip. She was about to put her things in her school satchel when she remembered there was a small suitcase on the top of the wardrobe in her parents' room.

Their bedroom stank even worse than the living room, and the bed wasn't made. There were more bloodstains on the pillows, she supposed from the cut on her dad's cheek. She stood there at the dressing-table looking at herself in the mirror for a moment.

She looked awful, she thought, it was no wonder no one wanted her. Even before she got the black eye and the scar on her cheek she hadn't been pretty. Dull, straggly, biscuit-coloured hair, sallow skin, even her eyes weren't a proper colour like brown or blue, they were a greenish colour that Mum had once said was like canal water.

It was no wonder her mum was angry that her pretty daughter got killed instead of the plain one.

Pulling up the bedroom chair, Adele climbed on to it to reach the suitcase, and as she lifted it down she saw it was covered in a thick blanket of dust. She put it on the bed and wiped it off with the edge of the bedspread.

There was nothing but a few old letters inside, but as she scooped them up, intending to put them into the dressing-table drawer, she suddenly remembered that the doctor had been asking whether they had any relatives.

She flicked through the letters, but they all seemed to be from the same person and addressed to her father. She opened one and saw it was from his sister in Manchester. Disappointed, she bundled them all up together, but as a few fell off the pile and she bent to retrieve them, she noticed one in quite different handwriting which was addressed to Miss Rose Harris, her mother's maiden name.

The envelope had turned a yellowish-brown with age, and it wasn't even sent to this address. But as she held it in her hand looking at it, she suddenly recalled Mrs Patterson's words earlier: '*I think she grew up in Sussex, by the sea.*'

This letter was addressed to Curlew Cottage, Winchelsea Beach, nr Rye, Sussex.

As her mother had never mentioned her parents, Adele thought they must be dead, but she was curious about who this letter was from and pulled it out of the envelope. It was from someone in Tunbridge Wells in Kent, dated 8 July 1915.

'*Dear Rose,*' she read.

I was so thrilled to hear from you after all this time. I missed you terribly after you left, and all the girls ask if I've had any news of you. I suppose it is a bit dull living right out in the country, but then it's dull everywhere when all people can talk about is the war. Lots of the girls at school have lost their fathers and brothers, I'm glad my father doesn't have to go and that I haven't got brothers old enough. I hope your father keeps safe.

Does your mother make you knit socks and scarves? Mine does.
I'm sick of grey wool. We were playing tennis this afternoon and
Muriel Stepford said she was going to try and become a nurse. She
said it was because she feels so sorry for all those wounded soldiers,
but we all think she's afraid she'll be left on the shelf as there's so few
men of her age left here.

Write soon, and tell me about what you do all day. Do you really
keep chickens and grow vegetables, or was that a joke? I can't
imagine you getting your hands dirty.

All my best wishes,
Alice

Adele read the letter three times, intrigued because it was
a tiny glimpse of her mother's past she knew nothing of.
Was this girl Alice a good friend? Had her mother and her
parents moved away from Tunbridge Wells because of the
war? Could her grandparents still be living in Curlew Cottage
now?

It was written sixteen years ago, four years before she was
born, but as she didn't know exactly how old her mother
was, she couldn't even guess at the age of her grandparents.

But she'd heard the doctor say he was going to ask Jim
about family, so she put it back with the other letters and
filled the suitcase with her things. Then she left the flat,
closing the door behind her.

The following morning, as church bells were ringing for the
Sunday morning service, Dr Biggs returned. He came in to
the Pattersons' for a little while, asked Adele how she was
feeling, and said he'd contacted the hospital where her
mother had been taken, and that she was much calmer.

'How long do you think they will keep her there?' Mrs
Patterson asked.

'I don't know at this stage,' Dr Biggs replied guardedly.
'Now, I'll just go up and see Mr Talbot.'

The doctor wasn't very long with her father, and when he came back down he looked flushed and annoyed.

'Run along outside in the yard with the boys,' Mrs Patterson said, giving Adele a little shove on the behind towards the door.

Adele went, but not right outside. She just closed the door through to the living room and waited outside it. She wanted to know what her father had said to make the doctor angry.

She didn't have long to wait. The doctor fairly exploded. 'That man is so dense, I might as well have talked to a brick wall,' he said. 'He is adamant Adele isn't his child. He said he met her mother when she was pregnant and he can prove it because he was still in France until then.'

'But by marrying Rose, surely that makes him responsible for Adele, whoever her real father was?' Mrs Patterson said.

'Technically yes. But you know the expression "You can lead a horse to water, but you can't make it drink",' the doctor replied. 'How can I walk away leaving such a young girl in the hands of someone so full of anger and spite? Anything could happen.'

'What are we going to do then?' Mrs Patterson asked.

'I shall have to get a care order. There's nothing else for it, Annie. Rose is mentally ill, I can't even say she will recover. Besides, maybe it's for the best in the long term – I suspect the child has been badly treated for many years. If I get her away from here now she'll be better off.'

'Did you ask Jim if there were any grandparents?'

'Yes, but he knows nothing about them. He said Rose had fallen out with her mother long before he met her, and she has had no contact with her since.'

Lily began wailing loudly at that point, shutting out anything further said by the adults. Adele waited nervously for Lily to stop crying, but she went on and on, drowning everything.

Adele went back into the living room a little later. Dr

Biggs smiled at her. 'I was just telling Mrs Patterson I thought it best if you stay home from school for a couple of days until that eye gets better,' he said. 'I'm sure you don't want anyone asking you questions about it, do you?'

Adele looked from him to Mrs Patterson, sensing they had planned something between them. She wondered why adults told children off for being deceitful when they themselves were all the time.

Chapter Four

As Adele ate her porridge the following morning, Mrs Patterson was tying Tommy's tie for him.

'It's high time a big boy like you learned to do it yourself,' she said, giving him a playful cuff on the ear.

'I like you doing it,' Tommy retorted, and reached out to tickle his mother under the chin, making her laugh.

The affectionate exchange made a lump come up in Adele's throat. In the last two days she'd seen many such little expressions of love between the members of this family, and each one was a sad reminder that she'd never experienced such affection from either of her parents. She had come to the conclusion that the fault must be hers, for after all they'd managed to show affection for Pamela.

'Is Adele taking me to school?' Tommy asked once his tie was tied.

'Of course not,' Mrs Patterson said, glancing over at Adele who was still sitting at the table. Adele had stopped taking him after Pamela was killed. 'Why should she? You're a big boy now.'

Tommy looked beseechingly at Adele. 'Please?'

'Adele isn't quite right yet,' his mother said briskly. 'She needs rest.'

'I don't,' Adele said, getting up. She was touched Tommy wanted her with him. 'I'd like to take him.'

Mrs Patterson hesitated.

'Please? I'd like to go out,' Adele pleaded.

'All right then,' Mrs Patterson agreed. 'But come straight back, the doctor said you were to rest.'

*

Adele hadn't considered that walking Tommy to school would bring back such vivid memories of Pamela. Tommy behaved just the way he always had, one minute running along with one foot in the gutter, the other on the pavement, the next swooping back to her, arms outstretched, pretending to be an aeroplane. Pamela had always held Adele's hand and complained that Tommy showed them up. Adele missed that little hand in hers, the scornful look on her sister's face, and the way she would break into giggles when Tommy pulled faces at her.

The primary school was a big old soot-blackened building of three storeys, the infants' classes on one side, the juniors' on the other, with separate entrances and playgrounds.

'See you at dinner-time,' Tommy said before running in through the gates.

Adele stood for a moment, watching through the railings as he was swallowed up by a throng of small boys. The junior girls were gathering on the far side of the playground, and for a brief moment she found herself automatically looking for Pamela amongst them.

It was fear of such reminders of her sister which had stopped her taking Tommy to school after Pamela's death. Yet although it felt very strange to be here once again, hearing the same old deafening noise of two hundred or more children all shouting at once, it was also oddly comforting. While she could see boys play-fighting and girls skipping about holding hands, just as they always had, she felt a kind of continuity of life going on regardless of Pamela's death.

She remembered the first day her little sister was due to go up to the junior school. She was really scared, asking Adele on the way there if it was true that the bigger children pushed the new ones' faces into the lavatory bowls. Adele promised her that it was just a silly story to frighten new children, and that anyway she'd be there in the top class to see no harm came to Pamela.

Adele was proud to have such a pretty sister. Even when Pamela lost her two front teeth she was still cuter and more endearing than any other girl in her class. She could see her now, skipping in the playground, her neat blonde plaits bouncing up and down as she jumped. Some of the girls in her class distanced themselves entirely from their younger siblings, but not Adele – she went out of her way to show off Pamela.

Last September, when Adele had to go on up to the secondary school, it was Pamela's turn to ask her sister if she was scared. 'I'll come with you if you like,' she volunteered as they walked down the road together. 'I'll tell all the big girls they've got to be nice to you, just like you did for me.'

Adele had laughed, it was funny to think of a little eight-year-old imagining she could boss big girls around. Yet Pamela's concern for her had made her less frightened to start at the secondary school.

She stood for some little while watching the children playing, wondering if someone would come to take her away today. While in one way she wanted to be taken, for it would mean the end of anxiety, a new start, the greater part of her was very scared. She could only liken it to starting at the secondary school, but at least there she'd known other children from the junior school. Many of them lived just a few doors away. Wherever they took her now, everyone was going to be a stranger.

'Are they coming for me today?' Adele suddenly blurted out as she helped Mrs Patterson peg some clothes on the line in the back yard. They had had a cup of tea together when she returned from the walk to Tommy's school and she'd sensed by the way Annie couldn't relax, jumping up from her chair every few minutes and tidying things, that something was up.

She saw an expression flit across the woman's face, and knew she was about to tell her a lie.

'I know some one *is* coming,' she said, looking hard at her. 'I just want to know if it's today.'

Annie Patterson had always liked Adele, right from the first day the Talbots moved in upstairs. It was raining hard that day, Jim and Rose were struggling to get their stuff upstairs, and Pamela, who was a newborn baby then, was screaming her lungs off. Annie had volunteered to take both the children in while the couple got themselves straightened out. She had only just discovered she was pregnant herself, with Tommy, so she was interested in children.

Even at four, going on five, Adele was a funny little thing, suspiciously well behaved, with an almost eerie adult manner. 'Mummy gets very tired,' she said soon after Annie had lifted the baby out of her pram to soothe her. 'I rock the pram for her a lot, but little Pammy doesn't like that much, she wants Mummy to cuddle her.'

Annie remembered how she asked Adele what she thought of her new little sister.

'She's nice when she's not crying,' she said thoughtfully. 'When she learns to walk I'll take her out all the time and Mummy can have some rest.'

That was just how it turned out too. By the time Adele was six she was pushing her little sister down the road in a pushchair. Annie recalled watching her from the front room window, and wondering how any mother could trust so young a child with a toddler. While it was true most of the other families in the street used their older children as nursemaids for the younger ones, Rose seemed too well bred to be so careless.

But Annie soon found that there was something about Adele which inspired trust. When Annie was expecting Michael, she let Adele take Tommy out along with Pamela to the park so she could put her feet up. She always welcomed the girl coming in to see him as she would read to him, play games and generally entertain him. She was a real little mother and very bright.

Many times over the years Annie had seen Adele with bruises, but she was such a good kid it never occurred to her then that she got them from her mother. It was only in the last two or three years that Annie had become suspicious. She noticed how much nicer Pamela's clothes were than Adele's, and Pamela looked plump and healthy too, while Adele was as skinny as a rake with an almost permanent cold. She often saw Rose holding Pamela's hand as they walked down the road, and it struck her that Rose never went out with Adele at all. Never once in eight years had she ever seen Rose kiss her elder daughter, give her a cuddle or even an affectionate pat on the head. Yet she'd seen her do all that to Pamela.

Now Annie was ashamed of herself. Not only had she let Adele down by not acting on her instincts a long time ago, now she was doing it again by conspiring with Dr Biggs about the welfare person coming to take her away.

She looked into the child's strange eyes and knew she couldn't lie to her 'Yes, my lovely,' she said with a sigh. 'Someone will be coming today.'

'Am I going to an orphanage?' Adele asked.

'Not if Dr Biggs can help it,' Annie said truthfully. 'He feels you'd be happier in a private house. Maybe with someone kind who has little ones of their own that you can help with. That sounds nice, don't it?'

Adele was fairly certain Mrs Patterson wasn't convinced it would be nice for her, or she would've said something earlier. But Adele nodded and tried to smile as if she was pleased. She knew she wouldn't get any kind of choice anyway, and she didn't want kind Mrs Patterson to feel bad about it.

*

A woman in a brown hat and tweed suit, who looked like a teacher, arrived just before twelve.

'I'm Miss Sutch,' she said, shaking Mrs Patterson's hand and smiling at Adele. 'We're going for a ride on the train out into the countryside, Adele,' she said. 'We've found somewhere lovely for you to stay until your mother is better.'

She picked up baby Lily and said what a pretty baby she was, and asked Michael how old he was and when he'd be starting school. Then she sat down at the table as if she was an old friend.

While they all had a cup of tea, Adele studied the woman. She guessed she was about forty, not exactly old, but getting on. She was tall and skinny, with freckles all over her face, and when she took her hat off, her hair was quite pretty, a kind of golden-red colour, short and curly. Mrs Patterson admired it and Miss Sutch ran her fingers through it.

'You wouldn't want it,' she laughed. 'If I let it grow I can't do a thing with it. When I was a child and my nurse used to force a comb through the tangles and make me cry, I thought curly hair was a curse.'

Adele thought she was a nice woman as she was neither stern nor condescending. She liked her gay laugh, and the way she didn't look about her as if there was a bad smell in the room. She even cuddled Lily and wiped the baby's nose on her own handkerchief as if she was a relative. But above all she seemed genuinely concerned about Adele's predicament and wanted to make things better for her.

'We've found a place at The Firs for you,' she said, looking Adele right in the eye. 'It's a family home in Kent. Mr and Mrs Makepeace have been taking children in for several years, mostly ones like you who need a temporary home for a while, and you'll be the oldest.'

She paused and smiled encouragingly. 'You are really lucky they have room for you just now. There's a swing in the garden, lots of books and games. Mrs Makepeace often takes all the children out for picnics and even to the seaside in the summer. You are going to love it.'

'Where will I go to school?' Adele asked nervously.

'Mr Makepeace is a teacher, so you'll have lessons with him, at least for the time being,' Miss Sutch said. 'Now, how does that sound?'

'Nice,' Adele said truthfully.

'Right then, we'd better get going,' Miss Sutch said. 'Have you got your things together?'

'She hasn't got much,' Mrs Patterson said, getting up and pulling Adele's little suitcase from beneath the couch. 'She'll need some new shoes, hers have got holes in them.'

'Mrs Makepeace will see to that,' Miss Sutch said cheerfully. 'So let's say our goodbyes to Mrs Patterson and then we'll be off.'

Mrs Patterson enveloped Adele in a warm hug. 'Be a good girl,' she said, kissing her forehead. 'And write to me to tell me how you are. Everything will turn out fine, you'll see.'

'Will Mum and Dad know where I am?' Adele whispered, suddenly nervous again.

'Of course they will,' Mrs Patterson said. 'Dr Biggs organized all this, love, so he'll be checking up on you, and them.'

Adele kissed baby Lily and patted Michael's head as he never let her kiss him. 'Thank you for taking care of me,' she said to Mrs Patterson. 'And say goodbye to Tommy for me.'

She felt a little odd as she walked down the street towards the Tube station with Miss Sutch. She had lived here for as long as she could remember, and apart from a day trip to Southend with the Sunday school she'd never been out of London. While it might have been miserable at home most of the time, all the good memories of Pamela were here, and she wasn't sure she wanted to leave those behind.

'You can always come back, you know,' Miss Sutch said suddenly, as if she'd read Adele's mind. 'I sometimes go back to the village I lived in as a child. I walk about and look at things, remember the good people and the ones who were nasty to me. Then all at once I find I'm glad I don't live there any more. You see, you change with different experiences. What suited you once won't suit you for ever.'

To Adele's surprise the train took them to Tunbridge Wells, the same place the old letter to her mother had come from. She would have told Miss Sutch about it, but the woman suddenly seemed flustered on their arrival, checking her watch and saying they'd have to get a taxi out to The Firs because she had to be back in London by six-thirty.

From what Adele could see of the town from the train, it looked interesting. The houses were old, but not rundown like the ones by stations in London. As they hurried to get a taxi, Miss Sutch said that in the 1800s people used to come to Tunbridge Wells to take the waters. Adele supposed that meant there was a well in the town which was like medicine. She would have liked to know more but Miss Sutch got into a conversation with the taxi driver about him waiting to take her back to the station.

Once they were right out of London the train journey had all been through open countryside, and Adele had been enchanted at the sight of new lambs frolicking in fields, primroses growing on the railway banks, and pretty cottages which looked as though they'd come straight out of story books. But once the taxi had left Tunbridge Wells and turned into narrow, winding lanes with thick hedges on either side and no more houses, she began to feel a little trepidation.

It began to rain heavily too, the sky becoming so black that the bare branches of the trees suddenly looked menacing.

'It's a long way from the shops,' she ventured.

'Now, why would you need shops?' Miss Sutch said sharply. 'Mr and Mrs Makepeace will make certain you have all you need.'

Adele didn't feel able to say she was scared of not knowing exactly where she was. It would sound suspicious and ungrateful, but she sat up straight and tried to take note of landmarks to make herself feel less lost.

The taxi turned off from the lane on to a muddy bumpy track, and Adele and Miss Sutch were thrown from side to side along the slippery seat while the driver cursed under his breath.

'If this rain keeps up it will be impassable soon,' he said, turning his head to look warningly at Miss Sutch. 'So don't you keep me waiting long now!'

'I'll just take her in and be right out again,' Miss Sutch assured him, then patted Adele's knee. 'I'm sorry, my dear. I meant to stop for tea and get you settled in, but you can see how it is for me. But you'll be fine. Mrs Makepeace is very welcoming.'

All at once Adele saw her destination straight in front of her. It was a plain red brick house with tall chimney pots, partially covered in ivy and surrounded by the tall fir trees from which it got its name. It was a very long way to even the closest neighbour.

'Such a splendid situation,' Miss Sutch said with a satisfied sigh. 'Of course it's a shame you couldn't have seen it for the first time in sunshine, but you've got the whole summer ahead of you for that. Now, driver, wait here, I shan't be long.'

Miss Sutch wasn't long, in fact she did no more than take Adele to the front door and ring the bell, and once it was opened by a stout woman with grey hair wearing a floral frock, she began making her excuses.

'This is Adele Talbot, you are expecting her, I believe? I shall have to love you and leave you as the taxi is waiting, and the driver getting grumpier by the minute because he's afraid of getting stuck in the mud.'

'I'm Mrs Makepeace, love,' the woman said with a smile, taking Adele's small case from Miss Sutch. 'Come on in and meet the others, it's nearly tea-time.'

Adele felt let down by Miss Sutch's haste to leave, which made it seem that the interest she'd shown when she first picked her up from Charlton Street was perhaps false after all. But Mrs Makepeace looked nice enough, and even if this place was very remote, she would have the company of other children.

'Goodbye,' she said, turning to Miss Sutch. 'Thank you for bringing me here.'

'Such a well-mannered girl!' Miss Sutch simpered, already backing away to the taxi. 'You'll have no trouble with this one, Mrs Makepeace. Now, I must dash.'

'That one could learn a few manners herself,' Mrs Makepeace said as she drew Adele into the hall and closed the door behind her. 'She's always the same, rushing like the March Hare. I often wonder if her boss knows how careless she really is. But then she has no idea what it's like to be without a home or family – brought up in the lap of luxury, that one! Now, let's go into the kitchen and meet everyone. We are one big happy family here so you've nothing to fear.'

The big hall was very bare, with just a shiny wood floor and an old sideboard, but there was a big vase of daffodils on it, and it smelled of lavender polish.

Adele's first impression of the kitchen and her 'new family' was surprise that both were so large. As Mrs Makepeace opened the door, she saw a huge table with what looked like a dozen children sitting around it, all staring at her.

'This is your new friend Adele,' Mrs Makepeace said, ushering her in and putting her case down by a dresser. 'Now, I'll start with the youngest. Mary, Susan, John, Willy, Frank,' she said, pointing out each child around the table. 'Lizzie, Bertie, Colin, Janice, Freda, Jack and Beryl. Now, what do we say to new friends, children?'

'Welcome,' they chorused as one.

'That's right, you are welcome.' Mrs Makepeace smiled broadly at Adele. 'Now, there's a spare seat waiting for you next to Beryl. I'll just make the pot of tea and we'll all start.'

Adele was sure she'd never remember everyone's name. The only one she'd caught was Mary's, who was just a baby, no more than eighteen months old, sitting up in a high chair chewing on a crust of bread, and the oldest, Beryl, who was perhaps eleven. The others ranged from three up to ten and were all quite unremarkable, as shabbily dressed as she was, and just as thin.

'Grace now, please,' Mrs Makepeace said as she put a giant-sized white enamel teapot on the table.

Everyone save little Mary jumped up and stood behind their chairs, bowing their heads over folded hands.

'We thank the Lord who put this food on our table,' Mrs Makepeace said. 'May we remember but for His loving kindness we might be hungry and neglected. Amen.'

The chorus of 'Amen' came with the scrape of chairs being pulled out again. 'Pass the bread, Beryl,' Mrs Makepeace ordered.

The mountain of bread spread thinly with margarine disappeared at the speed of light. Adele learned that the first two pieces had to be eaten plain, then on the third they could have jam. There was no fourth slice as it had all gone. The tea was watery, without sugar, and the final item was a small slice of cake which looked a little like bread pudding, but had no real flavour and the sultanas were very sparse.

For Adele it was enough, for Miss Sutch had given her an apple and a chocolate biscuit on the train journey. But she thought the other children were still hungry for they'd polished off their piece of cake even before she began hers, and kept looking at hers as if hoping she'd leave it on her plate.

They were all very quiet. Every now and then Mrs Makepeace would ask one a question and it was answered, but there was no conversation aside from that.

Despite its size, the kitchen had a homely quality, heated by the cooking range. A huge dresser took up one wall and it was crammed with china, ornaments and tin boxes. A wooden rack hung from the ceiling festooned with drying or airing clothes. There were pictures of royalty, animals and flowers cut from magazines stuck up on the pale green walls, plants on the window-sill and an enormous tabby cat asleep on an easy chair by the stove.

Grace was said again after tea, then Freda, Jack and Beryl, the oldest children, were told to remain behind to wash up, while Janice was told to take Adele and the others to the playroom.

'You won't start your duties till tomorrow,' Mrs Makepeace said to Adele. 'Beryl will explain all that to you later when she shows you your bed. So run along and get to know the little ones now.'

Janice, who was to inform Adele later that she was eight, wiped baby Mary's face and hands with a dish cloth, then, straddling her on her hip, led the way to the playroom, followed by the others in a crocodile. A small hand reached up for Adele's and when she looked down she saw it was Susan, the second to youngest, who was about three. She had a squint, and straggly, thin fair hair, and her little hand felt very rough; when Adele looked at it later she found it was scaly and sore.

The playroom was warm too. There was a coal fire behind a big fire-guard, and like the kitchen it had a well-worn appearance. A vast, dilapidated couch sat by the fire and there were several other equally shabby armchairs, a big table with a half-completed jigsaw on it, and several boxes of comics, books and toys.

It was nicer than Adele had expected, and through the large French windows was the garden, complete with a swing.

The rain made it look dreary, but to Adele who had never had a garden to go into, it was lovely. She was also pleased that most of the other children were little. Susan was still clinging to her hand and it made her feel really welcome.

'Where've you come from?' Janice asked, sitting down by the fire with Mary on her lap.

'London,' Adele replied, sitting down beside her and drawing Susan close to her. 'Is it all right here?'

'Frank! Don't touch that jigsaw or Jack will have your guts,' Janice shouted at one of the smaller boys. She looked at Adele, and grinned. 'Jack loves jigsaws and he can't stand it if anyone breaks them up before he's finished. Yeah, it's all right here. But I wish I could go home to Mum.'

Janice reminded Adele a little of Pamela. She wasn't pretty like her – her hair was mousy-brown, and her teeth were going black – but she was the same age and she had that same kind of confident look about her.

'You've got a mum then?' Adele asked.

Janice nodded. 'Most of us have. Mine's sick and my aunty could only take the baby, so Willy and I came here. That's my brother Willy,' she said, pointing to a small boy with red hair. 'He's four now. But if Mum don't get well soon I reckon they'll put us somewhere else.'

'Why?' Adele asked.

Janice shrugged. 'They only take kids for a short while here. Mr Makepeace makes what he calls assessments of us.'

'Where is he?' Adele had forgotten until then that there was a Mr Makepeace too.

'Dunno, he goes out a lot,' Janice said. 'Sometimes we don't see him for days.'

That remark led Adele to ask about their lessons, and Janice said they didn't have many. She said that those like her who could already read and write were told to read a chapter of a book, then write in their own words what it was about.

'Once a week Mr Makepeace puts a lot of sums up on the blackboard in the schoolroom,' Janice went on. 'We have to stay there till we get them right. But that's easy, he never gives us really hard ones. Then Mrs Makepeace gives us a spelling test too. The ones we get wrong she makes us write down till we can remember them.'

Adele wondered if Mr Makepeace set different work for older children like her. She was good at arithmetic and spelling already, but she wanted to get better still.

'What do you do for the rest of the time then?' she asked.

'We get jobs to do,' Janice replied, looking oddly at Adele as if surprised she didn't know that. 'Then we play outside if it's fine. It ain't real hard here. You don't get the stick unless you do something really bad. But I still wish I could go home.'

It was dark outside by the time Beryl came back from the kitchen and took Adele upstairs to show her the bedrooms. She was just a year younger than Adele, a slight, dark-haired girl who appeared extremely anxious about absolutely everything.

Adele was to share a room with her and Freda, who was ten. It was chilly, furnished only with iron beds, a locker each and a washbasin. It adjoined the nursery room where baby Mary and Susan and John, the two three-year-olds, slept. It seemed the older girls were expected to take care of the younger ones during the night.

'Mrs Makepeace gets really cross if they wake her up,' Beryl said, her dark eyes flitting around the bedroom as if she was convinced someone was eavesdropping on her. 'Freda never wakes up, so it's always me what has to see to 'em. You will help me, won't you?'

Adele assured her she would, and was then shown the other rooms. Lizzie and Janice had a room of their own, with two spare beds in it. The remaining five boys, including Janice's four-year-old brother, shared another, with ten-year-old Jack in charge.

'Bertie and Colin are holy terrors,' Beryl said with a sigh. 'They are always up to something like trying to sneak downstairs for more food, or having pillow fights. Jack ain't up to keeping them in line, he's backward you see, so if we hear them carrying on we have to stop them.'

By the time Adele finally got to bed she had identified why Beryl was so anxious. It seemed Mrs Makepeace delegated all the chores to the children, and as Beryl had been the oldest until Adele's arrival, she was blamed if things didn't run smoothly. Beryl hadn't elaborated further, but she didn't need to. Adele saw the bleakness in her eyes, the resignation in her voice, and recognized a similarity to her own situation at home.

'It's not as bad as the place I was in before,' she replied to Adele's blunt question about whether she or any of the other children were ill-treated. 'We got beatings all the time there, and we hardly had anything to eat. Just watch out for Mrs M. and do what she tells you, or you'll get it.'

Mr Makepeace was away for the whole of Adele's first week at The Firs, and for the first two days she thought she must have misunderstood Beryl, for Mrs Makepeace seemed so warm-hearted, caring and jolly. She laughed when Adele asked about lessons. 'Don't you go worrying your little head about that,' she said, as she rummaged through a cupboard of clothes and found a blue checked skirt and a pale blue jumper for Adele to wear. 'You've had a nasty shock, and I'm going to pretty you up, so you feel better.'

She washed Adele's hair for her, and combed it into two bunches, putting pale blue ribbons on each. 'That's better,' she said, patting Adele's cheek affectionately. 'Once that nasty scar has gone and you've got some roses in your cheeks you'll look a different girl.'

It was nice to be fussed over, to be able to confide in the woman about all the horrible things her mother had said to her. Adele could see it was true that Mrs Makepeace did get the children to do much of the work around the house, but she didn't mind, after all she was used to doing a great deal at home, and at least Mrs Makepeace appreciated it.

But on her third morning Adele discovered that Mrs Makepeace had a cruel and vindictive side to her.

Colin, a tow-headed eight-year-old, had been sent out to collect the eggs from the chickens. It was still raining hard and he'd run back with the eggs, but slipped on the wet grass and broke two of them.

He was crying when he came in, for he'd hurt his knee, but Mrs Makepeace made him cry even harder. 'You're useless,' she raged at him. 'It's hard enough feeding all you lot without one of you wasting food. Bertie and Lizzie will have to go without their egg for breakfast because you are so stupid. I hope they make you suffer for it.'

Adele was astounded when she made Colin eat an egg in front of two other children who'd been deprived of theirs. She could see by his tortured face he would gladly have gone without himself for two or even more breakfasts rather than risk his friends' displeasure. And Mrs Makepeace goaded Bertie and Lizzie to be angry with Colin. She kept asking how their bread and marge was without a boiled egg. She said they should ignore Colin all day.

It was the kind of sinister, manipulative cruelty that her own mother had gone in for. She could remember Pamela being given second helpings of pudding while she was left out. Or Pamela being forced to parade her new skirt or cardigan when Adele needed one far more. The only reason she didn't turn spiteful to Pamela was because she always knew that was exactly what their mother was aiming at.

Sadly, Bertie and Lizzie did react as Mrs Makepeace wanted. They were nasty to Colin all day. By bedtime he'd withdrawn right into himself, and Adele knew he felt lower than a worm, for that was just the way she used to feel herself.

From then on Adele found herself watching Mrs Make-peace more closely as she doled out her flamboyant affection, patting bottoms, kissing cheeks and tweaking hair, and calling them 'her little sweetheart'. The recipients glowed with delight, falling over themselves to keep her approval in any way they could, mostly doing extra chores for her. But it soon became clear that their subservience was as much from fear as adoration. At the slightest misdemeanour Mrs Makepeace would crush the love-hungry child with ridicule. She was a master at humiliation, homing in on weakness and insecurity.

Adele got the idea that all the children over five had been selected purposely, for there was a distinct type. There wasn't one independent, rebellious street urchin – every one was needy in some way. They all had younger brothers and sisters whom they were separated from and missed, which made them ideal nursemaids to the younger ones. Adele could recognize herself and her background in each one of them.

As the days went by she heard Mrs Makepeace reminding the children over and over again in honeyed words that the clothes they wore, the food they ate and the toys they had to play with all came from her and her husband. This wasn't true either, for Adele discovered that The Firs was a charity, and the Makepeaces mere wardens.

She had made this discovery while dusting Mr Makepeace's study. A pamphlet with a picture of The Firs was on the desk, and she couldn't resist reading it. She read that it was a charitable home for 'Distressed Children', a place of safety where they could stay until their family circumstances improved or long-term care could be found for them. Donations were required as Mr and Mrs Makepeace, the wardens, had to be paid, along with the housekeeping expenses. Furthermore, it was hoped that enough money could be raised to accommodate more children and give them better school and play facilities.

But whatever Adele thought of Mrs Makepeace, she liked The Firs well enough. She had three meals a day and the company of other children, and she was very glad to wake each morning knowing that she wasn't going to be slapped or shouted at for merely looking at her mother.

Then Mr Makepeace arrived home and the last of Adele's little anxieties floated away. Just the way all the children ran eagerly to him to be swung round or thrown up in the air said that he really loved the children in his care.

He was tall, perhaps six feet, with thick dark hair, a moustache and the loveliest, softest brown eyes Adele had ever seen. She thought he must have false teeth because they were so white and even, but when he laughed or smiled, which he seemed to do very readily, there was no give-away flash of anything that wasn't natural gums. He was a bit portly, but he dressed so beautifully with a waistcoat beneath his suit jacket that it hardly showed.

'Adele is such a pretty name,' he said when his wife introduced them. 'But then you are a very pretty girl. And how are you settling in?'

'Fine thank you, sir,' she replied, looking down because she was embarrassed at someone saying she was pretty when she knew she wasn't.

'Mrs Makepeace tells me you are a clever girl as well as being pretty,' he said, putting his hand under her chin and lifting her face up. 'A good reader, gentle with the little ones, a first-class potato peeler. So many talents. But I don't think you believe you are pretty too.'

'No, sir,' she whispered.

'Well, you're wrong,' he said, looking right into her eyes. 'Prettiness comes from inside, and I can see it's there in you. Another couple of years, a bit of filling out, and you'll be gorgeous.'

His voice was so smooth and deep she couldn't help but smile at him.

'There you are,' he chuckled. 'A smile that would melt anyone's heart. Now, come into my study for a moment and we'll have a chat about your lessons.'

He sat down at his desk and made Adele sit beside him. He took a book down from his shelf and asked her to read a passage. It was *The Mill on the Floss*, a book Adele had read not long before Pamela died. She had loved it and perhaps that was why she lost her nervousness and read it well.

'Excellent,' he said. 'We don't get many children as able as you here. Now, tell me what you were learning at school before you came here.'

He was so easy to talk to, she found herself telling him far more than he asked. About how she loved reading, that she'd been top of the class in arithmetic, but history was boring and geography didn't seem to have any use to her personally.

'But you might travel one day,' he said with a smile. 'How would you know how to decide which country you wanted to visit unless you'd studied them?'

Adele had never thought of that aspect, but then she'd never spoken to a man who knew as much as he did. He even seemed to know about the events which had brought about her needing a new home, and he asked how she felt about being brought here.

'It's nice,' she said shyly. 'But I am a bit worried I'll get behind with school work.'

'Mrs Makepeace isn't a teacher,' he said slightly reprovingly. 'And sadly many of the children here aren't able to learn as readily as you, Adele, and many of them don't stay here for very long. We have always stuck to just the rudimentary things, reading, writing, sums and spelling, for that is all that is necessary for most. Yet when we have a child here who can learn more, I am only too pleased to help them.'

*

Adele felt she was floating on air in the days that followed Mr Makepeace's return home. She lost interest in observing his wife and had stopped listening to Beryl's many whines about how put-upon she was. For the very first time in her life she felt special and she had Mr Makepeace to thank for it.

On his second day home he had called her in from the garden where she was helping with the weeding, and set her a test in arithmetic. When she'd finished that, he marked it, and praised her for getting every sum right, then gave her *A Tale of Two Cities* by Charles Dickens to read over the weekend, and said they would discuss it the following Monday.

As she got into the book she found herself imagining Charles Darnay as Mr Makepeace, which made it all so much more important and vital to her. To complete her happiness over that weekend, Mrs Makepeace relieved her of nearly all her chores, and while the rest of the children were working, or in the younger ones' case, out in the garden, she curled up on the playroom couch, lost in the drama of the French Revolution.

She finished the book late on Sunday evening, and when she went up to bed she found Beryl awake, stiff with disapproval.

'You aren't the first girl he's made a fuss of,' she said waspishly. 'He does that, then when he gets fed up he sends them away.'

Adele wasn't in the mood for Beryl. She was always moaning about something and she thought the girl was riddled with jealousy.

'He won't send me away,' she retorted confidently. 'He likes me.'

Chapter Five

Mr Makepeace took the pipe he was lighting from his mouth. 'How long have you been with us now, Adele?' he asked.

They were having a private geography lesson in the schoolroom. The room bore little resemblance to the classrooms Adele had been used to, being very small, with just one old refectory table, a few chairs, and a handful of dog-eared books on the window-sill. The only real indication of the room's purpose was the blackboard, which at present had a large map of the world clipped over it. Mr Makepeace had been pointing to various countries on it and Adele had to write down their names and capitals.

Anyone glancing into the room would have perhaps imagined she was receiving some kind of punishment, as it was a sunny spring afternoon and all the other children were playing outside in the garden. But although the sounds of their voices wafted in through the open windows, Adele had no desire to be out there with them. She was more than content to be having another lesson with her teacher.

'It's over a month now, sir,' she replied.

'And are you happy here?'

She was a little taken aback by such a question. Adults weren't in the habit of asking her such things. 'Yes, sir,' she said cheerfully.

He was leaning against the window-sill, the aroma of his pipe tobacco cancelling out the scent of freshly cut grass which had been wafting in previously. He was wearing an open-necked white shirt today and grey flannel trousers, and while he didn't look as impressive as he did in a dark suit, he seemed far more approachable and fatherly.

'Only "yes"! No explanation about what makes you happy here, or even a "but"?' he said mockingly.

Adele frowned in bewilderment and this made him laugh. 'Well, you could have said, "Yes I am happy here, but I still hate geography,"' he said, wiggling his pipe at her.

'But I don't hate it any longer,' she said quickly. 'Not since you began teaching me.'

'Does that mean you are happy here because of me?'

Adele knew that was the case, she adored him and lived for these private lessons. But she was reluctant to admit that; right from her early childhood she had learned it was safer not to reveal her true feelings about anything or anyone.

'Because of everything,' she hedged. 'I like the house, the other children, the garden.'

'And me?' he interrupted.

'Yes,' she said sheepishly. 'And you.'

'That's good,' he said, getting up from his chair and coming over to her. 'Because you grow more special to me every day,' he said softly, and bent to kiss the top of her head.

Adele felt a surge of pure joy run through her. She had adored him almost from the first time they met, hung on his every word and felt sad on days when he wasn't around. But she had never expected that he would ever feel anything like that for her. She was plain and dull, a girl destined to be overlooked.

'Does it please you that you are special to me?' he asked, and he knelt beside her chair and put his arm around her.

His voice was low and tender. The smell of his lavender hair oil, the tobacco in his pipe, and the way his fingers gently caressed her side made her feel quite faint. 'Yes,' she whispered. 'Because you're special to me too.'

He was looking at her in such an intense way she had to drop her eyes. 'Kiss me, Adele,' he said softly.

Slightly embarrassed, she gave him a quick peck on the

cheek. But he put his hand against her cheek and drew her back close to him. 'On the lips,' he whispered. 'That's what people who love one another do.'

Adele was so overcome by him saying that he loved her that she flung her arms around his neck and kissed him willingly, but his moustache tickled her lips and made her giggle and break away.

'You find me funny?' he asked.

His dark eyes bored into her, and his expression was stern.

'No, it's just your moustache is bristly,' she said hastily.

He got up from his knees and she was afraid she had offended him, but to her surprise he pulled her to her feet, then sat down again, drawing her on to his lap. 'So if I shave it off, will you try again?' he asked.

A small dart of anxiety pricked her. She wanted to be cuddled, but he wasn't doing it quite right. He was holding her very tightly against him with one arm, but his other hand was on her thigh.

'I should go now, it's time to help get the tea ready,' she said, trying to wriggle away.

'No it isn't,' he said, drawing her back against him. 'Mrs Makepeace has gone into town like she always does on Friday afternoons. You know we don't start tea until she gets back. We've got lots of time yet. Don't you want to be my special girl and have a little cuddle?'

He looked hurt, his big brown eyes so mournful that Adele felt obliged to put her arms around his neck and hug him tightly.

'That's better,' he murmured against her neck. 'I think of you as my little girl. I need to hold you.'

Later that day up in the bathroom, Adele sat on the stool drying baby Mary, while Beryl washed Susan and John in Mary's bathwater. This part of the day was one Adele always enjoyed. Mary was a chubby, placid toddler who responded joyfully to being tickled and played with. Susan and John were happy little souls too, content just to sit there in the bath laughing and splashing each other. Beryl was always less prickly and tense here, and Adele supposed that was because Mrs Makepeace never came to see what they were doing with the small children.

Adele wished she and Beryl could become real friends. It ought to be possible, there was only a year's difference in their ages, and they were together so much. But Beryl never initiated a conversation, she hardly ever laughed, and she appeared to be lost in a world of her own.

It didn't help that Mrs Makepeace was always on at her. Adele had often noticed that Beryl seemed bewildered and lost, and it was only when she was with the little ones that she came to life at all.

'You've got a bit sunburnt on the back of your neck,' Adele said, noticing the angry red patch as the other girl bent over the bath. 'Is it sore?'

'Yes, very.' Beryl grimaced, putting her hand up to touch it. 'I told Mrs Makepeace but she told me to stop moaning.'

'You'd have to have a leg coming off before she'd show any interest,' Adele said in sympathy. 'But there's some calamine lotion in the cupboard, I saw it there the other day. That'll soothe it. I'll dab some on for you once we've got these three put to bed.'

Beryl's thin face broke into a wide smile of appreciation. 'Thanks. That's what I miss most about home. Our mum always noticed stuff like sunburn or grazed knees. Did yours?'

Adele shook her head.

'She didn't!' Beryl looked shocked. 'What about yer dad?'

'He wouldn't have noticed if I was on fire,' Adele said. 'He wouldn't even look after me while Mum went into hospital.'

A month ago wild horses wouldn't have dragged that piece of information from her, but Adele was keener to keep the conversation going than to cling on to loyalty to a man who didn't want her around. 'What's your dad like?'

'Nice when he ain't drinking,' Beryl said wistfully. 'That's why us kids got taken away when Mum got ill. He went on a bender.'

'What's that?' Adele asked.

Beryl shrugged. 'Drinking all the time, not coming home and that.'

Adele wanted to ask a specific question about Beryl's dad but she wasn't sure how to approach it.

'Is your dad . . .' She hesitated for a moment. 'Well, affectionate to you?'

Beryl frowned. 'Wotcha mean? Does he hug me and stuff?'

Adele nodded.

'Yeah, all the time. Even more when he's got the drink in him.'

The conversation was abruptly ended when Susan got some soap in her eye and began crying. By the time the two older girls had washed it out, dried her and got her nightdress on, Adele couldn't think of a way to open the conversation up again.

What she really wanted to know was if Beryl's dad ever kissed her on the lips. Mr Makepeace had done it again to her after cuddling her for quite a long time. It made her feel creepy and confused. It was almost a relief when the lesson time was over, yet she was scared too that he would stop loving her if she didn't want to kiss him again.

She thought if she only knew how real fathers behaved with their daughters, she wouldn't feel funny about Mr Makepeace. It was no good thinking about Jim Talbot, she couldn't remember ever being kissed or hugged by him even when she was small, though she remembered him throwing Pamela up in the air to make her laugh.

How could she find out about ordinary dads? No one in this place came from what she'd call a normal family, at least not the kind she read about in books. Even books didn't make it very clear. Daughters always ran to their fathers, they said they hugged and kissed, and she had always supposed that was in the way she'd seen Mr Patterson greet his children. But there was no point in comparing Mr Patterson to Mr Makepeace anyway. Mr Patterson worked on the railways; he was a rough, tough man, quite different to a teacher.

Two weeks later, at tea-time, another girl, called Ruby Johnston, arrived at The Firs. She was ten, the same age as Freda. She looked ill, she was so thin and pale, her clothes were several sizes too large, and someone had hacked her brown hair off to less than an inch all over. She looked terrified when Mrs Makepeace brought her into the kitchen and she saw all the children sitting round the table. Adele felt really sorry for her because she remembered how she felt on her first day.

'Adele, you'll have to move up to the attic room to make room for Ruby,' Mrs Makepeace said after making all the introductions.

Adele glanced at Beryl and saw she wasn't pleased to hear this. Adele guessed she was thinking that now she'd have the sole responsibility for Mary if she woke in the night. Adele didn't welcome the change either. She didn't want to be alone in a room at the top of the house.

It was a nasty, tiny room which hadn't been used for years. Birds often got in there as there were gaps in the house's eaves. The walls were stained, there were damp, bare boards on the floor, and there was no electricity up there either.

Adele certainly didn't find Beryl and Freda great company, they were dull and slow-witted and afraid of their own shadows, but she'd got used to being with them. If she woke in the night it was comforting to know they were close. But apart from that, Adele was afraid that being in a room on her own would mark her out even further from all the other children.

Being the eldest set her apart anyway, and then there were the private lessons. No one had ever said much about them, but perhaps that was because they saw them as a kind of punishment rather than a privilege. Yet the time away from the other children did make her feel detached from them.

Every single lesson now Mr Makepeace wanted to kiss and cuddle her, and sometimes he didn't teach her anything.

It seemed so strange that she used to think it would be heaven on earth to have this man hold her in his arms, and now that the wish had come true, she didn't really want it.

The creepy feeling she'd got the first time was with her constantly now. When he stroked her arms and legs, ran his fingers through her hair and held her so tightly on his lap, all she could think of was that it wasn't right. But she didn't know why, or how to put an end to it.

He said he needed to touch her because he loved her, and that she was his special girl. He said he'd never felt this way about any of the other children who'd come to The Firs. So if she said she didn't like it, surely that was the same as saying she didn't like him?

'Adele!'

Adele started at the sound of Mrs Makepeace's voice. She had been so absorbed in her private worries that she hadn't noticed the others had finished their tea, or that she was being spoken to.

'I'm sorry, did you say something?' she asked guiltily.

'Yes I did, several times,' the woman snapped. 'You can take Ruby upstairs, show her where she'll sleep and run a bath for her,' she said. 'Find her a nightdress and some clean clothes that fit her. Then you'd better make up the bed in the attic. Freda can help Beryl put the little ones to bed tonight.'

Adele could sense that Ruby was even more scared as they left the kitchen and she was ashamed of herself for not being more welcoming.

'Where've you come from?' she asked, trying to make up for it. 'Was it London like me?'

'Deptford,' Ruby replied in a small voice.

Adele nodded. She knew that was in South London but had no idea what it was like. 'Is your mum ill?'

'She's dead,' Ruby said flatly.

Adele didn't know what to say to that, she knew adults always said they were sorry, but something in Ruby's tone told her that wasn't appropriate. 'Well, you'll be all right here,' she said, deciding to say something similar to what Beryl had said to her on her first night. 'Mrs Makepeace doesn't beat us or anything, and the other kids are nice.'

She ran a bath for the girl and while it was running told her to take off her clothes and put them in the laundry basket. Ruby did as she was told almost too fast, as though she thought she'd be punished. When Adele saw there were a great many bruises and marks all over her body, some old and some new, she felt a great well of empathy for her.

'After the bath you can help me pick out your new clothes if you like,' she said, afraid to say anything about the bruises. 'There's lots of nice stuff in the cupboard.'

Ruby's lips moved just slightly, as if she wanted to smile but had forgotten how to. Although she was so thin and pale she had lovely grey eyes and very long eyelashes – when her hair grew again she'd probably be very pretty. 'Are you the oldest here?' she asked.

'Yes, but only by a year,' Adele replied, very glad Ruby seemed less scared now. 'But you'll find Beryl thinks she's in charge because she was the oldest for a long time before I came.'

'She gave me a funny look,' Ruby said, and frowned. 'Will she be mean to me?'

'What, Beryl?' Adele giggled. 'She couldn't be mean to anyone, she's too much of a scaredy cat. No one will be mean to you here, Ruby. If they are, you tell me.'

Ruby got into the bath gingerly, with a renewed fearful look in her eyes, and Adele guessed she wasn't used to a real bath. Naked, she was so thin that Adele could see all her bones, and she wondered if Mrs Makepeace would give her extra food to fatten her up.

Adele made small talk while the other girl bathed. She told her a little about each of the other children, and something of the chores they each had. Then, when she sensed Ruby felt more comfortable with her, she asked who cut her hair so short.

'Aunt Anne,' Ruby said with a deep sigh. 'She's not a real aunty, just the woman Dad had it off with. She said it was the only way to deal with the nits I had. But that wasn't the real reason, she just hated me.'

Adele sat down abruptly on the stool, shocked that a ten-year-old would speak of something like 'having it off'. Adele had heard big girls use that expression sometimes, and she knew roughly what it meant. It was what men went to prostitutes for. But she wasn't going to say anything about that to Ruby, not when she'd been treated badly by this woman.

'It will soon grow again, love,' she said. 'And those bruises will go too. I felt better when I got here, and you will too in a day or so.'

'Did you think nobody in the world cared about you?' Ruby asked, her grey eyes full of pain.

Adele nodded. A lump had come up in her throat because she felt so sorry for the girl. 'But we've got one another to care about here,' she said. 'It's safe here, no one hurts us.'

Later that evening Adele lay in the bed in the attic thinking about Ruby. In the face of what the new girl had gone on to tell her later, she didn't think she had any reason to mind being alone up in this room. The old iron bed was a bit creaky and the mattress lumpy, but she was lying between clean sheets, there was light coming in from the landing downstairs, and she wasn't hungry or hurt.

Ruby had told her that her father had left her with Aunt Anne and her four children in their basement flat and gone off to look for work. Ruby said she didn't know exactly why Aunt Anne had suddenly become so nasty to her, but she thought it was because her dad hadn't sent any money. Whatever the reason, she locked Ruby in the coal cellar which was outside the front door and went under the pavement of the street above. She said it was bitterly cold in there, and dark too, and at night she had only a few sacks to lie on, and an old coat to put over her. Each morning Aunt Anne would drag her out to wait for the postman to come. When there was nothing from her father, she'd hit Ruby, then shut her back in the cellar with just a couple of slices of bread and a cup of water.

Ruby didn't know exactly how long she'd been in there, but she said her father had gone away in early February, and it was about three weeks after that when Aunt Anne had shut her in. It seemed her teacher at school and the neighbours thought her father had come back for her and taken her away when they didn't see her. She was only found and released because a gas man went down to the basement area to empty the meter and heard her crying. He called the police.

Adele felt sick as Ruby told her all this. Some of the marks on her body were from cigarette burns: she said Anne would force her into a chair and insist Ruby knew where her father was, and she would burn her to try to get it out of her.

'But I didn't know and I thought I was going to die in that cellar,' Ruby said, tears running down her cheeks. 'I prayed Dad would come back for me, but Aunt Anne said once that men didn't give a toss about their children, all they cared about was getting their cocks into a fanny, and once the woman was up the spout they were off. I suppose she was right.'

Adele had tried to hide her shock at the crude words

Ruby used, and indeed her bewilderment that a ten-year-old appeared to know so much more about what went on between men and women than she did. Adele did know that the rude word 'fucking' was part of being married and having babies, but Ruby's graphic words made it sound so ugly.

Yet hearing Ruby's terrible story had made Adele feel lucky. She hadn't spent one night hungry and cold since her mother was taken away. The doctor had cared enough to make sure she went to a decent home, and she had Mr Makepeace who loved her. She felt she ought to feel really happy; she might have ended up somewhere with someone like Ruby's Aunt Anne.

A few days after Ruby's arrival, Mr Makepeace went away on business again. As he always ate his meals in his living room, and often went out in his black car in the mornings, Adele didn't even think about him until the afternoon when they were due to have a lesson.

'Will Sir be back in time for lessons?' she asked Mrs Makepeace.

'No, he won't,' the woman snapped. 'He's gone away for a while. But you can help the younger ones with some reading and writing.'

'Today?' Adele asked.

'Today and every day until I tell you otherwise,' was the curt reply. 'So don't just stand there gawping at me, if you're as clever as my husband claims, you should be able to manage perfectly well. Take the middle group first, and the older ones can do some jobs for me.'

The middle group was the six- to eight-year-olds, Frank, Lizzie, Bertie, Colin and Janice. While they all liked having stories read to them, none of them read very well themselves. In fact, six-year-old Frank barely knew the letters of the alphabet, and when Adele had tried to teach him on several previous occasions he'd refused even to try.

Adele was about to point out the difficulty of having Frank in the class with the others when she sensed Mrs Makepeace was waiting for some sort of protest. She had that slightly mocking look on her face she always had when she was boiling up for something. One wrong word when she was like that meant a clout. So Adele said nothing and went out into the garden to round the five children up.

The lesson went much better than she expected, but then she did bribe the children by saying that if they each read a passage from a book in turn, and then copied six lines from it in their best handwriting while she helped Frank, she'd read them all a story.

Mrs Makepeace came into the schoolroom just as they were doing the writing part. She stood for a moment watching, and Adele carried on helping Frank write simple three-letter words. Perhaps she was impressed that all the children were working, because she soon turned on her heel and left without saying a word.

The older group later were no trouble at all, they got bored being out in the garden for long periods, and they were glad to have something to do. Even Jack, who was a little backward and couldn't read much better than an average seven-year-old, wanted to try. For the writing part Adele chalked up sentences on the blackboard, missing out an adjective, and got them to put their own in.

She had to suppress a giggle when she read one of Jack's efforts. He was a big, ungainly boy with a sloppy mouth and sticking-out ears, so gormless that she couldn't usually be bothered much with him. But this really amused her.

The sentence she'd given the children was, 'It was a – day, so Mrs Jones hung the washing in the garden.'

The others had slipped in 'lovely', 'nice' or 'windy', but Jack had put 'bloody'.

'Why bloody, Jack?' Adele asked, trying hard to keep a straight face.

'Mum always said, "It's bloody washing day" every Monday,' he replied.

She read them the first chapter of *Treasure Island* afterwards, and when the bell went for tea she felt very pleased with herself that both lessons had gone so well.

That first day was the only one when Adele managed to hold the attention of the classes. As each further day passed, their behaviour gradually grew worse. By the end of the week they were all larking around the whole time, and Adele got the blame from Mrs Makepeace because they were making so much noise.

All at once Adele found herself friendless because the children saw her as Mrs Makepeace's spy and excluded her from their games and conversations. Even the younger children kept their distance. Once in her attic bed she could hear the other girls chatting and laughing together downstairs and she felt they were laughing at her. On top of that, Mrs Makepeace was very sarcastic towards her, and any questions were met with, 'You're the clever one, work it out for yourself.'

Four whole weeks crept by, each one leaving Adele more miserable and isolated. Sometimes she was afraid that Mr Makepeace was gone for good, because his wife seemed so angry, and Adele felt she'd just wither up and die if he didn't return.

Then one morning as she was peeling potatoes for dinner, she heard his car draw up outside. She didn't dare run out to him of course, but her heart began to hammer and she rushed to the window to look at him.

She thought he looked as handsome as a film star in his dark grey suit and trilby hat. His face was bronzed from the sun and as he saw her at the window and smiled, his teeth flashed brilliant white.

Mrs Makepeace dished up the children's dinner, warned them to behave while they ate it without her, then took hers and her husband's into their living room. She emerged again over an hour later, just as Adele was finishing the washing up. The other children had skipped off to play outside, and Beryl was wheeling Mary around in her pram trying to get her to go to sleep.

'My husband wants to see you in the schoolroom after you've done these,' Mrs Makepeace said curtly, banging down a tray loaded with dirty plates and glasses.

Adele only nodded. The grim look on the woman's face was enough to know something had upset her.

When Adele finally got to the schoolroom, Mr Makepeace was sitting on the window-sill smoking his pipe and she rushed to him, throwing her arms around him.

'You've been away so long and it's been terrible without you,' she blurted out.

He laughed softly. 'I'll have to go away more often if I get a welcome like this when I get back,' he said.

'I missed you so much,' she said, and began to cry, spilling out how she couldn't teach the younger ones anything, and she hadn't got a friend in the whole place.

He moved on to a chair and drew her on to his lap. 'I'm sure it wasn't that bad,' he said, drying her eyes with his handkerchief.

'It was, it was,' she insisted. 'I couldn't bear it.'

He cuddled her to him and rocked her in his arms. 'I missed you too,' he said. 'But I have to go away now and then, I have business to take care of.'

When he began kissing and stroking her Adele was so pleased to be with him again that she found she didn't mind as much as before. He said he wished he could take her away with him, and that maybe when she was a little older he could.

Beryl was lurking in the corridor when Adele came out of the schoolroom an hour later.

'Teacher's pet,' Beryl hissed scornfully at her.

'You're only jealous,' Adele retorted. 'I can't help it if he likes me because I'm the only one of us who wants to learn anything.'

'That's not what he likes you for,' Beryl snapped back, her small face full of spite. 'He likes anyone who lets him stick his hand in their knickers.'

Adele stopped in her tracks, astounded by what the younger girl had said. 'That's a filthy thing to say,' she gasped.

'He's the filthy one.' Beryl shrugged. 'He tries it on all the bigger girls, that's why Julie ran away.'

Adele walked past with her nose in the air. She didn't believe Beryl, and she wasn't going to give her the satisfaction of thinking she'd upset her.

But as she helped Mrs Makepeace get the tea ready, spreading margarine on the bread, and laying out plates and cups on the table, she was still mulling over what Beryl had said.

Soon after Adele arrived at The Firs she recalled Mrs Makepeace laying into a couple of the children because they'd said a girl called Julie had run away. Mrs Makepeace said they were talking rubbish, and that Julie hadn't run away at all, but left because she was fourteen and old enough to go to work.

Adele was fairly certain that Beryl had concocted her nasty version of Julie's story with the aid of Ruby. The new girl had a dirty mind, she was always saying grubby things, and Beryl hung on her every word.

'What on earth's up with you?'

Adele jumped at Mrs Makepeace's angry voice. 'What do you mean?' she asked.

'Well, just look how much marge you've spread on that slice of bread,' she said, wiggling a tablespoon menacingly at Adele.

Adele looked down and saw that she had spread enough

marge for several slices. 'I'm sorry,' she said. 'I was thinking about something.'

'Well, stop it,' the woman snapped. 'Thinking isn't any good for girls in your position. You have to learn to work and do it quickly, that's all.'

Adele woke with a start that same night to hear a creak on the stairs coming up to the attic. She sat up in bed and looked towards the door, but she could see nothing because the light on the downstairs landing had been turned off.

A stair creaked again and all at once she saw a big dark shape in her doorway. She was just about to scream when she smelled lavender hair oil. 'Is that you, sir?' she whispered.

'Yes, my love,' he whispered back. 'Not a sound please, we don't want to wake anyone else up.'

'Is there something the matter?' she asked when he'd come right in and shut the door.

'No. I just wanted to be with you,' he replied.

As her eyes got used to the dark she could just make out that he was wearing his pyjamas, and he sat down on the bed beside her and made it creak.

'You've stolen my heart, Adele,' he said, taking one of her hands and rubbing it between his. 'All I can think about is you.'

Adele didn't know what to say. He had stolen her heart too, but it didn't seem right that he was creeping about in the dark to say such things.

'May I lie beside you?' he asked. 'I just want to hold you.'

Adele moved over, but the bed was very narrow and there wasn't much room for him too. 'You shouldn't be here,' she ventured nervously, suddenly thinking of what Beryl had said again.

'Why, my darling?' he said, scooping her into his arms. 'Didn't you ever get into bed with your father for a cuddle?'

'No,' she said. 'I wasn't allowed.'

'But you would have liked to?'

Adele remembered that Pamela had often gone into bed with their parents, especially when she didn't feel well. Adele had always envied her. She had tried to do it herself a few times when she was five or six, but her mother always ordered her back to her own bed. 'Yes, I would've liked to,' she admitted. 'But it's different with you.'

'Why is it?' he asked, kissing her forehead. 'I love you like you were my own daughter.'

That made it seem right, and she relaxed against him, and as he held her closely to him the warmth and comfort of his arms made her sleepy again.

She woke later to find herself alone in her bed, and the first rays of morning light were just coming in through the window. For a moment she thought she had dreamed he was there with her, but as she turned her face into the pillow she smelled his hair oil and knew it wasn't a dream.

Later that day in a lesson with the other older children he gave her a secret kind of smile, and when the lesson was over he asked her to stay on in the classroom for a minute.

Once the others had left, he came over to her. He smoothed her hair gently. 'You fell asleep before I could explain why I came,' he said. 'You see, I can't continue with our private lessons.'

'Why?' she asked.

He shrugged. 'I have to spend more time with the other children.'

A cold shudder went down Adele's spine. She wanted to ask if that meant she wasn't special to him any longer but she didn't dare.

'Don't look that way,' he said. 'I can't help it. The others need my help more than you do.'

Her eyes filled with tears, and he reached out and wiped one tear away with his thumb. 'It doesn't mean I've stopped caring for you. We just have to find other ways to be together sometimes.'

Her heart leaped, and she ran her sleeve over her damp eyes and smiled.

'That's better.' He laughed softly. 'It will be our little secret. But you mustn't tell anyone! Promise me?'

Adele nodded, happy again.

'Good girl,' he said. 'Now off you go and I'll see you later.'

In the days that followed Adele felt increasingly confused and worried because nothing at The Firs was the same any more. Prior to Mr Makepeace going away there had been no timetable, or strict routine, Mrs Makepeace had always told the children at breakfast the jobs she wanted them to do that day. It was a fluid arrangement, varying according to the weather, her mood, and whether anyone was receiving punishment. She normally stayed at the breakfast table reading the paper with Mary sitting beside her in the high chair, and the oldest children went off to do allocated jobs – laundry, cleaning the bathroom or sweeping and polishing the bedroom floors.

Now there was a timetable pinned to the kitchen wall, and every child over five was to have school lessons each day. Mrs Makepeace said nastily that they were all lazy good-for-nothings, and it was high time they realized they weren't on holiday. She said that any misbehaviour in the classroom or failure to do their jobs properly would mean there would be no outside play later in the day.

The middle group had to go straight into the schoolroom immediately after breakfast, during which time the oldest group, which included Adele, had to do all the cleaning and laundry. Mrs Makepeace no longer sat at the table with her paper, she rushed around like an angry hornet, lashing out at anyone she felt wasn't pulling their weight.

If baby Mary, or Susan or John, the three-year-olds, got in her way, made a mess or any noise, she became irate, often terrifying them by shouting at them.

Dinner had to be served on the dot of twelve and eaten in silence. In the afternoon the oldest group had their lessons, and Mr Makepeace was just as tetchy as his wife. Adele could hardly believe how hard he was on Jack and Freda, calling them stupid and often clouting them round the ear just for getting a sum wrong. He belittled Beryl and Ruby when they read aloud and stumbled over hard words.

Adele found the afternoons endless, for the lessons were aimed at the least able of the group, all stuff she'd done several years before. Sometimes Mr Makepeace would give her a book to read, or some mathematical problems, but mostly he didn't even acknowledge her presence in the room.

She would stare out of the window, watching the breeze fluttering leaves on the trees, and wonder what had gone wrong. It seemed to her that it had to be her fault, though she couldn't see why.

After tea the others were allowed out in the garden until bedtime, but Mrs Makepeace made Adele do mending. The pile of socks needing darning, and the heaps of shirts or blouses with missing buttons never seemed to grow any smaller. Adele got the idea Mrs Makepeace was digging out old clothes from the cupboards just to keep her busy.

It was all very reminiscent of how it had been at home, with Adele alone singled out for punishment. Mrs Makepeace never spoke to her directly, just dumped things in front of her or barked an order at her. So Adele did exactly what she'd always done at home, just did as she was told, never answered back, and kept her tears in check until she was alone in her room.

She was still crying late one night when Mr Makepeace crept into her room again. She didn't know he was there until he sat down beside her.

'What's the matter, my darling?' he asked.

'It's all so horrible,' she wept. 'I can't bear it.'

He got into bed with her again that night and rocked her in his arms.

'It's all my fault,' he said. 'My wife is jealous because she has guessed how much I care for you. I have to pretend I don't feel anything more for you than I do for the others. I'm so sorry.'

She fell asleep later, and like before, when she woke in the morning he was gone. But that day she felt better, for he'd said that one day soon he'd take her away from The Firs, and bring her up as his own daughter.

On the Saturday of that same week, a big black car came in the morning to take the middle group of children for a day out at the seaside. It was a beautiful morning, with a faint mist still lingering, promising to be very hot later, and as Adele watched the children climbing excitedly into the back of the car she would have given anything to be going with them.

'Lucky little bleeders,' Ruby said at her elbow. 'Who is that woman taking them anyway?'

'Someone from the church,' Adele said, looking at the plump woman in a pink dress leaning into the back of the car and organizing the children. 'I hope none of them gets sick, or she won't take anyone again.'

'No one wants big girls like us anyway,' Ruby said gloomily. 'We'll be stuck here till we're fourteen, then they'll make us go and work in a factory.'

Having thought about little else but Mr Makepeace all day, and found it far too hot to sleep, Adele was thrilled when she heard him creeping up the stairs to see her that night. But almost as soon as he lay down beside her she felt something different in his manner. He smelled of drink rather than his customary hair oil, and he put his hand over her mouth to shush her when she said something about the younger children's trip to the seaside.

He didn't seem to want to speak to her either, and kept kissing her on the mouth with wet, sloppy lips. Then all at once he was pulling up her nightdress and trying to touch her private places.

'Don't,' she said, pushing his hands away. 'It's not nice.'

'But it is, my sweet,' he said, his hands going back to the same place. 'This is what people who love one another do.'

She kept pushing him away, but when he kept on coming back she became really frightened. Beryl's words, things she'd heard Ruby say, all took on new meaning, and she started to cry.

'Don't be silly,' he said, and took hold of her hand, drawing it down the bed towards him.

She stiffened as he placed it on something warm and hard, about as thick as her wrist, but it was a few seconds before she realized what it was. She had only ever seen little boys' willies, soft, wiggly things no bigger than her thumb.

'No,' she cried out in disgust and tried to get away from him.

But she couldn't escape, she was trapped between him and the wall, and he was forcing her fingers round that big, horrible thing.

'Hold it nicely,' he said, his voice all gruff and insistent. 'See how hard and big it is. It likes to be held.'

He clamped his hand over hers, forcing her to hold it and rub it up and down.

'Shush,' he said, putting his free hand over her mouth when she tried to yell out. 'Mrs Makepeace will be very angry if you wake her, and this is our special secret.'

Adele tried to fight him off, but he had her half pinned down by his body. His breathing was getting harder and noisier as he made her rub him harder, and worse still he was trying to get on top of her and push her legs apart. Instinct told her what he was trying to do, and she struggled still harder to get free.

'I won't hurt you, darling,' he said hoarsely. 'I only want to love you. Let me do it, please.'

Adele was now beside herself with terror. The drink on his breath was making her feel sick, he was wet with sweat, and each time he thrust himself at her, he jarred her spine on the hard mattress. She wanted to scream out, yet she knew if Mrs Makepeace came she'd get the blame, and all she could do was wriggle and wriggle so he couldn't get that big thing in where he wanted to.

Just as she was getting too exhausted to fight him any more, he made a kind of deep throaty groan and all at once she felt something horribly warm and sticky on her hand and belly.

'Get off me,' she managed to stammer out as he removed his hand from her mouth, 'I'm going to be sick.'

He moved quickly as she retched, jumping out of the bed as if he was on fire. 'Quick to the bathroom,' he said. 'If anyone comes I'll say I heard you call out.'

Adele fled down the stairs and into the bathroom, just reaching the lavatory in time as she retched again, this time bringing up everything she'd eaten that day.

She didn't know how long she stayed on her knees clinging to the lavatory bowl, but it seemed like hours. She heard his voice whisper something at the door, but she told him to go away. She could smell him on her, the sticky substance drying like glue on her hands and belly, and that made her retch again and again.

Later she sat on the floor, leaning back against the cool tiles, too desolate even to cry. Her eyes had grown used to the darkness now, and it mirrored how she felt inside.

There was no sound from along the landing and she guessed he'd gone back to his own bed. She imagined him getting in beside his wife, and hated him so much she felt she could kill him with her own bare hands.

Later she washed herself all over and went back to her room. Yet the moment she was in there, she knew she couldn't get into her bed. The smell of him was in the room, she doubted it would ever go. He was just downstairs, and she knew he would do it again the moment he got the opportunity. She had to flee this house now while she still had a chance.

She pulled on her clothes, and stood for a moment looking out of the window, frightened to leave in the dark, yet even more frightened to stay. She had no money, nowhere to go, she wasn't even sure she could find her way to Tunbridge Wells. But being alone out in the countryside had to be safer than here.

Chapter Six

Adele shivered and buttoned up her cardigan as she hurried away up the drive towards the gate. It was twenty past two by the kitchen clock while she was helping herself to the remains of a loaf, a chunk of cheese and two apples which she put in a paper bag. The back door had squeaked as she opened it to leave, and she'd been frightened it might have woken someone, but as she glanced back at The Firs it was still in darkness except for the dim glow of the night light on the landing.

It wasn't cold, in fact the night air felt as balmy as a summer's day, but she guessed it was shock and fear that were making her shiver, and as she hurried up the dark lane she began crying again.

How could a man who said he loved her do such a thing? She didn't think she'd ever feel clean again, or trust anyone either. But even worse was that she felt it was her fault. Surely she should have heard warning bells that first time he tried to kiss her?

Another wave of nausea overcame her, and she had to stop for a moment and take deep breaths. In the light of what had just happened she could see now that all that flattery, cuddles and kisses were leading up to this. If she hadn't been so desperate for someone to care about her, she might have questioned why a man like him would single a plain girl like her out for attention and private lessons.

Scary as it was walking along narrow lanes overhung with trees, she found she could see well enough once her eyes had adjusted to the dark. Big tree trunks appeared to have ghoulish faces and she kept hearing strange rustling sounds in the hedgerows. On hearing a low bellowing sound she ran like the wind, only to realize later it was just a cow. Yet her disgust and anger with Mr Makepeace, and her fright at being all alone in dark country lanes, did serve to focus her mind. Going to London wasn't an option; if she ran to Mrs Patterson she would only end up in another children's home, perhaps even worse than The Firs. The only place she could go was to Rye to find her grandparents.

Their address, Curlew Cottage, Winchelsea Beach, near Rye had remained locked in her head ever since she read that old letter to her mother. Shortly after arriving at The Firs she had looked at a map in the schoolroom to see where it was, and she'd discovered that if she drew a line between London and Rye, Tunbridge Wells was right in the middle. She even remembered the names of two towns on the way there, Lamberhurst and Hawkhurst. If she could just find her way to the first of these towns, she'd be on the right road.

She knew of course there was no certainty her grandparents still lived there, or were even still alive. If they were there they might not want to help her, of course. But it was worth a try. If that failed she would have to take her chances with the police.

Soon after the first rays of morning light came into the sky Adele came to a signpost that told her she had only six more miles to go to Lamberhurst, and she almost began crying again with relief.

Much earlier she'd come to a crossroads and the signpost had confused her completely, because it said Lamberhurst lay to her right, and Tunbridge Wells to her left. She had believed she had to go through Tunbridge Wells first, and she had stood at that sign for some time wondering which way was the right one. In the end she plumped for the right fork, and hoped for the best. It was such a lonely winding road with barely any houses that she'd become convinced she was going round in circles.

So far not one car had passed her, but she supposed that was because it was Sunday. She had planned to hide if she heard a car coming because she was afraid any adult seeing her walking in the dark would stop and ask where she was going. She couldn't trust any adult now. They might be as bad as Mr Makepeace, and even if they weren't, they might insist on taking her back to The Firs.

The daylight and the conviction she really was on the right road cheered Adele considerably although she was getting very tired. As she continued to walk she made up her mind she would keep on going until noon, then find a nice spot in a field to have a little rest. She felt sure she could reach Rye by the evening.

Church bells ringing later in the morning told Adele it was eleven o'clock, but she was so tired and footsore she could barely put one foot in front of the other. It was also very hot, without a cloud in the sky, and she was finding the countryside too big, wild and lonely for her taste.

She had expected it to be like Hampstead Heath, where she'd been twice on Sunday school picnics – peaceful, sweet-smelling, yet with enough people around to feel safe. But the trees out here were more like forests, with thick undergrowth that gave her the idea bad men could be lying in wait there to jump out and attack her. Fields might look lovely from a distance, but in reality they were full of cow pats, mud, flies and stinging nettles.

Earlier she'd seen a footpath across the fields to Lamber-hurst, and it was obvious from the well-worn ground that it was a short cut. But she cut her leg on some barbed wire by a stile, and the next field she had to cross was full of cows. As soon as they saw her they began walking menacingly towards her; as she ran for her life she accidentally slipped in a sloppy cow pat, and now she stank of it.

She doubted she'd seen more than six people since

daybreak, and then only from a distance. There were hardly any houses either, and although the idea of having a rest in a lush green field had seemed so attractive earlier on, she didn't believe she would ever find one that looked safe and clean.

Her paper bag of food had split in her sweaty hands a couple of hours earlier, so she'd had to eat the bread and cheese, and one of the apples, even though she didn't feel hungry. But she'd no sooner eaten it than she was sick again, and she still felt bad now: her tummy hurt and she had a headache.

It was only sheer determination that stopped her sitting down by the road and sobbing her heart out. She knew she had to keep going a little longer. She began counting her steps, telling herself that when she'd taken five thousand she could stop.

When she'd counted three thousand she knew she couldn't go any further, and seeing a gate into a field where the grass looked soft, with no cow pats, she climbed over it. She sat down and took her shoes off, only to find a darn in the heel of her sock had given her a blister, and that was enough to make her cry again. She folded her cardigan up for a pillow and lay down.

Cold made her wake later, and to her dismay the sun was right down, so she must have been asleep for hours. When she tried to get up she saw her legs and feet were burnt by the sun, as were her face and forearms, and she was so stiff she could barely move. She couldn't stay where she was for it was too cold and she needed a drink, so she put her socks and shoes back on, and hobbled painfully to the gate and the road beyond.

She tried to pluck up courage to knock on the door of each cottage she passed and ask for a glass of water, but she was afraid of the questions the people would ask. She finally saw a horse trough with a tap at one end and got a drink just before the sun slipped down over a hill, and when she saw a barn with its door wide open, she slipped in, knowing she could go no further in the dark.

The night seemed endless. There was straw to lie on, but it prickled her burnt skin, and the rustling noises of mice, and perhaps rats too, frightened her. With only her cardigan to wrap around her she was shivering, yet her burnt face, arms and legs were red-hot. It was a relief finally to see the first light of dawn, so she put her shoes back on and hobbled back to the road.

There were more cars and trucks on the road now it was Monday, but though she looked hopefully at every one that drove past, no one stopped to offer her a lift. At times she wondered if she was on the right road, but at last she saw a signpost which said 'Hawkhurst 4 miles.' Soon she wasn't alone on the road. She saw men in working clothes on bicycles, and several women with baskets hurrying along. Later there were children too, shouting and laughing as they made their way to school, and as she got closer to Hawkhurst a bus passed her with every seat taken.

The shops were just opening in the little town, and the sight and smell of freshly baked bread in a baker's shop brought on hunger pains. She stood for a few minutes by the open door, tempted to rush in, snatch up something to eat and run off again. But she knew she couldn't run anywhere, not with such sore feet, and the man in the shop was watching her as if he knew what she had in mind. So she limped on, past a couple of tramps sitting on a low wall, and she thought they looked as hungry and despondent as she was.

It struck her that if she wasn't tired, hungry and homeless she might have found Hawkhurst a good place to explore. It was very old and pretty, the cottage gardens full of flowers, and many of the shops had bow windows like she'd seen on calendars and chocolate boxes.

Since arriving at The Firs she hadn't been out once, and

she had missed the hustle and bustle of Euston and King's Cross, the shops, cinemas and hundreds of people. Hawkhurst wasn't bustling, but there were enough people around to make her feel less frightened and alone. She stopped for a moment to look in a toy-shop window, marvelling at the china dolls, miniature tea sets, toy trains and lead soldiers. She remembered sadly how Pamela never got tired of looking at such things, and how she liked to pretend they had a big bag of money and could buy anything they liked. If Adele had a bag of money now she'd go into the café across the street and order bacon and eggs, a pile of hot buttered toast and a cup of tea. Then she'd ask someone if there was a bus to Rye so she didn't have to walk another step.

Just outside Hawkhurst a signpost told her it was eighteen miles to Rye, and with that she couldn't contain her tears any longer as she'd thought she was nearly there. It was impossible to walk so far.

There was a small stream by the side of the road, so she sat down on the bank, took off her socks and shoes and soaked her feet in the cool water, wondering what she should do. Her feet looked as bad as they felt, so swollen that she wasn't sure she'd be able to get her shoes back on, and there were blisters on each toe, both heels and on the ball of each foot. Her face was very sore from the sunburn too, and now the sun was getting hot again she knew it would be real agony before long.

'You've come this far, you've got to go on,' she said to herself. 'If you go to the police now they'll just take you back.'

The mere thought of Mr Makepeace's face was enough to bring back a vestige of the determination she'd felt the previous day. When her feet became numb with the cold water, she dampened her socks and put them back on, then her shoes. When she stood up they didn't feel quite so bad.

She had managed to walk another three miles when she

began to feel really ill. Her head was throbbing, her vision seemed distorted, and every bit of her ached. A signpost said it was another fifteen miles, and she leaned against it because she was sure that if she didn't prop herself up on something she'd fall over.

Ahead of her was a steep hill, the road shimmering in a heat haze, and she knew she hadn't got the strength to walk up it in the hot sun. It was so tempting just to slump down under the nearest tree, but she had a feeling that if she did, she'd never be able to get up again.

Hearing the sound of an engine, she looked round. An old truck was coming towards her, and realizing she really had no choice any more, she waved weakly at it.

It came to a rattling halt beside her and she saw that the driver was an old man in a greasy-looking cap. 'You want a lift?' he called out.

'Yes please,' she said, and forced herself to let go of the signpost and stagger towards him. 'Are you going to Rye?'

'That I am,' he said. 'Get in.'

Adele felt too ill even to consider that here was a piece of good fortune at last. She braced herself for questions from the old man, but he didn't ask any, although perhaps that was just because he knew he couldn't be heard over the noise of the truck.

She supposed she must have dozed off because one moment they were miles from anywhere, and the next they were coming into a little town that looked older than any place she'd ever seen before. She guessed by the sun that it was around five or six o'clock.

'Where you goin'?' the old man shouted to her.

'Winchelsea Beach,' she managed to get out, surprised that she even remembered the address any longer.

'Well, you'd better get out here then,' he said, and stopped the truck at a junction. He pointed a grubby finger straight ahead. 'It's a couple of miles that way.'

Adele thanked him and got out, waiting until he'd gone on round the corner before wearily crossing the road.

Everything looked so small, tiny little terraced houses jammed up against one another, their front doors opening on to the street. Leading off the main street were very narrow lanes, with even older houses, winding up to a church on the top of the hill.

It didn't look very inviting, The terrace Adele passed by looked every bit as dilapidated as the worst areas around King's Cross. There were a couple of very old ladies in black sitting on stools by their front doors, and they looked curiously at her as she limped on by.

The road, which seemed to have almost as many pubs as houses, wound round to a quay. Adele paused there, for ill and exhausted as she was, she felt cheered by the view. Many boats were moored up. In the main they were small fishing boats with furled sails, but a few larger vessels were being loaded or unloaded too. She couldn't actually see the sea, but she knew it couldn't be far away for she could smell it and taste the salt on her lips. A dozen or so fishermen were sitting on wooden crates mending nets, other men in cloth caps were standing around smoking. She guessed they were out of work as they had the same dejected stance she'd grown used to seeing during the last year in London.

The road continued over a bridge across the river and there was a windmill to her right. Shortly after crossing the bridge she saw a signpost marked with Winchelsea straight on and Rye harbour to her left. From there on there were no further houses, only flat marshland, with another river running close by the road.

Turning round to look back at Rye, Adele thought how pretty it looked. It was built on the only hill in miles of flat marshland. The houses were all crammed up together, so many different shapes, colours and sizes, and the church at the top towered over it like an ancient castle.

As she turned to go on, in the far distance was another smaller twin of Rye, also perched on a hill. Yet in between, apart from a ruined castle to her left, there was nothing else for as far as she could see but grass with grazing sheep and a few trees distorted by the wind.

With each step Adele felt worse. Her head ached, she was alternately hot and cold, and her feet hurt so much she felt that she might collapse at any moment. She tried very hard not to think of what would become of her if her grandparents weren't there, and instead just concentrated on dragging herself forward.

After what seemed like miles, the road swept round to her right and up into the small town on the hill which had been ahead for so long. But there was also an unmade-up road going off to her left towards the sea, and she thought that might very well be the way to Winchelsea Beach.

She hesitated for some few minutes, afraid to choose either road in case it was the wrong one, then in the distance she spotted a man on a bicycle coming down from the houses up on the hill.

He was old, wearing strange checked knickerbockers and a battered hat which was tied under his chin. As he came closer Adele waved to him to slow down.

'You want something, miss?' he said, stopping by putting his feet down rather than using his brakes.

'Do you know Curlew Cottage at Winchelsea Beach?' she asked.

'Why are you looking for it?' he asked, his bright blue eyes boring into her.

Adele was puzzled by that question. 'Because I want to see Mr and Mrs Harris who live there,' she replied.

'You won't see Mr Harris, he's been dead ten years or more,' the man said with a smirk. He had a very peculiar way of speaking, nothing like the way people spoke in London.

'What about Mrs Harris?' she asked.

'She's there still. But she don't like visitors.'

Adele's heart sank. 'But I've come all the way from London,' she said.

He made an odd kind of cackle, Adele didn't know if it was a laugh or not. 'Then you'd better go right back there,' he said. 'Children round here think she's a witch.'

Adele's heart sank even further and she swayed on her feet with exhaustion and disappointment. 'Just tell me which way to go,' she said in little more than a whisper. 'I can't go back until I see her.'

'It's up that track,' he said, and with that he swung his leg over the crossbar of his bike and took off.

Quite suddenly Adele felt utterly terrified. This place was barren, nothing but scrubby grass and sheep for miles. Rye was away on the horizon, even the other village up on the hill had to be at least half a mile away. A keen wind was blowing, and it whipped through her dress, tangled her hair and made her eyes and sunburn smart. She knew the sea was in front of her, yet she couldn't actually see it, any more than she could see the birds which were making eerie shrieking noises.

It had none of the soft beauty of the countryside she'd seen earlier in the day. Even the sheep who grazed here didn't look like other sheep she'd seen, they were thin and small with black faces. It was a hard landscape, as flat as a pancake, and she thought it was as arid as a desert. Anyone who chose to live here would have to be much the same, and with a sinking heart she knew she wasn't going to find a storybook grandmother who would welcome her with open arms.

But she couldn't turn back now, so she stumbled on past two tumbledown cottages which were little more than huts. Then she saw Curlew Cottage.

It was single-storey and covered in black tarred shingles like the buildings she'd noticed down at the quay in Rye. The windows were small, there was a latticework porch around the door, and the ground in front was all pebbles. Yet although it was neat enough, and there was smoke coming out of the chimney which meant someone was at home, it didn't look at all welcoming.

She could see why children would think a witch lived there. The cottage had a defiant air, daring the wind to tear it down, or floods to sweep it away. Surely no one normal would choose to live in such a bleak, isolated spot? With the horrible image of her demented mother tied to a chair so fresh in her mind, it seemed likely that at any moment that door could open and a hideous old crone would appear.

There was no fence or gate, and the path to the door was just old pieces of wood. She stood for a moment weighing up whether she was brave enough to walk across them.

But she had no choice. So, taking her courage in both hands, she walked to the door and banged on it.

'Who is it?'

The strident and irritated inquiry from behind the door made Adele move back a step.

'I'm your granddaughter,' she called back.

Adele expected that the door would open with a creak, a beaky nose would peer round it, and an almost skeletal hand would stretch out to pull her in. But that wasn't how it was.

The door opened wide, and the woman who stood there was oddly dressed in grey men's trousers, a baggy blouse and heavy boots. Her face reminded Adele of a conker kept too long in a warm place, weathered dark brown and slightly wrinkled. Her steel-grey hair was harshly pulled back, but her eyes were a vivid and beautiful blue, exactly like Adele's mother's.

'Who did you say you were?' she asked, her thin pale lips set in a guarded straight line.

'I'm Adele Talbot, your granddaughter,' she repeated. 'Rose, my mum, is ill, and I came to find you.'

It seemed to Adele that she was standing there for ever in

front of this woman who was staring at her as if she had three heads. But she couldn't focus her eyes any longer, there was a whistling noise in her ears, and suddenly everything began to spin.

Adele came to with water being splashed on her face, and opened her eyes to find she was lying on her back and the woman was bending down over her, a cup in her hand.

'Drink!' she ordered.

Adele lifted her head and feebly held out her hand for the cup, but it shook too much to hold it, and the woman had to put it to her lips.

'You fainted,' she said curtly. 'Now, who did you say you were?'

Adele repeated her name. 'My mother is Rose,' she added. 'Rose Talbot now, but she was Rose Harris.'

The woman's lips were quivering, but whether this was with emotion or just old age, Adele couldn't tell. 'After she went away to hospital I found a letter in her things that had this address on it. Are you my grandmother?'

'How old are you?' the woman asked, sticking her nut-brown face up close to Adele's.

'Twelve,' Adele said. 'I'll be thirteen in July.'

The woman put her hand up to her forehead, digging her nails into her skin, a gesture Adele had seen her mother make hundreds of times. Sometimes it meant 'I can't cope with this now,' and sometimes 'Get out of my sight if you know what's good for you.' It wasn't a good omen, but Adele knew she was in no position to retreat.

'They put me in a home,' she blurted out. 'But bad things happened there so I ran away. I didn't know anywhere else to go.'

The woman continued to stare down at Adele, her thick brows knitting together as if with puzzlement. 'What bad things? Where's your father?'

Her tone was cold and suspicious, and all at once the strain of trying to pretend she was an adult was too much for Adele and she began to cry. 'He doesn't want me, he said I wasn't his child,' she said through her sobs. 'And Mr Makepeace tried to do dirty things to me.'

'For goodness sake stop blubbering,' the woman said sharply. 'I can't be doing with that. Get up and come inside.'

Adele got only the briefest impression of the inside of Curlew Cottage before she lost consciousness again. It was like walking into the junk shop by King's Cross station, a musty smell of old books and furniture, a gloomy room stuffed with relics from the past.

Honour Harris stared down at the child on the floor, for a moment so horrified she didn't know what to do. Her heart was thumping dangerously, long-buried emotions threatening to surge up and spill over. She glanced at the door for a moment, considering running to get help, but seeking help for anything wasn't in her nature, so she shook herself, bent down, lifted the child up and put her on the couch.

The simple act of lifting her brought back Honour's natural instinct to protect any hurt animal. The child's skin was ferociously burnt by the sun, she was filthy, her hair matted, and when Honour removed her shoes and socks she let out an involuntary gasp. They looked like lumps of raw bloody meat, and it was clear she'd walked a very long way to get here.

Yet after a cursory inspection Honour felt it was exhaustion and hunger rather than illness which had brought about her collapse. That was something of a relief, for she could neither afford nor wanted a doctor coming here.

The kettle was already on the stove, hot enough for washing, so she got a bowl, a flannel and a towel. She stripped off the girl's filthy dress, leaving her in her vest and knickers, then proceeded to wash her.

Honour was fifty-two, and years of hardship living alone out on the marsh had taught her to deal only with the present. While she knew that this child, if what she'd claimed was true, was going to force her to look back at a part of her life she wanted to forget, for now that wasn't important.

After washing her as well as she could, she went into her bedroom and found a pot of ointment, good for soothing and healing burns. She applied it liberally to the child's arms, legs, face and the back of her neck, but decided against putting it on the broken skin of her feet.

'Just sleep now', she said, tucking a soft quilt around her. 'When you wake I'll have some food for you.'

Honour found the child's presence in her living room deeply disturbing. Questions kept arising in her mind, and she felt constantly compelled to go over to look at her. While relieved to find she was sleeping peacefully, Honour still had the jitters, and her own supper of bread and cheese was left uneaten on the table, for she had no appetite for it now.

No visitor had come into Curlew Cottage for years, and Honour found it odd that just one small person could make her suddenly aware of how cramped her living room had become in that time.

She looked about her at the spare mattress stacked against the book shelves, the piles of books on the floor, boxes of china, ornaments, linen and memorabilia from the past crammed into every available space, and she felt even more uneasy. When Frank was alive it had been such a comfortable, well-ordered room. But after he died she stopped caring about how it looked. She had brought the contents of Rose's old room in here when the guttering above it started leaking, but even after she repaired the guttering, she had no enthusiasm for putting the stuff back. She should have got rid of it all.

But most of it held precious memories of happy days as a new bride, so she couldn't. Why they hadn't sold it all before they took up permanent residence here, she didn't know.

Goodness knows, they could have done with the money. But Frank had always been so insistent that their ship would come in again and they'd need it all one day.

It was odd that the overcrowded room should suddenly start to bother her the moment this child stepped through her door. But then any memory of Rose always had a bad effect on her.

Honour got up from her chair again, this time to make some soup from the stock pot she had simmering on the stove. She got a small piece of chicken from the meat safe in the scullery, cut it into tiny pieces and added it to the stock along with a diced carrot and a small onion. Then, suddenly aware it was growing dark, she lit the oil lamp at the end of the couch.

When she glanced round a little later, she was suddenly struck by the child's resemblance to Rose at the same age. She supposed that while she was washing her it had been too gloomy to see her clearly.

By sixteen Rose had become a stunner. Honour could remember looking at her curvy body, her beautiful face with those wide blue eyes, full pouting lips and silky blonde hair and marvelling at the transformation. Yet at twelve, Rose had been as skinny and plain as her daughter was now. Frank used laughingly to say she looked like a stick insect with saucer eyes.

She hadn't noticed whether the girl's eyes were blue, but she thought not, and her hair was a dull light brown, but she had got Rose's defiant pointed chin and the same slender nose and full lips.

Honour hoped she hadn't inherited her mother's cruel nature too.

At twelve that same night Honour was dozing in her chair, wanting to go to her bed but afraid the child might wake during the night and not know where she was.

A rustle woke her with a start, and she opened her eyes to see the child sitting up on the couch looking frightened.

'So you've woken up at last,' Honour said sharply. 'Do you know where you are?'

The girl looked about her, then looked down at herself and saw her dress was gone. She touched her cheek as if to test if it was still sore. 'Yes, you are Mrs Harris,' she said eventually. 'I'm sorry if I've been a nuisance.'

Honour snorted. She was in fact a little touched that the child's first thoughts were for someone else. But it wasn't in her nature to say so, or to say anything welcoming. She was also relieved the child hadn't called her Grandmother. She wasn't prepared to accept that was what she'd suddenly become. 'I dare say you need to go to the lavatory. But you can't go out there in the dark now so I've put a chamber pot out in the scullery,' she said brusquely, and pointed the way with one finger.

She saw the child wince as she put her feet to the floor, but she didn't complain and hobbled out.

When she returned, Honour told her to sit at the table and silently put a bowl of soup and a glass of water in front of her.

She saw the child down the water in almost one gulp and wondered how long it was since she'd eaten or drunk anything. She waited till over half the soup was gone and then fetched another glass of water.

'Water is good for sunburn,' she said as she put it on the table. 'Now, are you going to tell me how you came to turn up at my door?'

Adele was confused. She could remember knocking at the door and this woman opening it clearly enough. She had a vague recollection of telling her who she was, but it had a kind of dream-like quality, so she wasn't sure how much she'd told her.

'Start at the beginning,' the woman said sharply. 'With

your full name, how you came by my address and where you've just walked from.'

That confused Adele even more, for it sounded as if this woman wasn't her grandmother after all. She was so gruff and peculiar. If Adele hadn't realized while she was peeing in the chamber pot that she'd been washed and some sort of cream had been put on her sunburn, she'd think the woman was ready to put her out the door if she didn't tell the story quite right.

Wearily Adele began, explaining who she was, how her sister had been run over and that her mother went mad a while after and had to be taken away to hospital. She explained about Jim Talbot not wanting her, about the letter she'd seen with this address, and then how she was taken to The Firs.

'In Tunbridge Wells?' Mrs Harris exclaimed. 'Whereabouts?'

Adele said she didn't actually know the whole address but she said it was nearer to Lamberhurst than she'd expected.

'Why did you run away from there?'

'Because of Mr Makepeace,' Adele whispered, and overcome with renewed shame at what he'd done, she began to cry.

'Don't start blubbing again,' Mrs Harris said impatiently. 'You can leave that part till later. Now, what does Jim Talbot do for a living?'

Adele thought that was a very strange thing to ask, the most unimportant thing in her entire story. 'He works in a builder's yard,' she said, thinking it was better to tell her exactly what she wanted to know. 'I always thought he was my real dad until the night Mum went crazy and attacked us both. She'd been blaming me for Pamela dying, and saying all kinds of other nasty things, but I heard Dad tell the doctor I wasn't his child and that he didn't want anything more to do with me or Mum.'

Adele was startled when the woman got up and moved around the room, fiddling with things as though she was nervous, but saying nothing. Even Mrs Makepeace had been quite sympathetic when she'd explained all this to her, and she wasn't any relation. Adele racked her brain to think of something further to say that would make this woman act as if she was aware she had someone else in the room with her. But she couldn't think of anything.

'Rose disappeared when she was seventeen,' Mrs Harris suddenly burst out, turning towards Adele and banging her fist down on the table. 'Not a word to me, not a single word, the heartless baggage. Her father had come back from the war sick, and she took off just when I needed help. So you tell me why I should care about the child she didn't even bother to tell me had been born!'

Adele was scared then. This woman had the same eyes as her mother and perhaps she was mad too. 'I'm sorry,' she whispered. 'She doesn't care about me either.'

'All these years I never knew if she was alive or dead,' the woman went on, her voice rising almost to a shriek. 'Her father asked for her so many times when he was dying, sometimes he even accused me of throwing her out. He never would believe what a minx she became after he went off to the war. She was his little girl. His treasure, he used to call her. He died believing it was my fault she didn't come home to see him. Do you know what that's like?'

Adele burst into tears again. She did know what it was like to be blamed for everything. And now it seemed she was going to be blamed for her mother's behaviour too.

'Oh, stop that blubbering,' her grandmother shouted at her. 'You're the one who turned up uninvited, telling me my daughter is mad, and wanting me to take you in. It's me who should be crying.'

From deep within her Adele felt anger rising. In a brief flash she saw images of all the injustices that had been piled on to her – the blame for Pamela's death, her mother's cruelty, being sent off to a home where the man she trusted betrayed her. And now this grown woman was being unfair too. Well, she wasn't going to take any more of it. She had to speak out.

'Then get the police and make them take me away,' she shouted back. 'I haven't done anything to you, except hope that you might care about your granddaughter. I can see where Mum got her nastiness from. It's you!'

She expected a blow. She quickly covered her head with her arms in self-defence when the woman moved towards her. But surprisingly no blow came, just a hand on her shoulder. 'You'd better get back on that couch and go back to sleep,' she said gruffly. 'You've been out in the sun for too long, and we're both overtired.'

Chapter Seven

'How on earth do I deal with this?' Honour grumbled to herself as she got into her bed later that night.

The candle was flickering in a breeze from the window, making the shadow of her bed posts on the wall move in a disconcertingly eerie manner, and she shivered.

It had been a tremendous shock to open her door and find that waif of a child there. In the last ten or so years she had done her best to erase Rose from her mind. She had been forced to, for the bitterness and anger she felt towards her daughter had almost destroyed her. Yet on the rare occasions Rose covertly slipped into her mind again, Honour had always imagined her living in luxury, the spoiled and cosseted wife of a wealthy man. She had never once considered that she might have had children.

If the news of Rose's present plight had come from any other source, Honour would undoubtedly have felt some kind of grim satisfaction. But to hear a mere child spilling out such a tale was utterly chilling.

Honour picked up the framed photograph of Frank from the bedside table. It had been taken just before he was sent to France in the spring of 1915. He looked so happy, dashing and handsome in his uniform, yet just two years later he was brought back to England a physical and mental wreck.

Honour knew that millions of young men shared the same horrors in the trenches as Frank did. A huge proportion of them didn't live to tell their loved ones about it either. She could well imagine the men's terror at seeing their comrades die and wondering when it would be their turn. She felt for every one of them who had endured living in mud, with rats and lice their constant companions. But Frank's story was even more horrific, for he had fallen into a fox hole after being shot in the leg and was buried alive beneath other fatally wounded men who tumbled in after him.

It was believed he was trapped there for three days before he was found. It was hardly surprising that he lost his mind as he became drenched in his comrades' blood, heard their death throes, and thought he would surely die too.

'What do I do, Frank?' she whispered at his picture. 'I don't want her here, not after what her mother did to us.'

Honour had known Frank Harris all her life. Her father, Ernest Cauldwell, was the local schoolmaster in Tunbridge Wells, and Frank's father, Cedric, owned Harris's, the most prestigious grocery shop in town.

Harris's was a splendid shop, all shiny walnut and white marble, stacked from floor to ceiling with every kind of delicacy. Honour remembered as a small child being morbidly fascinated by the fantastic displays of dead pheasants, rabbits and hares lying on a bed of greenery. Her mother had to hold her tightly so she wouldn't attempt to stroke them.

Frank and his younger brother Charles only stayed at the local school, where they had often been Honour's playmates, until they were eight, then they were sent to boarding school. But they remained friends, and always came to see Honour in their holidays. Both boys helped out in their father's shop as they got older, and Frank often delivered groceries on a bicycle with a big basket for goods on the front. Whenever he came past the schoolhouse, he always stopped to chat to Honour, and he often gave her a ride on the front of the bike.

By the time he left school at seventeen and came home to work for his father, Honour only had eyes for the tall, slender young man with bright blue twinkly eyes and a mop of unruly blond hair. Frank wasn't particularly handsome, but he had a joyful nature and he was kind, funny and interested in nature, music, art and books. With him as a friend Honour didn't need anyone else.

She was seventeen when she began officially 'walking out' with Frank, and both families were delighted. The Cauldwells might not have been wealthy like the Harrises but they were well respected. Frank often joked to Honour that his father kept begging him to marry her because she had brains, and that would improve the family business.

They were married in 1899, when Honour was twenty and Frank twenty-two. They moved into the flat above the shop, which had been empty for some years since the Harrises had bought a house on the outskirts of Tunbridge Wells. Honour remembered being deliriously happy at having such a lovely home. The Harrises were so generous, showering them with gifts of furniture, linen and glass – there was even a maid to do the rough work. And as Frank was the assistant manager in the shop, he was in and out all day, so she never felt lonely as some of her girlfriends did when they left their own families to be married.

Honour was always aware that Frank had no real love for the grocery business. He was a sensitive and artistic man who would have much preferred to be a gardener or even a gamekeeper than weigh out sugar and cut meat and cheese. But it was his father's dream that his eldest son should eventually inherit the business, and Frank felt obligated to him. He consoled himself in moments of irritation by saying that the shop ran itself anyway, as the assistants had all been trained so well by his father. He found time in quiet periods for his sketching and for walks in the country, and he often told Honour he considered himself the most fortunate of men.

Two years later, in 1901, Rose was born, a plump, adorable baby with white blonde hair, and made her parents' happiness complete. But just a few weeks after her birth, Cedric Harris had a severe stroke. Confined to a chair, and knowing he wasn't going to recover, he made the shop over entirely to Frank.

Until it became his sole responsibility, Frank had never realized just how much work there was in running the shop. All at once there were books to keep, orders to check, and suddenly there was no time left for sketching, walks in the country, or even playing with his baby daughter.

Honour knew she didn't help him adjust to the extra work load by constantly complaining that she was bored being alone all day with Rose. But she was young and unthinking, and she missed the carefree times they'd had previously.

The following year Frank tried to make it up to her by arranging a holiday for the three of them in Hastings, at the same hotel where they'd spent their honeymoon. But to their disappointment it was fully booked. They weren't happy about going to a strange hotel with a baby, so when one of their wealthier customers offered them the use of a small cottage in Rye, a place he claimed was much prettier than Hastings, they were delighted to accept.

Almost from the moment they stepped off the train, they fell in love with Rye. They were enchanted by the quaint old houses, the narrow cobbled streets, and the long and fascinating history of a place which had once been an important port. Frank wanted to sketch everything he saw, from the old fishermen sitting with their pipes outside the sail sheds, to ancient buildings and the wildlife on the marshes. Honour loved waking up in the morning to the smell of the sea, instead of cheese and bacon. It was wonderful to have Frank's complete attention, and she felt free for the first time in her life.

Rye had none of the genteel sophistication of Tunbridge Wells, or the heady delights of Hastings with its pier and concerts. Most of its residents had never been further than ten miles away from their home, they worked the land, they fished or built boats. They were friendly, simple people, who had to work too hard to keep their many children to concern themselves with fashion, world news, or even politics.

Honour found that there were none of the social restraints in Rye that she had had drummed into her from babyhood. She could run down the street with Rose in her perambulator if she wished, abandon her hat and gloves without raising an eyebrow. The outsiders who'd settled there were people like herself and Frank, attracted by the beauty and serenity of the town and the surrounding marshes. Many of them were writers, musicians and artists. Frank would point out the artists, sitting at their easels sketching and painting in the sunshine, and he became obsessed with the idea of having a holiday cottage there.

They heard about Curlew Cottage just two days before they were due to go home, and Frank wanted it even before they saw it. Honour tried to talk him out of it, pointing out that it was a long walk from Rye, water came from an outside pump, and the cottage was almost falling down. But Frank wouldn't listen: the rent was cheap, he loved it, and he was determined to have it.

'We have to have a little world of our own,' he said, his blue eyes shining with excitement. 'Everything back in Tunbridge Wells is Father's. His shop, his flat, his customers. We live our life secondhand. But I could cope with that if we could escape now and then.'

Put like that, Honour could only agree. She thought it would be fun to have holidays in such a wild place – they could get bicycles and explore everywhere, take dips in the sea, tramp miles on the marsh. It would be lovely for Rose as she got older, for there was no garden at the shop for her to play in. Honour was also excited at the idea of turning the tumbledown cottage into a real little home.

*

Honour could still look back on the first holiday they spent at the cottage and smile, despite all the trouble and hardship which came later. They were like a couple of children playing house as Frank whitewashed the walls and she hung cheap gingham at the windows for curtains. Every afternoon they'd take Rose for a walk, and fill bags with wood for the fire at night. They had almost no furniture then, just a cheap bed bought in Rye, a table and two chairs, and they hung their clothes on nails. They would go to bed with the windows wide open, listening to the sounds of the wading birds that lived in the many ditches and swampier ground. They could hear the sea washing over shingle, and the wind rustling the gorse bushes.

It was the happiest time, so much joy and laughter as they learned to cook on an open fire and mend the shingles on the cottage walls, and attempted to make a garden on ground which was barren and pebbly. On hot days they would strip off Rose's clothes and let her play in a tub of water, while Frank painted and Honour sat in the sun reading.

The following summer they bought two bicycles, and Frank made a little saddle for Rose on his crossbar. They would ride down through Rye and on to Camber Sands, sometimes even going as far as Lydd, where they would buy an ice-cream before returning home.

Later, after the collapse of the business, Honour often reproached herself. If she had pitched in and helped Frank in the shop, rather than encouraging him to go off to Rye any time he looked fed up, it might not have happened. Yet Frank insisted the blame was all his.

He claimed the shop had prospered in his father's hands because Cedric Harris loved it. He had the business acumen and the right obsequious mentality to butter up the gentry around Tunbridge Wells to keep their custom. Frank wasn't made that way, he couldn't fawn over people just so they would give him a weekly order. He didn't take pride in having twenty different kinds of biscuits, or ten varieties of tea. It irritated him that the customers felt they owned him.

Frank admitted just before he died that perhaps he let things slide purposely, because he had a horror of them ending up like their parents, sober and narrow-minded people who went to church every Sunday and followed the strict etiquette of their class. He said he wanted passion, danger, to know he was really alive.

Honour had smiled about the passion – that was one thing that even hardship didn't stop. Frank experienced danger too in the war, and she supposed they did truly know they were alive, when they were so cold they had to wear their coats inside the cottage, and had periods of near-starvation. But had she known how things would turn out, she wouldn't have been so eager to follow Frank's lead.

Cedric Harris died suddenly in 1904, and much to his widow and two sons' shocked surprise, he hadn't amassed a fortune as they'd supposed. After debts had been cleared there was only a couple of hundred pounds and the family home remaining. This he had left to Charles, the younger brother, on the understanding he was to take care of his mother, because he had already given the shop to Frank.

Antagonism between the two brothers began to erupt almost immediately. Charles worried that Frank seemed set on letting their father's business run into the ground. Frank's way of dealing with anything unpleasant was to avoid it. He didn't like to see his younger brother's irritation with him, so he took Honour and Rose off to the cottage even more often. During that time the elderly owner offered to sell it to them for a nominal sum, so Frank bought it and became even keener to go there more often.

The more he was away, the more the business sank. One by one, the wealthiest people in the town stopped coming in, and without a quick turnover of perishable goods there was a great deal of waste. But Frank and Honour weren't really aware of this until it was too late. They were totally immersed in their carefree way of life down on the marshes.

Rose was eleven when the shop finally collapsed. Frank went in one morning to find a couple of angry suppliers waiting for him. They hadn't been paid for months, and they wanted their money immediately. Frank paid them, but he couldn't persuade them to give him any further goods on credit.

The shop had survived eight years of Frank's neglect, but once the word got around it was in difficulties, it took only a few weeks to fail completely.

Even now, nineteen years later, Honour could still picture the way Frank looked when he came upstairs to her after locking the shop door for good. He was thirty-five then, but still as slender and boyish as the day they married. 'It doesn't matter,' he said, his face breaking into a wide grin. 'We'll sell the building and go and live in Curlew Cottage for ever.'

He made her believe it would be paradise, that the interest on the capital from the sale of the shop building would keep them. He would sell his paintings, and they'd raise a few chickens and grow their own vegetables. Everything would be fine.

Honour sighed deeply. Back then she was as naive as Frank. She didn't stop to think what living on the marsh in winter would be like, or that Rose would resent leaving her old school and friends behind. It didn't cross her mind that her own parents would see their only child's sudden departure from Tunbridge Wells as abandonment. She didn't know what real poverty meant then either, not until their capital was depleted.

Nor did she know then that just two years later England would go to war with Germany and Frank would enlist. If anyone had told her on the day the shop closed for the last time that within six years she'd be wishing for death to release her from the struggle to survive another day, she would have laughed at them.

The candle had burned right down to a mere stub while Honour had been reliving the past. It hurt to dredge it all up, to look at what a good life they could have had if only they hadn't chased dreams. If Frank had kept the shop going he could have avoided joining up, and perhaps he'd still be alive today. If they'd stayed in Tunbridge Wells maybe Rose would have turned out differently too.

But the past was past, and there was nothing to gain by wishing they'd done things differently. It was the present that mattered to Honour now, and until this evening her life, though often hard, had been tranquil and agreeable. She made just enough to live on with the sale of her eggs, preserves and rabbits, and she loved the marshes and her little home. She didn't want change, heartache or further responsibilities.

Especially not a child to take care of. She would be a constant reminder of Rose and all that grief she caused. She couldn't and wouldn't keep her here.

Adele woke suddenly at the sound of a cockerel crowing and for a second or two she thought she was still at The Firs and had dreamt the long walk to Rye.

But her feet were throbbing, her face felt as if it was on fire, and when she tried to sit up, a sharp pain in her back prevented her, and she soon realized this was no dream.

It was very early, for the light coming through the thin gingham curtains was still grey, and above the sound of birdsong, she could hear her grandmother snoring in the next room.

She was relieved to see that her imagination hadn't been playing tricks with her, and that her grandmother's living room was every bit as cluttered and odd as the brief impression she'd formed when she arrived.

The couch she lay on was in front of the stove, one of those old-fashioned ones with a fire inside it. It had gone out now, and she supposed her grandmother had to light it each morning. From her position on the couch, the front door was in front of her, the scullery behind, and her grandmother's bedroom door to her right beside the stove. To her left at the back of the couch were a table and chairs and all the clutter. It even blocked the light from the window back there.

She'd never seen anything like it: piles of cardboard boxes, a chest of drawers perched on an old sideboard. There was a stuffed russet-coloured bird with a long tail in a glass case, a big carved wooden bear which looked as if it could be a coat and hat stand, and a mattress stacked against the wall. She wondered what was in all the boxes. Could her grandmother be preparing to move somewhere new?

The bird, the bear and the table and chairs all looked as though they came from a rich person's house; even the couch she lay on was dark red velvet. It didn't seem to go with a woman who wore men's clothes and had no electricity.

Adele wanted to go to the lavatory, but when she tried to get up again, she found she still couldn't. She felt awful too, and very scared when she remembered how nasty her grandmother had been last night. She didn't dare call out, so she closed her eyes and tried to go back to sleep.

She must have dozed off again, coming to with a jolt as a door creaked. Bright sunshine was coming through the windows now and the sound was her grandmother coming out of her bedroom. She had a shawl around the shoulders of her flannel night-gown.

'I need to go to the lav,' Adele said hesitantly. 'I tried to get up, but I can't.'

'Why not?' her grandmother asked, peering down at her suspiciously.

'I hurt all over,' Adele said.

'You're just stiff I expect. I'll help you.'

Her help was merely to catch hold of Adele's two arms

and jerk her upwards. Adele bit back a scream of pain and wavered on her sore feet.

Her grandmother offered her arm to hang on to and Adele edged towards the scullery, wincing with every step.

'Slip your feet into those,' Honour ordered, nudging a pair of old slippers towards Adele with her foot. 'It's not far to the privy.'

When the back door opened, the view in front of her beyond the fence of the large garden was so beautiful and unexpected that Adele momentarily forgot the pain she was in.

Waving grass studded with wild flowers stretched all the way to Rye. To her right was the ruined castle she'd seen on her way here, and a river like a slick of silver ribbon winding its way through the lush grass.

A honking noise made her look up. A flock of large birds with long necks were flying over, and as she watched they swooped down on to the river, landing gracefully without even making a ripple.

'Wild geese,' her grandmother said. 'We get dozens of different kinds here.'

Adele suddenly became aware again of how much she hurt and hobbled on to the privy which her grandmother had pointed out, almost hidden beneath a bush covered in large purple flowers. When she came out again a few minutes later she saw her grandmother opening a rabbit hutch to let the occupants out into their run.

'I like rabbits,' Adele said as two very large brown and white rabbits came out and sniffed the air expectantly.

'They aren't pets,' her grandmother said coldly. 'I breed them for their fur and the meat.'

By the afternoon Adele was in despair, and convinced her grandmother really was a witch, for she had to be the nastiest person she'd ever met. All she wanted to do was lie down, close her eyes and go to sleep, but her grandmother said she must sit in the chair.

She had made her put on an old dress of hers while she washed Adele's, and she kept firing questions at her that mostly she felt too ill to answer. One moment she was cold, the next so hot she was sweating, but her grandmother didn't appear to notice for she kept going outside to do jobs.

She was cross when Adele ate only a few spoonfuls of soup for dinner, and then she plonked a jigsaw on a tray and ordered her to do it instead of staring into space.

Adele had always loved jigsaws, but her head spun as she looked at the pieces. She wanted to cry and say how ill she felt, but she was sure that if she did, it would only make the woman nastier.

She wished she hadn't come here now. It would have been better to have taken her chances going to Mrs Patterson.

'Drink this up!'

Adele started nervously at her grandmother's voice so close to her. She was holding out a cup of tea in one hand and a plate with a slice of fruit cake in the other. 'Come on, sit up straight, and don't mind the flecks of cream on the tea, it won't do you any harm. But I'd better go and buy some more milk, it goes off so quickly in this warm weather.'

Fruit cake was Adele's favourite, and at home it had been a rare treat. 'Did you make it yourself?' she asked.

'No, my cook made it,' her grandmother retorted. Even though Adele's mind seemed very fuddled she recognized the sarcasm. 'Now, behave yourself while I'm gone. Don't go poking around.'

Adele could only stare stupidly at the woman, not understanding what she meant.

Honour rode her bicycle to the shop in Winchelsea, glad to be away from the cottage and the girl for a while. She seemed so dim, hardly able to answer the simplest question. Halfway up the hill into Winchelsea she had to get off and walk because it was so steep, and by the time she got to the top she was perspiring heavily because the sun was so hot.

It was only then that it occurred to her the girl might be suffering from sunstroke. She remembered she'd had it once after a day on the beach at Camber Sands with Frank and Rose. In fact she'd been poorly for days.

All at once she felt ashamed she hadn't considered this before – after all, the girl had been out in the sun for two whole days. If that was the case, no wonder she couldn't eat the soup for lunch!

Honour considered asking the chemist for some advice on how to treat sunburn, but when she looked in the shop there were several women queuing, and she didn't want them to hear what she had to say. So she bought a pint of milk, put it in the basket on the handlebars, and rode home quickly.

She had left her front door propped open for the breeze, and the first thing that she saw as she stepped inside was the girl's legs sticking out from behind the couch.

Rushing in, Honour found her face down in a pool of vomit. She lifted her away from it, turned her on her side and quickly checked her airway wasn't obstructed. The girl was unconscious, her pulse weak, and when Honour touched her forehead she found it red-hot.

Glancing round, Honour saw the empty tea cup, the half-eaten slice of cake on the small table beside the chair, and guessed it was that which had made her sick and she'd tried to make her way to the privy.

For the first time in many years Honour felt scared. The girl had said she was in pain first thing this morning, but she'd taken no notice. She hadn't even put her to bed. Now it was obvious she was seriously ill. A doctor was needed, but how could she go to find one and leave the child alone?

It was terribly hot in the living room, so she picked the child up in her arms and carried her into her own bedroom and laid her down there. 'Adele!' she called, tapping the child's cheek sharply. 'Can you hear me?'

There was no response. Adele was as floppy as a rag doll, burning up, and Honour felt sick herself with terror that she was going to die. How would she explain that away? People already talked about her, she knew they were suspicious about Rose disappearing. What if they thought she had killed this child, or just left her to die?

'Cool water!' she said aloud, trying to calm herself. 'You've got to cool her down and get some fluid into her.'

When she stripped the child naked and laid her on some towels Honour saw the tell-tale purple bruising of finger-marks on her skinny thighs. She began to cry then, mortified that she'd been so obsessed with getting Adele to tell her about her mother that she had ignored that plaintive explanation of why she'd run away from the children's home.

'He did dirty things to me.' She should have picked up on that. But it hadn't registered because she was only thinking of herself and trying to safeguard her peaceful, reclusive life.

Adele's eyelids began to flicker as Honour sponged her down with the cold water, and she paused to hold her head up and make her sip some water. 'You must drink,' she pleaded. 'Just a few sips for now.'

Honour had always prided herself on being capable. She had nursed Rose through scarlet fever, Frank through his mental trauma and the pneumonia which ultimately killed him. She could mend a bird's broken wing, wring a chicken's neck and skin a rabbit. If a tile came off the roof she climbed up there and fixed it. But she felt weak and helpless as she sponged Adele, made her drink, then held the bowl as she vomited it back up.

On and on it went. She would get her cool enough to shiver, then cover her again, but within minutes her temperature shot up again and she was back to where she started.

It grew dark, and she lit a lamp. She listened and soothed Adele when she became delirious, calling out for her little sister and someone called Mrs Patterson. Hot one minute, cold the next, vomiting until there was nothing further to come up but bile. And all the time Honour kept seeing those purple fingermarks on her thighs, and felt rage that a man could do that to a child.

Midnight came and went, and Honour had already changed the bed sheets twice because they were soaked with sweat. She wanted to open the window to let in fresh air, but the moment she did so moths flew in, and the sound of them fluttering against the lamp was too distracting. Eventually she lay down beside the child, but although she was exhausted she was afraid to close her eyes even for a minute. Each time she looked at the girl's face, swollen and red with sunburn, she felt a sense of outrage that both Rose and that man Makepeace had treated her so badly.

It was four in the morning when Adele called out for a drink. Honour woke with a start and felt ashamed she had fallen asleep for a little while.

She was off the bed in a trice, rushing round to the other side to lift the girl's head and offer water. This time Adele drank half the glass before sinking back on the pillow. Honour sat by the bed waiting with the bowl, expecting her to vomit again, but the minutes crept by and this time she didn't. Honour felt her forehead. It was still extremely hot, and she laid a wet cloth on it to cool it. Yet instinct told her the danger period was past.

Honour blew out the lamp as the first light of dawn was beginning to creep into the room. Then, going over to the back window, she opened it to let some fresh air in. The sky was a pinkish grey, suggesting it would rain later, and that pleased her, not just because her vegetables needed rain, but because it would cool the air and help the child to get better.

'Her name is Adele,' she murmured to herself reprovingly.

She leaned her elbows on the window-sill, staring out across the marsh, and wondered why Rose gave her that name. Could the father have been French?

'Does it matter?' she asked herself. 'After all, you'll be packing her off once she's better.'

Chapter Eight

'You'll strain your eyes trying to read that book in this light,' Honour said sharply. It was early evening but raining hard outside, which made the room dark.

Adele put *Little Women* down reluctantly, wishing she dared ask if she could light the oil lamp. But she knew her grandmother never lit it until dusk, and that was a couple of hours away.

She had said earlier in the day that it would be two weeks tomorrow since Adele arrived here. It didn't seem that long to Adele, but then she'd been too ill to notice the passing days.

It had been very strange to wake and find herself in her grandmother's bed, with her beside her, and then to discover three whole days had passed without her being aware of anything. Her last clear memory was being given a piece of cake and a cup of tea and her grandmother going out. The tea didn't taste right, and the cake seemed all dry and nasty, then suddenly she felt really awful and she tried to get out to the privy. That was all; what happened from then on was just a blank.

She realized that she must have been very ill because of the way her grandmother was with her. She had to lift her out on to a chamber pot, wash her and comb her hair, and she fed her with a spoon like a baby.

Once Adele stopped wanting to sleep all the time, her grandmother propped her up on pillows and let her read. That was a real surprise because her mother had always been really nasty when she was too ill to go to school. She would snatch any book or toy away, claiming if she was well enough for that she could get up and do something useful. Her mother had never ever made special food that was easy to eat either. Grandmother made her something called junket. It was a bit like slippery blancmange and nice once she got used to it. Then there were soft-boiled eggs, rice pudding and lots of chicken soup.

But it was books she appreciated most. She forgot that she felt so bad while she read *Rebecca of Sunny Brook Farm* and *What Katy Did*. She didn't even think about her mother, Pamela dying or what happened at The Firs. She didn't really want to get better, it was lovely just to immerse herself in someone else's life and adventures. She didn't want to think about what would happen to her when she was well again.

Now she was on the mend and allowed up to sit in a chair, Adele had come to see how her grandmother lived. The chickens and rabbits she vaguely remembered out in the garden were her income. She sold the eggs from the chickens and she killed the rabbits for their meat and their skins. Along with this she made all kinds of preserves, and grew fruit and vegetables.

She had to work very hard, never stopping from early morning until the light faded in the evening, and Adele felt she would be very glad when she could hand her over to someone else as she had more than enough to do without unwanted visitors.

Adele hadn't considered whether she would like to stay here for good or not. There was no point – she knew adults took no notice of what a child wanted. But she did think her grandmother was the most peculiar and baffling person she had ever met.

As she'd looked after Adele when she was really ill, that was proof she did have a kind and gentle side. But she was brusque all the time now, and her posh way of speaking was at odds with her men's clothes and the way she lived.

She wasn't very talkative, and when she did speak she fired

questions. Mostly the answers to those seemed to make her cross. Adele wished she could think of something to say that would make her smile or even laugh.

Then when her grandmother did something really kind and nice, she tried to pretend she'd done nothing.

The second bedroom was one of those nice things. Adele hadn't even known there was another room, not until her grandmother said she'd moved the mattress back in there, and Adele was to sleep in there in future.

All the time she had been in her grandmother's bed, Adele had kept the image in her mind of how the living room beyond the bedroom door had looked when she first arrived. She remembered so clearly how cluttered it was that it was a huge shock on the day her grandmother helped her into it for the first time to find it quite different.

No boxes piled high, just an ordinary room. In fact 'Ordinary' wasn't the right description as Adele had never before seen such extraordinary things as her grandmother owned, but at least they were arranged in an ordinary fashion. The bird in the glass case was sitting on the sideboard. The bear coat stand was by the front door, and the table and chairs in the middle of the space they'd all taken up, with a vase of wild flowers on the table. The walls were covered in vivid paintings, there were shelves of books and ornaments, and even a lovely rug on the floor, the kind rich people had in their homes.

The mattress must have been hiding the door to the second bedroom. Adele fully expected it to be as bare and shabby as her room at The Firs had been, or why else would the door to it have been hidden? But to her absolute amazement, it was really pretty, with nice green and white wallpaper, curtains, a wooden bed with a carved headboard, even a dressing-table and a book-case full of books.

It was all extremely baffling. Had her memory been playing tricks?

She couldn't ask. Her grandmother didn't like being questioned, even though that was all she did. So she said nothing more than how nice the room was.

It wasn't until Adele heard the postman talking to her grandmother that the mystery was solved. He asked if she had got the wallpaper up all right and if she wanted any help moving anything. Suddenly Adele understood. That room hadn't been used for years, perhaps since her own mother moved out of it. All the stuff in it had been moved into the living room for some reason. But her grandmother had done it up and moved everything back while Adele was ill.

Why she had never said anything about it was another mystery, still unsolved.

She was making a nightdress for Adele now. She'd dug out some flannelette and sewed it on her sewing machine. Even when she admitted what she was making she didn't say it in a nice way, she just barked, 'Well, you'll trip up over that one of mine, it's far too big.'

Both the room and the nightdress might have given Adele the idea that her grandmother intended to let her stay, but Adele supposed she could hardly send her off to another children's home without a nightdress of her own. She wished she dared ask when this was going to be. But like asking for the oil lamp to be lit early, she didn't dare.

Another very peculiar thing was the way her grandmother reacted to anything Adele said about Rose. She would suddenly get up and walk out into the garden before Adele had even finished. The only time she'd ever listened right through was when Adele told her the whole story about Pamela's death and how much she missed her. Her grandmother gave one of her sniffs, and said that was how it should be.

Adele fidgeted in her chair. It was boring just sitting doing nothing. She wished her grandmother had a wireless, then it wouldn't seem so bad. For the last two days she had been allowed to sit out in the garden for a couple of hours in the afternoon. That was really nice, but seeing that old castle, the river and the hundreds of birds made her itch to go and explore. She was dying to see the sea too.

'Shall I make us a cup of tea? Or is it time for me to go to bed?' she blurted out. At least she could watch the sun go down from her bedroom window.

Honour glanced over at the child, and thought how much better she looked now. She had looked fearful all the time she was really sick; the skin on her face had come off in great flakes, giving her a piebald look, her hair was like dirty straw, and those odd, greenish-brown eyes seemed far too large for such a thin face. But good food, rest, a couple of afternoons sitting outside in the sun and a good hair-washing had done wonders. There were golden lights in her hair now, a faint blush to her cheeks, and her eyes were rather beautiful on closer inspection. She realized that the child was bored, and that was a further indication she really was on the mend. 'I'll make us some cocoa soon,' she said, removing a few pins from the sleeve of the nightdress.

She had got Adele to talk about her life in London over the last few days, and the child's descriptive ability was quite remarkable. With seemingly no effort she portrayed her home, family and neighbours so clearly that Honour felt as if she were there. Not that she wanted to see it that clearly. It stung to see Rose as a drunken harridan, married to a coarse, uneducated man and living in what sounded like a slum. Honour couldn't understand why, when Adele was clearly very intelligent, she showed no real anger or bitterness that her mother had treated her with such contempt.

But perhaps a child brought up without any love had no real conception of what that was?

After piecing together all the scraps of information about Rose, Honour thought it most likely that Adele's father was a married man and that she'd met him while working at The George in Rye.

Rose had resented having to leave Tunbridge Wells and all the friends she had there. She was sulky and difficult for some time, but she appeared to adjust eventually. It wasn't until four years later, when she was fifteen and got the job at the hotel, that she showed the first signs of being ashamed of where and how she had to live.

The George Hotel was for wealthy people, and Rose was suddenly talking of nothing else but what the guests wore, what they ate and how they looked. When Frank was brought home from France, Rose often stayed the night at the hotel when they had a special dinner or party there. Honour didn't question this or even ask if she was getting extra wages for working longer hours, because she was mostly too exhausted with nursing Frank to think about anything else. Yet she did remember wondering now and then if Rose was sweet on someone, for she seemed distracted, jumpy and overly concerned about her appearance.

Had that someone been a single and ordinary sort of man, she would surely have spoken about him, or even asked to bring him home.

Honour doubted she would ever learn the truth about what happened to Rose after she ran away. Perhaps it was better not to know why she ended up in a slum with a man she had nothing in common with. But whatever the reasons, Honour couldn't understand why they would prevent her loving her child. Women everywhere married men they didn't love, for money, status and many other reasons, yet they loved their children fiercely. And Rose, by all accounts, did love Pamela, Jim's child.

Since listening to Adele forlornly relating the events which led up to her mother being taken away, Honour had found it no longer mattered what Rose had done to her and Frank.

It paled into insignificance after what she had done to Adele. Not only failing to love, care and protect her daughter, she had heaped a huge burden of guilt for Pamela's death on to her young shoulders.

Honour knew she must try to lift that burden from Adele, but how? Honour wasn't, and never had been, a talker; she could get everything straight in her head, knew what needed to be said, but somehow the words never came out right. Even when young she had often been accused of being brusque, unfeeling and even callous. She didn't think she really was that way, it was just that she couldn't show her true feelings. The older she got and the more time she spent alone, the worse she became. And she wished this wasn't so.

Frank was the only person who knew she hid her soft centre behind a shell to protect herself. But they had been so close they could almost read each other's minds, and one word often sufficed where other people would have used dozens. If Frank was here now he'd know exactly how to help Adele. He had the patience to wait for the right moment, the insight into people's minds, and a very special gift of being able to draw confidences from almost anyone.

But Frank wasn't here, and Honour knew that she had to deal with this herself. While it was very tempting to do what she always did with anything which troubled her or got in the way, namely, pack it away like that surplus bedding and china, she couldn't do that this time.

The first priority was to find out what happened to Adele at The Firs. If a man supposed to be taking care of children was molesting them, then he had to be stopped.

'I could make the cocoa,' Adele said suddenly, breaking into Honour's reverie. 'You've been rushing around all day and you must be tired.'

Honour gulped hard, for Adele's sensitivity was further evidence that she'd spent her entire childhood trying to placate people. When Honour was twelve she wouldn't have ever considered that a grown woman could be tired.

'Not now, we'll do it later. I want you to tell me why you ran away from The Firs,' she said bluntly.

'I didn't like it there,' Adele said, and suddenly looked evasive.

'It was more than that, and you know it,' Honour said crisply. 'Now, just tell me and get it over with.'

'I can't.'

Honour saw her head had dropped down and she was wringing her hands. 'I know it's hard to talk about things that embarrass you,' she said firmly. 'But I have to know the truth. You see, I shall have to go to the police any day now.'

Adele looked up in alarm. 'Why? I didn't do anything wrong.'

'I'm sure you didn't. But when you ran away Mr Makepeace must have reported you missing to the police. They might be searching for you, and if I don't tell them you are here with me, I could get into a lot of trouble. I will also have to tell them the reasons you ran away, to make sure they don't send you back there.'

'They can't make me go back there!' Adele exclaimed.

'They could,' Honour said firmly. 'I may be your grand-mother, but you were put into the Makepeaces' care, not mine.'

'Can't I stay here with you?' Adele said, her eyes wide and fearful. 'Please, Granny?'

Honour knew that calling her Granny was a slip of the tongue, but it touched something deep within her. The girl had persisted in calling her Mrs Harris all this time, and Honour hadn't suggested something less formal because she didn't want to be moved by emotion.

'I doubt they'd let you stay here,' she said brusquely. 'They'd look at this place with no electricity or bathroom and they'd think that it was better for you to be in that big house with other children.'

'But I feel safe here,' Adele retorted.

Honour knew that two weeks ago that plea would not have meant anything to her. But her fright at thinking Adele was going to die, nursing her back to health, and the child's sweet, uncomplaining nature had altered her perspective. While Honour still had many reservations about her own suitability to take care of a young girl, and her ability to find the money to feed her too, Adele had crept under that hard shell of hers. And unless someone else came forward with a more suitable home for her granddaughter, she wasn't going to let her go without a fight.

'Feeling safe means you trust someone,' she said. 'Do you trust me?'

Adele nodded.

'If you trust me, then you can tell me what happened,' Honour said.

She waited. The girl was frowning, as if she didn't know where to start. Every now and then she would glance up at Honour, open her mouth to speak, then shut it again.

Honour felt like shouting at her to spit it out and be done with it, but she controlled herself and thought what Frank would say and do. 'Start with the bit you didn't like,' she suggested. 'Once you've said that it won't be so hard.'

'He got in my bed,' Adele blurted out in a rush. 'He—' She broke off and began to cry.

Honour was tempted to make it easier for her, to use the word rape. But she herself wouldn't have known what that meant at the age of twelve, and she felt sure Adele was equally innocent. When he began to recover mentally, Frank had said that telling her about the terrible things he witnessed during the war did help him to put them aside. Perhaps if Adele faced up to this awful business and spoke of it in her own words it would help her too.

'Come and sit next to me,' she said, patting the seat beside her.

Adele was out of her seat and on to the couch like greased lightning, and her desire to be held was so obvious that it brought a lump to Honour's throat. Involuntarily she found herself putting both her arms around the child to comfort her. 'Go on,' she whispered. 'I'm listening.'

'He put his hands under my nightdress and touched me,' Adele sobbed, burying her head against Honour's chest. 'He said it was his way of showing he loved me. He got on top of me and tried to put his thing in me.'

'Did he get it into you?' Honour asked, almost gagging at the brutal question.

'I don't think so, it was too big and I kept wriggling,' she whispered. 'But he made me hold it,' she added.

'And?' Honour said.

'I said I was going to be sick when stuff came out of it. He told me to run to the bathroom, and I did. I was sick too, again and again. He just left me there. I think he went back to his own bed.'

Honour closed her eyes and let out a silent sigh of relief that he hadn't penetrated the child, at least not that time.

'And how long after that did you leave The Firs?' she asked.

'That same night,' Adele said. 'I couldn't stay there, could I? So I just washed, got dressed and went.'

Honour felt she could breathe again at last. 'Yes, that was the right thing to do,' she said, smoothing down the child's hair. 'He was a very wicked man to do what he did to you, and you were very brave and sensible. Now we'll have some cocoa, and then you can tell me what Mr Makepeace was like when you first got to The Firs.'

Honour was shaking as she put the milk to heat on the stove, lit the oil lamp and drew the curtains. Adele was hunched up on the couch, her tears had died down to just a few snuffles, but she looked the picture of misery. It made Honour question whether she had done the right thing. She wouldn't forgive herself if she made the poor child ill again or gave her nightmares.

As they drank the cocoa, Adele told her all about Mr Makepeace, and as the story about the private lessons unfolded, and how important the man became to her, so Honour began to see the whole picture.

It was a sinister story, for as an adult she could see that the man had clearly planned ahead. He'd softened Adele up by telling her how clever and special she was, and unused to affection as she was, she wouldn't realize his caresses were improper. Alienating her from the other children would have made her even more dependent on him, and he probably thought he had her entirely in his power by that last night.

Honour had no doubt that if Adele hadn't run away that night, by now he would be using her whenever he felt like it.

'Was it my fault?' Adele asked a little later.

'Of course not,' Honour said a little sharply because she felt so tired and drained. 'He was the bad one. But you are safe now. It's all over.'

'But what if the police say I've got to go back to The Firs?' Adele asked in a small voice.

'They'll have me to reckon with if they do,' Honour said fiercely. 'I shall be making all the decisions about you from now on.'

'Does that mean you would let me stay with you, Mrs Harris?'

Honour looked at Adele and thought she looked like a frightened rabbit caught in lamp light. Such big eyes, still swimming in tears, and her lips quivering. If she could get her hair trimmed, brush it till it shone, feed her up to fill out those stick-thin limbs, and fill her mind with the beauty of nature till there was no room for the ugly memories she had now, Honour would feel she'd done something really worthwhile.

'I think Granny is a better thing to call me,' she said with a smile. 'And they'd better let you stay now after all the trouble I went to getting you well again.'

Part II

Chapter Nine

1933

Adele was deep in thought as she picked gorse flowers out on the marsh. Her grandmother used them to make gorse wine, which she sold in Rye along with her preserves, eggs and other produce. The large straw basket was almost full now, and Adele's hands were covered in small scratches from the prickly bushes. She barely noticed them, or the cold spring wind. In nearly two years of living with her grandmother she'd become hardened to such things.

Adele knew that she'd changed a great deal since the day she arrived exhausted and sick at Curlew Cottage. She had grown some four inches to five feet three, and though she was still slender, her limbs were now rounded out with muscle. She was delighted that her hair had grown long, thick and glossy and that her complexion was clear and glowing, but she hadn't yet come to terms with her budding breasts. They gave her more embarrassment than pleasure.

If anyone was to ask her what she considered to be the most dramatic change in her, she would probably claim it was her height. But in her heart she knew that it was being happy.

While the life she shared with her grandmother was some-times, particularly in winter, very hard, and absolutely nothing like the vision she'd held as a child of a perfect home, she had come to like it. Granny might be brusque and odd, but she was constant. Adele never had to brace herself for sudden rages, she was never belittled, or her efforts scorned.

Maybe she could do with a few explanations, like exactly what went wrong between her mother and grandmother; where her mother was now and if she was better. It would also be good to know if her mother had made any efforts to discover if Adele was being looked after properly, and whether Mr Makepeace was punished for what he did to her.

Granny wasn't one for explanations, however, especially when the subject matter was awkward. Yet Adele had come to see that she was wise and honest, and she had no doubt she would tell her these things when she believed the time was right, for beneath her crusty exterior there was a very tender side.

In the winter Adele never went to school without a big plate of porridge inside her and her coat warmed by the stove. On hot summer days when she returned home, Granny was often waiting with a picnic, which they'd eat after a swim at the beach. When storms came in the night, she always got up and came into her room to check Adele wasn't frightened. She was interested in what Adele learned at school, and she could often explain things far better than her own teacher.

During the first summer here, just about everything Adele had previously thought important was challenged. Back in London, money had dominated everything. Arguments between her parents mostly started over it, you couldn't pay the rent, buy food, or go to the pub or pictures without it. Adele had always thought that it was having money that made people happy.

Yet Granny set little store by it. She was careful with what little money she had, but it was only for basic commodities like oil for the lamps, flour, tea and sugar she had to buy; mostly everything else she made, reared, grew or gathered.

She kept the stove going with gathered wood, she grew vegetables, baked her own bread. Transport was her own two legs or her old bicycle. She made her preserves with whatever fruit or vegetable was in season; gorse flowers, elderberries and blackberries could be gathered for nothing. She wasted nothing – an old dress could be made into a skirt or blouse, vegetable peelings and even the chicken and rabbit droppings made compost for her garden.

But Granny saw no hardship in this, she took pleasure in living off the land, and Adele had learned to like it too.

In the beginning Adele had believed she would always yearn for London, with its shops, cinemas and crowds of people. Back at The Firs she had yearned for fish and chips, to ride on a tram, and the quiet of the countryside unnerved her. Yet in that first summer here, once she was well enough to go out, Granny introduced her to her beloved marshes and Adele had discovered a world more beautiful and exciting than anything she had ever dreamed of.

It wasn't a bleak and barren place as she had first thought. It was a home for all manner of plants, birds and other wildlife. When they went out on wood-collecting walks, Granny would point out different birds and name them. She could identify each call or cry, knew every plant and herb. Slowly Adele found herself enveloped in its magic, and she loved to walk on her own, relishing the peace and beauty. She would remember that in London in summertime the leaves on the trees hung limply, daubed with dust and soot. She would recall the unpleasant smells of sewers and rotting food, hot sticky nights when she couldn't sleep, and the constant noise of traffic, and people shouting and fighting. The sounds that came in through her bedroom window here were all gentle ones: the bleat of a sheep, the hoot of an owl, the crash of waves on the shingle beach.

Her grandmother kept her back from school right through till the start of the autumn term in September, but to Adele's surprise she didn't feel lonely without other children. There were so many books to read, and she could draw and paint, sew and knit. Her grandmother also taught her to swim and to ride her bicycle.

Adele smiled to herself as she remembered the very first time she saw her grandmother in a bathing suit. It was a very

147

old-fashioned knitted one, royal blue with a red stripe across her chest, almost like a baby's romper suit that covered her right down to her knees and elbows. Yet she had a good figure for a woman in her fifties, still lean and taut with shapely legs. And she could swim like a fish, diving into the waves with all the glee of a child. She said her father had taught her when she was only five, even though in those days it wasn't considered proper for a girl. He'd had a sister who drowned in a river and because of that he believed all children should learn to swim as water attracted them.

Honour was a good teacher, surprisingly patient and very encouraging. Whether she was showing Adele how to make jam and bread, to tell the difference between weeds and flowers, or ride a bicycle, she had a knack of explaining just enough so Adele could grasp the idea, then she'd stand back and let her do it herself.

Adele could do things now she would never have been able to imagine in London. She could skin a rabbit as well as her grandmother, she could cook and lay a fire and get it going with only one match, pluck a chicken and chop wood.

As Adele continued picking the gorse flowers, her mind was on the future rather than the many skills she'd already learned. In three months' time in July she would be fourteen and able to leave school and find work.

The Slump, or Depression as some people called it, continued, growing worse every month as more businesses folded. Although Adele rarely saw a newspaper, she could see the real effects of unemployment in Rye when she went to school. The men stood around on the quayside in groups, their faces etched with anxiety and almost certainly hunger. She saw their wives with drawn faces looking longingly in shop windows. And many of the children in the meanest streets in Rye were so pale, thin and lethargic that Adele often felt guilty that she had more than enough to eat.

Her grandmother had very strong views about the plight of the poor, though she didn't consider herself to be one of them. She got angry about something called the Means Test, because it meant some families had to sell their furniture and other belongings to qualify for dole money. She thought it was immoral that the rich continued to buy motor cars and expensive clothes and go on holidays to France or Italy, yet paid their servants starvation wages. When she heard how two men had been arrested for stealing a sheep on the marsh because their families were so hungry, she marched into Rye and gave the police a piece of her mind. As she pointed out, the families of those men would only suffer more if they were sent to prison. And what was one sheep when the farmer didn't even know how many he had?

Adele had got a sketchy knowledge of what was going on elsewhere in England and the rest of the world through occasional trips to the pictures in Rye. On Pathe News she saw dockyards at a standstill, haggard men waving banners pleading for work, enormous queues outside soup kitchens in America, gangsters killing one another in places like Chicago, and the somewhat sinister rise to power of a man called Adolf Hitler in Germany.

She sometimes felt a little guilty that she cared less about the real world than the make-believe one of the Hollywood films she and her grandmother saw. But it was good to watch glamorous film stars dancing and singing wearing gorgeous clothes, to glimpse a world where houses were like palaces, and everyone had big cars, fur coats and swimming pools.

Her grandmother was very fond of remarking that 'Hollywood was dope for the down-trodden masses', and she was probably right, but even so Adele couldn't help but think that if she could only get the right job, then maybe she could buy lovely clothes, stop Granny from working so hard, and make her proud of her.

*

'Excuse me!'

Adele jumped at the unexpected sound of a male voice and turned to see a boy with a bicycle behind her.

'I'm sorry. I didn't mean to startle you,' he said apologetically.

His posh voice and good clothes set him apart from the local boys she knew by sight. He was perhaps sixteen, fresh-faced, tall and slender, with very shiny dark hair.

'I didn't hear you ride up,' she said, blushing furiously because she knew she must look like a tramp to someone who wore grey flannels with a knife-edge crease, and a tweed jacket like something from a tailor's window.

On school days Adele looked much like her classmates, often better dressed than many of them because her grandmother was good with the needle, and she had a pinafore dress and blouse as good as any bought in a shop. But away from school, clothes had to be practical, and Honour had made her a pair of trousers which she wore tucked into Wellington boots, topped by a much-darned navy blue jumper. One girl at school had said sarcastically that she looked like a replica of her grandmother.

'It's the wind, it kind of whines, blocking out everything else,' she added nervously.

'I should've rung my bell,' the boy said with a smile. 'But that seemed awfully rude. I only wanted to know if I can ride to Rye Harbour this way.'

He had a nice smile and lovely dark blue eyes, and she liked his good manners. Most boys she knew were very uncouth. 'You'll find it hard to ride,' she said. 'It's boggy in places and there's lots of shingle. It's a lovely walk, but easier to get there by road on a bike.'

'I was just exploring really,' he said, and looked curiously at her basket of gorse flowers. 'Why are you picking those?'

'To make wine,' she said. 'My grandmother makes it.'

He looked surprised. 'What's it like?'

'She doesn't let me drink it,' Adele said with a grin. 'But I've sipped it. It's kind of sweet, and smells like the flowers. They say that one glass makes you drunk, two makes you dead drunk.'

He laughed. 'Is your grandmother drunk all the time then?'

'No, she only sells it,' Adele said reprovingly. In two years she had become very used to people trying to ridicule her grandmother, and very adept at defending her.

'I was only joking,' he said. 'I've never met anyone who made wine before, my parents get theirs from a wine merchant. Could I buy a bottle of it for them to try?'

Adele didn't really know how to answer that question. Granny always sold all her wine to a man in Rye. He gave her the bottles, and he sold it on to his customers along with the elderberry, dandelion and other wines she made. 'I'd have to ask her,' she said. 'Are you here on holiday?'

'Not exactly,' he said. 'My grandmother has just died, so I came down with my parents to help my grandfather organize the funeral. He lives in Winchelsea.'

'Would your grandmother be Mrs Whitehouse? My grandmother mentioned only yesterday that she'd died. If so I'm very sorry.'

'Yes, that's her,' he nodded. 'She was over seventy, and frail, so it was to be expected. I didn't know her very well. Mother used to bring us down here occasionally when I was very young, but I suppose she and my grandfather found noisy brats too much of a trial. We're staying until I have to return to school after the Easter hols.'

'School?' Adele exclaimed without thinking. Everyone she knew left school at fourteen and he was certainly a lot older than that.

'Well, yes,' he said, clearly puzzled by her remark. 'Have you left then?'

'No, but I will be leaving this summer,' she said. 'I was just thinking about finding a job when you came along.'

He gave her a long, cool stare, and Adele felt he was weighing up her shabby clothes and the wine-making and deciding she wasn't the sort of person he should be chatting to.

'I expect that will be hard down here,' he said eventually, but his tone was sympathetic, not patronizing. 'We went into Rye yesterday afternoon and my parents both remarked that people there must be suffering badly with the Slump. What kind of job are you aiming at?'

'Anything that pays,' she retorted, and even to her own ears she sounded as brusque as her grandmother.

She expected him to take his leave and ride off, but to her surprise he dropped the bike on the ground and began plucking the flowers off the gorse bush. 'I'm Michael Bailey, and if I help you'll be finished quicker,' he said with a grin. 'Then maybe you'll show me the walk to Rye Harbour? That is, if you haven't got anything better to do?'

His grin was so warm and genuine that Adele couldn't help but smile back.

'I'm Adele Talbot,' she said. 'But I have to take these flowers home before they dry out.'

'Is that a polite way of saying you can't or won't come with me?'

Adele had had very little contact with boys so she certainly hadn't learned to be deliberately evasive. She had meant just what she said, that she had to take the flowers home, though perhaps she ought to have added 'first' to make it clearer. But as he'd given her time to think about it, she wasn't sure it was right to go for a walk with a complete stranger.

'Why would someone like you want to go for a walk with me?' she asked defensively.

He put his head on one side and looked at her appraisingly. 'Someone like me?'

'Well, look at you!' she said, blushing again. 'A real gent. If your folks saw you with me they'd have a fit.'

He frowned. 'I can't see why,' he said, sounding as if he really didn't know. 'Why shouldn't we walk and talk and even become friends? Don't you get lonely all by yourself out here?'

Adele shook her head. Perhaps she was strange, some of the girls at school said she was, but she never felt lonely out on the marsh, she loved it. 'There's too much to see to feel lonely.' She shrugged. 'I look at the wild geese, check to see the first new lambs, find wild flowers. I feel much more lonely when I'm in town surrounded by people.'

She expected that he'd give her one of those smirks that said he too thought she was strange, but as she raised her eyes to look at him in defiance, she saw instead understanding and approval. For the second time she was struck by his eyes, not just by their dark blue colour, but by the intensity of his stare.

'I often feel lonely surrounded by people too,' he admitted. 'Even my own family make me feel that way. And back at my grandparents' place it's so gloomy, all they can talk about is the funeral arrangements. That's why I took off this morning. But I don't know the marsh, I don't know what to look out for. Come and show me!'

Once the basket was full, Adele took it home, and after only the briefest of words with her grandmother, she sped out again to meet Michael. She felt surprised at herself, for normally if she saw anyone walking on the marsh she went in the opposite direction. When she'd first come to live here, Granny had told her that 'Marsh People' were a sort of joke to the town people, considered to be at best eccentric, at worst mad. Adele had had plenty of evidence that this attitude was widespread, so she avoided town people – even girls from her class at school could be very superior. But maybe, as Michael didn't really come from here, he hadn't heard of it.

*

Michael abandoned his bike, and Adele led him along the way she always walked to Rye Harbour, a path that involved jumping over a few water-filled ditches, a plank over a stream and taking in several of the willow shelters that shepherds erected to give the sheep and their new lambs some protection during bad weather.

Within minutes Adele stopped feeling nervous because it was obvious to her that Michael was genuinely interested in exploring the marsh, and his enthusiasm reminded her of the way she'd been when she first saw it.

They saw dozens of new lambs, some obviously only a few hours old, their little legs still very wobbly, and she was sure by Michael's wide smiles that it was the first time he'd seen any so young.

'What on earth's wrong with that one?' he asked, pointing out one lamb looking very odd and bloody.

'It's not hurt,' Adele said. 'The shepherd has just tied another dead lamb's skin round it.'

'Why?' he asked.

'It's been orphaned. Some ewes die while giving birth, just as some lambs don't make it either. So the shepherd skins the dead lamb, puts the skin around an orphaned one, and then the mum who's lost her baby thinks it's hers because of the smell, and she feeds it.'

Michael looked staggered. 'I always thought shepherds fed orphaned lambs by bottle!'

'They might on an ordinary farm where there's only a few sheep,' Adele said. 'But there's hundreds out here – imagine trying to get out here four or five times a day with dozens of bottles of milk! Besides, it's better for lambs to be brought up in a flock rather than as pets, they can become a real pest when they are fully grown.'

'Wouldn't you be tempted to rear one?' Michael asked, looking at one little lamb bleating pitifully for its mother.

Adele smiled. 'Oh yes, they are so sweet. Last spring I was

over here every day looking at them. I kept hoping I'd find one alone that I could take home. I didn't think my grandmother would turn it away, she loves animals. But perhaps it was as well the shepherd always got here before me. Grown-up sheep aren't much fun.'

She told him about Misty, the rabbit that her grandmother had given her as a pet.

'She's just beautiful, the lightest grey colour, like dawn light. She's so tame she comes hopping into the house and lies down by the stove. She's the best thing I've ever had.'

'Does your grandmother keep lots of rabbits then?' he asked.

Adele nodded ruefully. 'She breeds them and then kills them for the meat and the skins. I thought she was so cruel when I first came to live with her. Not only killing rabbits that are so sweet, but wringing the chickens' necks too. But I see it differently now. It's just a way of making a living.'

Michael asked her then why she lived with her grand-mother, and Adele told him the same thing about her parents as she told everyone else: that her mother had become ill and her father thought it best she came here to live.

But Michael wasn't satisfied with that explanation, and as they continued their walk to look at Camber Castle, he kept asking more questions. What was wrong with her mother? How often did her father visit her, and why if her mother was ill didn't she come and stay here too?

Adele liked the fact that someone as nice as Michael could be really interested in her, but she didn't want to reveal her background, so did her best to change the subject. Michael was persistent, however, and kept on asking her the same thing, only rephrasing the questions in different ways.

'Why don't you tell me the truth?' he said eventually as they reached the ruined castle. He looked at her sternly. 'Is it that bad?'

*

Adele thought that if she was to tell him the whole truth, he would consider it pretty bad. But that wasn't the reason she didn't want to reveal it. It was loyalty to her grandmother. She'd taken her in when no one else cared, and so it seemed right not to bandy around that her daughter was mad, and a bad mother. Granny often used the word 'standards', and to Adele that meant keeping family secrets secret, maintaining some dignity even if your dress was shabby and your grandmother distinctly odd.

Adele had come to admire her oddity. Honour Harris treated everyone the same, whether it was the man she sold her wine and preserves to, policemen, acquaintances in Rye, or ramblers who came to the door asking for a drink of water in the summer. She was proud, cool and impervious to flattery, cheap jibes or any kind of blackmail. Adele had noticed with some delight that most people became quite obsequious to her after just a brief meeting.

She strode into Rye to sell her goods with the belief they were better quality than anyone else's. She didn't wait humbly for the shop proprietor to see her. If he didn't drop everything the moment she walked in, she went somewhere else. The manager of the Home and Colonial store had once described her to Adele as 'a real character'. He was right, she was quite unique. Hard, capable, bombastic and sharp-tongued, she was also fair, honest and unexpectedly generous. She could always spare a penny or two for beggars, especially those who were crippled ex-servicemen. When she knew a family was in dire straits she would make up a bag of vegetables, eggs and some chicken or rabbit to help them out.

'Actions speak louder than words' was the proverb Granny lived by, and Adele had clear proof of that. From the moment Honour knew what Mr Makepeace did to Adele, she had taken action. She had never divulged what transpired when she went to the police to inform them that her granddaughter was with her, but months later she announced she was now Adele's legal guardian. There was a legal document to prove it, and even more important to Adele, her grandmother had never shown the slightest hint that she regretted it.

'How well do you know Rye?' Adele asked Michael as they walked into the ruin of Camber Castle. She wasn't so much deliberately ignoring his questions, as hoping to sidetrack him.

'I know my way around it,' he said with a grin. 'It's very quaint, isn't it, but I suspect you want to know if I've learned all its history?'

'I suppose so.' She smiled. 'My grandmother is an expert on it, she can walk you around it telling you tales of the ship-building, the smuggling and its royal connections. She's almost as passionate about it as she is about the marshes.'

'My grandfather told me Rye and Winchelsea were once islands but the sea receded and created the marshland, but that's about all I know,' Michael replied.

'It's more important to know that Rye was one of the Cinque Ports and that Henry VIII built this castle,' Adele said reprovingly. 'Some people claim he built it to lock up Anne Boleyn, but I don't believe that, he built it as a defence in case of an invasion. It's my favourite place.'

To others the castle might only be an old ruin, but to Adele there was something mysterious and wonderful about the way nature had taken it over, bushes sprouting out of the thick stone walls, ivy clambering up stone stairs, and lush grass and wild flowers growing inside. Even in winter she often walked here, as once inside the outer walls, sheltered from raw winds from the sea, she could sit and dream. Primroses and cowslips bloomed earlier here than anywhere else on the marsh, birds nested here, and often, if she sat very still, rabbits would come out of their burrows and scamper about near her.

She would imagine Henry VIII arriving here on horseback

in a velvet cloak trimmed with ermine, with a procession of noblemen, the servants scurrying to get things ready for him. Sometimes she could almost see it.

The castle was the place where she did all her thinking, a place to run to when she felt the world was against her. A couple of hours alone here and everything came right again.

'It is a lovely old place,' Michael said, gazing around him reflectively. 'But I want to hear about you,' he added, putting one hand on her shoulder.

'When you've been down here for a bit longer you'll find out about "Marsh People",' she said with a giggle. 'We're supposed to be not quite right in the head on account of the wind. Some children think my grandmother is a witch.'

'I don't think you can be both a witch and a grandmother.' He laughed. 'Witches don't marry. Has yours got a black cat?'

'No cats, she doesn't like them because they kill birds. But I reckon she could do a few spells if she had to.' Adele smiled.

'Well, get her to do one for my folks,' he said, sitting down on the grass and leaning back against the castle wall. 'It would take real magic to make them happy.'

Adele looked at him in surprise. She might have only met him a couple of hours ago, but he came across as the sort of person who basked in a golden world where everything was perfect.

When he saw her surprise he gave a hollow laugh. 'Oh, I know what you're thinking, the privileged boy at public school! But my mother is always flying into terrible rages, then she stays in bed for days on end. Father rages back at her and makes her worse. If he'd just stay around a bit more, be kind to her, she might change. But he's as cruel as she is barmy. Mostly I'm glad when the holidays are over and I can go back to school.'

All at once Adele realized that this was why he'd wanted

to come for a walk with her. He probably had no intention of unburdening himself, but just wanted to be taken into another kind of life for a while. In a way it was the same as when she and Pamela used to go and watch other people at Euston station. A way of escaping reality.

Yet it also seemed to be some strange twist of fate that Michael should pick her of all people to talk to. Who else would have any real empathy with him? 'Is your father cruel to you too?' she asked tentatively, her heart expanding with sympathy for him.

'Sometimes, but it's mostly Mother. But then she is very demanding, suspicious and extraordinarily difficult.' He paused, giving Adele a faintly embarrassed grin. 'She ruined my sister's wedding by having a tantrum,' he went on. 'My sister-in-law refuses to come to our house any more because of something she said. Father always claims it's her nerves and gets her medicine for it. But I think that makes her even more confused and frightened.' He stopped again, and this time there was no grin, just a bleak, sad look and suspiciously damp-looking eyes.

'Sometimes I think what she really needs is just someone to talk to,' he added with a sigh.

Adele noted that he had both attacked and defended his mother, which suggested he was torn both ways. She also remembered that her own mother had often said that nobody ever listened to her.

'My mother used to complain that my dad didn't listen to her,' Adele ventured, very tempted to break her code of secrecy about her parents just this once.

'I don't think there's many married couples who communicate,' he said sadly, pulling his knees up to his chest and leaning his chin on them. 'I watch my friends' parents and they are much the same as mine. In public they are so polite, they put up this united and devoted front, like actors in a play. But at home when there's no one but children or servants around it's quite different. They either ignore one another, or snipe away with sarcasm and mockery.'

'Really?' Adele exclaimed. She had always imagined that rich people had everything they wanted, including greater happiness.

Michael nodded. 'My elder brother Ralph and sister Diana are both getting like it too. All they seem to care about is their social life, filling their houses with other people, going off to the races, to concerts and the theatre. Sometimes I think they are afraid to be alone with their husband and wife. When Ralph's first child was born Ralph went away on business. He didn't have to, he could have put it off, what could be more important than sharing such a moment with his wife?'

Adele had never met anyone, except perhaps Ruby back at The Firs, who had told her so much about their family at a first meeting. She thought she ought to be suspicious of Michael because of it. Yet instinct told her he wasn't normally so open. She thought maybe he'd been tripped off by his grandmother's death, or he sensed something in her that made it seem right to confide in her.

'Where I used to live it was tradition for a man to go down the pub when a baby was being born,' she said hesitantly. 'That amounts to the same thing, doesn't it?'

'No, they are celebrating the birth of the new baby,' he said indignantly.

Adele smiled. 'Maybe they say that's what they are doing,' she said. 'But from what I've seen, most working-class people drink to escape reality. They don't want to think about having an extra mouth to feed, just as they don't want to remember there's rent to pay, and that they'll be lucky if they're still in work next week.'

'It seems we are looking at this from opposite ends,' he said with a smile. 'Do you know any couple who married for love and stayed that way?'

'My grandmother did,' Adele retorted. 'Grandfather died a couple of years after the war. Every now and then she tells me something about him and her face goes all soft. She's got some of the pictures he painted in the cottage, she's always looking into them like she's seeing him.'

'He was an artist then?' Michael looked quite taken aback.

'Yes, and a good one too, but he was wounded in the war and never painted again. When they first married they lived in Tunbridge Wells, they had a quite different life there I think. More like yours, I suppose.'

Michael looked really interested at that. 'So they weren't real "Marsh People"?' he asked with a smile. 'Your grandfather came here to paint? That's pretty romantic.'

Adele had thought it terribly romantic when her grandmother had explained how it all came about. She loved to hear how they'd brought all their grand furniture down from Tunbridge Wells in a horse-drawn cart. She imagined the bear coat stand, the stuffed bird and the china cabinet all piled up, with Granny and Grandfather sitting on the back with Rose between them.

'Granny's not exactly one for going over the past, and why and how things came about.' Adele shrugged. 'But there are things about her that give you big clues. She's very well educated, her father was a schoolmaster, and some of her furniture is really fine, like it came from a big house. And Grandfather was an officer in the army, not an enlisted man.'

'Intriguing,' Michael said thoughtfully. 'You are too, Adele. You've got a young girl's face, but the mind and manner of someone far older. Why do you think that is?'

'The wind on the marshes I expect,' she joked, afraid he was nudging her into a situation where she might say too much. 'Come on,' she said getting up. 'We'll never get to Rye Harbour at this rate.'

*

It was just on six when Adele got home, having parted from Michael where he'd left his bike earlier in the day. She was very cold now, and she went straight over to the stove to warm her hands. Her grandmother was sitting mending a pair of socks. She'd put some bread to rise by the stove, and there was also one of her vegetable soups simmering.

'Umm,' Adele said, sniffing the air. 'I'm starving.'

'Didn't the young man buy you tea and cake?' Grandmother said in a caustic manner.

Adele wheeled round in surprise. 'How did you know I was with a young man?'

'I have eyes,' she retorted. 'The marsh is flat, you can see for miles. If you were trying to hide him then you failed.'

Such a remark was typical of her grandmother. She said things just as they were, no beating around the bush, no trick questions or subterfuge.

'Of course I wasn't trying to hide him. He just got talking to me and I showed him the way to the harbour.' Adele felt foolish now – she might have known her grandmother would spot them together.

'And his name?'

'Michael Bailey,' Adele said. 'He's down here because his grandmother, Mrs Whitehouse, died. You mentioned her the other day.'

Granny nodded. 'Then he must be Emily's child. The Whitehouses had two sons too, but they lost them both in the war.'

'Do you know his mother then?' Adele asked.

Her grandmother wrinkled her nose. 'Yes I do, an uppity little madam, though she may of course have grown out of that. I haven't seen her for donkey's years.'

Adele would have liked to have known why her grandmother had formed that opinion, but she thought it might lead to repeating what Michael had told her. 'Michael's really nice,' she said instead. 'He really liked the marsh too, I don't think he's ever seen a newborn lamb close up before.'

'That's city folk for you,' her grandmother said with a wry smile. 'As I recall, the man Emily married was a bumptious chap. Far too full of himself for my liking. I'm glad the son isn't like that too.'

Adele was surprised that her grandmother didn't ask her more about Michael. Girls she knew at school said that their parents were always suspicious of anyone of the opposite sex. But then, as Granny knew his family perhaps she didn't need to ask anything more.

When Adele asked if she could go for a bike ride on Monday, she was even more surprised that her grandmother agreed readily. The only comment she made was not to go too far, as the weather in April was unpredictable.

Granny was right. Adele and Michael got as far as Camber Sands and it began to pour with rain. They sheltered under a tree for a while, but when the rain showed no sign of stopping, they had to head for home.

Yet even getting soaked didn't spoil the day. Michael was such good company, he could talk about anything and everything. He told her about his friends at school, his home in Hampshire, and how he wanted to fly aeroplanes.

'Father sniffs every time I say it,' he laughed. 'He's a barrister, you see, so he thinks I ought to be one too. I told him once that he'd already sucked Ralph into the law, and he needn't think I was going to follow like a sheep. But I think he imagines when I go up to Oxford that will change my mind.'

Adele had already decided she wouldn't like Mr Bailey one bit. Michael had said he was complaining at being stuck in Winchelsea with a doddery old man, and if he had his way he'd be off the moment his mother-in-law's funeral was over. Adele thought it was hardly surprising Mrs Bailey was nervy if she had such a heartless husband.

'Maybe he doesn't think you'll make a living flying planes,' she said.

'Well, he's probably right there.' Michael grinned. 'But I don't care about money. The first time I got up close to a little bi-plane, something about it just bowled me over. It belonged to a friend of my father's and he took me up in it. That was it, my fate sealed.'

'I think it's wonderful you've got a real ambition,' Adele said staunchly. 'But he might be right about you changing your mind once you're at Oxford.'

She knew now that Michael was nearly sixteen, and he had two more years of school before Oxford. She had thought he must be very clever to go there, but Michael insisted he was only average, and he didn't think he'd stand a chance of getting into Oxford if it was purely on merit, rather than having been at the right school first.

'I won't change my mind,' he said firmly. 'I've only agreed to make an effort to get into Oxford because they have a flying corps there. I'm going to do it, come what may.'

Mrs Whitehouse's funeral was two days later, and the rest of Michael's family didn't arrive until the morning of that day. Adele was intending to walk up to Winchelsea and just happen to be near the church at the time of the funeral. She wanted to get a look at them all, but her grandmother was horrified when she realized that was what Adele had in mind.

'You'll do no such thing,' she said sharply. 'Have a little respect, girl! Do you think they'd appreciate you gawping at them at such a time?'

'I was only curious about them,' Adele said lamely. 'Michael's told me a lot about them.'

'Curiosity killed the cat,' her grandmother said tartly. 'I daresay the boy will be back to see you when it's all over. And you'd better invite him in so I can get a good look at him.'

Adele thought that sounded ominous, but she hadn't reckoned on Michael having such a winning way with people. He didn't turn up till two days after the funeral, and in his arms he had a bundle of wood for the stove that he'd picked up by the river on the way down from Winchelsea.

'I hope you don't think me impertinent, Mrs Harris,' he said, when Honour opened the door to him. 'But I saw all this lying around and thought you might be glad of it.'

'What a kind thought,' she said. 'Though I don't know that your parents would approve of you roaming down here. But come on in, it's a miserable raw day.'

Adele felt shy and awkward about Michael being in her home. Out on the marshes they were equals, but she expected he would think Granny's house with its lack of electricity and outside lavatory a slum compared with his grandparents' big house.

But Honour asked him about the funeral, and how his grandfather was bearing up, even mentioning that she knew him to be a good chess player, and Michael looked very comfortable and at ease with her as he had a cup of tea.

Honour was intending to make and bottle up her ginger beer that day. The mixture of yeast, ginger and sugar had been fermenting by the stove in a big pot for the past week. 'May I help?' Michael asked, when she mentioned it.

The bottles Honour was intending to use were still outside, unwashed. Never one to let a pair of willing hands go unused, she set Michael to the task in the scullery. She gave him a bottle brush, hot soapy water, and made him scour them out and remove any labels.

Adele was frightened he'd get fed up and want to leave, but he didn't. He cleaned the bottles in no time, bringing them into the living room all sparkly, just as Adele and her grandmother had finished straining the yeast mixture, added lemon and water, and were ready to fill the bottles.

'So when is it ready to drink?' he asked, as he took over

lifting the heavy bucket of cloudy ginger beer to pour it into the funnel Honour was holding in a bottle.

'It needs to sit for at least a couple of weeks,' she replied. 'It's delicious. Adele will give you some that's ready to drink now. It's not alcoholic like my wine, and they say ginger is good for the circulation. I'm proof of that. I rarely have cold feet or hands.'

'Then I'd better start drinking it,' Michael said with a wink at Adele. 'One of the drawbacks to being a pilot is cold hands and feet.'

Adele was astounded to see how quickly he won her grandmother round. She not only said he was welcome to call any time if he was at a loose end, but thanked him heartily for his help and the wood.

He came every day after that, and never failed to ask what he could do for Honour before he suggested going for a walk or a bike ride. He shinned up on to the roof to fix a loose tile, he collected wood, helped weed the vegetable plot, and secured a climbing rose right round the trellis porch at the front door. He blanched when Honour killed some rabbits one day, yet he still stayed to help her skin them.

Yet it wasn't so much what he did or what he said that made Honour like him. It was just the way he was. He didn't have a condescending bone in his body – he was genuinely interested in the way she made a living, and openly admired her ingenuity and resourcefulness. Honour said she liked his intelligent questions, muscle and lack of squeamishness.

'He's a fine boy,' she said late one night as she and Adele were having their nightly cocoa. 'I never would have believed Emily Whitehouse could produce anything but a brood of gutless snobs.'

'I think from what Michael's told me that his mother is a bit nervy,' Adele confided, hoping that wasn't betraying his confidence.

'So was her mother,' her grandmother said with a wicked

smile. 'I said to her once, "Stick up for yourself, woman, don't let Cecil use you as a doormat." She sort of whimpered and said words to the effect that a husband should be masterful.'

Adele was astonished. 'I didn't know you knew her that well!' she exclaimed.

'We were friends.' Honour pursed her mouth the way she always did when there was something she didn't want to enlarge on. 'She was a lot older than me of course, but we were friends nevertheless. That kind of changed when I began cleaning for her at the start of the war, though. I had to, I needed the money. I helped out a few times too when young Emily came running home with her children because that husband of hers wasn't treating her right.'

'Why haven't you told Michael all that?' Adele asked.

Her grandmother didn't answer for a little while. But eventually she looked at Adele and gave a ghost of a smile. 'I don't like admitting I had to clean for anyone, especially a friend,' she said. 'But more than that, I didn't think it was a good idea to tell him I had any connection with his grand-parents, or his mother.'

'Why? He'd be fascinated!'

'Yes, he would be, he's that kind of a lad. And he's also the open kind who would go home all excited and tell his parents. I don't want that. As I remember, both of them were fearful snobs. I suspect they'd frown on Michael being friends with you.'

Adele had already come to that conclusion on her own. She knew people who lived out on the marshes didn't mix with people in the big houses in Winchelsea.

'You don't frown on it though, do you?' she asked.

'Of course not,' her grandmother said vehemently. 'My background is every bit as good as theirs, and I'm pleased you've got such a nice friend. But, my dear, you must remem-ber he will be going back to Hampshire and I can't imagine his parents coming down very often to see poor old Cecil. You may not ever see him again.'

Later that night as Adele lay in bed listening to the wind howling across the marsh, she thought about what her grandmother had said and felt sad because she knew it was true. Michael was such fun to be with, they laughed at all the same things, they could talk about anything, and she wished he could stay here for ever.

But she knew she had to be realistic. He probably wouldn't have made friends with her if there'd been anyone else around to pal up with. Once he was back at school he'd soon forget about her. She was going to miss him, but she wasn't going to get silly about him like the soppy girls in love stories.

For the last week Michael was there, the weather turned really warm, and they had many wonderful times together. They paddled in the sea, shrieking with laughter because it was so cold. They built a bridge out of branches across one of the streams on the way to Rye Harbour, and had a competition to see who could make their gob-stopper last longest. Adele had never had one of those giant sweets before as she rarely had any money to spend on such things, but Michael had bought them, and explained they changed colour as you sucked them. It made Adele laugh when he kept making her open her mouth to see what colour hers had turned to.

They tried having races across the top of the shingle banks. Adele taught him to kind of ski down the steep parts. She showed him the millions of baby eels in one of the streams and he taught her to count in French. Yet it wasn't so much what they did, it was that everything seemed to be such fun when they were together. They could just look at each other and start laughing over nothing.

On the morning of the day Michael had to go home again, he called round at Curlew Cottage just as they were finishing breakfast.

'I won't intrude, Mrs Harris,' he said very politely. 'But this is a thank-you for being so welcoming.' He handed Honour a very pretty tin tea caddy, full of tea.

'How very thoughtful of you, Michael,' she beamed, admiring the tin.

'I got you a book,' he said to Adele, handing over a parcel. 'I hope you haven't already read it.'

Adele opened it and found it was *Lorna Doone*. 'No, I haven't read it,' she said, delighted with the surprise. 'Thank you, Michael. I shall start reading it today.'

'Will you stay and have a cup of tea with us?' Granny asked.

Michael shook his head. 'I can't, they'll be waiting to leave.'

'Run along to the end of the lane with him then,' she said, giving Adele a little nudge. 'Goodbye, Michael. I hope to see you again one day.'

Michael had his bike out in the lane. He picked it up and looked at Adele.

'I'm going to miss you,' he said glumly. 'Will you write back if I write to you?'

'Of course I will,' Adele agreed. 'You make sure you tell me all your news. But you'd better be going. You don't want to make your parents angry.'

She watched as he rode off, the bicycle wheels wobbling as he went over the rough ground. Towards the end of the lane he stood up on the pedals and went faster. As he turned on to the Winchelsea road he waved without turning his head.

Adele still had the book he'd given her in her hands. She opened it and saw he'd written a message for her.

To Adele, a story about a boy who meets a girl out on the moors and can't forget her. I'll never forget you either.
   With all my best wishes,
   Michael Bailey. Easter 1933

Chapter Ten

1935

'I don't believe I'm ever going to find a real job,' Adele said wearily as she slumped down on the grass by her grandmother's chair.

It was almost the end of August, two years since she left school, yet she still hadn't found permanent work. She had managed to get temporary jobs, a few weeks here and there in the laundry when they had a busy spell with holidaymakers in the town, haymaking in a farm in Peasmarsh beyond Rye. She had picked strawberries and raspberries, dug up potatoes, cleaned the fish shop in town after it was closed for the day, and done dozens of other little jobs too. She had written letters to just about every company and business in Hastings as well, and travelled over there on the bus time and time again, but no one wanted to take her on permanently, in any capacity.

'They all say they want someone with experience,' Adele complained. 'But how can I get experience if no one will give me a chance to show what I can do?'

'Times are hard,' her grandmother said, and gave her a little pat on the head.

Adele was only too aware that there were millions unemployed, and indeed that men had taken their own lives because they couldn't provide for their families. Hardly a week went past without a hungry man looking for work knocking on the door to ask if they could spare some food. Honour always gave them a bowl of soup and some bread – she'd even parted with the last of Frank's old clothes. These men usually came from the Midlands or the North of England, though there was terrible poverty in Rye and Hastings too.

On a hot sunny day like today it wasn't obvious, but back in the winter Adele had seen ragged, barefooted children begging along the High Street. Every week there were yet more men hanging around dolefully by the quay, hoping for a day or two's work. Some families had sold every stick of their furniture, and old people died in the winter because they had no coal to burn.

'Maybe I'll have to go to London,' Adele said gloomily. 'I met Margaret Forster in town. She said she'd had a letter from Mavis Plant and she's managed to find a job in an office there.'

'You are too young to go to London,' her grandmother said forcefully. 'I don't want you living in digs, at the mercy of unscrupulous people. And something will turn up here, I'm sure of that.'

'The papers keep saying there's work now for those who want it, but that's rubbish,' Adele said angrily. She was hot and tired and her feet hurt. It hadn't helped that Margaret Forster had been crowing about her job in the Home and Colonial. She boasted about a new pink crêpe-de-chine dress, and she said she was going to the pictures that night with another girl from the shop. Adele had only been to the pictures twice in the last year.

What made her really furious was that she was sure she was being turned down because she lived on the marsh. Interviews always went quite well until she was asked where she lived. She was intelligent, quite attractive, well-spoken and good-mannered. Why did they think she had a fatal flaw just because of where she lived?

'We can manage perfectly well even if you don't get a job for another year,' her grandmother said calmly. 'With all your help I'm producing twice as much as I did three years ago, and getting better prices.'

'I can't bear to see you work so hard,' Adele blurted out. She had observed her grandmother even more closely since she left school, and noticed she hardly ever sat down during the day. Between the chickens and rabbits and making jam or wine, she never stopped. 'I should be making things easier for you now, not making you have to work even harder.'

'If I work harder now it's because I choose to,' Honour said crisply. 'I like what I do, I'm not a martyr. Now, go and wash your face and hands, get yourself a drink and go and sit in the shade for half an hour. Tomorrow's another day, and who knows what will appear?'

'Nothing will appear,' Adele muttered as she washed her hands in the scullery. The water suddenly trickled to a halt, and that was the last straw. They got drinking water from a pump in the garden, but rain water ran into a tank at the side of the cottage and that fed the tap in the scullery for washing. It hadn't rained for a couple of weeks and the tank was obviously empty.

Everything in this cottage was such hard work. The stove had to be lit and fed with collected wood. A bath meant heating pails of water and filling up the tin bath, which then had to be emptied. The privy didn't have a flush, every now and then they had to tip some lime down it, and it always smelled. There was no electricity, just candles and oil lamps. They didn't even have a wireless.

Since she left school Adele had become far more aware of the way some other people lived. It wasn't that she was jealous exactly that so many of them had gas and electricity, wireless, gramophones, boilers to do the washing in and even electric irons, she just thought it was a little unfair that some had so much, and some so little. She had been top of the class at school, yet she couldn't get a job, while Margaret Forster, who was the class dunce, landed one in the Home and Colonial. Most women of her grandmother's age had time to sit in a chair with a book. Yet she had to eke out a meagre widow's pension by skinning rabbits. And those rabbit skins were made into coats for women who did absolutely nothing all day.

Snatching up a large enamel jug, Adele went out to the pump in the garden and pumped furiously until she'd filled it. Then she filled a bucket too. As she carried the water back inside, she wondered how on earth Granny would manage when she was a really old lady. When she wasn't fit enough to pump water or collect wood.

'I'll take care of her,' she said to herself. But that thought made her start to cry. How could she take care of someone else when she couldn't even get a job?

Honour came in and caught her crying. 'What are you blubbing for?' she said in her customary unsympathetic manner.

'Because everything's so bloody hard,' Adele burst out.

'Don't you dare swear in my house,' her grandmother retorted, 'or I'll scrub your mouth out with soap. And stop feeling sorry for yourself, there's millions far worse off than you.'

Adele ran into her room and slammed the door, flung herself down on her bed and cried even harder. She stayed there, even though she knew Honour was getting the tea ready, and when she wasn't called for it, she cried harder still because it was obvious Granny didn't care if she was upset or hungry.

She knew she was being irrational and wallowing in self-pity, and it wasn't the lack of modern conveniences here, or even the absence of a job which was causing it. She loved this place, and she didn't really care if she had no money to go to the pictures. Even her anxiety that Granny worked too hard didn't really wash, as she'd only stepped up her output of produce because she had Adele to help with it.

Maybe she was grouchy because of Michael?

She hadn't really expected to see him again after that Easter holiday two years ago, but he did keep in touch by letter, and that July he'd come again to stay in Winchelsea with his grandfather.

They had three glorious weeks during which they met every day. They swam, went on bike rides and took long walks. One day they'd taken the bus into Hastings and Adele got to eat fish and chips again for the first time since she left London. Michael won her a fluffy dog on the rifle range, they'd had candy floss, ice-creams, and winkles from a stall on the pier. That was the best day of her whole life, and she knew Michael thought so too.

But he had to return to Hampshire, and she had to find a job, and even though Michael continued to write, he admitted he didn't know how he could swing it to come to Winchelsea again as his grandfather wasn't too keen on visitors.

During the Christmas holidays he came back again briefly. He and Ralph, his elder brother, had been sent to check on their grandfather. Michael called at Curlew Cottage, bringing Adele a present of a blue scarf and matching gloves, and a box of expensive chocolates for Granny, but he couldn't stop because his brother was waiting for him back at their grandfather's.

Then, the following February, Mr Whitehouse died. Apparently his housekeeper had come back from her afternoon off and found him dead in his armchair. He'd had a heart attack.

Adele felt very guilty that she was almost pleased because it would mean Michael would come back. He did come for the funeral, but it was arranged from Hampshire, and his family all drove up together for the service and went back the same day.

He wrote afterwards and explained why he couldn't call in, but he said he thought he'd be coming back to help clear the house out later on in the year. He said then that he kept thinking about her, and wished they lived closer so he could see her more often.

His letters kept coming all through Easter and on to Adele's fifteenth birthday in July when he sent her a pretty topaz necklace. He said it made him think of the gold in her hair the previous summer, and for the first time ever Adele began to think of him as a sweetheart rather than just a friend.

All through the summer holidays Adele was almost holding her breath, hoping against hope that he would come and they could relive the fun they'd had the previous year. He finally turned up in late August, with his parents, and while they were sorting out his grandfather's house, he managed to get away now and then to see her.

Something had changed slightly. Not just that he'd shot up in height and his voice was deeper, it was more than that. They were so pleased to see each other, they wanted to repeat all the things they'd done before, but there was a strange kind of shyness between them, which led to long silences and awkwardness. Adele caught him looking at her too intently, then when she asked why, he'd blush and insist it was nothing. She found herself very aware of his maleness when he sat close to her, noticing his long eyelashes and the curve of his lips, and when he stripped off to his bathing trunks to swim, his chest and upper arms had lost the boyish skinniness of the previous year; now he had muscle and a manly shape.

They didn't have the previous year's endless time together either. Michael had to be back in Winchelsea at set times. Yet they had a picnic on the beach one hot day, went to Camber Castle, and on his last day they walked into Rye where he took her to the tea shop up by the church and they had hot buttered crumpets and cakes.

Adele loved wandering around Rye almost as much as the marshes. It was all so old and pretty, with narrow alleyways, steep cobbled streets and many beautiful ancient houses. Michael liked the gun garden below the Ypres Tower which was built as a prison during the Napoleonic war. He took a photograph of Adele sitting on one of the cannons, and joked that she looked like a pin-up girl.

It was when they were walking back home that he held her hand for the first time, and just the touch of his skin against hers made her feel giggly and unbelievably happy.

As they got to where the road forked off to Curlew Cottage, he said he would have to leave her there. Then he kissed her.

The kiss wasn't like the ones at the pictures where the heroine melted into the hero's arms as the film ended. He sort of lunged at her, his lips grazing hers only momentarily.

'I wish things could be different,' he said, looking embarrassed and anxious. 'But maybe they can be next year when I go up to Oxford. You will wait that long for me, won't you?'

At that moment Adele thought he merely meant he hoped she wouldn't find another boyfriend. She said that of course she'd wait for him.

It was only after they'd parted that she suddenly realized that he was trying to say far more than that. But he couldn't without hurting her feelings.

Adele knew that while they were just friends the fact that she came from the marshes and wore shabby clothes hardly mattered. But in thinking of her as a sweetheart he could see trouble looming ahead, not only with his parents but just about everyone he knew. She guessed that he was hoping that by the time he got to Oxford, she might well have transformed herself into the sort of girl his family and friends would accept. Maybe he even hoped she might come to Oxford to work, so they wouldn't have the geographical problems either.

Adele took a long hard look at herself in the mirror that night, and she could see so well what Michael's set wouldn't approve of. Constant exposure to wind and sun had given her an almost gypsy-like complexion. Her hands were rough and she bit her nails, her hair was natural, streaked blonde by the sun, while town girls wore hats and went in for permanent waves. Even her greenish-brown eyes seemed to suggest she was a wild creature. Her stare was too bold and she rarely blushed or giggled like her friends from school did.

She wondered if going to a hairdresser and buying new clothes could transform her into one of those elegant young women she saw in films. Somehow she doubted it. Even if by some miracle she could find the money, that wouldn't change the way she walked, her eyes, or even the way she was inside. She'd grown like that by living in a wild place; she had muscle from hard work, from running through fields and chopping wood. Nothing could turn her into a delicate hothouse flower.

Michael didn't write again for some two months, and by that time she had decided he'd thought better of daydreaming about such an unsuitable girl. This seemed to be confirmed when he finally wrote again and said he was learning to drive and his father was going to buy him a car if he did well in his exams. The letter had a stilted tone to it, almost as if he were writing to an aunt, not a girl he had kissed and said he hoped would wait for him.

No further letters came, only a Christmas card to both her and her grandmother, and so Adele was astounded when he turned up again in May, driving a blue sports car and wearing a very smart dark suit. He said he'd had to come to Rye to pick up some papers from his grandfather's solicitors and he was driving back that night.

Over a cup of tea, he talked of going up to Oxford in October, commiserated with Adele who was still without a permanent job, and asked Honour about her wine and preserves, but he seemed very formal and adult.

Later he asked them both if they'd like a ride in his car to Hastings. Honour said she had too much to do, but urged Adele to go.

It was only once they were in Hastings walking along the promenade that he seemed to revert to the old Michael, and suddenly blurted out that things were really bad at home.

'It's all over Harrington House,' he said, referring to the house in Winchelsea. 'Father wants to sell it, but it seems Grandfather made some sort of trust for Mother, and he can't do anything with it without her permission. Mother won't agree, and they fight all the time now. Every time I'm home from school I get dragged into it. It's awful. I think I'm going to go away to Europe in the summer hols, I can't face the thought of the whole summer being like being in the middle of a war.'

They drove up to Fairlight Glen later and went for a walk, and he asked Adele if she thought he was doing the right thing.

'Maybe you should give the car back to your father and get a job well away from them for the summer?' she said a little sharply. 'That way you'd be independent. As long as you take money from them they'll expect you to be at their beck and call.'

He laughed then and ruffled her hair. 'Such a wise little girl,' he said with more tenderness than mockery. 'Not even sixteen yet telling me not to be a parasite.'

'I didn't mean it like that,' she said heatedly. 'I can hardly shout, I'm living off Granny! I just think that working would give you a much better excuse to distance yourself from them. Going travelling looks like running away.'

'Yes, I expect it does,' he said thoughtfully.

He said nothing further about his problems and they slipped back to the old easy way they'd had when they first met. When he got her home he came in to say goodbye to Granny, and left later saying he would keep in touch.

Adele reached out beside her bed for the letter he'd sent her a few days after that visit.

'*Dear Adele,*' she read.

I just wanted to thank you for listening to my troubles. You are the best listener I know, but perhaps that's because of the way you live with your grandmother, in touch with nature, at one with the seasons. I envy you that life, I'm surrounded by opinionated people with loud braying voices, who care for nothing but material things. I long for the stillness and serenity of the marshes. I will always treasure the good times we have shared and even if I don't take your advice and still go travelling in Europe, a part of me will be there with you.

You never did tell me your secrets, and I know you have them for how else would you have come to be so understanding of others? Maybe they are too painful to reveal? If that is the case you must feel that I am a little feeble with my constant moans about my home life.

I hope you find work soon, I shall be thinking about you whatever I do this summer.

My very best wishes.

Michael

Adele always found herself a little choked up when she read that letter, and today even more so because she felt lonely. She had done her best to try to lose her romantic thoughts about Michael. She knew quite well that they could never come to anything. But that still didn't prevent her wishing.

He hadn't taken her advice, just as she'd known he wouldn't. Three postcards with the briefest of messages had come from Paris, Rome and lastly from Nice. She doubted that after seeing those places he would ever want to come back to Romney Marshes.

Harrington House looked forlorn. Adele rode up there on her bike every now and then to check if there were any new developments. It was an imposing red-brick double-fronted house over two hundred years old, but the windows were dusty and the porch, which stood right on the pavement, was full of blown-in rubbish. It looked very much as if no one had been in the house since the last time Michael went there.

'It's no good thinking about him,' she thought sadly. 'If you can't even find a job, what hope have you got of keeping him as a friend?'

The following morning when Adele got up, she saw some blood on her nightdress. She knew immediately what it was, as Granny had explained about menstruation two years earlier. All her schoolfriends had started a couple of years ago, and she had begun to think there was something terribly wrong with her, so she was pleased to find she was normal after all.

'Well, that explains your behaviour last night,' Granny said dryly when Adele informed her. 'I always got down in the dumps at that time when I was a girl, it's a sign of the changing feelings that come with being a woman. You have had a bitter lesson in the past about what men can be like, so I'm sure I don't have to warn you to be on your guard in future.'

Adele blushed scarlet with embarrassment and rushed outside to let the rabbits out of their hutches.

She knew of course that this was Granny's blunt way of pointing out that she was now physically capable of having a baby, but she was shocked that she would use what happened at The Firs as a warning. In all this time she had never once referred to it, not even in the most oblique way.

Adele had tried very hard to forget it ever happened, but the memories jumped out on her unexpectedly from time to time. Perhaps that was why her periods were so late. She was still nervous of men, especially when they looked too closely at her. Michael was the one exception, he never made her feel uncomfortable or threatened. She knew that if he was ever to kiss her again, she would welcome it. But she couldn't imagine ever wanting things to go further than that. She'd be too afraid of evoking frightening memories of Mr Makepeace again.

Once she'd let all the rabbits out into their pens, and found a few clumps of dandelion leaves for their breakfast, she picked up Misty to stroke her.

Honour didn't allow the buck rabbits in with Misty, as she said Adele would only be upset when her babies had to be killed. Adele had often thought she would like to live her whole life like Misty, petted, well fed and protected from the nastiness of breeding. But then she supposed that would mean she'd end up an old maid without any children or grandchildren.

She was still stroking Misty and contemplating the mysteries of love, sex and marriage, when she heard a car coming down the lane. There were too many bushes and trees at both sides of the cottage to see who it was, so she walked round the side path.

To her astonishment Michael was getting out of a big black car.

'What a surprise,' she said, blushing furiously because he was in a formal suit and tie, and she hadn't even brushed her hair this morning and was wearing the old rag of a dress she always did her chores in. 'I thought you were still travelling the world.'

He smiled, but it was a forced, troubled one. 'I had to come back,' he said, grimacing. 'Oh hell, I don't know where to start.'

At that point Honour came out of the front door. She must have heard what Michael had said, for she asked if his mother was all right.

'No, she's not, Mrs Harris,' he said. 'May I talk to you? Or are you too busy?'

'Not too busy to see you, Michael,' she said welcomingly. 'Come on in.'

Thrilled that he was back, yet anxious because all did not seem well, Adele put Misty back in her pen, then joined her grandmother and Michael indoors.

'Mother and Father have separated,' he burst out. 'Mother is going to live at Harrington House. I don't understand what it's all about and I'd be very grateful if you wouldn't say anything about it to anyone.'

'I'm sure you know me well enough to know I wouldn't dream of that,' Honour said crisply. 'Have you brought your mother down here, or are you just checking the house out for her?'

'No, she's here. I drove her down yesterday,' he said. 'We stayed the night in a hotel because it was too much for her to come straight here. She is very upset.'

For a moment Adele's heart leaped. It was sad of course that his parents were splitting up, but he'd said they weren't happy anyway. Her pleasure was because she thought she'd see Michael more in future.

'It's to be expected that she would be upset,' her grandmother said sympathetically. 'She's been married a great many years. I am very sorry, Michael, it must be very troubling for you, especially when you are just about to go up to Oxford. But I'm sure your mother will have adjusted by the time you have to leave.'

'But that's the real trouble,' he said. 'I have to go now, at least back to Alton to return Father's car. I can't stay with her and I don't know how she'll manage. She's never looked after herself.'

'Of course she can look after herself, she's a grown woman,' Honour said dismissively.

'She's never had to do it,' Michael insisted. 'She's always had servants to take care of her and the house. There isn't anyone at Harrington House, not a cook or a maid, no one.

And I haven't the first idea how to get someone for her. That's why I came to see you. What do I do, Mrs Harris? I can't just drive off and leave her there alone.'

'That's perhaps the very best thing to do,' Honour said. 'She'll soon learn to take care of herself.'

'Granny!' Adele said reprovingly. 'Poor Michael's worried enough without you being tough.'

Michael looked gratefully at Adele. 'I'm worried sick. We brought a box of food with us, but I can't even trust her to make a meal for herself. I told you what she can be like, when she's upset she just goes to bed and stays there. Our housekeeper at Alton had the knack of persuading her to get up and get dressed, but on her own she'll stay there for ever until she dies of starvation.'

'Poppycock!' Honour exclaimed. 'People have a very strong sense of self-preservation. She might lie in bed for a couple of days feeling sorry for herself, but once she gets hungry she'll soon get up. She's not a young and foolish girl, she's a mother of three grown-up children. It's time she started behaving like an adult.'

'You are probably right, Granny,' Adele said cautiously. 'But poor Michael can't be sure of that once he's gone. What if I went up there to help her?'

'I couldn't ask you to do that,' Michael said quickly. 'I didn't come here for that. I just thought Mrs Harris might know how to get a maid or a housekeeper.'

'Now, do I look as if I employ a maid?' Honour gave a wry smile. 'I left that kind of thing behind years ago. You could place an advertisement in the newspaper. There's so many people desperate for work you'll soon get someone.'

'But that would take time,' Michael said despairingly. 'I don't even know if Mother would know how to interview anyone. And in the meantime she's likely to get in a fearful mess. Do you know anyone in Winchelsea, or even Rye, who might come in?'

'I don't, Michael.' Honour shook her head. 'But maybe you could ask in the shop in Winchelsea. Or the neighbours?'

Michael grimaced. 'I don't want to have to confide in anyone local,' he said. 'It won't help her in the long term if word gets around that she's a bit —' He broke off.

Honour nodded in understanding. 'No, I don't suppose it would. I can't understand, Michael, why your father didn't bring her up here and get the household sorted out for her. I know it's none of my business, but he does have a duty to care for her. Has he thrown her out, or did she run away?'

Michael hung his head and didn't respond, Adele and Honour looked at each other. 'Answer me,' Honour ordered. 'It won't go any further than this room.'

'There's lots of things I don't understand,' Michael said haltingly. 'They've been having huge arguments all year about Harrington House. My grandfather left it to my mother and I think my father tried to force her to sell it. I was in Europe when it all blew up and she hasn't explained anything to me.'

'Are you saying he told her she could get out if she wouldn't sign?' Honour asked.

'I think so,' Michael said, his eyes brimming with tears. 'But Ralph and Diana, that's my brother and sister, seem to be blaming Mother too, so maybe there is something more I don't know about. I got home from France the night before last, to find Father ordering the maid to pack Mother's bags.'

'I see,' Honour said thoughtfully. 'It sounds to me as if your mother needs a lawyer as well as some domestic help.'

'My father *is* a lawyer! On the way down here Mother kept saying that all his lawyer friends would side with him and no one would listen to her.'

'That's foolish talk,' Honour said dismissively. 'Her father, your grandfather, was a well-respected man in these parts. He was also highly intelligent, so if he left his house solely to your mother, he had a good reason for it. She should go to his lawyer in Rye. The days when a man was automatically entitled to a woman's money and property as soon as he married her are over.'

Adele had listened to all this in silence, watching both Michael and her grandmother. She could sense that Granny's sympathies lay with the other woman and she very much wanted to relieve Michael of his immediate anxiety about her.

'I could help your mother,' she said impulsively. 'I know I don't know anything about what maids do, but I can cook and clean.'

'I couldn't possibly ask that of you,' Michael said. But a faint ray of hope came into his eyes.

'You aren't asking. I'm offering,' she said. Then, looking at her grandmother, she said, 'You wouldn't mind, Granny, would you?'

'Not as a temporary measure, not if you really wanted to,' Honour said cautiously.

'Then that's settled it, I'll go,' Adele said, and smiled at Michael. 'That is, if you think she'll accept me?'

'Accept you?' Her grandmother's voice rose with indignation. 'She'd better be grateful! You are worth a great deal more than being someone's maid.'

'She certainly is,' Michael said, and smiled warmly at Adele. 'But then it would only be until I can get someone permanent.'

'She'll need to be paid. I'm not having her acting as a lackey for nothing,' Honour said tersely.

'Granny!' Adele gasped.

'Mrs Harris is quite right,' Michael agreed. 'I know we pay the housekeeper at Alton two pounds a week, but her husband works for us too and they have their own cottage in the grounds. Suppose I offered two pounds ten shillings a week, would that suit you?'

It sounded like a fortune to Adele. She knew some families lived on much less than that. But before she could say anything her grandmother spoke out.

'You will point out to Mrs Bailey that my Adele was not intended for domestic work, she was top of her class at school. If she is to live in, she must be allowed a couple of hours off every afternoon and one full day a week. She is not to be slapped or bullied either. And your mother must understand that this can only be a temporary arrangement.'

Adele could only gasp at her grandmother's cheek.

'I will relay your views,' Michael said, and Adele saw his mouth twitch with amusement. 'But are you sure you want to do it, Adele?'

'I'm happy to do it,' Adele said. She even felt excited. Harrington House was a lovely old place, and however difficult Mrs Bailey was, she didn't think she could be any worse than her teacher at school, or even her grandmother. While she hadn't learned to cook many different dishes, Granny always said that if you could read a recipe book, you could cook. And they must have electric light at Harrington House, maybe even gas too. 'Will we go now?'

Michael looked at Honour for confirmation this was all right with her. She nodded her agreement.

'Well, if it's all right with you, Adele, it would be best. Then I can introduce you to Mother myself and show you around.'

'That's fine,' Adele said. 'I'll just go and put something presentable on. I won't be long.'

As Adele was brushing her hair, the required hundred strokes Granny always insisted on, and twisting it up into a neat bun at the back of her neck, Honour spoke to Michael.

'Adele is a good, honest and hard-working girl, and I am sure she will give excellent service to your mother,' she said, her expression serious and concerned. 'But you do understand that I will whisk her away immediately if I feel she is being treated unfairly?' she added, giving him a stern look. 'Make this clear to your mother, Michael.'

'I promise,' he said. 'I shall come back down just as soon as I can, but you never know, by the time I get back to Alton,

Father might have seen he was wrong to push Mother out.'

'You must try and find out the whole story,' Honour said. 'You need to know exactly what is going on. Ask your brother and sister what they know too.'

Michael sighed. 'They are always influenced by Father. Whether he's right or wrong, they'll back him up.'

'You must try and stay neutral,' Honour said, her tone softening with sympathy. 'Help your mother by all means, it's right that a son should do that, but at the same time make sure she knows she has to help herself too. You are not her keeper.'

He smiled weakly. 'I'll do my best.'

Adele stared out at the road in front of her as Michael drove. In her tidiest dress, dark blue cotton with white collar and cuffs, a dress her grandmother had helped her to make with work in mind, she thought she looked appropriately attired for what lay ahead. She was suddenly very apprehensive. Not only because she had no idea of what helping Mrs Bailey was going to entail, and whether she could actually do it, but because of Michael.

This was going to change everything between them, that much was certain. Whenever she'd thought of him this summer it was with memories of walks, bike rides and picnics, and she'd hoped there would be more in the future.

But by going to work for his mother, that would be ruled out. She might not know how the upper classes ran their homes, but she knew gentlemen didn't have maids for friends. It just wasn't done.

'Will Mrs Bailey tell me what she expects of me, or do I just do what I think needs doing?' she asked nervously.

He glanced round at her and he looked terribly worried. 'I really don't know,' he said with a big sigh. 'Back in Alton the staff all have their set jobs, and our housekeeper keeps them in line. I don't know if Mother even gave her any instructions. I can only ever recall her sitting at her desk writing letters, or arranging flowers. Of course she may have done much more than that and I never saw it.'

'Well, will she tell me what she wants to eat, and when?'

'I don't know,' he said. 'Oh hell, Adele. I think you'll have to play it by ear. It might be as well just to cook what you think is right. She doesn't eat much at the best of times.'

It was beginning to sound as though Adele was being sent to take care of a very difficult spoiled child. But she reminded herself that Granny and home were just down the road, and if the worst came to the worst she could just walk out. They had agreed that for the time being Adele would go home every evening after supper. She thought she could cope with almost anything if she could leave at seven.

As they drew up in front of the house, Adele saw that the windows were still dusty and that the door brass hadn't been cleaned for a very long time. While that was hardly important, she wondered how neglected the inside was.

She became scared then, wishing she hadn't been so impulsive in offering her help.

'You'll be fine,' Michael said, as if reading her thoughts. 'My mother is difficult, but she can also be very charming. Show her you genuinely want to help her, and she'll show her appreciation.'

Michael opened the door and walked in, beckoning Adele to follow. 'Mother!' he shouted, once in the hall. 'I've got someone to give you a hand.'

The hall was large with a wide oak staircase going up from it. It had a flagstone floor which looked none too clean, and some very dreary pictures on the wall. It certainly wasn't as nice as Adele had expected.

Mrs Bailey appeared at the top of the stairs. She was a small and slender woman with delicate features, wearing a pale green dress. Her hair was beautiful, somewhere between red and blonde, and she wore it in loose waves just touching her shoulders. Adele knew she was a couple of years older than her grandmother, but she looked closer to thirty. If it hadn't been for her red-rimmed eyes, she could have passed for a film star.

'I can't find any coat hangers,' she said petulantly. 'It was all very well you telling me to hang up my clothes. But how can I without anything to put them on?'

'Never mind that now,' Michael said, looking up at her. 'I've brought someone to help you. Come down and meet Adele Talbot.'

The woman didn't move for a moment, just stared at Adele. She had blue eyes just like Michael's, and milky-white skin as clear and unlined as a child's. Adele thought she was childlike in every way, with her unabashed stare, little-girl mouth and petulant manner.

'Is she a maid?' she asked as she began to come down the stairs. She moved very elegantly, and Adele saw she was wearing pale green high-heeled shoes which matched her dress exactly. 'Where did you find her? Has she got references?' she added, as if Adele wasn't there.

Adele decided it would be best to act in the way her grandmother did. Straight to the point, state her case, and if Mrs Bailey didn't like it, well too bad. 'No, I'm not a maid,' she said. 'I am just a friend of Michael's and when he told me you needed help to settle in here, I volunteered. I can cook, clean and do laundry. If you want my help I'll stay, if not I'll go.'

'But you are just a child,' she exclaimed, looking Adele up and down. She looked back to Michael. 'How do you know this girl?'

'I met her when we were down here two years ago,' he said. 'Adele lives at Winchelsea Beach, I called in this morning to ask if they knew of anyone to help you. Adele kindly offered her help. She is very capable and trustworthy.'

Mrs Bailey said nothing, just waved her hands in a

distracted manner. Adele sensed she was the kind who couldn't make a decision about anything.

'I know you don't know anything about me, ma'am,' she said. 'But my grandmother is very well known around here. She suggested I came as a temporary measure to help you out. As I understand it, you don't have any other help right now?'

'No, I don't,' Mrs Bailey said. 'But Michael, surely you could have got me someone more mature?'

'Where from?' he asked. 'There isn't a shop where you can go and buy staff and expect them to start work straight away.'

'Why not the grandmother then?' she said. 'Or is she very old?'

The woman's assumption that she had only to bleat she needed help and anyone from the working classes would drop everything for her riled Adele. 'My grandmother wouldn't work for anyone,' she said sharply. 'It's me or nobody. Now, I don't wish to be rude, but if you think I am unsuitable, just say and I'll go home.'

'She's very outspoken,' Mrs Bailey said to Michael, her voice shaking a little.

'I trust her,' he said. 'Now, come on, Mother. You know I have to leave soon with the car, and I don't want to leave you here all alone. Give Adele a chance to show what she's made of, you are lucky to get her.'

'I need to talk privately to you,' she said to her son. 'Come into the drawing room.'

Michael excused himself and asked Adele to wait. He and his mother went into the room on the right of the hall and shut the door behind them.

Adele could hear their voices, Michael's very low, Mrs Bailey's high and indignant, but she couldn't hear what they were saying. To her left was a dining room, with a vast table and eight chairs around it. A rather dingy room, she thought, and very dusty, but then no one had been here for a while. She took a step or two into it and saw a large kitchen beyond. It was disappointingly old-fashioned – she had imagined anyone living in such a big house would have far better. She just hoped there was a real bathroom – Mrs Bailey looked the kind to lie in bubbles half the day, and Adele didn't fancy lugging pails of water to her.

About fifteen minutes later Michael emerged from the drawing room alone, looking pleased with himself. 'Mother's come round now,' he said. 'And she asked me to apologize for offending you. She has agreed the terms, and I'm to show you round while she has a rest.'

He showed her the kitchen first, and said he didn't have a clue how to light the stove, but he knew it ran on coal and was kept permanently alight. Adele examined it and found it wasn't much different to the one at the cottage, just bigger and newer. 'I can light it,' she said.

It seemed it heated water too, and pipes ran to a bathroom upstairs, much to Adele's relief. There was also a small electric stove which could be used to cook on any time the stove wasn't lit. Adele was also pleased to see a big, cold larder as keeping food fresh in the summer was the biggest problem at Curlew Cottage.

The Baileys had brought a box of food with them, including a piece of ham which Adele quickly put in the larder. She thought that whoever had packed the box knew what they were doing – it contained just about all the basic necessities, and a few luxuries too, like cake and biscuits.

'Will Mrs Bailey do the shopping?' she asked.

'She isn't used to doing it,' Michael said. 'So I expect she'll get you to do it.'

'And will she give me the money for it?'

'No, I expect it will be on account,' Michael said.

'I don't know that they'll give tick here,' Adele said. 'You might have to arrange it before you leave.'

That was one of dozens of questions she asked him as he showed her round the house, and most he didn't know the answers to. Adele began to feel very sorry for Michael, he looked so worried, and she couldn't tell him everything would be all right, as she was far from convinced of that herself. How did she know how often rich people had clean sheets? Or what they expected to have for breakfast? She just hoped her grandmother would know.

The whole house was full of dust. And there were so many ornaments in every room that it would take a whole day to clean each one thoroughly. But at least she found some coat hangers for Mrs Bailey. There were hundreds of them in a box under one of the beds. This was just as well because Mrs Bailey had strewn the whole of the big bedroom with her clothes.

'I'll have to go now,' Michael said when they got back down to the hall. 'I honestly don't know what I would have done if you hadn't agreed to come here, Adele. I would never have had the effrontery to ask you – I hope you know I didn't come hoping you'd offer?'

Adele smiled. She knew he was speaking the truth. 'Stop worrying, Michael. I may not turn out to be the ideal house-keeper. But your mother will live in a clean house and I'll get food for her. That's all I can promise.'

He reached in his pocket and pulled out a printed card. 'That's my home address, telephone if there's any problems. If I'm not there, ask to speak to Mrs Wells, she's our housekeeper. She's very fond of Mother and she'll help you. But I'll be telephoning here anyway.'

'I've never used a telephone,' Adele admitted. 'What do I do?'

'When it rings you just pick it up and say "Harrington House",' he said. 'If you have to ring me, you pick up the receiver and ask the telephonist to get this number. For local numbers, like the doctor, you just dial the number and wait for someone to answer it. Always be careful what you say though, the operators tend to listen in.'

'I hope I can remember all that,' Adele said anxiously.

'You'll soon catch on,' he said. 'I'd better say goodbye now, and go and see Mother before I take off. You've been a real brick.'

Adele went into the kitchen and unpacked the rest of the box of groceries while he was saying goodbye to his mother. The stove had been cleared of ashes, so she screwed up some newspaper, laid some kindling over it and lit the paper with a match. Hearing the front door open and close, she went to the dining-room window to look out. Michael was just getting into the car, and his face looked so drawn with anxiety it made a lump come up in her throat. He was too young to be sorting out his parents' problems.

'We all have to grow up sometime,' she thought as he pulled away. 'Look at you, behaving like a ten-year-old last night, this morning you find you've turned into a woman, and now just a few hours later you're starting work.'

She was on her knees adding coal to the burning kindling piece by piece, and blowing to get the coal to light, when Mrs Bailey came into the kitchen. 'It's elevenses time,' she said. 'I like coffee and biscuits. I'll take it in the drawing room.'

Adele had never drunk, nor made, a cup of coffee in her life. The closest she'd ever got to coffee was seeing Americans drink it in films.

'I'm sorry, ma'am,' she said, 'I don't know how to make coffee. I could make you some tea once I've got the stove going.'

The woman's eyes opened wide with incredulity. 'You don't know how to make coffee?'

'No, ma'am,' Adele said, feeling very foolish. 'Do you?'

'I don't have to know,' Mrs Bailey said indignantly. 'One has a maid to do these things.'

'I'm not a real maid,' Adele said, thinking there was no

point in beating about the bush. 'I'm just helping out till you get a real one. Now, the whole house is full of dust, this stove isn't hot yet, and your clothes are all over the bedroom, and will have to be put away before I can make up your bed. I'm only going to have time to do essential things today. So it will be tea once the stove is hot enough. By tomorrow I may know how to make you coffee.'

'Well!' Mrs Bailey gasped out. 'I have dismissed girls for less cheek than that.'

Adele shrugged. 'I only came because Michael was worried about you,' she said, even as she spoke wondering how she got to be so bold. 'I got the idea I was to help you settle in, not do absolutely everything myself while you drank coffee in the drawing room. Why don't you go and hang your clothes up? I've put a box of hangers in your room.'

Mrs Bailey flounced out of the kitchen, leaving in her wake a faint smell of lily of the valley. Adele half smiled, and continued to add coal to the stove. Somehow she doubted she'd last a week here, she didn't think she had what it took to be a real maid.

It was nearly noon before the stove got hot enough to boil the kettle – she had found the electric stove didn't work. She made a pot of tea, put it on a tray with some sugar, milk and a strainer, then carried it upstairs to Mrs Bailey's bedroom.

To her dismay she found the room in an even worse mess, clothes and shoes all over the floor and bed, and Mrs Bailey sitting on the edge of the bed crying.

Adele's first thought was that it was because of the coffee. 'I'm sorry I couldn't make you coffee,' she said. 'But I've brought you tea now.'

'I can't sort all this out,' Mrs Bailey sobbed out. 'Molly, my maid in Alton, always saw to my clothes. She had them all arranged in colours, with the matching shoes beneath. I can't do it.'

For Adele, who had just the dress she was wearing, the shabby one she worked at home in, and one skirt, blouse and cardigan, arranging her clothes had never presented the slightest problem. She couldn't believe one woman could have so many dresses and shoes. But she couldn't bear to see people cry, and she supposed it must have been hard for Mrs Bailey to leave her old home.

'You come and sit here and drink your tea,' she said, putting the tray down on a low table by the window. The chair by it was very shabby, and she thought maybe old Mr Whitehouse used to sit up here all day looking out at the street. 'I'll hang your things up.' She took Mrs Bailey's arm and led her over to the chair, then poured a cup of tea for her.

Mrs Bailey continued to sniffle as Adele made a start on the clothes. Fortunately the wardrobe was vast, with rails at the bottom for shoes. Within just a few minutes she had a bunch of green things hanging up, another of pink, and another of blue. 'You've got beautiful clothes,' she said admiringly. One blue dress had a bodice covered in sequins and chiffon sleeves, Adele didn't think she'd ever seen such a lovely dress.

'Most of them are out of date now,' Mrs Bailey said, and with that began to cry harder. 'We wore such short things during the Twenties, and now the fashions are so different. I don't know what I shall do.'

Adele was at a loss as to what to say to that. She didn't think Mrs Bailey would have anywhere here to wear such glamorous clothes, anyway. Most of the women of her class wore tweed during the day.

'Have you any old friends here?' she ventured. 'Ones from before you were married?'

'A few maybe,' Mrs Bailey sniffed, dabbing at her tiny little nose with a lace-edged handkerchief. 'But I won't know what to say to them. I can't say I've separated from my husband.'

'Why?' Adele asked.

'Because of the shame of it of course,' Mrs Bailey exclaimed. 'It just isn't done!'

'I'm sure they'd all be sympathetic,' Adele said. 'Lots of people get divorced these days.'

She didn't know that for gospel, but her grandmother was prone to claiming there was an epidemic of divorce. Mind you, Granny thought that was disgraceful, she believed you married for life, even if he turned out to be a louse.

'I'll never divorce him,' Mrs Bailey suddenly screeched out. 'He can shove me out of my home, turn my children against me, but I will never let him be free to marry that floozy.'

'So that's it,' Adele thought. 'Another woman.'

By the time seven o'clock came round Adele felt she could understand why Mr Bailey wanted to get shot of his wife. As Michael had said on the first day they met, she was very demanding. She whined about this, cried about that, and kept creeping up behind Adele while she was scrubbing and polishing to ask for something she could easily get herself.

At first Adele broke off what she was doing to get the slippers, cardigan, book or whatever Mrs Bailey wanted. But when she rang the bell in the drawing room, just as Adele was scrubbing out the bath, only for a drink of water, Adele lost her temper.

'A glass of water?' she exclaimed. 'You've got legs, haven't you? You know where the tap is!'

Mrs Bailey's eyes grew larger than millstones in surprise. 'Are you suggesting I get it myself?'

'I'm not suggesting, I'm telling you,' Adele retorted. 'If this house was clean, and you were an invalid, then maybe I'd get you a drink of water. But the house is filthy, and you are as able as I am. If you had any gumption at all you'd be sorting out your own house, arranging things to make it nice, not sitting there doing nothing like a bloody potentate.'

'But you're being paid to do my bidding,' Mrs Bailey said snootily. 'And how dare you swear at me?'

'You'd make a saint swear,' Adele snapped. 'I only agreed to come and help you out until you got trained staff. I expected to do cooking, cleaning, making beds and lighting fires, but you've had me hanging up your clothes, fetching cardigans, and dozens of other trivial things you could do yourself. You'll be wanting me to wipe your nose soon.'

'I've never been spoken to like that before.' Mrs Bailey's big blue eyes filled with tears. 'Get out of my house now.'

'No, I won't,' Adele said stubbornly. 'I still haven't finished cleaning the bathroom for you, and neither have I made you your supper. When I've finished that I'll go, but not before because I promised Michael I'd stay till seven. And I'll be back in the morning, and the next, until you've got proper staff, whether you approve of me or not. You know why? Because your son is convinced if you are left alone you'll stay in bed and die of starvation.'

With that Adele turned on her heel and walked out of the drawing room and back upstairs to finish the bathroom.

It was only much later, when she let herself out of the house at seven, having left Mrs Bailey eating her supper, that she realized just how impudent she'd been.

But as she walked wearily home back down the hill, she had no intention of retracting a single word she'd said. She knew she'd done a very good day's work, and no one, however rich or high and mighty, had a right to treat another person like a personal slave.

Just a couple of weeks ago her grandmother had been talking about how it was for her growing up. Although her schoolteacher father wasn't rich, it was unthinkable at that time for girls in the middle or upper classes to work. Honour had filled her days with sewing, reading and playing the piano. She had said that until girls married they weren't even allowed to talk to a young man without a chaperone either.

The war in 1914 had changed everything. These same cloistered women were suddenly nursing, driving ambulances or running tea wagons for troops at the railway stations. Once they'd tasted freedom they didn't want to return to the old order of sitting at home waiting for a suitable husband to present himself. Not that there were enough suitable young men any longer – the war saw to that.

Her grandmother had explained, too, that it was the war that relieved working-class girls from a life of obedience and drudgery in service, one of the few career choices open to them before. Suddenly there was a wealth of other opportunities in factories and offices, all more attractive than lighting fires, washing clothes, cooking and cleaning for the wealthy.

Maybe there wasn't that abundance of work available any more, but Adele knew she mustn't begin to think she should be grateful to Mrs Bailey for allowing her to be her skivvy.

She must keep it in mind that she was doing the woman a favour. And gaining some experience of how rich people lived and behaved. As soon as a real job came up, she'd be off.

Chapter Eleven

1936

Adele moved to the far end of the drawing room to look at the overall effect of the Christmas tree she'd just finished decorating. It was over seven feet tall and she'd placed it in the alcove beside the fireplace and covered the tub it stood in with red crêpe paper.

She smiled with pleasure. The silver tinsel was draped perfectly, and the glass balls were well spaced out, each one with a small candle close to it so the light would reflect on the balls when the candles were lit, just the way she'd seen in one of Mrs Bailey's magazines. She'd even managed to fix the fairy at the top straight, no easy feat standing on a chair and stretching over prickly branches.

She felt optimistic that this Christmas was going to be a happy one, unlike last year's which had been absolute misery. But then, in sixteen months of working for Mrs Bailey she felt she'd come a long way. She not only knew a great deal more about running a household, but she had also come to know her employer well, and learned to read the danger signs that heralded disaster.

Her grandmother said it was stupidity which made Adele stay longer than one week, and sheer cussedness that kept her there afterwards. Perhaps she was right, because Mrs Bailey had to be the most difficult, selfish, idiotic woman in the whole world. She was beautiful, rich by Adele's standards, and quite charming when she chose to be, but that wasn't often.

Adele couldn't count the tantrums the woman had thrown in those first few months. Each day she had to brace herself for what she'd find when she let herself in the front door. In the first few weeks Mrs Bailey often hurled her supper tray against the drawing-room wall. Adele would get in the next morning to find a congealed mass of leftovers along with the broken china and whatever ornament had been knocked down by the tray. Apparently Mrs Bailey was incensed that there was no one there to remove it to the kitchen.

Adele kept cleaning the mess up each day until one day she rebelled and left it there. It just so happened that Mrs Bailey's solicitor called that morning, and Adele purposely showed him into the drawing room, and left him staring at it in astonishment while she called Mrs Bailey to tell her he was there.

'How could you let such an important man see that mess?' Mrs Bailey screamed after he'd gone. 'I didn't know where to put myself.'

'Well, think on that before you throw any more food and china,' Adele retorted, past caring if she got thrown out. 'Because I'm not clearing it up again, and if it gets left there you'll have rats coming in to eat it.'

Looking back, that was one of the more easily solved problems. Mrs Bailey was terrified of mice, let alone rats, so she never threw food again. But she would throw the entire contents of her wardrobe on the floor and leave it for Adele to hang up again. She would demand fires to be lit all over the house when she wasn't using the rooms. She ran baths and forgot them until the bathroom was flooded. She would stand by the telephone listening to it ring while Adele was in the garden hanging the washing up, then complain that she'd missed a call. Sometimes she drank so much in the evenings that Adele would find her out cold on the floor, often in a pool of vomit. But the most irritating thing about her was that she seemed unable to understand she was never again going to have a team of staff to jump to her every whim.

Jacob Wainwright, the solicitor in Rye, arranged that John Sneed, the gardener who had worked for Mrs Bailey's parents, would come back to look after the garden and do any odd maintenance jobs. Mr Wainwright also eventually found a Mrs Thomas, and got her to come in two mornings a week to do the laundry and the rough work like scrubbing the floors. That left Adele to do everything else, but she accepted this when Mr Wainwright explained that Mrs Bailey couldn't afford more staff.

Adele liked Mr Wainwright. He was big and hearty, with a bulbous red nose which suggested he was over-fond of port. He commiserated with Adele, praised her for getting the house back into such good shape, and said he admired the tough line she took with her mistress. He said it was imperative that Mrs Bailey learned to do some things for herself, for the time might come when she would have to move into a far smaller house and manage without any help.

By that Adele realized Mrs Bailey hadn't got a bottomless pot of money, so she made economies where she could. It was fortunate that her grandmother had trained her well in this department because if she ever asked Mrs Bailey what she'd like to eat for dinner, she always said she wanted lamb, steak or some other expensive food. So Adele stopped asking and just cooked what she thought was appropriate. And Mrs Bailey invariably ate it without complaint.

It was just over a year ago that Adele had finally been compelled to come and live in Harrington House. She had no real choice, for her employer was a danger to herself. Aside from her drinking, she never remembered to put the spark guard in front of the fire when she was out of the room or going to bed. The hearthrug was peppered with burn holes, and it was only a matter of time before a fire would break out and burn the house down.

Aside from being able to have a real bath and use an inside lavatory, Adele hated living in. The job had never seemed so bad when she could go home at night and tell her grandmother what she'd been doing. They often had a good laugh at some of the sillier things Mrs Bailey got up to.

Now Adele had her day off on one of the days Mrs Thomas came in, and left something cold for Mrs Bailey's dinner. On fine days she and Granny usually went for an afternoon walk, collecting wood as they went, or sometimes they'd go into Rye, have tea in a shop and go to the pictures together. When it was wet or very cold they'd just stay in by the stove and talk.

Honour always had a recipe for her to take back to try, and she would talk through any problems Adele had run into during the week. It was through this that Adele got further insight into the way her grandmother had once lived. She knew how everything should be done, from the right thickness of starch for the bed linen, to which kind of glass you used for any drink. She had a huge fund of dinner and supper ideas, and she was well versed in etiquette too.

She always asked about Michael, and whether he'd been to see his mother. He did telephone every week, and sometimes if Mrs Bailey was out he and Adele would have a chat. He had joined the University Flying Corps as he said he was going to, and he was always eager to talk about the flying lessons, his friends in Oxford and playing cricket. He never spoke of girls though, and that convinced Adele he was avoiding the subject deliberately for fear of hurting her feelings. She felt sure he must have a girlfriend, and did her best to persuade herself that she didn't care.

But although he telephoned his mother every week, he'd only visited three times: last Christmas, at Easter and in the summer, always staying only one night. As for the rest of the family, they hadn't been once.

Adele sympathized with them, for Mrs Bailey's behaviour was as disturbing as her own mother's had been. There was only so much nastiness, embarrassment and hurt a person could take before love disappeared.

When Mrs Bailey was at her worst, Adele often thought about Rose and wondered where she was now, and how she lived. But she hadn't the slightest inclination to see her again, and she supposed the Bailey children felt much the same way about their mother too.

Mrs Bailey had been absolutely dreadful back in November of last year, refusing to get out of bed, crying all the time and not even bothering to wash herself or do her hair. But she finally perked up when Michael said he was coming for Christmas, and then announced she was going to invite some old childhood friends for drinks on Christmas Eve.

Christmas had always been a disappointment to Adele. She could remember how she and Pamela had always got excited once the lights and decorations went up in the shops. At school they put on a nativity play, the Salvation Army band played carols outside Euston station, and the feeling of joy and hope grew larger and larger as Christmas Day drew nearer. But it was always an anti-climax. Their father would invariably come home from work late on Christmas Eve so drunk he could barely stand, and that would tip their mother into one of her blackest moods. Adele could remember taking Pamela out for walks on Christmas Day, for there was always far more jollity on the streets than there was at home.

Yet coming to live with her grandmother had cancelled out some of those sad memories. Her grandmother didn't have much money to spare on frivolity, but she put a great deal of effort into Christmas. She bought little treats and surprises, decked the cottage out with holly and paper chains, and told Adele stories of the wonderful Christmas parties she went to as a child. When she talked nostalgically of eight-foot trees alight with hundreds of candles, of huge tables laid with silver and sparkling glasses, of singing round the piano, and games of musical chairs, pin the tail on the donkey and blind man's bluff, she often had tears in her eyes. Adele sensed that she was remembering her own parents, her husband, and perhaps Rose too as a little girl. She admitted that the Christmas after Frank died she felt so low she stayed in her bed all day, and she hadn't attempted to celebrate Christmas in any way at all until Adele came to live with her.

It was because of this blight on her own family that Adele tried so hard last year to make everything lovely at Harrington House. She got armfuls of holly from the garden and tied it with red ribbon, polished up the best glasses, and spent hours making dainty mince pies, sausage rolls and other little festive canapés Granny suggested. And all that alongside buying and preparing the Christmas Day dinner.

Michael arrived late in the afternoon on Christmas Eve, but Adele barely saw him because she was so busy in the kitchen. Then just before six he came charging in to get her, saying his mother was throwing another tantrum because she hadn't got anything to wear that night.

The guests were due at seven, so Adele flew upstairs. Mrs Bailey had said earlier in the week that she was going to wear her silver satin cocktail dress and Adele had pressed it and hung it up on her wardrobe door, with silver shoes beneath it. In Adele's opinion it was the perfect choice, a very fashionable mid-calf length, cut on the cross, with a flash of black embroidery from one shoulder to her breast. Mrs Bailey looked lovely in it.

The sight that met Adele's eyes as she entered Mrs Bailey's bedroom was alarming. She was dressed in just a satin petticoat, her hair all wild, and she'd done her old trick of dragging the entire contents of the wardrobe on to the floor. The silver dress was torn into pieces and tossed on to the bed.

'What on earth have you done that for?' Adele asked incredulously, knowing she'd have to work a year or two to buy such a dress. 'It's a beautiful dress and you look so lovely in it.'

'It made my skin grey,' Mrs Bailey screamed at Adele, and came rushing at her, as if about to strike her. Adele put her hands out to stop her, and as she caught the woman's arms she could smell whisky on her breath.

'I'll make your skin grey if you start showing off now,' Adele said fiercely, and pushed her down into the chair. 'Your friends will be here soon, do you want them to see you acting like a madwoman?'

Adele found a dark red crêpe dress and forced her to put it on. She brushed her hair for her, fixed two glittery combs one each side of her head, and then powdered her face and put a little rouge on her cheeks. But as she bent down to pick up a pair of black shoes for her to put on, Mrs Bailey kicked her up the backside and she fell forward, banging her head on the end of the bed.

It was all Adele could do to stop herself from kicking the woman back. Her head hurt and she guessed she'd have a bruise there the next day.

'You're a nasty piece of work,' she snapped at her. 'I've a good mind to go home right now, and leave you to cope alone tonight. But you aren't going to show Michael up, not if I can help it.'

Somehow she managed to get Mrs Bailey to put on some lipstick and the right jewellery, and got her downstairs. Mrs Bailey immediately poured herself another large drink.

Michael watched his mother pacing the drawing room and he was pale with fright. 'What am I going to do?' he whispered to Adele. 'Perhaps I should send the guests away when they come, she's going to be awful, I just know it.'

'You can't do that on Christmas Eve,' Adele said. 'I'm sure she'll start behaving once they get here.'

At first it looked as if Adele was right. Mrs Bailey greeted her old friends with warmth and charm, introduced Michael to them all, like a perfect mother, and even told them all that Adele was her treasure, as she handed round the food.

There were five couples in all, two of whom Adele knew by sight as they lived in Winchelsea, and it seemed to her that everyone was there to show that their sympathies lay with Mrs Bailey and they would support her now she was living alone. Michael began to relax, the fire was blazing, the drawing room looked lovely and so did his mother. She had a drink in her hand but she didn't appear to be drinking it. Every time Adele looked at her she was engrossed in animated conversation, and she looked really happy for once.

About nine o'clock Adele was just coming back from the kitchen with more hot sausage rolls when she heard the crash from the drawing room. She rushed back in to find Mrs Bailey lying on the floor, with her dress right up showing her stocking tops. She had presumably fallen over the side table for it was overturned, and the glasses on it were all spilt on the carpet.

The other guests were looking down at her in astonishment.

Adele ran to help her up, but Michael got there first. 'It's those shoes again,' he said. 'You said you were going to get rid of them because the heels are wobbly.'

Adele gave him ten out of ten for making up such a plausible excuse so quickly. It was clear to her that Mrs Bailey had been drinking after all, and constantly refilling her glass. There was nothing wrong with the shoes.

'She made me wear them,' Mrs Bailey said, slurring her words and pointing none too steadily at Adele. 'She does everything she can to embarrass me, but then she's in the pay of my husband.'

Everyone looked at Adele, and she was so shaken she let the tray of sausage rolls slip a little and to add to her distress they began to slide off on to the floor.

'You see what I mean?' Mrs Bailey said triumphantly. 'But what can you expect from a girl from the marshes?'

Adele fled to the kitchen and burst into tears. She had done her very best to make the house welcoming, she'd spent hours cooking and arranging everything, and she so much wanted Michael to have a happy evening and to stop worrying about his mother. It hadn't worked and she would get no thanks for trying.

The guests all left very soon afterwards. Adele heard Michael apologizing to them in the hall as he helped them into their coats. She thought he was apologizing for her and that made her cry even harder.

She heard him go back into the drawing room, and it was then she got her coat to leave for good. But as she came out of the kitchen with it on, he was coming towards her across the hall, the tray of sausage rolls in his hands.

'I'm so sorry, Adele,' he said, his lips quivering. 'That was awful for you. She's drunk of course, out cold in a chair. Goodness knows what her old friends thought, it will be all over the county by tomorrow.'

He made Adele go back into the kitchen and sat her down at the table. His face was white and strained but he wiped her tears away with a handkerchief and kissed her on the forehead.

'I shouldn't have subjected you to this,' he said. 'Has she been like this to you before?'

It was only because Michael looked so troubled that Adele didn't tell him the truth. He didn't deserve to hear what his mother was really like, not on Christmas Eve.

'She has her nasty moments,' was all she said, and took her coat off because she knew she couldn't leave him alone to deal with his mother.

'But that was last year,' Adele murmured to herself as she picked up the empty box of decorations to put away. 'It won't be like that this time.'

So much had happened on the world stage this year that even self-obsessed Mrs Bailey had been forced to see she wasn't the only person with problems. In January King George died, and the whole country was plunged into mourning. That was hardly out of the way when the newspapers began printing stories about King Edward's love affair with the married American woman Wallis Simpson. Civil war broke out in Spain in July, Mussolini seemed to be trying to take on the world, and sinister rumblings in Germany were getting louder and louder. Two hundred men marched from Jarrow in County Durham to London, with a petition about the 75 per cent unemployment in their town. Then finally, just a couple of weeks ago, King Edward decided to abdicate from the throne so he could marry Wallis Simpson, and the whole of the country was thrown into turmoil and heated debate.

Adele doubted that Mrs Bailey was really concerned about her country or those less fortunate than herself, but she had calmed down considerably. Her tantrums, screaming fits and heavy drinking bouts were all less frequent. She even appeared to have reconciled herself to being an estranged wife because she got the drawing and dining rooms redecorated to her taste. Adele didn't much care for the dark red striped wallpaper in the dining room, it was too gloomy by day, but the pinks and greens in the drawing room were beautiful. Mrs Bailey had also been doing some voluntary charity work with a couple of other women, and had gone to France for a week back in the spring with an old girlfriend.

There were still times when she took to her bed and wouldn't get up. She still showed little regard for all the hard work Adele did. But on Adele's seventeenth birthday in July she had given her a little silver locket on a chain. She didn't say anything other than 'Happy birthday', but Adele thought maybe she was like Granny and just couldn't put her feelings into words.

Now Michael had somehow managed to persuade his brother Ralph, his wife and children, and Mr Bailey to come for Christmas. They would be arriving tomorrow, Christmas Eve, and Adele fervently hoped the family could patch up their differences.

*

'I didn't expect to see you today!' Honour exclaimed in surprise as Adele walked into the cottage the following afternoon.

Adele took off her coat and shook the rain off it before closing the door. 'I just needed to see you,' she said.

'What's the matter?' her grandmother asked, getting out of her chair.

'Nothing at all,' Adele said, and lifting a basket up on to the table she took out a brightly wrapped present, a small pudding in a china basin, a bag of tangerines and a tin. 'I just wanted you to have these for the morning,' she said.

'Don't tell me you aren't coming home tomorrow?' her grandmother said, and the catch in her voice told Adele her instinct had been right, and she was feeling very alone.

'Of course I'm still coming in the afternoon,' Adele said, and reached out to pat Honour's cheek affectionately. 'I wouldn't leave you alone on Christmas Day even if Wallis Simpson was calling in to give me a few of her old dresses.'

Honour thought Wallis was a she-devil, sent directly from hell to overthrow the monarchy. Yet despite her loathing of the woman, she often remarked that her clothes were sensational.

'What's in the tin?' she asked, getting up to look.

'A Christmas cake,' Adele said with a smile. 'Made and iced by my own fair hands.'

Adele watched as her grandmother lifted the lid, but instead of the expected questions, or even a little sarcasm that the icing wasn't too smooth, she saw a tear trickle down Honour's cheek.

'I didn't take the ingredients,' Adele said hastily. 'I bought them, but I didn't think there was anything wrong with putting two cakes in the oven at the same time.'

'It's beautiful,' her grandmother said, her voice soft and low. She wiped away the tear and smiled. 'You've gone a long way from that little waif I took in five years ago. That was the best day's work I ever did.'

A tingle went down Adele's spine at hearing the love in her grandmother's voice.

'A pudding too!' Honour exclaimed. 'So mind you don't stuff yourself up at the house and have no room for your dinner here!'

'I'll have to go back now,' Adele said. 'Open the present in the morning.'

Her grandmother shook her head. 'No, I'll wait for you to come. So don't let them keep you there too late.'

As Adele walked back through the driving rain to Winchelsea she offered up a little prayer that by the end of Christmas Mrs Bailey would tell her she was going back to her husband in Hampshire.

She didn't want to be a servant any longer, she knew what it really meant now. A couple of years ago she had thought that it was purely earning money by taking care of someone richer. To her it had been no different to a bricklayer building a house for someone else, or a butcher selling his meat to his customers.

But it wasn't like that at all. The reality of a servant's place in society had been driven home today when Michael and his family arrived. His father had stuck his hat and coat in her arms and walked into the drawing room, and the others had followed suit, even the two children. As though she was a coat stand.

Michael sort of shrugged and gave her a tight-lipped smile. He at least hung his coat up himself, but he went on in after the rest of them and closed the door behind him.

Michael had sat drinking ginger beer in her granny's kitchen, he'd helped skin rabbits, and collected wood, like one of the family. Yet although Adele cleaned up his mother's vomit, coaxed her into eating, washed and ironed her clothes and slept in her house to make sure she didn't burn it down, she couldn't talk to Michael in front of his family. She could say 'Merry Christmas', or 'Shall I take your hat, sir?' But not 'How are you getting on at Oxford? Do tell me all about it!'

To them she belonged in the kitchen with the pots and pans. If she was working elsewhere in the house she was supposed to be quiet and invisible, without any rights, personality or feelings. Right now they were probably sitting in the drawing room enjoying the warm fire and the decorated Christmas tree, anticipating tomorrow's roast goose and plum pudding. Yet she knew they wouldn't stop to think how it got to their table, or of the planning and preparation that went into making their Christmas a merry one.

'It's time you moved on,' she murmured to herself as she approached Harrington House. 'It was only ever meant to be a temporary job.'

As Adele opened the front door, Mr Bailey came out into the hall. She had always imagined him looking like Michael, tall, slender and dark-haired, but in fact he was almost the exact opposite. He was no more than five feet seven, portly, and what was left of his hair was grey.

She knew him to be in his fifties, and fond of overeating and drinking, judging by his fat belly and high colour. He was short on charm and tolerance too – he had barked orders at her several times when she was serving luncheon.

'Oh, there you are,' he said sharply as she wiped her wet feet on the doormat. 'I rang the bell and there was no reply.'

'I have a couple of hours off in the afternoon,' Adele said. 'Didn't Mrs Bailey tell you?'

'She's having a nap,' he said. 'But we expected you to be on call while there are visitors.'

Adele felt a surge of irritation but she forced herself to smile. 'I'll just go and take my coat off, then I'll come and see what you want,' she said.

'We want tea for the children,' he snapped at her, his

colour rising. 'And they can stay in the kitchen with you until their bedtime.'

Adele might have been tempted to say she wasn't a child-minder, and that expecting her to prepare the supper with two excited children under her feet wasn't fair or right. But she knew if she did Mr Bailey was likely to take it out on his wife or Michael.

As it turned out, Anna and James, Ralph and Laura Bailey's children, were no trouble. In fact Adele suspected they'd spent most of their young lives in the company of servants as they looked far more relaxed and happy in the kitchen than they had earlier in the dining room. Anna was six, James four, two small attractive replicas of their blonde, blue-eyed mother. Ralph took after his father: although he was a little taller and had a fine head of dark hair, he was already developing the same high colour and a paunch.

After a tea of sandwiches, scones and cake, Adele gave the children a large jar of buttons to play with. She'd found them in one of the kitchen cupboards when she first started here.

'You could sort them into colours, or make pictures with them,' she suggested, tipping them out on to a tray. She arranged a few into a flower shape to give them the idea and gave each of them a tray to stop the buttons falling on the floor.

Once the children were occupied, Adele laid the table in the dining room for supper. Mrs Bailey had requested soup, followed by cold meat and pickles, and as the soup was ready, requiring nothing more than heating up, Adele thought she had plenty of time to make the stuffing for tomorrow's goose, then whisk the children upstairs and get them into bed at half past six, ready to serve the supper at seven.

She thought it was odd that Laura Bailey didn't come upstairs while she was getting her children into their night-clothes, but then she'd already noticed that the pretty blonde came from the same mould as her mother-in-law, and didn't do anything much for herself.

'Will you read to us, Adele?' Anna asked once she was tucked up in bed with her brother.

'I can't, I've got to get the supper,' Adele replied. 'And you've got to go to sleep otherwise Santa Claus won't be filling your stockings.'

The stockings, two large red linen ones embroidered with the children's names, were hanging on the bed posts. She and Pamela had only ever had a pair of their father's socks, and the contents had been meagre compared with what these two children would get.

'Please read us a story,' Anna pleaded. 'We promise we'll go to sleep straight afterwards.'

She looked so adorable with her blonde hair tumbling down over the shoulders of her pink nightdress that Adele hadn't got the heart to refuse. 'Just a quick one then,' she agreed.

There was no clock in the bedroom, and Adele got so involved in the story of the witch who lost her magic wand that she didn't realize how long she was with the children.

After she'd tucked them in, kissed them goodnight and got back to the kitchen, she saw to her horror it was well after seven.

'And what time can we expect our supper?'

She spun round from stirring the soup on the stove at Mr Bailey's sarcastic question. He was standing in the doorway which went through to the dining room, his hands on his hips. 'In just a few minutes, sir,' she said, and began to explain why it was late.

'I don't want excuses,' he said, cutting her off curtly.

Had Mrs Bailey said such a thing to her, Adele would have reminded her that she only worked until seven, but Mr Bailey was intimidating.

She quickly took the dish of cold meats and put them on the table, lit the candles, got the baked potatoes out of the oven, and popped the bread rolls in to warm them.

Once the soup was piping hot and everything else was on the table, she rang the gong. Then, as the family came into the dining room and sat down, she tipped the soup into the tureen she had warmed.

Ralph Bailey was saying something about the midnight service at the church as Adele came in with the tureen. It was heavy and hot, and her thoughts were whether it would be better to put it on the table and serve it into the soup bowls there, or to put it on the sideboard. But Mrs Bailey was placing a table mat beside her, so presumably she wanted it put there. Suddenly Adele's foot slid from under her. She tried to hold on to the tureen but couldn't, and it clattered to the floor, breaking on impact and spilling vegetable soup all down her front and hands and halfway across the room.

'You blithering idiot!' Mr Bailey shouted, jumping up from his seat at the head of the table. 'What on earth are you doing?'

Adele was mortified at the accident. Her right hand was scalded, and as she looked down and saw the mess, and the large flat button she'd slipped on, she began to cry.

'I'm sorry,' she exclaimed. 'I slipped on a button.'

She was down on all fours immediately, desperately trying to pick up the china from the mess of soup and small pieces of vegetables.

'A button!' Mrs Bailey said, her voice shrill with indignation. 'What is a button doing on the floor?'

From her position on the floor Adele gabbled out how the children had been playing with them and one must have rolled in here. Laura Bailey said something about her blaming the children for her own stupidity. Mr Bailey called her useless, and Ralph asked what they were going to eat now.

'Come on now,' Michael's voice rang out over all the

others'. 'Adele couldn't help it, it was an accident. She should have finished work now anyway, and there's plenty of other things to eat.'

He came round the table, pulled Adele up from the floor, and saw her red hands. 'Go and rinse them in cold water,' he said gently, his eyes full of sympathy. 'I'll clear this up.'

Adele scuttled away crying. But their angry voices still reached her, even over the sound of the running water.

'Only you could take on a numbskull as a maid,' she heard Mr Bailey say, presumably to his wife, and Ralph joined in with some sarcastic remark about how she hadn't unpacked either his or his wife's suitcase. 'Really, Mother,' he went on, 'you must get yourself some trained staff.'

Michael came out into the kitchen a few minutes later with a bundle of soup-stained tablecloth in his hands. 'I wiped up the worst of it with this cloth I found in the cupboard in there,' he said. 'I hope it wasn't a family heirloom?'

'No, it's just an ordinary one,' she said, taking the bundle from him. 'It will wash. It's not as nasty as all the drunken vomit of your mother's I've cleared up in the past.'

She knew that was a cruel remark to make, but then they'd all been cruel to her. 'You go and eat your supper,' she said, turning away from him so she didn't have to see the stricken look on his face. 'Mind you don't slip in what's left of the mess. I'll wash the floor after they've finished eating.'

After he'd gone Adele closed the kitchen door behind him and held her burnt hand under the kitchen tap. She wondered how people got to be as heartless as the Baileys were, and fervently hoped something nasty would happen to each of them to teach them a lesson.

Later, she heard the family leaving the dining room, and a short while afterwards the bell tinkled from the drawing room. She ignored it, and lifted the bucket of hot water out of the sink to go and wash the floor over. As she surveyed the dining room, she grimaced. They hadn't taken care to avoid the remaining vegetables on the floor, there were squashed pieces everywhere, and she expected they had walked some of it into the drawing room too. But clearly spilled soup hadn't affected their appetites as there was not a scrap of food left on the table.

She had finished cleaning the floor and was just stacking the crockery from the table on to a tray when Mr Bailey came in.

'Are you deaf? We rang for coffee,' he said belligerently.

'I finish work at seven,' she said, looking straight at him. 'I'm only still here clearing away this lot because it's Christmas.'

'If that's your attitude you can get out now,' he said, waving one podgy finger at her.

Adele knew how hard it was to get a job and she'd come to like having money of her own. She was on the point of apologizing when it suddenly struck her that if she backed down now she would lose all dignity, and that was far more important to her than mere money.

'That's fine by me,' she said, taking her apron off and dumping it on the table. 'I'd much prefer to cook a Christmas dinner for my grandmother who will actually appreciate the effort I put into it.'

He seemed to puff up in front of her, and for a moment she thought he was going to strike her. 'How dare you?' he hissed. 'You throw soup across the room and don't answer bells. What sort of a maid are you?'

'The quitting kind,' she said more bravely than she felt. 'I've had quite enough of being insulted. I don't deserve it.'

'You insolent little baggage!' he exploded. 'My wife said you could be very sharp, and now I see the truth, you've been taking advantage of her good nature.'

'What good nature?' Adele retorted, angry now and prepared to fight him with every weapon she had. 'You know as well as I do what she's like, isn't that why you threw her out? If it hadn't been for me she would have starved to death in a filthy house.'

'Get out now,' he said, pointing to the door, his finger quivering with rage.

'I'm on my way,' she said, walking towards the kitchen to collect her coat. She paused in the doorway, looked back at Mr Bailey and grinned. 'The goose is ready for the oven tomorrow, you'll need to put it in about six in the morning as you light the fires. The stuffing and vegetables and puddings are in the pantry. Have a Merry Christmas.'

He leaped forward and slapped her hard across the face. 'I've never known such incredible insolence,' he shouted at her. 'How dare you? Who do you think you are?'

'I don't think I'm anyone, I know who I am,' she said, resisting the desire to clutch at her sore cheek. 'And I'm a much nicer person than you are, that's for certain.'

He caught hold of her upper arm and she braced herself for another blow, but he didn't hit her, just half dragged her towards the hall and opened the front door. 'Get out this minute,' he yelled at her, regardless of the fact that it was raining hard and she had no coat.

'Then you'd better take your wife home with you when you go,' she retorted as she stepped out into the rain. 'She won't find anyone around here to wet-nurse her like I did.'

The door slammed behind her before she'd even finished the sentence.

It was raining twice as hard as it had been earlier in the day, and by the time Adele passed under the old Landgate to go down the hill, she was soaked through to her underwear and her shoes were waterlogged. Tears mingled with the rain on her face, but they were tears of anger rather than remorse.

'Adele, wait for me!'

She turned her head at the sound of Michael's voice and

saw him haring down the road towards her, but she trudged on resolutely.

'Adele, I'm so sorry,' he gasped out as he caught up with her.

'It's me who should be sorry for you,' she said tartly. 'Your father is unspeakable.'

'I know he is,' he agreed, panting from running. 'I can't make any excuses for him.'

'He slapped me and threw me out,' she said indignantly. 'He had no right to do that. I've done my best for your mother. I feel sorry for her now, I'm beginning to see why she's so demented.'

'Please come back,' he begged her. 'Mother went quite pale when she heard you'd gone. She knows she can't manage without you.'

'Good,' Adele said defiantly. 'I hope your entire family suffers, they deserve it.'

'Me too?' he asked grabbing hold of her arm.

'No, not you,' she said, shaking off his hand. 'I used to think I was unlucky with my mother. But now I've met both your parents you deserve more pity. Now, go home and leave me alone.'

'If you think I'm going to let you walk home alone in the dark and rain you are mistaken,' he said.

'My grandmother will turn on you,' she warned him. 'Don't chance it, Michael.'

'I'll take the risk,' he said. 'I have to apologize to her.'

They didn't speak the rest of the way for once they were down on the marsh the wind was so strong they could hardly keep upright, and the rain was like being under an icy shower.

Honour was already in bed when they got to the cottage, so Adele had to tap on her bedroom window and ask to be let in. Her grandmother opened the door holding a candle and wearing a shawl over the shoulders of her nightgown.

'What's happened?' she asked, then seeing Adele had no

coat on she hauled her in quickly, telling Michael curtly that he'd better have a good excuse for bringing her home soaked to the skin.

Once inside, Adele blurted it all out in a torrent.

'And you, Michael? Why didn't you stand up for her?' Honour asked as she lit the oil lamp.

Michael explained that he wasn't there at the last part. 'I didn't know Father was going to be like that,' he said. 'He did keep saying, "Why isn't she answering the bell?" and I said I'd go and see, but he told me to stay put. My brother told me not to interfere when I heard Father shouting. I'm so ashamed that I didn't step in then.'

'It was spineless, but I suppose understandable, given that he's bullied you all your life,' she said crisply. She pushed Adele towards her bedroom, telling her to take off her wet clothes quickly.

Michael stood there hanging his head as the rainwater dripped off him on to the floor.

'You'll have to stand up to your father sometime,' Honour said tartly. 'Bullies thrive on weakness in others. But I suppose you aren't a complete coward as you did go after Adele and were brave enough to face me. But you'd better go home now and get out of those wet clothes.'

'I'm so sorry, Mrs Harris,' Michael said.

Honour could see he was trembling with both cold and shock. 'You shouldn't have to apologize for your father,' she said. 'I shall of course take action about this, but I think that for the sake of peace tomorrow in your house, you should say nothing more than that you escorted Adele home.'

'I'm so ashamed,' Michael said in a small voice. 'I don't want to be part of a family who treat people so badly. Ralph is almost as bad as Father too.'

'You can't help the family you are born to,' Honour said more gently. 'Now, go home, Michael.'

Chapter Twelve

Honour watched Adele drift off to sleep on the couch and smiled to herself. She had been fighting against sleep since they finished their Christmas dinner, but had finally lost the battle.

Honour thought she looked so pretty lying there with her hair all loose about her flushed face and her legs curled up beneath the skirt of her new dress. The dark rose-pink wool suited her so well, and Honour was thrilled that it fitted to perfection as it was the most extravagant garment she'd ever made. She'd not only had to buy the pattern because all her old ones were so old-fashioned, but because it was cut on the cross it took nearly five yards of fabric.

When Adele tried it on she joked that she looked like Wallis Simpson. Honour didn't think she looked one bit like that gaunt scarecrow of a woman, but she had got the idea for the dress from her – the draped bodice, slim three-quarter-length sleeves, and the hip-hugging swirl of a skirt was almost Mrs Simpson's trademark. However, Honour thought it suited Adele far more because she had a perfect figure and lovely shapely legs.

'She'll need some high-heeled shoes and a decent coat and hat to go with it,' Honour thought, gazing at her granddaughter reflectively. She found it quite strange that after years of seeing clothes just as a way to keep warm, never caring what she looked like, suddenly it was so important to her that Adele should be well turned out.

'Michael, I suppose,' she murmured to herself.

Right from the first time Honour met Michael three years ago she'd sensed something special between him and Adele, even though they were little more than children at the time. Honour liked him immediately for his lack of guile, his innate good manners and his open curiosity about the way she lived.

She had expected that Adele would be nervous of any male after what had happened to her at The Firs, and that she herself would be very defensive if anyone came near her granddaughter. But there was nothing threatening about Michael, he had a kind of purity, an openness, and a warm heart. She had always hoped that one day their friendship would turn to romance.

When Michael went up to Oxford, and Adele became his mother's maid, Honour thought the spark had gone out and felt saddened. Yet last night, wet and upset as they both were, she'd seen that it was still alight. Michael was so tender and protective towards Adele, and she was concerned that her actions were likely to give him grief.

Sadly, what Honour had to do now was likely to extinguish that spark rather than fan it into a fire, but the Baileys had to know that she would not allow anyone to get away with hurting or humiliating her granddaughter.

She got up from her chair and walked around the room straightening things for a few minutes, checking to see how deeply Adele was sleeping. Once she was satisfied, she covered her with a blanket and hoped she wouldn't wake before she got back.

She crept silently to her bedroom, and looked at herself critically in the dressing-table mirror. She was beginning to look her age – her skin was growing crêpey, and she was getting a moustache. As for her steel-grey hair, it was hard to imagine it had once been a rich chestnut. Her navy blue dress with its lace collar and cuffs was her best one, indeed the only decent dress she owned. It was very old-fashioned, but then she'd made it the year before Frank died. Luckily the moths hadn't got into it and it still fitted her. Adele had said just this morning that she associated it with happy days, as the first time she'd seen her wearing it was the day Honour took her to enrol at school. Since then it had been worn only on Sundays and at Christmas.

Honour fixed a few stray hairs back into her bun, dabbed a little powder on her nose, then put on her hat. It too was navy blue, a no-nonsense felt hat with a small brim. Adele had once joked that it made her look even more formidable. That was the effect she wanted to create today.

The velvet collar on her coat was almost worn away, but she covered it with her foxtails. Frank had bought them for her on their honeymoon, and said they were essential for a lady of quality. She wasn't so sure she liked the idea of a couple of dead foxes hanging round her neck any more, their glass eyes were a bit too realistic. But they did smarten up her coat.

Finally, her best shoes. She didn't relish walking up the steep hill to Winchelsea in them as they were tight. But appearance was all when you were going to confront the enemy. She wanted to look like their equal, not the old witch who lived on the marsh.

A biting north wind almost cut Honour in half as she made her way up the lane. The sky was the colour of lead and she thought there might be snow later. The River Brede was swollen almost to the top of its banks from the previous day's heavy rain, and it was very lucky it had stopped when it did – another inch and the banks would have burst.

It was only on days like this that Honour fell out of love with the marsh. It looked so bleak and cruel, a forbidding place only suitable for wild birds and sheep, and even the sheep were huddling together for warmth.

Outside Harrington House, she pulled her hat on more firmly, arranged the foxtails more securely and took a deep breath before ringing the bell.

A child was crying upstairs, and it was some time before

she heard footsteps in the hall. The door was opened by a young woman with dishevelled blonde hair and red eyes as if she'd been crying. She was clearly Ralph Bailey's wife.

'I wish to see Mr and Mrs Bailey,' Honour said, quickly stepping over the threshold before the young woman could refuse her.

Laura Bailey was startled. 'It's not really convenient right now,' she said feebly, then glanced over her shoulder as another wail came from upstairs.

'It's convenient for me, so I suggest you go and see to your child while I go right in, I know the way,' Honour said. And she marched swiftly towards the drawing-room door and opened it.

Adele had described the whole family so vividly that Honour felt she already knew them well. Emily was on the couch by the fire, her son Ralph beside her. Myles Bailey was in an armchair opposite. All three looked up in shocked surprise at her entrance, and judging by the tension hanging in the air, she guessed she had interrupted an argument. Thankfully Michael wasn't present. She hoped that wherever he was, he would stay there.

The room was very untidy, strewn with bits of wrapping paper and abandoned toys. Honour noted the Christmas tree in the alcove, and thought Adele had done a fine job in dressing it so prettily.

'Who are you?' Ralph burst out indignantly, jumping up off the couch. 'And what do you mean by walking in here uninvited?'

Honour guessed by his mother's puzzled expression that she hadn't yet recognized her as her mother's old friend.

Honour looked Ralph up and down, noticing he was a carbon copy of his father at the same age. 'You haven't changed,' she said crisply. 'You were very rude even as a small boy. I am Mrs Harris, a friend of your late grandparents, and I'm also Adele's grandmother.'

Myles jumped out of his chair. 'Now look here,' he blustered, 'we had no choice but to dismiss Adele, she was extremely insolent, so if you've come here to plead for her job then you are wasting your time.'

'I'm not given to pleading with anyone,' Honour retorted archly. 'I came here to tell you what I think of you and to collect her belongings and what's due to her.'

Emily looked astounded. 'Mrs Harris!' she exclaimed, her small hands fluttering with agitation as it dawned on her that this was her mother's old friend. 'It's been a great many years since we last met. Why on earth didn't Adele tell me she was your granddaughter?'

'Would you have treated her with more respect and kindness had you known?' Honour asked, raising one eyebrow quizzically. She thought the passing years had been much kinder to Emily than they had to her. Her hair had retained its rich colour, and her complexion was still like porcelain. But Adele's observation that she looked like a china doll was very true – her blue eyes were glasslike and a little vacant, and even her lips had a little-girl pout.

Honour thought her powder-blue two-piece with frills at the neck was unsuitable for her age, yet she had hardly changed from how she looked as a young mother back in 1913.

'You should be ashamed of yourself, Emily,' Honour went on. 'Adele came and helped you out when there was no one else, just as I often did for your mother. She'd had no training except what she'd learned from me, yet she has run this house, and run it well. She has been discreet, loyal and kind to you. Yet you allow your husband to slap her and put her out in heavy rain.'

'Now look here,' Myles butted in. 'You can't come crashing in here disturbing us on Christmas Day. The girl was insufferably rude. Goodness only knows what she's said to my wife in the past. I had no choice but to dismiss her.'

'You had no right to do that, she worked for your wife, not you. Adele merely stuck up for herself,' Honour spat at him. 'You, Myles Bailey, are a bully.'

She launched into a vitriolic account of the worst aspects of Adele's service in the house, sparing nothing. Each time Ralph or Myles tried to silence her she rounded on them with more. Emily began to cry, and Honour turned on her.

'That's right, cry,' she hissed at her. 'That's all you're good for now. Adele fed you, cleaned up after you, cooked, sewed, ironed and washed, even left her home to keep an eye on you. Not once has she blabbed to the neighbours about you, she hasn't stolen anything, or taken advantage in any way. Look at that tree! She did that, with no help from you, along with cooking and making the whole house welcoming for your family. What have you done in return? Nothing! No Christmas present, no words of praise. You allowed him to shove her out into the rain without even a coat, for dropping a soup tureen.'

Honour could see the effect she was having on all three of them. Emily was pale and shaking, Ralph incredulous that anyone had the nerve to speak to his parents in such a manner, and Myles was puffed up with rage. Knowing that they'd probably had a miserable Christmas with no servants to wait on them, Honour hoped that by coming here and confronting them she had made it the worst one in their family history. But she wasn't finished with them yet, her blood was up, and she demanded to collect Adele's belongings from her room and two weeks' pay in lieu of notice.

Myles strutted around the room as though he was in a court room and the evidence he had just heard was a tissue of lies. 'I find all this quite unbelievable,' he said. 'Tell me, Mrs Harris, if the position as Emily's maid was as terrible as you claim, why didn't the girl just leave?'

'There are some people in this world who allow compassion to override their good sense,' Honour said sharply.

'Adele was afraid to leave for fear of what Emily would do to herself. On top of that she didn't want Michael worried or to interrupt his studies.'

'Ah, now we get to the core of it,' Myles smirked nastily. 'She's set her cap at my son, hasn't she?'

'What tosh,' Honour snorted. 'They were friends long before she came here to work, in fact she only came as a favour to him. But she's hardly seen him since then, as Emily can confirm. So don't you dare to imply that my granddaughter has behaved improperly in any way with your son, or you'll be skating on very thin ice.'

His face turned a few shades redder, and he pulled out his wallet, removed a couple of notes and thrust them at her. 'Take that and her clothes and go,' he said.

'I want an apology first,' Honour said, taking the money but standing her ground. 'And a promise Mrs Bailey will give her a good reference.'

'Of course I'll give her a reference,' Emily said, suddenly agitated again and her blue eyes full of fear. 'But I'd rather Adele came back to work. I don't know quite what I'm going to do without her.'

'She can't come back, you silly woman,' Myles burst out. 'I'll find you someone else.'

Honour looked sharply at the man. He had no saving graces: he was a bully and a bigot and so puffed up with self-righteousness it was a wonder he wasn't airborne.

'An apology?' she said, raising one eyebrow and fixing him with her sternest look.

'All right, I'm sorry I lost my temper with the girl,' he said, not meeting her eyes and his voice a mere rumble. 'But please go now, we've had the worst Christmas ever, my grandchildren and daughter-in-law are distressed, and Michael hasn't been here all day.'

Honour felt triumphant. 'How different it might have been if you'd treated Adele like a human being,' she said silkily before turning to the door. 'I won't trouble you for her clothes now, I'll just get her coat from the kitchen. I'm sure Michael can bring the other things down to us tomorrow?'

'Not Michael,' Myles retorted. 'I don't want him coming anywhere near you again. Ralph or myself will drop them off to you.'

As Honour walked home, hobbling now in her tight shoes and holding Adele's coat over her arm, she had plenty of food for thought. She had wanted to laugh when she saw their kitchen, it was absolute chaos, with unwashed plates, saucepans and half-eaten food everywhere. She had touched the stove and found it was only warm – clearly they hadn't thought to stoke it up, and it was almost out. There would be no hot water for baths tonight or in the morning, and who would be pressed into washing up?

But the glee she felt knowing that Adele's departure had hurt them worse than it had hurt her granddaughter was diluted by the thought of Michael. It wasn't right that such a nice young man should be wandering around on his own on Christmas Day, or that his loyalties should be pulled in all directions.

The following day was even colder and darker. Honour had barely managed to open the rabbits' cages to feed them, the wind was so strong. When she tried to hang sacks over the hutches to give them some protection, it was all she could do to hold on to them.

'I'm not going out of that door again today,' she said as she came back indoors and warmed herself by the stove. 'I must be getting old,' she added when she saw Adele watching her. 'I never used to notice the cold.'

She was feeling a little uneasy, wondering how to tell Adele that she went to Harrington House yesterday. Her granddaughter was still sound asleep when she got back, and by the time she woke, Honour was back in her chair reading as if she'd been there all the time. She would have to admit it, she had the money for her after all, and someone would be bringing the rest of her things down later. But she didn't want to – Adele wasn't going to be happy about not seeing Michael any more.

'Do you think I could be a nurse?' Adele asked suddenly.

'A nurse!' Honour exclaimed. 'What brought that idea into your head? I thought you'd had enough of being at people's beck and call?'

'It's not the same thing as being a skivvy,' Adele retorted. 'It's a real job, something worthwhile. I know I'm not eighteen till the summer, but it might be worth making inquiries.'

Honour thought about it for a while, glad to be distracted from thoughts of the Baileys. 'You'd make a good one,' she said eventually. She really thought Adele would make a first-class nurse, she had the patience, the compassion and plenty of common sense, along with being strong and capable. But it wasn't in Honour's nature to reveal her innermost thoughts.

Adele seemed very satisfied with her reply anyway, and went on to explain that the idea had come to her last night in bed, and how she thought she could apply to the hospital in Hastings. Indeed she appeared to have thought it all through, including the fact that if accepted as a student nurse she'd have to live in the nurses' home.

'What was that?' Honour interrupted her suddenly on hearing a scrunch on the pebbles outside. She got up and looked out of the window, just in time to see a glimpse of Ralph Bailey disappearing back up the lane. 'Well, that's to be expected, he didn't even have the guts to knock on the door.'

Adele jumped up. 'What are you talking about?' she asked.

'It was Ralph Bailey. He crept up like a thief in the night with your things, left them on the doorstep and beetled away. He must have left the car down the road or we would have heard it.'

Adele went to the front door and opened it. The small suitcase she'd taken to Harrington House was on the doorstep. 'Oh dear,' she sighed, picking it up and coming back in, shutting the door behind her. 'They haven't returned my coat, I suppose they forgot that.'

Honour had to tell her then. 'Your coat is in my room, I got it yesterday,' she said.

Adele said nothing as her grandmother outlined the bare bones of what took place while she was asleep. She sat in her chair by the stove with a blank expression, neither approving nor disapproving. 'I got ten pounds out of him too,' Honour finished up. 'I only asked for two weeks in lieu of notice, but I wasn't going to say that was far too much.'

Adele still said nothing, but got up to open her case. On top of the clothes and a couple of books there was an envelope.

'It's a reference,' she gasped, once she saw what was inside. She read it quickly and smiled. 'What on earth did you say to them to make them come round?'

'Read it to me?' Honour asked.

'*To whom it may concern*', Adele read.

Adele Talbot has been my housekeeper for the past sixteen months. She was honest, diligent and very hardworking. It was with deep regret that I had to let her go due to a change in my circumstances.
    Yours sincerely,
    Emily Bailey

'Well, would you believe it?' exclaimed Adele. 'What a turn-up! Did you force her to write it, Granny?'

'Force her! Of course not,' Honour said. 'I did point out she ought to give you one. But from the tone of it she regrets losing you.'

'I hope she'll be all right,' Adele sighed. 'She really isn't able to take care of herself.'

'Now look here,' Honour said gruffly, 'you are not going to waste one more minute of thought on that woman. We all reap what we sow. I know her husband is a bully, but that doesn't make her incapable of making a bed or cooking a meal. She's her family's concern, not yours.'

'I don't think any of them care but Michael,' Adele said wearily.

'Well, that's her fault too,' Honour said tartly.

'Was it your fault then that Rose doesn't care about you?' Adele retorted.

Honour bristled. 'I gave Rose all the love in the world,' she said indignantly. 'She was just a self-centred minx.'

'Why haven't you ever told me what went wrong between you?' Adele asked.

'It's nothing to do with you,' Honour said defensively.

'I think it has everything to do with me, Granny,' Adele retorted, her tone a little sharp. 'It affected how Rose was as a mother to me. So please tell me.'

Honour sighed. She had known for a very long time that she ought to talk to Adele about Rose, both the events in the past and more recent developments. Yet the right moment had never presented itself. But perhaps this was the right moment now. Adele was almost an adult, and she was mature enough to understand.

'I've already told you that your grandfather came back from the war with shell-shock,' she said carefully. 'You can't really adequately explain to anyone just what that is like, it's something you have to witness to understand. Frank would sit all day just where you are now,' she said, indicating the chair Adele liked best, in its place by the stove.

'He would just stare silently into space. Now and then he would jerk his head in fright as if he'd heard a gun fired close by. His fingers were never still, he picked at his buttons, at loose threads in his trousers, and often at his face until he drew blood.' She paused for a moment, not knowing if she should illustrate it more vividly, or play it down in order to leave Frank with some dignity.

'It wasn't fair,' she said heatedly. 'Frank had always laughed a great deal, had wild ideas, and could talk about any subject under the sun, but that man I loved was gone. In his place was this withdrawn, nervous, often frightening stranger who put such demands on my strength and patience that I sometimes felt I couldn't cope.'

Adele nodded in understanding.

'But that particular day, when all this came about with Rose,' Honour went on, 'I had at long last seen a slight improvement in him. It was 1918 then, the war still rumbling on in France, and it was late spring. We went for a brief walk together during the afternoon, and he hadn't flung himself down on the ground as he had always done previously. He had managed to drink a cup of tea unaided, only spilling a few drops, and he had told me he loved me. That meant more than anything – you see, he rarely spoke at that time, and when he did it was just to rant about terrible things he had seen in the war. Mostly he didn't even seem to know who I was.'

'And where was Rose?' Adele asked.

'At her job in the hotel,' Honour said. 'But she was due home as soon as she'd turned down the beds for the night. I was looking forward to her coming in so I could tell her about the improvement in her father, and I decided I would mark the occasion by giving her the dress I'd been making in secret for her.'

Honour leaned back into the couch, half closing her eyes, and Adele could see that she was reliving the events as she continued with the story.

'Daylight was beginning to fail as she came out of her bedroom wearing the dress,' she said.

Honour could see it all as clearly as if it had happened yesterday. The table was laid for supper, Frank was in his chair by the stove, and she was lighting the oil lamp as Rose came out of her bedroom. She turned, fully expecting Rose to be striking a pose in the doorway, with giggles to follow as she twirled around the room to show off the dress.

With her blonde hair, pretty face and curvy figure, Rose looked good in anything, but that evening as Honour looked round at her, she looked simply stunning, for the blue of the dress matched her eyes perfectly. She felt an immediate flush of pride and satisfaction that the long hours she had spent making the dress had turned out to be so well spent.

But Rose wasn't striking a pose, there were no twirls or giggles. She was scowling.

'It's horrible,' she said, holding out the long skirt distastefully as if it was made of dirty sacking. 'How can you expect me to wear it? It's like something a schoolmistress would wear.'

Honour was shocked speechless. Since Frank had been brought home they had been struggling to survive on Rose's wages. The only way Honour had been able to buy the material for the dress was by selling her pearl brooch. It would have been far more sensible to have used that money to buy food, or even pay the doctor's bills, but she knew how hard it was for a young girl to wear the same old worn dress day in, day out.

Maybe the blue dress with its high neck and little pin-tucks on the bodice wasn't the height of fashion, but it was wartime and clothes had to be practical when you lived out in the country – surely Rose could see that?

'It was the best I could do,' Honour said eventually, sorry now that she'd parted with the brooch which had been a wedding-day gift from her parents, and the only thing she had left of them. 'I think you should count your blessings, Rose, there are plenty of girls around here who would give anything for a new dress,' she added sharply.

Perhaps Frank picked up on the friction in the room for

he began jerking his head, dribbling and making alarming noises in his throat.

Honour moved over to soothe him, but Rose merely looked disgusted and scornful. 'It's humiliating enough being so poor that I've got to wear a rag like this,' she spat out. 'But it's even worse to have a father who's like the village idiot.'

Adele gasped, for the way her grandmother had related the story had brought sharp images of her mother's cruel remarks back into her mind. 'What on earth did you do?' she asked.

'At the time I was so appalled by her callousness, I didn't say or do anything,' Honour said sadly. 'Later I wished I'd slapped her, or even forced her into a chair so I could pass on some of the horror stories Frank had spilled out in his more lucid moments. Perhaps then Rose might have appreciated the enormous sacrifice men like him made when they enlisted to fight for King and Country.'

'So what happened then?' Adele asked.

'She was gone by morning,' Honour said with ice in her voice. 'Slunk out like a thief in the night with our money and the few small valuables we had left. She left us to starve.'

Adele couldn't speak for a moment. She had never credited her mother with a kind heart, sensitivity or any other redeeming qualities, but it was a shock to hear that even as young as seventeen she'd been that callous.

'I see,' she said eventually. 'Of course, you could've told me this years ago.'

Honour winced at the reproach. 'If I have kept information from you, I had good reason,' she said haltingly. 'When you first came here you were very sick, you'd experienced terrible things, and the only way I knew how to heal you was by instinct. I had been deeply hurt by your mother too, and I dealt with it by casting her out of my mind. I suppose I tried to make you do that as well.'

'But it doesn't work like that,' Adele said. 'Secrets make things much worse. I understand now why you were bitter about Rose, I sympathize too, but it doesn't explain why she was so nasty to me. Does it?'

'No, Adele, it doesn't,' Honour agreed. 'I can only make assumptions about that.'

'And they are?'

'Well, Rose couldn't have been carrying you then, the dates are all wrong. So either she left here with a man, or she went to London looking for fun and adventure and met your father there. Either way, the man must have abandoned her, and it would have been very hard for any woman having a baby outside of marriage.'

'So she chose to marry Jim Talbot as an alternative to the workhouse or coming home, tail between legs?' Adele said.

Honour grimaced. 'I doubt she even considered coming home. She must have known what her disappearance did to us. I dare say she thought we could never forgive her.'

'Would you have?'

Honour sighed. 'I really don't know. I was furious with her, Frank was completely dependent on me, and we had barely enough money to feed us. Yet maybe if she'd turned up at the door with you in her arms I might have softened. I can't honestly say. Could you forgive her if she turned up here tomorrow?'

Adele thought about it for a few seconds. 'I doubt it,' she said eventually. 'But then she's not going to come back here, is she? Not knowing there are two of us against her. I take it she was told I was here?'

'Yes, when she signed the paper that made me your legal guardian,' Honour said.

Adele thought about this for a moment, remembering that her grandmother wrote and received many letters at that time.

'But that was years ago. Was she still in an asylum then?'

'Yes. In a place called Friern Barnet, in North London,' Honour replied. She'd had enough of questions for one day, but she sensed Adele wasn't going to stop until she knew everything.

'Is she still there?'

Honour hesitated.

'Well?' Adele prompted. 'Either she's still there or she isn't. If she isn't, she must be well again.'

'No. She's not there any more,' Honour finally admitted. 'She escaped.'

Adele gasped. 'And you kept it secret,' she said reproachfully. 'How and when did she escape?'

'Not long after she'd signed the papers about you. About nine months after you came here,' Honour said, hanging her head. 'It seems she got herself into a position of trust so she was allowed out into the grounds now and then. She may have hidden in a delivery van, no one really knows.'

'If she could do that she must have got better,' Adele said thoughtfully.

'Possibly,' Honour said. 'I hope so. I did think at the time it was the signing of the papers that made her escape and that she'd come here.'

'But she didn't.' Adele gave a long-drawn-out breath.

Honour couldn't swallow for the lump in her throat. She could feel Adele's hurt, and she had no idea what she could say to make it go away.

'No, she didn't. But maybe she felt you would be happier without her.'

Adele shrugged dismissively. 'If I was to believe she cared anything for my happiness I might start believing in fairies too,' she said sarcastically. 'But now we've got started on this unlocking of secrets, what happened to Mr Makepeace?'

A cold shiver ran down Honour's back. How could she tell Adele that she met disbelief in the police station when she reported that wicked man? Would it make Adele feel any better to know she wrote many letters to the charity which ran The Firs, yet they didn't remove the man from his position or even investigate her claims?

The only victory Honour had won in that first year Adele was with her, was to become her granddaughter's legal guardian. But even that wasn't much of a victory when it transpired the authorities were relieved to be spared the task of keeping her themselves.

'I reported him,' she said truthfully. 'Both to the police and to the charity. I was never told what happened to him.'

To Honour's relief, Adele didn't ask any further questions. Maybe that was because she was naive enough to believe that reporting him automatically meant he'd be punished. She got up from her chair, picked up her suitcase and walked over to her bedroom to unpack it. When she got to the door she turned. 'I don't suppose I'll ever see Michael again now,' she said sadly. 'So it's just you and me again, Granny.'

Honour's eyes prickled with tears. She glanced at Frank's painting on the wall which had always been her favourite for it was of Camber Castle with the river in the foreground. He'd painted it in a spot where they often had picnics. He had always been so good at expressing his feelings, both verbally and through his painting, and she knew he would say this was the perfect time for telling their granddaughter how much she was loved and valued.

'I love you, Adele,' she blurted out. 'You transformed my life by coming here. I wish I could do something to make everything right with Michael. I wish I could tell you something about your mother that would make you happier about her too. But I can't do anything more than tell you that you mean everything to me.'

Adele looked at her in astonishment for a few seconds and then began to laugh.

'Oh, Granny,' she said, tears coming with the laughter, 'I'm not so sure I like you getting soppy. It's not you.'

Honour couldn't help but smile. 'You know what's wrong with you, girl?' she asked.

Adele shook her head. 'Tell me,' she said.

'You are far too much like me for your own good.'

Chapter Thirteen

1938

'Nurse Talbot! Mrs Drew's dressing needs changing!' Sister MacDonald called out as she passed the sluice room where Adele was about to empty and wash a bedpan.

'Yes, Sister,' Adele said, and once Sister was out of view thumbed her nose at the bossy woman who ran Women's Surgical with an iron hand.

It was 1 January and the hospital was short-staffed on every ward because of an outbreak of influenza. Adele wasn't feeling too good herself, not because she'd got flu, but because she and several other student nurses had stayed up late to see the New Year in and celebrated with cheap sherry. She was sure Sister MacDonald knew this as she'd been hounding her all day.

She had started her nursing training at the Buchanan Hospital in Hastings in April. The pay was just ten shillings a week, and the hours very long, but she shared a nice room in the nurses' home, she got three meals a day, and she had made dozens of new friends. Angela Daltry, her room-mate, was a lovable, scatterbrained girl from Bexhill, and as they almost always worked the same shifts, they spent much of their spare time together.

Nursing wasn't anything like Adele had expected. As she'd never even been in a hospital until she began her training she supposed she'd romanticized it, imagined herself as a kind of angel of mercy, wiping fevered brows, taking temperatures and arranging the flowers. She did know that people would vomit, bleed and need bedpans of course, but she hadn't anticipated it being quite so relentless, or that as a student nurse she'd be the main one to deal with all the mucky jobs. She had never imagined so many rules either. Everything from not sitting on beds to making sure not a single hair escaped from her starched cap. Sister MacDonald was exceptionally fussy, and she had eyes in the back of her head. Adele was hauled over the coals on her very first day on the ward for eating a toffee. One of the patients had given it to her, but to hear Sister rant and rave about it, anyone would think she'd stolen a whole box and shoved them all in her mouth at the same time.

Yet despite the drawbacks, she loved nursing. It was so rewarding to see people gradually getting better after operations, to know that although she was only one very small cog in the hospital wheel, it was vital work. The patients were grateful for her care, they took as much interest in her as she did in them, and there was so much gaiety and laughter with the other nurses.

With the clean bedpan back in its rack, Adele grabbed the dressings trolley and made for Mrs Drew. She was a plump woman in her early forties, with greying hair, who had almost died of a ruptured appendix, and Adele had grown very fond of her.

'Time to change your dressing,' she said as she pulled the curtains round the woman's bed.

'Not again,' Mrs Drew sighed, and put down the magazine she was reading. 'I sometimes think you wait for someone to look really comfortable, then pounce on them.'

'Of course we do,' Adele laughed. 'We've got to do something to justify the enormous amount of money we get paid.' She folded down the sheets and blankets to just below the woman's stomach, then lifted her nightdress to expose her dressing over the abdominal stitching. She removed it gingerly. 'It's healing very well,' she said. 'I expect you to be able to go home very soon.'

'I'm in no hurry,' Mrs Drew said with a smile. 'It's nice and warm in here, and a real treat to put my feet up. Soon as I'm home my lot will all expect me to wait on them again.'

Mrs Drew had six children ranging from eighteen down to a three-year-old. She had ignored the pains in her stomach for months because she had no time for herself and she couldn't afford doctors' fees.

'Sister will tell them what's what,' Adele said with a grin. 'You've had major surgery, you've got to take it easy when you get home, no carrying heavy shopping, coal buckets or even your toddler. Your husband or one of the older children will have to do it all for you.'

Mrs Drew gave Adele a withering look. 'Some chance,' she said. 'I'll get back home to find the place like a midden. If you've got any sense, nurse, you'll stay single. Once the honeymoon's over it's down hill all the way.'

Adele had met many stoic women like Mrs Drew since she began nursing. They always put their husband and children first, their own needs ignored. Mostly they had brought up their large families in poverty, with appalling housing conditions, yet somehow managed to retain a lively sense of humour. Mrs Drew had a particularly black one – she called her husband Eric 'The Pig', because he grunted rather than spoke to her. She claimed she'd thought of rounding her kids up and dumping them on an orphanage doorstep to get a bit of peace. Yet her face broke into a wide smile when Eric walked into the ward to visit her, and she wrote separate little notes for each of the children, because they weren't allowed into the ward.

'I bet if you could start all over again you'd still marry Mr Drew,' Adele said as she cleaned the wound before redressing it.

'I suppose so. I'd clout him round the ear the first time he grunted though,' Mrs Drew chuckled. 'Are you courtin'?'

Adele shook her head.

'Haven't you even got your eye on anyone?'

Adele giggled. For a woman who often said marriage and

240

children was a mug's game, Mrs Drew was very keen on seeing everyone else getting paired off.

'I suppose I have,' she admitted, thinking of Michael. 'But it's not going to work out. His parents will never approve of me.'

'I'd be over the moon if my boy Ronnie found a nice girl like you,' Mrs Drew said. 'You're clever, pretty and talk nice. His parents want their heads seeing to.'

Adele pulled the woman's nightdress down and tucked the covers back over her. 'I've often thought that about them myself,' she said with a wink. 'Now, you have a rest, Mrs Drew, no gallivanting off up the ward to talk to someone.'

As Adele wheeled the dressings trolley back down the ward she wondered where Michael was right now, and if he'd been to Winchelsea to see his mother over Christmas. She had been working on both Christmas Day and Boxing Day, so she hadn't been able to get home. But she had two days off as from tomorrow and she hoped her grandmother would have lots of gossip for her.

Michael had written to her last January to apologize again for his parents' behaviour. It was an odd sort of letter, she could feel deep sadness in it, and a great deal left unsaid. Reading between the lines, she felt his father had laid into him about her and almost certainly insisted he was never to contact her again. Michael probably felt he ought to obey his father, maybe he even thought there was nothing to be gained by continuing their friendship anyway, but being a kind person he wouldn't say all that as it would add insult to injury.

Adele waited a couple of weeks and wrote a cheery letter back to him at Oxford. She told him she was applying to go into nursing and that he mustn't feel bad about anything because things had turned out for the best. She said she had no hard feelings towards either him or his mother, and hoped Mrs Bailey was managing all right.

It was almost three months before he wrote again, just a few days before she started as a probationer. He said he was thrilled she was going to be a nurse as it was in his eyes one of the most important jobs anyone could do. He also said he thought she was born for it. He asked if she would meet him if he came to Hastings, but he couldn't say when that would be. His hopes that his parents would get back together again had been dashed.

The rest of the letter was taken up with flying and the Corps at Oxford. He was jubilant that he was now a fully qualified pilot and said he was seriously considering a career in the RAF once he'd got his degree.

As a probationer, Adele didn't have time to think about Michael much. There was so much theory to learn, with tests every week, and every evening and day off was spent studying. Then there was the coronation of George VI in May and Adele was roped in to help make bunting and other decorations for the hospital. Some of the nurses went up to London to watch the celebrations there, but all the probationers were expected to help at the hospital tea-party in the grounds, either serving teas or escorting the patients who were well enough to attend down to it. For Adele this proved to be a real initiation into the social life of the hospital, as that day she got to know many more people – the clerical and domestic staff along with doctors and other nurses.

It was that day she began to see that England might really have to go to war again. The rumblings about Adolf Hitler and his ever-increasing power in Germany had been going on for so long she hadn't taken much notice. She was horrified of course by the way he was treating Jewish people, but it wasn't until she overheard one of the doctors echoing something Michael had said in his last letter about the man being set on ruling the whole world that she realized what that really meant.

He would have to be stopped, and it would be young men

like Michael who would be called upon to do it. A chill ran down her spine as she looked around her and saw Raymond and Alf, the two young porters, who always teased the student nurses. They would have to go too, so would most of the doctors here, all her friends' fathers and brothers, and it would be just the same way as it was in the first war, women taking over men's jobs. Waiting and hoping that their sons, husbands or brothers wouldn't be on the casualty lists.

All at once Adele understood why she had been accepted so readily for nursing training. She'd chosen to believe she was exceptional, and that she'd shone at her initial interview. But that probably wasn't the way it was at all. England would need hundreds more nurses if war really was coming, and perhaps anyone able and willing to train could get in. But though it was a bit disappointing to know she wasn't that special, it made her that more determined to prove herself.

Michael came to see her at the start of his long summer vacation without any forewarning. He was only staying a couple of days with his mother before going up to Scotland and he took the chance she'd be off duty. As luck would have it she was; she'd had the day off, and though she usually went home to see her grandmother, on this occasion she had stayed in the nurses' home to do some studying.

Some of the other nurses saw him waiting for her in the hall and they teased her unmercifully about it afterwards. It seemed that calling there, rather than arranging to meet in town, implied a serious romance. It also meant Matron would be watching her like a hawk in future.

It was pouring with rain, so they went in his car to a tea shop in Battle. It was a pretty place with gingham curtains and tablecloths, and lots of bright copper pots hanging from the beams.

Adele was still in the first throes of enchantment with nursing, having just started on the ward after her probationary theory lessons, and she could talk of nothing else as they drank tea and ate crumpets and cakes. Michael was almost as one-track-minded. He was off to stay with some people who sounded impossibly grand, with a castle on a loch and a private plane which he would be able to fly. Neither of them mentioned the marshes – it was almost as if they were both trying to be different people.

He looked so suave in grey flannels and a blazer, and he often lapsed into undergraduate slang which she didn't always understand. He had also grown very handsome; his hair was much longer, his face thinner, and while he was ordering more tea from the waitress, the light from the window caught his angular cheekbones, and she felt a surge of what could only be desire.

Yet however lovely it was to see Michael again, Adele was left with a sinking feeling that he had weighed her up and found her lacking. She couldn't blame him – in her cheap cotton dress, with bare legs, prattling on about taking temperatures, bedbaths and the like, she must have looked and sounded so ingenuous.

She knew he must meet many girls both at Oxford and through friends like the ones in Scotland. She imagined them all terribly well bred, speaking as if they had plums in their mouths and wearing clothes straight out of fashion magazines. Why would he stay interested in someone his parents disapproved of? Especially when there were countless girls out there all prettier, smarter and less trouble than her?

Michael had to be back at his mother's for dinner at seven, and when he dropped her back at the nurses' home he kissed her cheek.

'Next time we'll arrange it well in advance so we have more time,' he said. 'I'd like to take you to dinner or dancing.'

Adele took a deep breath before replying. She wanted Michael on almost any terms – he made her legs feel wobbly, her heart pound, and she could look into his dark blue eyes for ever and never get bored. But she was a realist, and however much they felt they had in common five years ago when they first met, they were grown up now and poles apart. Even if his parents hadn't been so against her, it still couldn't work, and she didn't want Michael to feel he had some kind of debt to pay back to her.

'No, Michael,' she said firmly. 'No dancing or dinner, just drop me a postcard once in a while so I know what you are doing.'

She had expected that he would look relieved, even laugh and say he was glad she hadn't grown out of being so direct, but to her surprise he looked stricken and turned off the car engine.

'You don't like me any more?' he asked. He put one hand on her cheek so she couldn't turn away from him and his eyes bored into her.

'Of course I like you, silly,' she said and made an attempt at a laugh. 'You will always be a special friend, but that doesn't mean you've got to keep turning up and giving me treats to make up for your father being so horrible to me.'

'Is that why you think I came here today?' he asked.

'Well yes,' she said. 'Maybe you didn't actually decide that was the reason, but I think it is. You don't have to feel bad about all that, I'm nursing now, the experience with your mother helped me get there. I haven't got any hard feelings towards you, or her.'

He put his other hand on her cheek too, cupping her face between his two hands. 'You've got it all wrong,' he said. 'I don't want to take you to dinner because I feel guilty, it's because I want you to be my girl.'

'But you can't possibly want that,' she said, feeling almost faint at the touch of his hands on her cheeks. 'How could I ever fit into your world?'

'Look at you,' he said with a tender smile. 'You're beautiful, Adele, capable and strong, you could fit in anywhere you chose to. But I don't want to get you to fit in anywhere at all, I just want you as you are, wherever you are. I like your values, your lack of conceit, your kindness. I like you, a great deal!'

Before Adele could say anything, he kissed her. Not a snatched, embarrassed kiss like the first one two years ago, but a real sweetheart's kiss, and the first Adele had ever had. His lips were far softer than she expected, and his arms went right round her, pulling her close to him. The tip of his tongue parted her lips a little, and suddenly she understood how lovers could stand in railway stations and shop doorways kissing for hours. She thought she could even ignore Matron if she was standing on the steps of the nurses' home, watching them. She wanted to stay in Michael's arms for ever.

'Now will you come out with me again?' he said when the kiss ended. He was still holding her tightly and rubbing his nose against hers. What could she say but yes? When she finally got out of his car she was so happy she felt like running into the nurses' home and screaming out to everyone that Michael Bailey wanted her to be his girl.

But it was just as well she didn't make a public announcement, for it seemed as if she and Michael were jinxed. He came back early from Scotland just to see her, but she had been put on nights and all they had together was a couple of hours in the afternoon walking along the promenade. In September, when he arranged to come again, his car broke down, leaving him stuck twenty-five miles from his home in Alton. He came anyway when it was fixed but they only had time for some fish and chips and she had to go on night duty. He was there again in the morning when she came off duty, but she was so tired she fell asleep in his car on the way to get some breakfast.

In October he had to go back to Oxford, and as it was his final year he had to buckle down and study. But he wrote to her every week and he begged her not to get fed up with waiting and fall in love with a young doctor.

Adele could only smile at that. She worked such long hours that by the time she came off duty the only thing she wanted was her bed, and she had to study for her exams too. Besides, it was strictly forbidden for nurses to fraternize with doctors, and even if it had been allowed, not one of them would hold a candle to Michael.

She daydreamed a great deal about him though, reliving his kisses, remembering every compliment, every joke they'd shared. Yet all the same she held herself in check, not daring to think ahead, for apart from his father's animosity towards her, there was now the very real threat of war.

Every day there was something on the news which seemed to bring it closer and closer. Mr Chamberlain, the Prime Minister, might make soothing speeches, but he wasn't really fooling anyone now. Michael mentioned the RAF more and more in his letters. Sometimes Adele got the idea he was actually hoping for war. He claimed that if it came it would be fought in the skies, not in trenches like the last one, and he said it with excitement and relish.

How could she think ahead when Michael looked set for the most dangerous profession she could think of?

Adele kept nodding off to sleep on the bus ride home to Rye that evening. But each time her head touched the cold window she woke with a start. She knew the road so well now that she didn't need to try to peer out into the darkness to see where they were. Even with her eyes closed, she knew by the bends in the road, the steepness of a hill and even the number of people getting on or off, how far the bus had come. There was a pig farm at Guestling, she could always smell it long before they passed it. She knew when they were stopping at the turn-off for Pett by the wheezing of the fat woman who always got off there.

She came to with a jerk as the bus drove into Winchelsea, and as always she got ready to look at Harrington House. To her surprise there was a Christmas tree ablaze with electric lights in the window of the drawing room, and she was suddenly wide awake, looking to see if Michael's car was there. It wasn't, but she saw a fleeting glimpse of a woman drawing the curtains upstairs in Mrs Bailey's bedroom. She thought it was probably the housekeeper who Granny said had arrived during the summer. She was a widow by all accounts and the gossip was that she was very religious. Adele wondered what she made of Mrs Bailey's drinking.

As the bus went through the Landgate and down the hill Adele got up, rang the bell and walked to the front to get off.

'Mind how you go,' the conductor said, opening the door for her. 'It's icy and you can't see in the dark.'

Adele wrapped her scarf more firmly round her neck as the bus pulled away and left her in pitch darkness. It was freezing cold with a raw biting wind coming off the sea. Yet however cold it was, the silence was wonderful. In the nurses' home and the hospital it was never quiet. She suddenly remembered the first winter she lived here, and how scared she'd been coming home from school when it was dark. She mistook the wind moaning in the trees for spooks, and always felt someone was lying in wait to grab her.

It was her grandmother who cured her of that. 'Don't be ridiculous,' she said sternly. 'If a man wanted to lie in wait for a girl passing by, he'd pick somewhere a little less chilly and somewhere more likely to catch someone. As for spooks, if there was such a thing, do you really think they'd pick the open countryside when there's hundreds of ancient houses in Rye to haunt?'

'She isn't afraid of anything,' Adele thought as she picked her way carefully past ice-covered puddles in the lane. She didn't think she'd want to live all alone in such a remote place when she got old.

But as she smelled the wood smoke and saw the welcoming light in the window, she forgot that she was tired, hungry and cold. It was so good to be home again.

'That was really scrumptious,' Adele sighed as she scraped up the last of the treacle pudding and custard which had followed chicken, roast potatoes, parsnips and Brussels sprouts. 'No one makes such good dinners as you, Granny.'

'It's easy enough when you've got fresh produce,' Honour retorted, but she was smiling with pleasure at the compliment. 'I expect the vegetables you get at the hospital are weeks old.'

'And cooked to a pulp,' Adele said. 'Everything tastes the same. Now, come on, tell me all the gossip!'

'Now, when do I ever see anyone to get gossip?' Honour said. 'Without you here it's not often I need anything at the shop in Winchelsea, so I can't tell you anything about the Baileys, not even if Michael came for Christmas.'

Adele blushed. She hadn't realized she was being so transparent.

'He'll be back off to Oxford soon,' she said. 'But he sent me this for Christmas.' She fished down the front of her jumper and brought out an oval gold locket.

Honour came closer and peered at it. 'It's real gold,' she exclaimed. 'It must have cost a fortune!'

'I know,' Adele grinned. 'All the girls were envious. It opens up too, for a picture. I wish I had one of him to put in it.'

'Do his parents know he still keeps in touch?' Honour asked, and raised one eyebrow.

'I shouldn't think so,' Adele replied.

Honour sighed deeply but made no comment.

The following day it was even colder, and apart from going out to feed the chickens and rabbits, they stayed huddled round the stove all day, Adele copying up some notes she'd made in a lecture, and Honour knitting. The following day it was just as cold, but Adele noticed there wasn't very much firewood, and as she was going back to the hospital in the evening, she insisted that she would go out alone to collect some.

It felt good to be outside bundled up in her old clothes and boots, dragging the little cart behind her. She never walked much in Hastings, after a long day on the ward she was always too tired, but she missed the fresh air and the solitude that had been so much of her life before nursing.

Within an hour she had filled the cart, for the high winds in the past few weeks had tossed a lot of driftwood up on to the beach. She was just coming back over the shingle bank with one last armful to put in the cart, when to her surprise she saw Michael in the distance.

He was coming from the direction of Rye Harbour, tramping along with his head down in the wind. He wasn't dressed for a walk in such a wild place, he appeared to be wearing a long city-type overcoat over a suit and he was bareheaded.

'Michael!' she shouted, but the wind was too strong for him to hear. She ran the rest of the way to the cart, dumped the wood and then ran back to meet him. It was only when she was about two hundred yards from him that he looked up and saw her.

'Adele!' he shouted jubilantly, and broke into a run. 'I never expected to see you. I thought you'd be working.'

He told her he'd come down on Christmas Eve, but his car was playing up and he'd taken it to a mechanic down by the harbour to fix. He'd got a lift down there this morning from a neighbour of his mother's, expecting to drive it away repaired, but it needed a new part, and it would be another day before it was ready.

'I should have gone home the road way,' he said, looking down ruefully at his smart black shoes all covered in mud.

'These shoes aren't meant for tough going, but I remembered the first time you showed me the way to the harbour, and I felt I had to come that way again. Then suddenly there you are in front of me.'

'Would you have knocked at the cottage if you hadn't seen me?' she asked, feeling it might have been wiser to have run home, changed into some decent clothes and waited for his knock.

'I don't think I would have. I'd thought about it already and decided I wasn't brave enough to face your grandmother.'

'Why on earth not? She doesn't bear a grudge and she knows we keep in touch,' Adele said. 'I showed her the locket the night before last, and she didn't say anything sharp about it. Thank you for it by the way. It is so lovely, but you shouldn't have spent all that money on me.'

She parted the collar of her coat to show him she was wearing it. 'I've got something for you too, nothing grand like this, but I was waiting till you got back to Oxford to send it.'

He smiled. 'Look at you!' he said. 'You look so beautiful with your rosy cheeks and that woolly hat.'

Adele blushed. 'I look a fright more like,' she said. 'Why is it you always turn up when I'm unprepared?'

'I don't believe you could look any more gorgeous than you do now, even if you'd had hours to prepare,' he said, staring at her intently until she had to drop her eyes from his. 'You do know I've fallen hopelessly in love with you?'

Adele heard what he said, but she could only think he was joking. He couldn't be serious. Could he?

Yet as she lifted her eyes he didn't appear to be joking. His eyes were so soft and tender, his full lips, red with the wind, were slightly apart as if waiting breathlessly for her reply.

'Are you serious?' she asked, her voice cracking.

'Never more so,' he said, and reached out for her. 'I've tried to tell myself a hundred times that I was imagining it, but it doesn't go away.'

He kissed her then, their cold lips suddenly turning warm on contact with each other, and the heat building up the tighter he held her. Adele forgot that they were out on the marsh, forgot the cold, the wood in the cart and that her grandmother would be expecting her back. Nothing mattered at all but the glorious feeling welling up inside her.

'Let's go to the castle,' he said, taking her hand and leading her back that way before she'd even answered. 'We'll be out of the wind in there.'

There were sheep sheltering in the castle and Michael made Adele laugh by running at them to shoo them out. 'That was mean,' she said. 'This is their house.'

'It's not, it's ours,' he said, taking her in his arms. 'You brought me here the first day we met and I blabbed out all that stuff about my parents. Do you remember?'

She nodded. She could still recall exactly how she felt that day, liking and trusting him, yet afraid to say too much about herself.

She looked about her, feeling a surge of affection for this old castle where she'd spent so much time in the past. There was no whine of the wind inside its crumbling stone walls, and even if the sky above was as grey as the stones, there were leaf buds on the trees that had taken up residence within its shelter. It was a haven for many animals and birds, and now for her and Michael too.

'You never did tell me your secrets,' he said pointedly, taking her hand and leading her to a grassy bank to sit down. 'Surely you can tell me them now that I've told you I love you?'

Adele ignored the bit about the secrets, it was the loving part which bothered her. 'You can't mean it, Michael,' she said, turning to him and taking his face between her two hands. 'Have you thought what your parents would say about it?'

'Yes, and I don't care. I'll be twenty-one this summer, I'll be joining the RAF and I can do whatever I want with my life. I don't owe them anything.'

'You do, Michael,' she insisted. 'They are your parents, they kept you all through school and Oxford. If they cut you off you'd hate it.'

'Would I?' He raised his eyebrows. 'Father doesn't really care about me – he might throw money at me, but that's just a way of controlling me. Mother loves me, but she never thinks about what I want or need, it's all me, me, me with her. I'm supposed to support her, fight her corner and be shown off as her clever boy.'

Adele felt he was being very realistic about both his parents as she couldn't argue about anything he'd said. Yet how could a girl from the marshes move over into the kind of world he came from?

He laid her back on the grass and kissed her with such passion that she forgot all her anxieties and found herself swept away to a magical place where nothing mattered but the moment.

It was only when his hands slid under her old coat and touched her breasts that she came to her senses.

A picture of Mr Makepeace shot into her mind. In the rapture of being kissed she'd forgotten that men would promise anything to get what they wanted.

'I've got to get home,' she said, pushing his hands away and sitting up. 'The lunch will be ready. I've got to leave on the five o'clock bus, and I need to spend some time with Granny before I go.'

He half sat up, leaning on one elbow, and looked at her in puzzlement. 'But I don't know how long it will be before I can get down here again,' he said.

'You'll have to make time then,' she said sharply, getting

to her feet. 'I can't roll around on the grass whenever it suits you, I've got responsibilities.'

'Why are you cross?' he asked as he got up. 'What did I do?'

The confusion she remembered so well with Mr Make-peace came back. She had trusted him too, and then he had betrayed that trust. How could she tell if Michael was saying he loved her just to have his way with her, or if he really loved her and touching was just part of that?

She knew perfectly well from her nurse friends that boy-friends did fondle breasts, squeeze and stroke bottoms, and often put their hands under skirts. The nurses often discussed how far they let men go before backing away. It seemed to be almost a game that was played, the girls gradually allowing more liberties with each date. Adele didn't want to play games, she wanted to know exactly where she stood. Yet she couldn't tell Michael any of that, she was much too embarrassed by the whole thing.

He took her hand in his as they walked back to where she'd left the wood cart. He said nothing, and Adele glanced at him several times, wondering what he was thinking.

'I'm sorry,' she blurted out eventually, unable to bear the silence. 'I was just a bit scared.'

'Scared that I would rape you?' he retorted, and when he turned towards her she saw his face was tense and angry. 'I love you, Adele. I would never try to force you to do anything you didn't want to do. I thought you would know that.'

Adele felt both foolish and scared. She had believed that what Mr Makepeace did to her would never affect her again – after all, it was nearly seven years ago and he had rarely crossed her mind in the last four. She felt she ought to give Michael an explanation, she didn't like to see him upset, yet a great part of her still felt indignant that he'd touched her breasts. She was struggling not to cry because she felt so confused.

They reached the wood cart, and Michael moved to pull

it, but to Adele the sight of him in his smart city clothes wheeling along a cart with old pram wheels was another reminder of how different their backgrounds were.

'Don't,' she said, grabbing the handle from him. 'I'll do it.'

'Can't I even touch your cart now?' he said sarcastically.

She began to cry then, and half running, half walking, she pulled the cart behind her over the rough ground, shedding part of the load as she made her way back to Curlew Cottage.

Michael bent and picked up some of the wood, baffled by why Adele was behaving so strangely. He had no intention of snatching the cart back from her, just the speed at which she was going suggested she might whack him with one of the sticks.

But he followed her, intending to drop the wood he had picked up by the cottage and then be on his way. He was cold and hungry, his feet hurt, and he was very disappointed that after the delight of meeting up with Adele unexpectedly, it should end so badly.

But as they drew closer to the cottage, Mrs Harris appeared in the doorway. Adele picked up even more speed, and because of the noise of the wind, Michael couldn't hear what she was saying to her grandmother. She abandoned the cart outside the front door and darted indoors. Mrs Harris came walking purposefully towards him.

'What have you done to make her cry?' she asked, her expression stern and defensive.

'I didn't know she was,' he said honestly, putting the wood down and brushing off his coat. 'I was walking back from Rye Harbour and I ran into her. We went over to Camber Castle for a while, and suddenly she said she had to come home. I don't know what's wrong with her, you'd better ask her. Perhaps she'll talk to you.'

Honour gave him a sharp look. 'She left here perfectly happy.'

'Obviously telling her I loved her upset her then,' he said curtly, and began to walk away.

'Don't walk away from me, Michael Bailey,' she said in a voice like thunder. 'Come back here.'

Michael didn't dare disobey her, and turned. 'Look, Mrs Harris,' he said, 'I really don't know what's got into her. Tell her I'll telephone her at the nurses' home tonight. My car's broken down so I can't offer to drive her back to Hastings.'

'You'll be around tomorrow morning then?' she asked.

Michael nodded.

'Come to see me then,' she said. 'I think it's time we had a talk on our own.'

Honour waved as the bus drove off. Adele had gone right to the back seat, and just the way she was slumped and her feeble wave told Honour that she would be crying all the way back to the nurses' home.

Honour stood there watching the bus drive up to Winchelsea, its headlights illuminating the old Landgate. Sighing, she turned to go home. She had always hated January, the cold, the early darkness, and because it was the month Frank died. Today she felt even more forlorn than she usually did at this time of year. The postman had told her this morning that it had just been announced that all schoolchildren were going to be issued with gas masks, and she guessed Adele's secret demons had come back to taunt her.

But while it was terrible that the Government were seriously concerned that the Germans might attack British civilians with gas, her primary fear was for Adele. She hadn't of course admitted what had happened today between her and Michael, but Honour could make an educated guess.

Michael arrived at the cottage soon after nine the following morning. Honour asked him in and offered him a cup of tea.

He looked apprehensive and she had no doubt he thought she was about to lay into him.

'Did you speak to Adele on the telephone last night?' she asked.

'No, they said they got no reply from her room,' he said.

Honour thought about that for a moment. She knew Adele must have been there, but wouldn't speak to him. 'That's a shame,' she said eventually. 'I had hoped you would have straightened out whatever was wrong.'

'I tried,' he said, and there was a note of anger in his voice. 'But I don't know what I'm supposed to have done to upset her.'

'You said yesterday that you told her you loved her. Do you really mean that?' Honour asked.

'Of course, I wouldn't have said it if I didn't mean it,' he said with some indignation. 'But I don't think she feels the same way.'

'Why do you think that?'

He looked down at his hands in his lap. 'I can't put it into words.'

'Perhaps Adele can't put her feelings into words either,' Honour said, 'I know I can't. It's easy to talk about how you feel about flowers, animals and things like that. But it's much harder to discuss thoughts and emotions.'

He said nothing and continued to look at his hands.

'You've got to remember that when Adele went to work for your mother that put her on an entirely different level to you,' Honour said, trying to be gentle and win his trust. 'She was a servant, you were to all intents and purposes her master. She knows your parents will never accept her as your equal.'

He looked up and there was hurt in his dark blue eyes. 'I told her I don't care about what they think. Adele is my equal in my eyes. Look at you, Mrs Harris. You may live here on the marsh, but you are more than my mother's equal, and you know it.'

'Yes, I am, but then I was a gently brought up schoolmaster's daughter, and I married into a good family too. Such a background gives a girl confidence in her own worth, which doesn't get broken even when personal circumstances change.

'Adele doesn't have that confidence. She was brought up amongst the working classes, and has experienced things which only serve to endorse her belief she is not worthy.'

He looked startled. 'Are you trying to tell me something about her past?'

'It isn't my place to tell you that,' Honour said, suddenly aware that Adele would never forgive her if she divulged details without her permission. 'But if you do love Adele, you will have to win her complete trust so she feels she can tell you herself.'

Michael's expression changed to one of suspicion. 'There's something about her mother, isn't there?' he said. 'When I first met her she told me she came here to live because her mother was ill. But she's never mentioned her since. Where is her mother? Why doesn't Adele see her?'

'We don't know where her mother is,' Honour said. 'For my part I don't care, she ran away from here when her father was desperately ill, without a thought for either of us. I didn't even know I had a grandchild until Adele turned up at my door nearly seven years ago.'

Michael's eyes widened and his jaw dropped.

'I'm not going to tell you anything more,' Honour said firmly. 'You have to get the whole story from Adele. All I ask is that you treat her gently, she has been hurt and bullied enough in the past.'

She made another pot of tea, and as she busied herself she kept an eye on Michael. He was deep in thought, probably even more puzzled now than when he first came in.

Last night she would have raged at him, warned him that if he ever laid a hand on Adele again, he'd have her to reckon with. But in the early hours it had come to her that that wasn't a wise course. She didn't want to frighten him away, and in any case a gut feeling told her that her granddaughter had probably overreacted to what was nothing more than an attempted fumble. He was a sensitive, highly intelligent young man, and if anyone could reach and heal that damaged part of Adele, it would be him.

'Now, what's all this I hear about you intending to join the RAF?' she asked brightly as she put the fresh tea on the table.

Chapter Fourteen

'Don't do that, it's horrible,' Adele exclaimed, grabbing Michael's hand in which he held a blade of grass. They were lying in the spring sunshine, up on Beachy Head near Eastbourne. When she had dropped off to sleep for a moment Michael had run the blade of grass around her nostril.

'Well, wake up then,' he said, grinning broadly. 'I want to talk.'

It was now Easter, some three months since their tiff at New Year. Michael had made a special overnight trip down to see Adele again a few days later to make things up with her. She was very tearful and apologetic, saying she didn't know why she'd been so funny with him that day. Michael took her out to dinner and once she seemed relaxed again, he persuaded her to tell him about her mother and her childhood in London.

It was shocking to hear what she'd been through, and it saddened him to realize she couldn't trust him completely if she'd held so much important detail of her life back from him. But as she spilled out all the hurt and sadness of the past, he could almost see her relief at finally sharing it, and it made sense of many of the things he'd been puzzled about in the past.

Michael had been very reluctant to leave Adele that night as she was in an emotional state, and he couldn't even say for sure when he'd see her next. He wrote to her when he got back to the camp, telling her how much he loved her, and how happy he was that there were no further secrets between them. When he telephoned her a couple of days later, she was more like her old bright and bouncy self, telling him not to worry about her because she really was fine, just sorry she'd been so moody and odd at New Year. They hadn't been able to see each other again till now, but when they'd talked on the telephone it was as if nothing had ever happened.

'So what do you want to talk about?' she asked, turning from her back on to her stomach and leaning up on her elbows. 'Oh, I know, about how handsome you'll look in your uniform.'

Michael laughed. 'No, I already know that, and that I'll be the best pilot the world has ever seen.'

'That doesn't leave much to talk about then,' she said. 'Unless you want to hear about bedbaths, temperature charts or the patients in my ward.'

Michael was staying with his mother for the entire Easter holiday, supposedly swotting up for his Finals when he returned to Oxford in a few days' time. Adele had managed to get three days off to spend with him, but tomorrow she would be starting in the Gynaecology ward.

They had been lucky with the weather, it was unusually warm and sunny for April, and Michael, who had just been accepted into the RAF, was very excited and could talk of little else.

'I thought you might tell me more about The Firs,' he said, bending down to kiss her forehead. 'It seems to me that something pretty drastic must have happened there to make you walk all the way to Rye.'

Michael found that one of the most frustrating things about conducting much of their love affair on the telephone, or by letters, was the inability to discuss anything serious. They told each other about day-to-day things, work, friends, bits of gossip, but scarcely anything else. Michael was still eager to know more details about Adele's childhood, and as he mulled over parts of what she'd previously told him, he realized she had said virtually nothing about the place she called The Firs, that she ran away from. Obviously it must have been a ghastly place or she wouldn't have felt the need to run to a complete stranger. Michael thought that most people would elaborate on what was so bad about it, if only to justify themselves. Unless, of course, whatever had happened there was so bad they felt unable to talk about it.

The cryptic comments Mrs Harris had made about Adele's past that time when she ordered him to come and see her kept coming back to him. He had fully expected a roasting that day, to be told he would not be allowed to go out alone with Adele in future. Surely that was what most girls' parents or guardians would do if they suspected a young man of 'trying it on'?

Yet Mrs Harris was calm, and didn't accuse him of anything. It was almost as if she was fishing to discover what Adele had told him about her past.

When Adele eventually admitted that her mother had been put in an asylum, Michael thought that was her guilty secret. It was only much later that doubts set in. Why should she be afraid to reveal that? He had an equally crazy mother, so he wasn't likely to be horrified. There had to be something more, and he became determined to find out what it was.

Michael wasn't very keen to spend the whole of the Easter holidays with his mother – it was always an ordeal staying with her for longer than a couple of days. But he could hardly arrange to stay for just the three days Adele was free, and disappear each day. So he had to grit his teeth, take his mother shopping and to visit old friends in the hope that when he did start going out alone she wouldn't kick up a fuss. Fortunately she didn't seem suspicious about his need to go to Brighton to buy a special book, going out to lunch with a friend from Oxford in the vicinity, or his excuse for today which was just a long walk on the Downs. Maybe she was as bored with his company as he was with hers. He just hoped no one would report back that he'd been seen with Adele, for that was guaranteed to bring on one of her turns.

The joy of being with Adele again, and his excitement at his recent acceptance into the RAF, had meant he hadn't yet got around to any gentle interrogation about The Firs. For the last two days he'd been a bit of a Flying Bore, talking non-stop about it, and of course the strong possibility of war and what it could mean to them. Adele might find herself transferred to a military hospital, or even to a civilian one in London, and he had no real idea where he would be based. But time was getting short now, and after today he probably wouldn't get to see her till late June or July.

'Come on! Tell me about it,' he urged.

'You don't want to hear about that place,' she said dismissively. 'It isn't interesting and I wasn't there that long.'

'It's interesting because you ran away from it,' he insisted. 'Why did you?'

'I've already told you. I wanted to find out if I had got grandparents. It just took longer to get there than I imagined it would. Now, give me a kiss and tell me that you love me.'

She lay on her back and held out her arms. Michael looked down at her and smiled at her beauty. Cheeks pink with the sun, wind-tossed hair and eyes almost the colour of amber. Most girls these days seemed to go for the artificial kind of dazzling beauty inspired by Hollywood. They curled their hair, shaped their eyebrows to give them a look of permanent surprise, and often wore so much makeup they looked old beyond their years. But Adele wore her hair loose when she wasn't on duty and it bounced and shone, inviting his touch. She didn't powder her nose or strive to change her body shape with corsetry. She was as natural and graceful as a swan. And he knew he'd love her till he died.

'Do you love me?' he asked, leaning on his hands either side of her, and bringing his face down close to hers.

'Of course I do,' she giggled, fluttering her long lashes.

'Then say it,' he said.

'I love you, Michael,' she said softly, looking faintly bashful.

'How much do you trust me?'

She frowned then. 'With my life? Will that do?'

'Then surely you can tell me what happened at The Firs?'

'Nothing happened, I just didn't like it.'

'You're lying to me,' he said firmly. 'Now, tell me the truth. If you don't, it will stand between us all our lives.'

He could read her thought processes in her eyes. A look that said she wanted to reveal it, but didn't dare. Then a slight narrowing of her eyes as she tried to think of something plausible to fob him off with.

'I've gone over everything that happened that day in January on the marsh,' he said. 'Trying to think what it was that upset you so suddenly. Then I remembered. I touched your breast.'

Her eyes turned fearful then, and all at once he knew the disturbing ideas that had kept creeping into his mind at night were right. By day he could dismiss them – she was after all very earthy, she could talk about bodily functions without embarrassment, she wasn't nervous or shy. Yet she always called a halt when kissing became too passionate. She didn't press her body against his the way other girls he had taken out did.

'It made you remember a man who hurt you at The Firs, didn't it?' he asked, and he could feel tears welling up in his eyes because he couldn't bear the thought.

'Yes,' she gasped. 'But don't ask me any more.'

Michael lay down beside her and drew her into his arms with her head on his shoulder. 'I'm not asking you anything more,' he said gently. 'You are just going to tell me what happened.'

'I can't,' she said, and he felt her shudder as she began to cry.

'I want to marry you, Adele. I want us to be together for ever and have children. How can we do that if there is a ghost of someone evil standing between us?'

He waited a few moments before continuing. 'Your grandmother knows, doesn't she? So you must have told her when you first got there. She was a stranger to you then. I'm not, we've known each other for going on five years. You aren't just my love, but my best friend too.'

'It was the warden,' she suddenly blurted out, covering her face with her hands. 'I thought he was wonderful because he took a special interest in me. No one had ever been that way with me before.'

She poured it out in a fast torrent once she got started, but kept her hands over her face. Michael didn't interrupt her, but just let it flow out. When she'd finished, she sobbed and sobbed while he held her.

Michael was deeply shocked. He couldn't imagine how any man could do such a thing to a child in his care. But it did make sense of so many aspects of Adele's personality. When he first met her he'd found it curious that she appeared to have no other friends when she was so likable. He also found her very mature for her age, yet it was a maturity mixed with a don't-come-too-close manner.

Looking back, Michael was sure he'd loved her right from the start for she was always on his mind, but that manner of hers, lack of experience with girls on his part, and of course his circumstances had prevented anything more than friendship. Yet it shamed him to think how he had gone off to the Continent, then to Oxford, blithely enjoying himself, flying planes, drinking with his friends, even taking other girls out, while his friend had that secret locked inside her. He had let her take care of his mother, which not only subjected her to more ill-treatment, but prevented her from having any fun and a life of her own. And now, acting like an amateur psychiatrist, he might have hurt her even more.

'Have I made it worse?' he whispered to her, feeling utterly helpless at seeing her so upset.

She gave a hiccupping sob. 'I thought I'd put it behind me. I never thought about it.'

'But it came back when I touched you?' he whispered, tears running down his cheeks too. 'I'm so sorry, darling.'

'Don't you be sorry,' she said in a small voice. 'You couldn't know, any more than I could. It took me by surprise and I didn't know how to deal with it.'

She sat up then and blew her nose and dried her eyes. She turned back to him and tried to smile. 'I bet you wish you hadn't pestered me to tell you now?'

'Yes. No, I really don't know,' he said sadly. 'I have to believe it's better to have no secrets between us, but I'll be afraid to ever touch you again.'

'You mustn't be,' she said, taking his hand in hers and kissing his fingers. 'It's all different now, that other time it just caught me unawares. It's out now, over.'

They sat side by side, hands linked, for some time. It was such a clear day they could see for miles over a patchwork of fields. Behind them beneath the cliff they could hear the sea pounding on the rocks, seagulls wheeled and squawked overhead. The sun was warm on their heads, the breeze soft on their faces, and as they sat there silently, Michael could sense that Adele was glad she'd finally been able to tell him.

'You are lovely, Michael,' she said suddenly, lifting one hand and running it down his cheek. 'So patient, so understanding. If I had known it would feel this good to let all that out, I would have done it long ago.'

Michael was deeply touched. 'There's a time for everything. I probably wouldn't have understood if you'd told me before. Loving you has made me understand a great many things better, even my parents.'

Adele nodded. 'I understand a little better now why my

grandparents chucked everything up and went to live on the marsh. I used to look at Granny's lovely things and imagine what their old home in Tunbridge Wells was like. I even felt cross that she didn't live like that any more. But I don't feel like that now, just the way she is sometimes tells me she and Frank had the kind of love most of us want.'

'That's what's wrong with my parents,' Michael said thoughtfully. 'I don't think they ever really loved each other. Mother was beautiful and much admired, and Father was rich, ambitious and shrewd. They married because everyone else thought they were a good match. I don't suppose they ever stopped to think that they hadn't got a single thing in common.'

He had told Adele the previous day that nothing had been resolved between his parents. They were both equally unyielding. When Emily got proof that Myles had a mistress, rather than divorce him, she insisted he came down to Winchelsea every other weekend so she could pretend to her friends that there was nothing wrong with their marriage.

Myles played along with this charade because he was afraid Emily might start a scandal which could jeopardize his legal career. Michael despaired of them, and he was sick of being stuck in the middle with loyalties on both sides.

Adele knew that when the Baileys did find out that she and Michael were not only still seeing each other, but planning a future together, there would be an uproar. His parents were at least united in thinking she wasn't good enough for their son. But Michael didn't seem concerned about that.

'Were you serious about wanting to marry me?' she asked.

'Of course,' he said, looking surprised she thought otherwise. 'But we'll have to wait until you've finished your training.'

'And saved some money,' she laughed.

'But we could get engaged,' he said eagerly. 'This summer when you are nineteen.'

Adele got to her feet and spread her arms out wide with joy. They were just twenty or thirty yards from the cliff edge at Beachy Head. The bright blue cloudless sky, the sea, the white cliffs and the deep green of the grass were so very beautiful it brought a lump to her throat. 'I could scream with happiness,' she said.

'Don't do that,' Michael said nervously as he noticed some ramblers coming in their direction. 'They might think you are about to jump off the cliff.'

'If I did, I'd fly,' she said, and flapping her arms, she ran yelling down over the grass away from the cliff top.

Michael began to laugh then too, relieved that he'd found out the truth, happy that his days at Oxford were now numbered and that soon he'd be flying for a living. He waited until the ramblers were nearly upon him, then he got up, waved his arms wide and ran full tilt down to Adele. He hoped the ramblers would think they were a pair of escaped lunatics.

Two months later, in June, Honour washed and dried the tea things, then switched on the wireless to listen to the six o'clock news. Michael had brought round the battery wireless for her a few weeks earlier. He said someone he knew in Oxford was throwing it out, though she didn't believe that, it looked too new. But wherever it came from, she loved it. The evenings flew by listening to plays and comedy programmes.

She sat down in her chair and picked up her knitting. She thought perhaps Michael was right in suggesting she ought to get the electricity put on too. Oil lamps and candles were all very well, but the light wasn't really bright enough for reading now that her sight wasn't quite so sharp.

The news was as gloomy as it always seemed to be these days. More about Germany invading Austria and all Austrian Jews being given two weeks' notice by their employers. Just the previous week she and Adele had gone to the pictures together and had seen Adolf Hitler on the Pathe News. Honour had of course seen his picture in the papers, but to see him in action on a screen brought home to her what a real threat he was. He was filmed at some kind of rally, shouting and bawling with his eyes rolling and his arms waving like a madman's. She couldn't think why anyone should want to follow such a nasty little man, and as for those ridiculous salutes everyone gave him! If she was in Germany she'd be tempted to give him a very rude salute with two fingers.

Adele had made her laugh when they got home by sticking a bit of black wool under her nose and goose-stepping round the living room in an imitation of him. Yet however much they laughed about this man, and however much the Government insisted England would not be drawn into another war with Germany, Honour wasn't convinced.

The final piece of news on the wireless was a little jollier. A new zoo had been opened in Regent's Park, and they said it was the biggest and finest in the world. She thought she would like to go and see it. Perhaps she and Adele could go on the train later in the summer.

A rapping on the front door took her by surprise. It was extremely rare for anyone to call on her in the evening.

'Who on earth could that be?' she muttered to herself, irritated at being interrupted when she'd just got comfortable.

She opened the door, and there stood a woman. She looked a real floozy, in a bright blue dress that was too tight, with red lipstick, blonde hair, very high-heeled shoes and no stockings or hat.

'Yes?' Honour asked, wondering how anyone dressed that way could be wandering around the countryside.

The woman just smirked at her, and Honour realized there was something strangely familiar about her. 'Do I know you?' she asked.

'I should say so,' the woman replied. 'I *am* your daughter!'

Honour reeled back in shock. Yet she knew it had to be true, for the only person she'd ever known with eyes that particular blue was Rose. 'W-w-what are you d-d-doing here?' she stuttered, feeling quite faint.

'I came to see you, Mother,' Rose said, giving the last word a sarcastic twist.

'I don't want to see you,' Honour said quickly, trying to pull herself together. 'You lost all right to visit my home the day you stole my things and disappeared.'

'I thought you might have mellowed as you took Adele in,' Rose said, and walked in, closing the door behind her, before Honour could stop her. 'Where is she?'

Honour had never seriously considered that Rose might come here one day, and now she was suddenly frightened. The Rose who had walked out of here going on twenty years ago might have been defiant, insensitive and heartless, but she had been softly spoken and well-mannered. This Rose was coarse in both voice and behaviour, and for once in her life, Honour was intimidated.

'She's working,' she said, giving her daughter the kind of look that would once have made her quake. 'And I haven't mellowed towards you. I don't know how you've got the nerve to come here after all this time.'

Rose merely smirked, opened her handbag and took out a packet of cigarettes. 'Everything's just the same,' she said as she lit one and gazed reflectively round the room. 'You, the cottage and the furniture. It's like time's stood still for nearly twenty years. I thought you'd be really old and wrinkly, but you don't look so bad.'

Honour was astounded at her insolence. 'Clear off,' she said. 'Go on, go. I don't want you in here.'

'I'll go when I'm ready,' Rose said, languidly exhaling smoke. 'I have a perfect right to come and ask about my daughter.'

'You don't,' Honour retorted. She wasn't used to feeling afraid and she didn't know how to deal with it. Even when desperate out-of-work men used to come to the door asking for something to eat, she had never lost her nerve. She sensed Rose had come to make mischief, for if her motive had been purely to see Adele, surely she would have used charm rather than menace.

She supposed that most people would consider Rose still very attractive, considering she was thirty-seven now. She was much heavier than she'd been at seventeen, but her figure was still good and her eyes very beautiful. But she looked so hard and brassy, her skin had a greyish tone, her teeth were dingy and even her blonde hair had lost its silky sheen.

'You lost all rights to Adele when you were committed to an asylum,' Honour said firmly. She wasn't going to let herself be browbeaten. 'If I'd only known you had ill-treated her before that, I would have come and taken her away. So don't think for one moment you are going to walk back into her life and undo all the good I've done.'

'Who said anything about walking back into her life? I only want to know about her,' Rose shot back.

'You escaped from the asylum. Where did you go?' Honour asked.

Rose perched on the arm of the couch and crossed her legs, flicking her cigarette ash towards the stove and missing. 'Back to London, where else?' she said.

Honour snatched the cigarette from her fingers and put it in the stove. 'How did you live?'

'A bit of this, a bit of that,' Rose said vaguely. 'I got by.'

Honour's hackles rose. That sounded very much as if she'd been selling herself on the streets, and to look at her that seemed very possible.

'And your husband? Jim Talbot. Where is he?'

Rose shrugged. 'How would I know? He scarpered when

they put me away. Now, tell me about Adele. Have you got a photo of her?'

'No, I haven't,' Honour snapped. 'She's training to be a nurse. She's happy. So get on your way and don't come back.'

'Is she courting?' Rose asked, as calmly as if she hadn't heard what Honour said.

'She has a young man, yes,' Honour said starchily. 'A very nice young man too. And I am not going to tell you where she is nursing, so don't bother to ask. The last thing she would want is you turning up to see her.'

'How do you know that?' Rose sneered. 'I bet you've smothered her, the way you did me. Girls don't like that, you know.'

'I did not smother you.' Honour's voice rose indignantly.

'Yes you did. I had to eat what you said, do what you said, go where you said. I never got a choice about anything. You dragged me away from a nice school and home, to here!' Rose's eyes flashed dangerously. '"We're going to live in the country, and it will be such a big adventure,"' she said, mimicking Honour speaking in a simpering way. 'Country! It's a bloody marsh, with the wind howling and not a soul for miles. Adventure! It was hell. What sort of a mother were you?'

'You loved it when we came for holidays,' Honour said defensively. 'Maybe it didn't turn out to be all your father and I hoped, but when we lost the shop we really had no other choice.'

'Oh yes we did, we could have lived with Grandma,' Rose retorted, and smirked as if she'd won a couple of points. 'I was eleven then, remember, not a baby. I heard things, saw things, I knew what was going on. You and Father might have been happy without all our relatives and friends around us, but I wasn't. Why didn't Father get a job like anyone else?'

'Do you really think you are in any position to criticize

your father's actions, in the light of what you did to Adele?' Honour asked. 'She was twelve when her sister was killed, and you blamed her for it. Later you tried to kill her. When she turned up at my door she was so sick I thought she was going to die. I thought she'd be scarred for life after what she'd been through. You did that to her and you'd known nothing but love from the moment you were born.'

Honour paused just long enough to catch her breath. 'I know what your game is, Rose. You're trying to suggest that your wilful neglect of Adele is somehow my fault, and that I owe you something now. Well, it won't wash. You were the selfish little baggage that robbed your parents and ran away with a fancy man. I had to listen to your father crying for you when he was dying, and I can never forgive you for that.'

'When did he die?'

'January 1921,' Honour spat at her. 'He began to get his wits back after you'd gone, sometimes I wished he hadn't because then he wouldn't have known what you'd done. The war broke his spirit, but you broke his heart.'

It was only then that Rose dropped her defiant and insolent stance. 'When I left I meant to send you money,' she said. 'But nothing worked out like I planned. You don't know what I went through.'

'Oh yes I do,' Honour said. 'You ran off with a rich man and you thought he'd marry you. But he skedaddled once he knew there was a baby on the way. You married Jim Talbot so you wouldn't end up in the workhouse. Then you spent the whole of Adele's childhood making her pay for your mistakes.'

She knew by Rose's expression that she was right.

'You can do whatever you like in this world,' Honour said. 'But there's one drawback. You have to deal with the consequences. You can't blame anyone else for those.'

'Just tell me how Adele is and I'll go,' Rose said sullenly. 'That's all I want, nothing more. Did she do well at school?'

'Yes, she did, she's a bright girl, just as you were.' Honour said sternly. 'It was hard when she left school, there wasn't much work, but she got a job as a housekeeper and now she's a year into her nurse's training. She loves it, she was born to be a nurse.'

'And what does she look like now?'

'She's tall, about five feet six, her hair's light brown, and she's lovely,' Honour said with some pride. 'Not a beauty in the way you were, but people take to her, she's a kind, hardworking, happy girl. And if you want to do something right for her at last, stay away.'

To her surprise Rose didn't come back with any cheek. 'I'll go now,' she said, getting up. 'I'm sorry if I upset you.'

Honour nodded and opened the door. She didn't trust herself to speak, not even to ask how Rose was intending to get back to London.

Rose left without another word, clip-clopping over the pebbles in her high-heeled shoes. After Honour had closed the front door, she went to the back door. Through the bushes she could see her daughter walking down the lane. She stooped momentarily to light a cigarette, then continued. It was only once she knew Rose had got to the end of the lane and the main road that she felt she could breathe again.

Her legs felt weak and shaky, she was sweating and her heart was thumping. As she closed the back door and locked it, she began to cry. She had never felt so terribly alone, or so frightened.

Chapter Fifteen

At the end of the lane, a black Ford was parked up by the river. Johnny Galloway had his arm leaning on the open window. Rose walked over to the car and got into the passenger seat.

'Did you see 'er?' Johnny asked.

'I saw my mother,' she replied grimly. 'But not Adele. She was working.'

Johnny Galloway was a spiv from South London. He had the look of a ferret, small and wiry, with oiled black hair slicked back from his face and a penchant for loud checked suits. He had the tenacious manner of a ferret too, holding on to Rose for dear life and pandering to her every whim.

They had met some three months ago in The Grapes, a Soho pub close to the restaurant where Rose worked as a waitress. She had known Johnny was a villain, but then most of the men who drank in The Grapes were. He was also illiterate, but he was smart enough to hide his criminal activities behind the front of a couple of legal businesses in Rotherhithe. That first night he plied her with drink until closing time, kept telling her how beautiful she was, and later paid for her taxi home without insisting he came too. In Rose's book that made him a prime prospect.

Rose had never had any qualms about going to bed with a man if that was what it took to open his wallet. But she had realized after only a couple of drinks that Johnny was different to most men. He was the type who was at his most generous and attentive during the chase, so Rose had given him a good one. She arranged to meet him, then stood him up. She would kiss him passionately, then tell him she couldn't go any further until she was quite sure of him. Sometimes on dates she barely said a word to him, on others she sparkled like a diamond.

She knew she intrigued him; other men had remarked that she was a fascinating combination of lady and whore with her posh voice, good manners and sensuality. But for Johnny she'd added another dimension to her character, that of a good woman who had been wronged.

By letting it slip that her husband had her committed to an asylum to get his hands on her money, she evoked Johnny's sympathy. When she laughingly spoke of her subsequent escape she portrayed herself as wily and brave. Johnny chose to think her heavy drinking was due to her grief at one daughter dying and the other being taken into her mother's care, and that was fine by her.

What she hadn't expected, though, was that Johnny had a soft heart. He got the idea that if Rose could be reunited with Adele the sadness of her past would be wiped out. She raised all the objections she could think of, including that her mother would have told Adele a great many lies to make her hate Rose. But Johnny insisted that if she were just to turn up on the doorstep, without any prior warning, Adele would see for herself what her grandmother had been doing.

Rose found herself in a tricky situation. She was scared stiff of seeing her mother, and she had no real desire to see Adele, apart from natural curiosity about how she'd turned out. But she knew that if she didn't do what Johnny suggested, he would find it strange, perhaps even suspect she'd been lying to him. She didn't want to lose him, he bought her nice presents and gave her a good time. So this morning when he'd suggested a drive down to Rye, she felt unable to back away.

Once she got to the cottage she could of course have turned away and told Johnny there was no one in, but for some reason she didn't understand, she felt compelled to go through with it. Whether that was out of curiosity or just faint hope her mother would be overjoyed to see her, she couldn't say.

'Was yer mum all right with you?' Johnny asked, lighting two cigarettes and giving one to her.

'No, she was a right cow,' Rose retorted, inhaling deeply on the cigarette because she was still trembling from the ordeal. 'She was always as mad as hell that my father left me his money and not her. I don't think she really believed that Jim made off with it after he'd got me committed either. Now she wants to keep my Adele from me out of spite. She seems to forget I've had to live in a slum and work my fingers to the bone just to send money for them.'

Johnny put his arm around her shoulder, his narrow face wreathed in sympathy. 'Don't get upset about it, luv,' he said. 'At least you tried. When yer daughter gets 'ome and 'ears you bin there, she'll be pleased as punch.'

'I don't expect the old bag will even tell her,' Rose said dourly. 'I knew it was a stupid thing to do. I shouldn't have listened to you.'

'Don't you go giving up just yet,' he said. 'You caught 'er on the 'op. My old lady used to chew me ear off every time I went 'ome, blamed me for every bloody thing that went wrong in 'er life, but she'd sleep on it, and the next day she'd be as nice as ninepence. Now, if we was to stay down 'ere tonight you could go back in the morning when she's 'ad time to think it over. I betcha she'll be okay then.'

Rose put her head on Johnny's shoulder and forced herself to cry because she wanted his sympathy for the hostility she'd got from her mother. She had of course expected it, and if nothing else it bore out her long-held conviction that the woman was totally heartless.

But she hadn't expected to feel confused.

Everything had been so cut and dried in her mind before going through that door. She wanted confirmation that her childhood home was a hovel; that the child she'd never loved was unlovable. That her life would have been very much worse if she'd never run away from home.

But the cottage wasn't a hovel. Primitive certainly, not one modern amenity, yet it was clean and bright with a rustic charm, flowers on the table, a smell of polish and soap in the air. It brought back so many memories she didn't want. And her mother must have found something to love in Adele, because why else would she have been so fiercely protective of her?

'There, there,' Johnny said comfortingly. 'Why don't we go into 'Astings and find a guest house for the night? We could go on the pier and 'ave a good time. 'Astings is a good place, I used to go there when I was a nipper.'

Rose didn't want a night of forced gaiety with Johnny in Hastings, and she certainly didn't want to have to share a bed with him. But if she insisted on going back to London tonight, he'd be disappointed and suspicious. It seemed better to pretend she was weighing up the possibility of going back to see her mother tomorrow, even though she had no intention of doing such a thing.

She sniffed and dried her eyes with a handkerchief. 'I don't know if I'm brave enough to try again,' she said. 'But maybe I'll feel differently in the morning.'

Johnny's face lit up. 'That's my girl! So it's off to the bright lights of 'Astings then?'

'Why not just go to Winchelsea?' she said, pointing it out up on the hill. 'I expect we could get a room at the pub there. We'll have to say we're Mr and Mrs Galloway though!'

He beamed, his little shoe-button black eyes almost disappearing. 'That'll be a pleasure, sweetheart,' he said.

In less than half an hour, Rose and Johnny were sitting in the bar of The Bridge Inn, Johnny with a pint of beer and Rose with a large rum and black. She didn't really know why she'd suggested staying here, perhaps it was a touch of nostalgia because she had often sat outside here with her father when she was small, him with a pint and her with a glass of lemonade. But the room was luxurious by her standards, all pink chintz with a big soft bed. All she needed now was to get some drink down her so she could show some enthusiasm for sharing it with Johnny, so she merely put on more makeup, brushed her hair and made for the bar.

'Don't you go letting it slip I'm local,' she warned him in a whisper as they sat down with their drinks. 'I don't want it to get back to my Adele that I was staying here with a man.'

'Okay,' he said, though he looked a little puzzled. 'But what if someone recognizes you?'

'That's not likely,' she said. 'I wasn't much more than a kid when I left here. But should anyone start talking to us, just go along with whatever I say.'

But no one did speak to them, not even the fat girl who waddled over to collect their dirty glasses.

'We should've gone to Hastings,' Johnny said after his fourth pint. The pub was as quiet as a church, the old men sitting in companionable silence, the only sounds that of the snap of dominoes on a table, the odd cough or a subdued welcome to a newcomer. Even the few dogs lying at their masters' feet were passive. 'We could've got fish and chips and gone on the pier. I don't reckon much on this place at all.'

Rose didn't reckon much on the pub either, even if it was quaint, yet as a child she had thought Winchelsea was wonderful. It consisted of little more than one street, a pub and a couple of shops, but the old houses and cottages were all so different, the gardens so pretty and the people could be relied on to speak to her.

She could remember coming up here on a message, and being excited by the post office which was packed with goods from floor to ceiling. It was very dark, but sold everything from knitting wool, mops and buckets to sweets. She could be in there for over an hour contemplating the many glass sweet jars with their delectable contents, before she finally decided what to spend her penny on.

She used to dream of it being her shop, weighing up the sweets on the big brass scale and putting them in the little paper cones.

But then she'd always wished they lived here too. To be able to swing on a garden gate and chat to people who walked by. Her mother had a friend here whom they used to visit sometimes, and that house had always reminded her of her grandmother's in Tunbridge Wells. Rose couldn't remember much about it now, except there was a big piano and a lovely garden. She wondered if she'd be able to recognize it if she walked along the road.

Both she and Johnny got a bit drunk, and before Rose knew it they were ringing the bell for closing time. As they went upstairs to their room Rose considered pretending to pass out so she didn't have to have sex with Johnny.

Fortunately Johnny became so excited the minute she got into bed beside him that he came before even getting inside her. He fell asleep immediately afterwards and Rose sighed with relief.

She was tired and drunk, but even though the bed was very comfortable, she couldn't drop off. It was too quiet, the only sound was the soft rustling of the curtains moving slightly in the breeze through the open window, reminding her sharply of summer nights as a child. She remembered how her father always crept into her bedroom before he and her mother turned in. He would tuck the covers round her more firmly, kiss her forehead, and close the window if it was windy or raining.

Rose had guessed her father was dead when they brought the guardianship papers to her in the asylum, as only Honour's name was on them. She hadn't reacted at all then, for she could only think of him as he was when she last saw him, a pathetic wretch who could do nothing for himself. She was just glad he was out of his misery.

But now, perhaps because of the memories this place evoked, and her mother's angry words earlier, she suddenly felt a pang of remorse. She could picture him now as he was when she and her mother saw him off at the station when he went to France. He was leaning out of the train window, smiling and blowing them kisses. He had never been distant or stern like other girls' fathers. He'd always been so warm, vibrant and loving. An intelligent, kindly man who saw life as something to be enjoyed to the full. 'My two best girls,' he used to say as he hugged them. It was sad that he'd spent the last couple of years of his life not knowing where she was.

'Wotcha wanna do today?' Johnny said over breakfast the following morning.

The landlady had laid up a table in the bar, and the sunshine was streaming through the open windows. Johnny looked pleased with himself – if he'd had a tail he'd have been wagging it. There had of course been more sex that morning, and Rose was too sleepy to find an excuse. Yet to her surprise she had enjoyed it, he'd taken her mind right off the past, and the prospect of spending the whole weekend with him was looking far more attractive than she'd expected.

'I don't think there's anything to be gained by going back to my mother's,' she said as she scraped up the last of the egg yolk with a piece of toast. 'I'll try writing to her instead. Let's go to Hastings, it's another lovely day and we should make the most of it.'

'That's my girl,' Johnny said with a broad grin. 'I'll show you what a crack shot I am on the rifle range.'

'I think I'd like to take a little walk first,' Rose said thoughtfully. 'You know, just look at the place again, see what's changed.'

'You go on yer own then,' he said. 'I'll stay here, pay the

bill and sit in the sun till you come back. That is, unless you want me along?'

'No, I'd rather be alone,' she said. One thing she had always liked about Johnny was that he always sensed when she wanted to be alone. He hadn't insisted on coming into her mother's like some men would do. Rose often thought that if all men understood that need in her, she might have kept relationships going longer.

She was transported back in time as she walked along the main street. The roses around the cottage doors, cats basking in the sun on window-sills, the mellow red of old pantiles, and front doors propped open to let in fresh air – everything the same as it was all those years ago when she was a small child. Rye had always seemed such a wide-awake place, full of people, bustle and sounds. Winchelsea was its sleepy neighbour, and even now on a Saturday morning there were only a few people about: a couple of women with shopping baskets making for the shop, an old man with a walking stick taking the air. She could hear a wireless through one open window, and the sounds of children playing in a garden, but it was so quiet she could also hear the birds singing and the buzz of insects.

She recognized the house she used to go to with her mother immediately, and the faded painted sign of Harrington House reminded her of other things. The lady there often gave her mother her own daughter's outgrown clothes. Rose could remember a blue velvet dress that she had adored. But she rarely got a chance to wear it, not living down on the marsh.

The only thing that was different about the little town was cars. She supposed there must have been some when she was a child, but she didn't remember any. There were several now, including a sleek black one right outside Harrington House.

She remembered then that the lady there had been called Mrs Whitehouse. She had always jokingly called her Mrs Red

House, to her mother at least, because the bricks on the lady's house were red.

Crossing over, she walked back up the street to buy some more cigarettes in the post office. She was disappointed to find it wasn't quite the same any more; there were still as many jars of sweets on the shelves, and knitting wool too, but it didn't have that stuffed-to-capacity look she remembered.

She bought a packet of Woodbines, and for old times' sake a picture postcard of Winchelsea.

'You've brought the sunshine with you,' the woman behind the counter said with a smile. 'They say it's going to last for a few days yet.'

The woman was about the same age as Rose, fat with a red, jolly face and black hair pulled back tightly. She didn't have a Sussex accent so Rose was absolutely certain she wasn't someone she'd been to school with.

'I used to come here as a child,' Rose confided. 'It's all still exactly the same.'

'Nothing much ever happens here,' the woman replied with a slight grimace, as if she held it against the place. 'My hubby and I bought this shop ten years ago now, and I bet I could tell you every single event in that time.' She laughed merrily. 'You'd be bored though, it would only be about who was born, married or died.'

Rose felt like lingering and hearing about people she had once known. 'There used to be a lady called Mrs Whitehouse in Harrington House. Is she still living there?' she asked.

'No, she and her husband died a while ago,' the shopkeeper replied. 'Their daughter lives there now.'

Rose realized this daughter must be the one-time owner of the blue velvet dress, and that intrigued her. 'What's she like?' she asked. 'I seem to remember her as being very beautiful and elegant, but that was a long time ago.'

'Oh, she's still that.' The woman smiled. 'A bit cuckoo though.'

'In what way?' Rose inquired.

The shopkeeper leaned her elbows on her counter, obviously glad to share a bit of gossip. 'Everyone knows she's separated from her husband, but she pretends everything's hunky dory between them. He comes down here from their old home just for the odd weekend, I suppose that's to make things look better.'

Rose thought if she kept this woman chatting she could maybe ask a few questions about her mother and Adele. 'Why would a separated couple want to pretend they are still together?' she asked.

'Well, Mr Bailey is a barrister,' the woman said.

The hairs on the back of Rose's neck suddenly rose at that name.

'I dare say he's worried about a scandal,' the woman continued. 'Important men are like that, so I've heard tell.'

'What did you say his name was?' Rose asked. It surely couldn't be the Mr Bailey she knew. Yet he had been a lawyer, and he did once say he had a relative in Winchelsea.

'Bailey, Myles Bailey,' the woman said. Then, perhaps seeing the shock on Rose's face, she blushed. 'Oh Gawd. My hubby's always telling me I should think before I open my mouth. Do you know him?'

'No. No, I don't,' Rose said hurriedly. 'I used to know another Bailey around here. But it wouldn't be the same family. I must go now, someone's waiting for me.'

As she stepped out of the shop into the hot sun, Rose felt sick. She rushed over the road to the pub, and sat down on the bench outside in the shade, opening her handbag with trembling hands to find her cigarettes.

Bailey was a common name, but Myles certainly wasn't. It had to be him, even though she knew he lived somewhere in Hampshire at the time she met him. When he said he had a relative in Winchelsea she had assumed it was a very distant one. But then she supposed a man intent on seducing a young waitress would hardly be likely to tell her it was his in-laws, when he hadn't yet admitted he was married.

'There you are!' Johnny's voice from the pub doorway made her jump. ''Ad a good look round?'

She nodded, feeling unable to speak.

'You all right, girl?' he asked, coming closer and peering at her. 'You're as white as a sheet!'

'I feel a bit queasy,' she said. 'That fried breakfast after all the drink last night, I expect. Could you get me a glass of water?'

Chapter Sixteen

Honour smiled to herself as she stood at the sink in the scullery. Michael was with Adele in the garden, sitting on a rug under the apple tree, and she guessed that the tiny parcel he was just giving her held an engagement ring.

It felt like a good omen that the sun had come out again for Adele's nineteenth birthday. It seemed to have been raining ever since the hot spell in June when Rose had suddenly appeared. Honour had been feeling very low since then, half expecting that her daughter would appear again.

She wished she had managed to establish why and how she came. It must have been by car, the bus had gone earlier, and she surely couldn't have walked from Rye in those high heels. What did she really want? Was it forgiveness, or something more sinister?

If it was forgiveness she certainly hadn't made any effort to win it. Perhaps she'd merely been passing in a man friend's car and felt compelled to call in? But would any reasonable person call at a place where they weren't sure of a welcome?

Because she couldn't rationalize why her daughter had called, Honour felt unable to tell Adele about it. Yet neither could she forget about the visit, it was like having a sore place in her mouth which her tongue kept visiting.

Yet Rose couldn't have been seriously intent on seeing her daughter again or she would at least have sent a birthday card today.

In view of that, perhaps she was right to keep it to herself.

Adele's cry of delight made Honour cast her more gloomy thoughts aside and look back at the couple in the garden. She thought the sight would make a wonderful picture,

Michael kneeling up on the rug, looking so dashing in his new RAF uniform, and Adele as pretty as a May morning in a pink and white print dress, gasping with delight at the ring he was putting on her finger.

Honour wiped a stray tear from her face with the corner of her apron. The engagement ring Frank had given her was made of daisies, as he knew he'd have to ask her father's permission to marry her before a real one could be bought. They had been at a tennis party and had given the chaperone the slip that afternoon, and if it was found out they'd been lying in long grass kissing each other they would have been in serious trouble.

She had wanted Frank with intense passion from the very first kiss; it was only through lack of opportunity that she was still a virgin on their wedding day. Honour sensed that Adele and Michael felt that way too. She could feel a current flowing between them, they reached out for each other's hands all the time, their bodies seemed to sway together as they walked. It was going to be hard for them to have a long engagement, but with the threat of war growing each day, getting married quickly was not a sensible thing to do.

'Granny!' Adele called out. 'Come and see!'

Honour glanced in a small mirror and arranged her face in an expression of 'Whatever now?'

'I'm busy,' she said with pretended crossness as she stepped out of the back door.

'Not too busy to see this,' Adele thrilled out, her voice shrill with excitement. 'Michael's asked me to marry him and he's bought me a ring.'

It was a beautiful ring, a single sapphire surrounded by tiny diamonds, and Honour knew it must have cost a fortune. It was on the tip of her tongue to say Michael would have been wiser to have kept the money in a bank for when they were married, but the expression on his face stopped her.

He was looking at her granddaughter with such tenderness

and joy that Honour couldn't diminish his gift. 'It's beautiful,' she said instead. 'And I hope you'll always be as happy together as you are now.'

'You don't object then?' Michael said anxiously. 'Maybe I should've asked you first, but I didn't know how.'

'I couldn't be happier,' Honour said, feeling a little dizzy with the unexpected emotions washing over her. 'You'll make a fine husband for my granddaughter. I couldn't have chosen anyone better myself.'

Michael had thought of everything, it seemed, he even had a bottle of champagne in his car packed in a box of ice and a set of real champagne glasses. Honour would once have thought that was suspiciously suave, but she knew this lad and guessed he had spent many long weeks planning it all, not to be flashy but to make Adele feel really special.

They drank the champagne in the garden, and Adele was soon very giggly as it went straight to her head. They chatted idly, about Michael's flying and Adele's nursing.

'I don't want to cloud your happiness,' Honour said a little later. 'But when are you going to tell your parents, Michael?'

'Tomorrow,' he said firmly. 'Father's coming down for the weekend along with Ralph and Diana and their other halves and children. There will never be a better moment. I'm going to suggest that the next time they are all there again, Mother invites Adele too so she can meet them all formally.'

Honour felt a pang of fear, even though Michael looked supremely confident. 'Good for you, Michael,' she said.

A look of anxiety swept across Adele's face though. 'What if . . .' she said, and then faltered.

Michael took her hand in his. 'I don't care if they don't approve,' he said firmly. 'It will be their loss not mine if they can't welcome you to our family. I won't have anything more to do with any of them.'

Honour admired his courage and said so. 'But take it easy,'

she warned him. 'It takes a while for any parent to accept that their child is old enough to pick a wife or husband. You might be wiser to leave them to mull it over before insisting that Adele is invited to your mother's home.'

'Granny's right,' Adele agreed. 'I couldn't bear to go there until I'm sure they've come round. I'd be happier just meeting your mother again first.'

'Mother will be all right,' Michael said, reaching out and touching Adele's cheek. 'I told her a few weeks ago that I'd been seeing you.'

'You didn't say!' Adele said indignantly.

Michael smiled. 'Do you tell me absolutely everything?'

Adele grinned. 'I only leave out boring things. That wasn't boring. What did she say?'

'Not a great deal, but she certainly didn't go off the deep end.'

'But your father won't see it like that, he'll only remember that I was your mother's housekeeper, and rude to him too.'

'Maybe so, but he's not entirely unreasonable,' Michael insisted. 'These aren't Victorian times, there's a war brewing too, and he's shrewd enough to realize I'll only become more determined if he opposes me.'

Michael felt very confident during the family dinner on Saturday night. His parents were both in mellow moods, both his brother and sister seemed pleased to be here with their families, and Mrs Salloway, his mother's housekeeper, had surpassed herself by making a truly delicious meal of steak and kidney pie served with fresh vegetables grown in the garden.

They had all spent the afternoon on the beach with the children, who had then been fed in the kitchen and were now in bed. The lighted candles on the table, the gleaming silverware, and the soft, warm breeze coming through the open windows were setting a tranquil scene for his announcement.

He wasn't that bothered for himself if they opposed the marriage. Three years at Oxford, and now mixing with men from all walks of life in the RAF, had made him very aware that he could manage quite well without his family.

In fact sometimes he hoped for an excuse to distance himself from all of them for he was sick and tired of his parents' ridiculous games with each other. He also found Ralph and Diana's snobbishness appalling.

But for Adele's sake he was going to give it his best shot. He didn't want her to feel second-rate or shamed. She was a far better person than all his family put together, and just the thought that they might look down on her as being somehow inferior made him angry.

His eyes flitted around the table. His father at the head, slurping down yet another glass of red wine, as if excess drink would make the weekend go faster and he could get back to see his mistress. Diana next to him, still toying with her food, was a younger version of their mother in looks, the same reddish-gold hair and blue eyes and her blue chiffon dress gave her the same elegant prettiness. Sadly, she had inherited their father's pomposity, and his abrasive manner.

Her husband David next to her was unprepossessing, thin with stooped shoulders, a weak chin and thinning sandy hair, but then he hadn't needed looks to attract Diana – his family's wealth did that.

Ralph's wife Laura, sitting beside Michael, had put on a lot of weight recently and with her blonde hair arranged in loose curls she looked cherubic. Michael liked Laura; she was lazy, especially when dealing with her children, but a good woman nevertheless, who deserved better than bullying Ralph for a husband, and she looked pretty tonight in pale green silk.

Ralph, the other side of Laura, was on his second or third helping of food, stuffing it in as if he hadn't eaten for a week. He too was putting on weight fast, something Diana had pointed out earlier. But then he was greedy in every way, for money, food and attention.

Then finally his mother at the foot of the table, as immaculate as ever, her hair swept sternly back off her face and arranged in two sleek coils at the sides of her head. Michael assumed that was the latest fashionable hair-style, even if it did give her the look of a telephonist, for she studied fashion magazines constantly. She was wearing a lilac dress with little-girl puffed sleeves. Michael had noticed she always wore something that gave her a slightly young and vulnerable look when Father was visiting. But at least she had laid off the wine tonight and perhaps that was because Myles had been quite pleasant to her all day.

Michael could not imagine Adele having anything in common with any of them, except perhaps Laura.

Mrs Salloway came into the room and began collecting up the empty plates. Michael approved of this excellent housekeeper; her cooking was first class, she was calm and pleasant, and she handled his mother's moods very well.

'The steak and kidney pie was marvellous, Mrs Salloway,' he said. He always strived to show his appreciation of her as no one else ever did. 'What treat have we got for pudding?'

She smiled, her plain lined face lighting up. 'I've made one of my summer puddings,' she said. 'I hope it will be all right, the blackcurrants are almost over now.'

'I'm sure it will be scrumptious,' he said.

When she disappeared back into the kitchen Ralph gave Michael a scornful look. 'Why d'you always suck up to the staff? They get paid for what they do.'

'People need to feel appreciated as well as being paid,' Michael pointed out, trying not to show his irritation at his brother's lack of sensitivity. 'If Mrs Salloway left, mother would be hard pressed to replace her.'

'That's true,' Myles said. 'She might be forced to get another girl like that appalling one from the marshes.'

'She wasn't appalling,' Michael snapped back, horrified that somehow Adele had cropped up before he could make his announcement as he'd planned.

'No she wasn't, Myles,' his mother piped up. 'I missed her when she left. She was bright and gay and had a good heart. Mrs Salloway might be a better housekeeper, but she's very gloomy.'

Michael thought fast. While he was heartened by his mother's support for Adele, she might change tack if he made his announcement immediately. Yet to delay would be a betrayal of his love for Adele.

He took a deep breath. 'I had intended to wait until we'd got to the brandy before telling you my news,' he said, looking around the table. 'But under the circumstances I will tell you it now. Yesterday I asked Adele Talbot to marry me, and she accepted.'

'Who is Adele Talbot?' Diana asked, her sharp nose quivering as if she'd smelled blood.

'The appalling girl from the marshes, no less,' Ralph said with a snort of derision. 'Good God, Michael. You must be having us on!'

'You mean Mummy's old maid?' Diana brayed out. 'Oh surely not, Michael!'

He looked around the table and saw horror on every face. Even Laura, whom he had always counted as an ally, looked shocked beyond belief. His mother looked panicked.

'I knew Adele long before she came here to help Mother out,' he said, trying hard to keep his voice firm. 'I met her when I was sixteen. She was just a friend then, and every one of you should be grateful to her for the way she took care of Mother. She became a nurse after she left here. I kept in touch and our friendship grew into love. She is my fiancée now, and with or without your approval I will marry her.'

'But she's common,' Diana retorted, her mouth twisted into a sneer.

'I wouldn't call her common,' his mother said, giving her daughter a disapproving look. 'I would call her most un-common. My mother thought a great deal of her grand-mother, Honour. She always said it was the most apt name for the woman to have.' She turned to Michael then. 'But I'm sorry, Michael, even if I know Adele is neither common nor appalling, I can't approve of you marrying her. I've got nothing against her personally. But she is most unsuitable for a boy of your background and education.'

'Thank you for that, Mother,' Michael said with heavy sarcasm. 'But what you all consider unsuitable means nothing to me. Suitable to me means a woman I love, respect, and who has the same aims and ambitions. I don't share aims and ambition with anyone in my family. Neither do I see any real love around this table.'

'You are a fool, son,' Myles roared out suddenly. 'You marry some little upstart from the marshes and you'll live to regret it. You've got a fine career ahead of you, but she'll hold you back.'

'How will she hold me back?' Michael asked. 'She's as well read as I am, she speaks the King's English, she can hold a knife and fork properly. She's a kind, good, beautiful person. I can't make that claim about any of you. But I'm not going to argue any further with you, I intend to marry Adele with or without your blessing. If you can't accept her for being the woman I love, then I have nothing more to say to any of you.'

At that point Mrs Salloway came into the room carrying an enormous summer pudding. Clearly she hadn't heard the raised voices as she was smiling. Michael realized there was no way he could sit down again and eat pudding, so he made for the door.

'Where are you going?' his mother cried out, rising from her chair too.

'Away from all of you,' he said sharply. 'To be with people who actually care about my happiness.'

He ran upstairs, threw his belongings into a case, grabbed his uniform and was back downstairs opening the front door, when his mother came rushing out of the dining room. 'Don't go, Michael,' she pleaded, tears in her eyes. 'You're all I've got.'

'I'm not,' he said sharply. 'You've got two other children with unhappy marriages and four grandchildren too.'

'But you know you've always been my special child,' she implored him, wringing her hands. 'I couldn't bear it if I lost you.'

'If you want to keep me, then you must accept Adele,' he said. 'When you can do that, let me know.'

He left then, the sound of her crying ringing in his ears. She was still standing at the open door as he drove away.

By the time Michael had driven down through the Landgate towards the marshes, he knew he was in no fit state to drive back to Biggin Hill. He'd had two large gin and tonics before dinner and then wine. While by no means drunk, he was upset, and it would be folly to risk having an accident.

He thought he would go down to Curlew Cottage. He didn't want Adele to know what had occurred tonight, but she was back at the nurses' home in Hastings, and he was pretty certain Mrs Harris would be sympathetic and give him a bed for the night.

The oil lamp was still glowing in the living room as Michael drew up. She was probably listening to the wireless and he hoped she wouldn't be frightened by a knock on her door so late in the evening.

'It's me, Michael,' he called out as he knocked. 'I'm sorry to disturb you.'

Honour was in her nightclothes as she opened the door. 'Adele went back to Hastings this morning,' she said, looking more surprised than nervous.

'I know,' Michael said, then asked if he could come in.

It struck Michael how different Honour Harris was to anyone in his family as he explained the bare bones of his predicament. She remained totally calm, listening carefully without any interruptions, without even a display of hurt that his family didn't believe her granddaughter was good enough for him.

'I'm so sorry,' Michael finished up. 'You shouldn't have to hear this. I'm ashamed of being related to them all.'

'You can't help that, any more than Adele can help the stock she comes from,' Honour said crisply. 'I'm not surprised at their reaction of course, I expected it. I dare say if I had remained in Tunbridge Wells in the kind of life I had had, I would've been equally bigoted if my daughter had wanted to marry a man outside our social circle.'

She got up, stirred up the stove and put the kettle on.

'Of course you can stay here tonight, Michael. You can sleep in Adele's bed. I very much admire your courage, and your loyalty to my granddaughter, but I want you to think carefully before you cut yourself off from your family.'

'But we can make our own family,' Michael insisted. 'We've already got you. I don't want any of my relatives with their poisonous ideas and their warped views.'

'You may believe that now,' she said as she put tea in the pot. 'But once you have children of your own you may feel differently. I didn't have any brothers or sisters, but I sometimes felt I'd deprived Rose of my parents' love and attention after we left Tunbridge Wells and came here.'

'Are you trying to say you think Adele and I shouldn't marry?' Michael asked incredulously. 'I can't believe someone as strong and forthright as you would bow to my family's ridiculous prejudices.'

'The strongest tree is the one that can bend,' she said tartly. 'I'm not saying you shouldn't marry Adele, but I am advising caution and not burning bridges.'

'Wait, you mean? Hope they'll come round?'

Honour shrugged. 'There's a great deal more to think about than just your parents' views. War is coming, that's almost a certainty. You will be right at the front of it as a pilot. What if you are killed and Adele is left a widow, perhaps even with a child? As long as there is breath left in my body I will help her, but I will be sixty next year. I might not be around.'

'So what do you suggest then?' he asked. 'I can't bring myself to tell Adele how hateful they were. I'm certainly not going back to them cap in hand.'

'First we have a cup of tea,' Honour said with a smile, and disappeared out into the scullery for the cups and milk.

After she'd poured the tea, and given Michael a slice of Adele's birthday cake, she sat down again and looked sternly at him.

'You only have to tell Adele that you told your family of your intentions,' she began. 'You can say they weren't enthusiastic, she doesn't expect them to be anyway. Meanwhile, write to both your mother and father. Say you are saddened by their attitude and ask that they give Adele a chance to show what a special person she is. You could also announce your engagement formally in a newspaper, and plan to marry when Adele has finished her nursing training. That way it makes it quite clear to everyone that you are both entirely serious and committed.'

'And if they still don't come round?' Michael asked.

'You go ahead with the wedding. And you will have to reconcile yourselves to the fact that I'll be the only family guest.'

Chapter Seventeen

January 1939

Michael glanced at Adele as he pulled up outside the Clarendon Hotel in Bayswater. She was biting her lower lip and looking up at the hotel with trepidation. 'Why so scared? I want to make love to you, not chop you into pieces,' he said.

Adele giggled nervously. She certainly wasn't afraid of Michael, he was kind, funny and in her opinion the most handsome RAF officer in England. She also thought she must be the luckiest girl alive to be loved by someone like him.

She thought the hotel looked quite grand too. It had marble steps up to the front door, and black iron railings in front of the basement area. It was only a five-minute walk to Kensington Gardens and in a very nice part of London.

'I'm not scared of you,' she said. 'Only of the people in the hotel not believing we're married.'

'Hotel owners don't care about such things,' Michael said firmly, leaning over to kiss her. 'Especially in London. Lots of the chaps in my squadron have stayed here, and they say the owner has one foot in the grave.'

It was two weeks into the New Year of 1939, and they had been engaged for six months, yet they had spent little of that time together. Adele always seemed to be on duty when Michael got leave, and several times when they'd managed to be off together, Michael's leave was cancelled at the last minute. He sometimes drove down from Biggin Hill and hung around until Adele came off duty, but that often meant they had only a couple of hours before she had to be back in the nurses' home.

It had become tortuous, both of them yearning to be

alone together somewhere warm and comfortable. Sitting in Michael's car parked in a secluded country lane was fine during the summer, but not so inviting on a cold winter's night. They hadn't even had Christmas together, as Adele was on duty, and it was on Christmas Eve, when Michael had driven down to Hastings just to give her a present, that he'd suggested going to a hotel for the night when she got her weekend off in January.

He said he wasn't trying to push her into having sex with him, he only wanted longer with her, away from other people, and Adele knew he meant that. She also knew that however much she'd always intended to wait until they were married, they couldn't. Each time they kissed it got harder and harder to stop at that. She knew that one day they'd get so carried away it would just happen, and almost certainly without taking any precautions.

So it was wiser to plan for it, to go somewhere snug and private, where there would be no going home alone afterwards.

'Are you ready then?' Michael asked, stroking her cheek with one icy-cold hand.

She took his hand and kissed the palm, tickling it with the tip of her tongue. 'Yes, I'm ready. If we stay out here any longer I'll turn into an icicle.'

Michael took charge at the reception desk, talking to the stooped old man and signing the register, while Adele stood well back, trying to look as if she was accustomed to staying in hotels.

It seemed so big to her, with an enormously high ceiling, and the imposing staircase leading off the hallway was reminiscent of the kind she'd seen in films. But the decor was shabby, with scuffed paintwork, chipped varnish and worn carpets, and a faint smell of mould and stale cooking lingered in the air.

'We're right up the top, darling,' Michael said in the posh voice he always used when he was trying to be very grown-up and sophisticated. He picked up their small suitcases and led the way.

They were puffed out by the time they got to the fourth floor, and Adele had to stifle her giggles as a chambermaid paused using the noisy vacuum cleaner to look at them while Michael struggled to open Room 409.

The room was rather dark as the window was small and the ceiling sloped down to it. There was a double bed with a dark blue counterpane, a chest of drawers and wardrobe, and they were all dark wood.

'It's —' Adele exclaimed, then broke off, not knowing exactly how to comment.

'Grim?' Michael suggested.

'No, not grim,' Adele said thoughtfully. 'Maybe basic would be a better word.'

'At least it's got an electric fire,' Michael said, switching on the one-bar heater fitted into an old fireplace.

Adele stood there awkwardly as Michael warmed his hands by the fire. She had thought of nothing but this moment ever since he had telephoned to say he had booked the room. She had planned her wardrobe meticulously, her new camel coat, with the fur tippet Michael had given her for Christmas, best brown high heels and a stylish broad-brimmed hat she had bought from one of the other nurses. All the way on the train to Charing Cross she had been bubbling with excitement, imagining that it would all be seamless, a kind of whirl into romance and passion the minute they got into this room.

But instead she felt peculiar, as if Michael was a suave stranger, not a man she felt she knew inside out.

Michael had announced their engagement in *The Times* back at the end of July. He had said his father liked to think of himself as a very liberal man, and that when friends and relatives got in touch he wouldn't want to admit he didn't approve and would eventually come round.

It had looked that way when soon after the announcement Mrs Bailey wrote to Adele and invited her to tea. Although the chilliness of the invitation suggested she hoped to browbeat Adele into agreeing to break with Michael, it hadn't turned out that way. Mrs Bailey was surprisingly pleasant, and insisted that if Michael had only confided in her in advance of his announcement to the whole family she would have been prepared.

She didn't actually give her blessing, because she thought Michael was too young to think of settling down, especially with the threat of war hanging over them. She also pointed out that the RAF didn't approve of their pilots getting married, and Michael's superior officer might very well not give his permission.

But she did say she wasn't opposed to a long engagement as she wanted whatever would make Michael happy.

Adele remembered only too well how self-centred Mrs Bailey was, and she guessed she was more concerned with holding on to her son because she couldn't cope without him, rather than wanting his happiness. But at least she had met them halfway. Mr Bailey was still hostile.

He hadn't written to Michael, gone to the camp to see him, or even telephoned. Michael said he didn't care, but Adele knew that wasn't strictly true. He loved his father, why she couldn't imagine as she'd found him totally obnoxious, but she was intelligent enough to know she hadn't seen enough of the man to make any real judgements.

'That's better,' Michael said as the fire began to warm the room. 'So what shall we do?'

Adele gulped. She wished she knew how women were supposed to behave at times like this. 'I don't know,' she said in a small voice.

'What's wrong?' Michael asked. He moved nearer to her.

'I don't know that either,' she said, hanging her head. 'I just feel strange.'

He came closer still and tilted her face up to his with one finger. 'A case of the screaming hab-dabs?' he suggested, one dark eyebrow raised questioningly. 'Why don't we go out for a bit? Take a walk in the park, get some lunch.'

Adele nodded.

He hugged her tightly to him. 'I feel a bit weird too,' he admitted. 'Maybe it wasn't such a good idea after all.'

'It was a good idea,' she insisted. 'We wanted to be alone together, and we still do.'

It was after four in the afternoon and dark when they returned to the room. They'd walked round Kensington Gardens, had a couple of drinks each, eaten lunch in Queensway, and then had their photograph taken in a studio close to the hotel. The drinks had dispelled Adele's nerves and it was so cold outside that she couldn't wait to get back into the room.

They had left the fire on while they'd been out, and the room was now really warm. While Michael drew the curtains, Adele took off her coat, hat and shoes and jumped up on to the bed and bounced. When it creaked ominously she laughed and sat down.

'Do you think there's other people like us staying here?' she asked.

Michael unbuttoned his tunic and took it off. 'You mean incredibly intelligent, with fantastic looks and hopelessly in love?'

'Are we all that?' Adele asked.

'And more,' he said, leaping up on to the bed beside her. 'I bet people who pass us in the street turn round to have a second look.'

Adele lay back on the bed. She was wearing the dusky-pink

wool dress her grandmother had made her the Christmas she walked out of Harrington House. It was getting worn now but the way it was cut made her look so elegant and shapely she felt she could never part with it.

Michael leaned over her and began taking the pins out of her hair. 'Your hair is like the seasons,' he said, running his fingers through it. 'Blonde streaks in summer, a reddish-gold in autumn, and now chestnut-brown, with little glints of gold. Once we're married I'd like you to wear it loose all the time.'

'It's too long and straight for that,' she said. 'It reaches right down my back.'

'So much the better,' he said, lifting a strand of it up to his nose and sniffing it. 'Just the thought of it tumbling over your bare shoulders makes me excited.'

Adele giggled. 'I've heard of men getting excited by breasts and legs, but never by hair,' she said.

'It was your hair that I remember most about you that first day we met,' he said. 'It was all wild and tangly with the wind. I used to think about it all the time when I got back to school.'

'I must have looked like a beggar that day,' she said reprovingly. 'I was wearing those horrible old trousers and a jumper that had been Granny's. I can't imagine why you didn't cycle on by.'

'You looked entirely at one with the marsh,' he insisted. 'As natural as the plants and birds. I think I fell in love with you that day, I certainly knew you were going to become important in my life. Was it like that for you too?'

'I suppose it was,' she said reflectively, remembering how happy she had felt that evening after they parted. Meeting Michael had been the point in her life when she began to feel she might be worth something after all. 'You were the first boy I ever really spoke to, there was something about you that felt so comfortable and right. Of course I didn't dare read anything more into it, you being a gentleman and all that.'

'I wish you could stop seeing yourself as some kind of underling,' he said reprovingly, looking right into her eyes. 'Your grandmother is every bit as much of a lady as my mother, for all that she skins rabbits and wears men's clothes. You are like that too, there's an almost regal quality about you. Whoever your father was, I know he must have been out of the top drawer.'

'Sometimes I wish I could see my mother again,' Adele said thoughtfully. 'There's so much mystery I'd like to clear up, including who my father was. Every day on the wards I see families exposing their true feelings when one of their number is sick or even dying. But people shouldn't wait until there is a crisis before they forgive one another, or just speak their minds.'

'Would you be prepared to forgive your mother?' Michael asked thoughtfully. 'Or do you just want to tell her what you think of her?'

'I might be prepared to forgive if I got some sort of sensible explanation as to why she was so nasty to me,' Adele said pensively. 'I certainly don't want to spend the rest of my life feeling bitter about her, like Granny does.'

Michael leaned up on his elbows and looked at Adele. He knew she had no idea what a beautiful person she was, both inside and out. Her skin was a peachy colour, clear as a child's, her eyes an extraordinary mixture of green and brown with thick, long dark lashes. Yet it was her compassion for others which moved him even more than her looks. She felt for every one of the patients on her ward, listened to their stories, tried to help in any way she could. He knew that in her off-duty hours she often visited patients who had no other visitors, taking them fruit, sweets and magazines to read. She was the agony aunt of the nurses' home too – everyone turned to her when they had problems.

'I love you, Adele,' he said, his voice gruff with emotion. 'I will for ever.'

He kissed her then and as her arms wrapped around him the world outside their room ceased to exist.

Adele had expected to feel embarrassed and even fearful when the moment came to take off their clothes. But somehow she went from fully dressed to naked between the sheets without even really being aware of anything but the heat of their kisses, and the thrill of his hands stroking her skin. It was wonderful to feel that naked chest she'd so often admired on the beach, pressed against her breasts. She gasped with wonder as his fingers delicately probed inside her.

She could feel his nervousness, that he might frighten or hurt her, that he was doing it all wrong, and she found herself murmuring words of encouragement and moving against him deliberately to excite him still further. She knew the real test for herself was to touch his penis, for if anything was going to bring back the horrors of the past, it would be that. But it just happened in the same smooth way their clothes had come off, and the moan of pleasure from him dissolved the last of her anxiety.

Some of the more worldly nurses at the hospital and even women patients discussed lovemaking occasionally, and their commonest complaint was about men who rushed to get inside them. But Michael didn't even attempt it, seemingly more intent on pleasing her.

They had turned off the light, but the fire was still on, turning the ceiling gold. Just enough light to see Michael's tender expression, the redness of his lips, and the occasional glint of white teeth. But sight wasn't necessary now, for his skin felt like satin beneath her fingertips and she could sense the places he wanted to be touched. She could hear and feel his breath on her face, hear the endearments and sense his love. She could smell his body, a warm, musky aroma of sweat, soap and the cigarettes he'd smoked earlier, and it was so lovely that she found herself licking and biting him, and tasting the saltiness of his skin.

It was she who guided him to come inside her. She felt like she was on fire, and she had to have him. He fumbled a little as he drew the sheath on, and she averted her eyes momentarily for his penis suddenly looked so large and hard, and she braced herself for pain.

But there was no real pain. There was a brief second when she felt kind of stretched too far, but it passed quickly, and the thrill of at last being possessed by him more than made up for it.

'Is it good for you?' he whispered, his mouth against her neck.

'It's wonderful,' she murmured truthfully. 'I love you, Michael.'

'Oh my darling,' he whispered as his breath came faster and faster. 'It's so good, so beautiful. I love you so much.'

When he suddenly gasped out her name and stopped moving, Adele felt for a moment as though she had been left hanging on a precipice. But as she held his hot, quivering body in her arms, and realized he was crying against her shoulder, she understood what had happened.

'Some of the chaps at the camp say flying is better than sex,' he whispered. 'But I've never had a flight as thrilling as that.'

Adele laughed softly.

'Was it good for you too?' he asked anxiously, lifting his head to look at her.

She could only nod, so full of emotion she could find no words, and pulled his face down to kiss him again.

They got up later, washed and got dressed and went out to find something to eat and drink. It was now nine in the evening, too late to go to the pictures or see a show as they'd planned. Michael led her to a restaurant close by which one of his friends had told him about, and they ravenously ate a huge mixed grill, washed down with a bottle of red wine.

'I wish we could get married right away,' he said suddenly. 'I'd give anything to be able to come home each night to you.'

Adele put her hand over his on the table. 'You know perfectly well that isn't possible. I'd be out of a job as nurses can't be married. And the RAF don't like their young pilots married either.'

'Yes, but that doesn't stop me wishing it,' he said wistfully. 'I can't even say when we'll get another weekend together.'

Adele knew from things Michael had told her that none of the young airmen at Biggin Hill took the thought of what war really meant seriously. Flying was their passion, and between training flights they played football, rugby and cricket, or piled into cars and went roaring off to the nearest pub where presumably they created mayhem. They played practical jokes on one another, had bizarre initiation rites for new recruits, and the reason marriage wasn't encouraged was to foster close bonds between the men of the squadron.

But even if life at Biggin Hill was mostly one long round of fun and jollity, where newspapers were rarely read and talking politics was taboo, she knew Michael was very aware of the reality of England's precarious situation with Germany.

Ordinary civilians could believe Neville Chamberlain had really secured 'peace in our time', but Michael had observed the Government's recent massive rearmament, seen the recruitment campaigns, and the new Hurricanes and Spitfires arriving at Biggin Hill. He might rhapsodize that these machines flew in excess of 300 miles an hour, and pretend to go along with popular opinion that a pilot's role in warfare was reconnaissance and dropping bombs, as it had been in the last war, but he knew better.

They were being trained in dog-fights, they had to learn how to use guns, and they had to sit on a parachute, something which hadn't been known in the previous war. Adele knew just as he did that airmen would be at the sharp end of any action, and that this war wouldn't be fought in trenches, but in the air.

All the young flyers were blasé about the danger they might be asked to face, but Adele sensed that their lovemaking had suddenly made Michael realize that it wasn't the lack of parental approval that might separate them, but death.

A chill ran down her spine. Recently at the hospital there had been a flurry of extra training in dealing with wounds and burns for all the student nurses. She knew medicines, bandages and other supplies and equipment were being stock-piled. But until now it had all seemed like fire drill, necessary in case of an emergency, but fairly unlikely. Suddenly she felt that everyone was foolish to be so unconcerned.

'Then we'll just have to make the most of any time we do get together then,' she said, forcing herself to sound gay and untroubled. 'We've got all night together and all day tomorrow. Let's just think about that.'

Rose came out of Temple Underground station and stood for a moment consulting a map. It was the first week in February and the snow that had fallen the previous day was still thick and white on the roofs of buildings and trees. On the streets and pavements it had turned to treacherous black ice, and it was bitterly cold.

Rose had dressed for glamour, not warmth, and she was regretting it now, for her feet in their high heels had turned to blocks of ice, and she was in danger of slipping on the ice. Johnny had bought her the blue coat with a grey fox collar back in the autumn, and it had seemed very warm then. But in reality it was only suitable for mild weather as the wind blew right through it. If she hadn't anchored the small pill-box hat on to her hair with a couple of hat pins, it would have blown off just in the draught of the Underground.

She wished she had caught a taxi too, but she had less than ten shillings left for the rest of the week. Yet if everything went well today she might never have to catch a Tube again.

Walking cautiously along, holding on to walls and railings, she finally came to the Inner Temple. It wasn't a part of London she was familiar with, and it was something of a surprise to find it was like a rabbit warren of very old buildings, each one of them home to seemingly dozens of lawyers.

She had seen the announcement of Adele and Michael Bailey's engagement quite by accident. People left newspapers in the Soho restaurant where she worked all the time, and they put them in a heap in the storeroom for laying down on the kitchen floor after it had been washed.

Rose had taken a bundle of the papers home last November to twist into firelighters, and as she was sitting at the table with them, she found herself reading snippets here and there. When she came upon the Births, Deaths and Marriages in a copy of *The Times*, it brought back a memory of her mother reading those announcements – she always said she liked to see if there was anyone in there she knew.

Rose only scanned the names idly, but when she saw the name Bailey in the Engagements section, she looked at it more closely. To her shock and utter amazement it said Michael Bailey, son of Myles Bailey QC from Alton in Hampshire, was engaged to be married to Adele Talbot of Winchelsea, Sussex.

For a moment she thought she was going to have a heart attack. She could hear her heart thumping like a steam-hammer, and sweat broke out on her forehead. She had to pour herself a glass of brandy to steady her.

Rose had often thought about Myles Bailey after her trip with Johnny to Winchelsea in the summer, but once she got over the shock of him looming up in her life again quite by chance, mostly she thought about it all with wry humour. He hadn't ever known exactly where she lived, she'd always been so vague about it. But when his wife went to live in the house in Winchelsea, he would have remembered that his young mistress had lived nearby. Maybe he was afraid she'd gone back there to live after he left her.

It had amused her to imagine him being afraid of running into her when he visited his wife, and she even considered writing to him at Harrington House, some kind of cryptic message so he would know she was keeping tabs on him. But she hadn't done anything – it was all too long ago to want to make mischief for him.

But she couldn't find anything even vaguely amusing about the announcement in black and white in front of her. She couldn't possibly ignore that Myles's son was intending to marry her daughter. She had to stop them.

They were brother and sister!

Rose penned several letters to her mother explaining everything and asking her to put a stop to the marriage, but she tore them all up because she kept remembering the contemptuous way Honour had looked at her on the last visit. She would never believe Rose could be motivated by morality; she would just see it as some kind of dastardly attempt to spoil Adele's chance of a good marriage.

Rose couldn't eat or sleep as she frantically tried to work out the best way of dealing with the problem, but as always when she was troubled, she drank more, and found herself unable to think clearly. Weeks and weeks slipped by in which she did nothing but go to work, then drink herself into oblivion each night. Johnny kept pestering her to try to find out what was wrong, and when she wouldn't tell him he stopped coming round. Without Johnny's company and his handouts of money and gifts, she felt even worse, and drank more. She fell behind with the rent, she was in real danger of losing her job, and even worse, she could feel herself sliding into the same black world she'd got into after Pamela's death.

Then at Christmas it came to her that she should go to

Myles. He could deal with it, and if it caused him the kind of nightmares she'd been having, then it served him right. She went to the library and looked through *Who's Who*, and found both his home address and that of his chambers in London.

It was only once she saw him listed in that big leather-bound book that she fully appreciated that he was now a very successful and important man. And when she weighed that against all the suffering he'd put her through, pound signs began to pop up in her head and the question of morality began to take a nose-dive.

She became focused once she'd decided on her plan. She stopped drinking in early January and worked extra shifts at the restaurant so she could pay off her back rent, get her hair done and buy some new clothes.

Finally, she made an appointment to see Myles for today. That had been the most difficult part. She gave her name as Mrs Fitzsimmons, and a false address in Kensington. She told his secretary it was an extremely delicate matter concerning her father's estate, and Mr Bailey had been recommended to her by a friend.

Rose found the right chambers, and saw Myles's name in gold lettering amongst others up on a board inside the porch. She was ten minutes early, and although she'd planned to get there at the exact time of her appointment to cut down on the possibility of anyone having time to ask her awkward questions, she was too cold to stay outside any longer.

The great age of the building was even more apparent as she walked up the bare stone staircase. The steps had become concave and smooth from millions of feet over the years, and it had a musty smell of old books and papers. At the top a half-glassed door opened into an area where there were chairs, a desk and thankfully a warm fire.

A middle-aged woman wearing glasses smiled welcomingly at Rose from behind the desk.

'Mrs Fitzsimmons,' Rose said. 'I have an appointment with Mr Bailey at four.'

'Do take a seat,' the woman said, getting up. 'I'll inform Mr Bailey you are here.'

Rose sat down, resisting the desire to slip off her shoes and warm her feet at the fire. She felt queasy with nerves and she'd kill for a drink, but she took her powder compact out of her handbag, powdered her nose and applied a little more lipstick.

She thought she looked good. The fox collar and the hat enhanced her peachy complexion, and the tiny veil stopping at her eyebrows drew attention to her eyes. She wondered if Myles would recognize her instantly.

She had only just put her compact away when she was taken by surprise by the receptionist telling her Mr Bailey would see her now. She got up, smoothed down her coat, and followed the woman along a narrow corridor past many small rooms in which people were working as quietly as if in a library.

Rose's first reaction on seeing Myles was surprise to find he was neither as tall, handsome or striking as the image locked in her head. He was tubby, flabby and ruddy-faced, no more than five feet eight, and the thick mane of floppy, rich brown hair had gone. He wasn't bald, but his hair had receded so far back that he was almost so, and what was left was dark grey. Yet she felt she would have known him if they'd passed in the street by his eyes. They hadn't changed, and the memory of them had stayed with her, for Adele's were an identical greenyish-brown. She had been forced to live with that constant reminder of the man who had ruined her.

'Mrs Fitzsimmons!' he said heartily, holding out his hand to her without actually looking directly at her. 'Do come in. You have some problem with your late father's estate I believe?'

Rose had expected he would recognize her immediately.

She had anticipated him staggering back in shocked surprise and gasping out her name. When he did neither of these things, proving he had no memory of the face of the young girl he'd claimed he loved, it made her even more determined to hurt him.

She shook his hand and smiled, then waited until the receptionist had gone, closing the door behind her. It was a warm and comfortable room, with a roaring fire with a club fender around it, leather buttoned-back armchairs and a mahogany desk, and the walls were lined with thick books. On the wall there was a large photograph of three children, obviously his, as the older boy looked very much like the young Myles she remembered. The younger boy in the front of the picture had to be Michael – he was around six, with very dark hair and an impish grin with missing front teeth.

Myles sat down when she did, and leaned back in his chair with a smile on his plump, overfed face, perhaps delighted that his new client was blonde and attractive. 'Now, how can I help you?' he asked in an oily tone.

'You can try to remember me,' Rose said.

'We've met before?' he asked with a frown.

'Oh yes,' she said. 'Would the name Rose ring a bell? Or do I have to remind you of The George Hotel in Rye?'

His smile vanished, his eyes opened wide and he sat up straight.

'Rose!' he exclaimed, and coloured up still further. 'My goodness me! What a surprise! How are you?'

'Well enough,' she said archly. 'A great deal better now than I was twenty years ago when I waited in vain for you.'

'I-I-I,' he stammered. 'It was the only thing I could do. Things were so difficult for me. And I left a letter.'

'You were a deceitful coward,' she snapped at him. 'Didn't I deserve better than just a letter? If you'd told me about your wife and children when we first met I'd never have got involved with you.'

'You know why that was,' he said, looking very flustered and not a little afraid.

'I was little more than a child,' she spat out.

'Now look here,' he said, rising from his chair. 'You begged me to take you to London with me, if you remember I was completely against the idea. I only agreed because you said your father was violent towards you, and you were supposed to find a job which you never even attempted.'

'I haven't come here today to rake over all that,' Rose said dismissively. 'The hard facts are that you abandoned me when I was carrying your child.'

'That was nigh on twenty years ago,' he said incredulously. 'In the light of all the other lies you told me at that time, there was no reason why I should have believed that either. So what has brought you here today, Rose? If not to rake over the past?'

'Sometimes the past can jump up and slap you in the face,' she said. 'That's what has prompted this visit. Our daughter, Adele, is planning to marry your son Michael, so I believe.'

If she had thrown a bucket of cold water over him she couldn't have hoped to give him a bigger shock. His mouth fell open, he blanched, and his eyes grew wide as he clutched at his head.

'Adele is your daughter?' he said in a strangled voice.

'*Our* daughter,' Rose corrected him. 'You know only too well that I was pregnant!'

'I don't believe this,' he gasped. 'It's too extraordinary.'

'Why is it? You don't believe that a girl who has a grand-mother living at Winchelsea Beach could meet up with your son who also had grandparents living in Winchelsea? It would've been extraordinary if they hadn't met when there are probably less than two hundred people living in that whole area.'

Rose paused for a moment, guessing he was racking his brain for something to shoot her story down with.

'Now, if you'd told me when we met that you were married and your in-laws were Mr and Mrs Whitehouse, I wouldn't have even gone for a walk with you. After all, my mother, Honour Harris, was a friend of your mother-in-law.'

At that he put his elbows on his desk and cradled his head in his hands. 'I don't know what to say,' he gasped out. 'I never connected Adele with you. And she was living in my wife's house as her maid!'

This much was news to Rose. Honour had said she'd been working as a housekeeper, but she hadn't said who for. Clearly her daughter was a chip off the old block, grabbing a good opportunity when it came along. It was a shame though that she had unwittingly to grab her own brother.

'Oh God! What am I going to do?' Myles gasped.

Rose half smiled. She guessed that Myles Bailey QC didn't often make such an admission. His court wig was sitting on a dummy head in the corner. His court gowns hung on the door. He was used to wringing the truth out of defendants and witnesses, but not to being held accountable for his own indiscretions.

'You'll have to tell your son that Adele is his sister,' Rose said. 'That is, if you don't want him to make an incestuous marriage.'

'What proof do you have that Adele is my child?' he asked suddenly, and she saw his eyes narrow with guile. 'Adele's name is Talbot. Where did that name come from if you are Rose Fitzsimmons now?'

'That name was just a smokescreen,' Rose said airily. 'My married name is Talbot. I married Jim Talbot just before Adele was born, purely so she could have his name. But should you think he is her real father, add up the dates. You took me away with you from Rye in March of 1918 when I was seventeen. I was with you right up till the day you dumped me in King's Cross in January the following year. I was already three months pregnant then. I married Talbot in May and Adele was born in July.'

'That isn't proof I am her father,' he retorted.

'Anyone who met me during those ten months we were together would vouch that I spent my days waiting for you to come home from your "business matters". I even told the doctor I saw in King's Cross your name. Then of course there are such things as blood tests.'

Myles was silent for quite some time, and Adele could see a vein throbbing on the side of his head. He was sweating, pulling at the collar of his shirt as if it was strangling him.

'What do you want, Rose?' he asked eventually. 'Somehow I don't believe it's just the desire to make sure Adele and Michael finish their relationship.'

Rose decided to ignore the question about what she wanted for the time being. 'I was rather hoping you were going to tell me how you think we should go about ending the relationship,' she said with a defiant toss of her head. 'Obviously it has to be done, but one way might be less destructive than another.'

'I am not speaking to Michael at the moment,' he said. 'If I was to go to him and tell him this he wouldn't believe me.'

Rose gave a little chuckle as she guessed why this was. 'So you didn't like the idea of your son marrying my Adele? Not good enough for your golden boy, eh? A girl from the marshes marrying the KC's son?'

He had the grace to look a little ashamed.

'Your wife will divorce you if this gets out,' she said. 'It could get out too, very easily. What will your other children have to say about it? What will it do to your standing here?' She thumbed towards the door. 'Incest is a very nasty word. For all we know it might have already happened. And Michael an officer in the RAF too.'

It was very satisfying to see him seriously frightened. He

reached for a cigar from a box on his desk and lit it with shaking hands.

'There is another way,' Rose said as she watched him sucking on the cigar as if it were a teat. 'You could go to Adele and tell her the truth. Ask her to break it off with Michael and beg her not tell him why. That way there will only be the three of us who know about it.'

'Why can't you tell her?' he asked.

'Because it would mean going back into her life,' she said. 'She went to live with my mother when I was ill many years ago. To go back for something like this would only cause her more pain.'

Myles looked at her sharply. 'Somehow I don't think you are suggesting any of this to prevent anyone's pain,' he said. 'What do you really want?'

Rose riled up. 'None of this would have come about if you'd been honest in the first place,' she hissed at him. 'You left me destitute in London with a baby in my belly. To avoid giving birth in the workhouse I had to marry a man I didn't even like. You ruined my life, and it's time you paid for that.'

'Aha,' he exclaimed, his eyes narrowing. 'Now we're getting to the real issue. It's money you want, isn't it?'

'Yes,' Rose said with a shrug. 'I do. I want a thousand pounds.'

'A thousand!' he exclaimed.

'You can afford it.' She shrugged. 'It's only fifty pounds for every year of Adele's life, I'm sure you've spent a great deal more than that on each of your other children.'

'And if I refuse?'

'Then I go to the papers with the whole sordid story. It's up to you.'

She fished in her handbag and pulled out a card from the restaurant she worked in. She put it on his desk with complete confidence. 'You bring the cash to me there next Monday evening,' she said. 'I have already written down everything about you and me, and Adele's birth, and given it to a friend to hold just in case anything happens to me, or Adele.'

'What if she won't keep quiet about it?' he asked.

Rose shrugged. 'You'll have to make it worth her while, won't you?'

'If I agree to this, what assurance do I get that you won't ask for more later?'

'You assured me you loved me,' she reminded him. 'I was naive enough in those days to think that meant you would never desert me. I might be many things, but I am not a blackmailer. I'm just asking for what's owed to me for a ruined life. Just be glad I'm not about to ruin yours.'

Chapter Eighteen

Adele, with a group of other nurses, walked up the steps of the nurses' home just after six in the evening. It was 15 February and the other girls had been teasing her about the Valentine she'd received from Michael the day before.

He'd made it himself, a picture of a Spitfire with a tiny photograph of himself stuck in the cockpit. On a cloud in front of the plane was an equally tiny picture of Adele's face, but he'd drawn her in an angel's costume.

'My head's in the clouds since I first met you,' the poem read.

> The sun is out and the skies are blue,
> You are my angel, the girl of my dreams,
> I spend all day dreaming up schemes,
> To carry you off to a wondrous place,
> To see you dressed in wedding lace.
> You are my Valentine for ever and a day.
> When can you next come out to play?

Adele thought it was sweet and wonderful but the other nurses had been teasing her by saying that they hoped he flew planes better than he wrote poetry.

'You're all just jealous,' Adele giggled, and when she saw Mr Doubleday the caretaker standing in the hallway looking stern, she playfully reached out and tweaked his cap down over his eyes.

'Now then, Nurse Talbot,' he said gruffly. 'Enough of that horseplay. There's a gentleman to see you. I've shown him into the sitting room.'

'Is it Michael?' she asked eagerly.

'If Michael's the fly-boy then it isn't,' Mr Doubleday said dryly. 'And your cap's on crooked.'

Mystified, Adele opened the door of the sitting room and there to her shock sat Myles Bailey. 'Good evening,' she said politely, but a cold shudder went down her spine because she knew he hadn't come all this way for a social call.

'I need to talk to you, Adele,' he said. 'Is this room fairly private or can we expect hordes of other nurses to come in any minute?'

'It's only ever used for visitors,' she said. 'I doubt anyone else will come in now, everyone's gone off to get changed and eat their supper.'

'You look very nice in your uniform,' he said, looking her up and down in a way she found most disconcerting. 'How are your studies coming along?'

Adele sat down opposite him. She was puzzled that he was being so nice, but she hoped it might be because he was coming round to her marrying Michael. 'All right, I think, though it's hard to swot up for the exams after a long day or night on the wards. It's nearly two years now, only one more to go before I'm an SRN.'

He cleared his throat and looked awkward and nervous.

'Nothing's happened to Michael, has it?' she asked in alarm.

'No, he's fine as far as I know,' he replied. 'But I did come here to talk about him, and you.' He gave a big sigh, and Adele's heart leaped, sure he was about to bumble out some kind of apology.

'This is a very delicate matter, Adele,' he said. 'It's not something I ever expected to crop up, and it's going to be hard for me to tell you about it.'

Adele was confused now. He didn't look as though he was struggling to word an apology, but his voice was too soft and hesitant for anger. Her heart sank again, for she sensed that whatever he had to say, it wasn't going to please her.

'You can't marry Michael,' he blurted out. 'You are brother and sister.'

Adele giggled. 'Don't be silly,' she said.

'I'm completely serious,' he said reprovingly. 'You see, it seems I am your father, Adele.'

She could only stare at him in astonishment. It seemed like a joke, yet common sense told her it couldn't be. Myles Bailey was a very serious man.

'I had an, er . . .' He paused and coughed, looking as though he wished the floor would open up and swallow him. 'I once had an affair with your mother.'

Adele could only stare at him in disbelief, thinking he'd gone mad. 'No, Mr Bailey,' she finally managed to get out. 'My mother doesn't live anywhere near here. You don't know her.'

'I do, Adele, or at least I did twenty years ago. I met Rose in Rye when she worked at The George. She came away with me to London.'

Adele was stunned. Her grandmother had once said she thought Rose had run off with a married man, but how could it be Mr Bailey? A travelling salesman, a soldier or sailor maybe, but not a pompous lawyer with thinning hair and a red face!

'No, that can't be right,' she insisted, yet a small voice inside her was telling her that no man would admit such a thing unless it were true.

She got a vivid mental picture of herself in bed with Michael and a creeping, prickling sensation ran up her spine. 'This is some desperate measure to try and split Michael and me up, isn't it?' she said indignantly. 'How could you!'

'No, Adele, it's not,' he said. 'We may have got off on the wrong foot, but do you really think I would cook up a story like that? I'm a lawyer, for goodness' sake!'

'What difference does that make?' she hissed at him. 'Two

years ago you slapped me round the face and threw me out in the rain. I dare say most people would say a lawyer wouldn't do that either.'

'I regret that now,' he said, wiping his forehead with a handkerchief. 'I was under a great deal of strain at the time, and of course I had no idea who you were then.'

Adele suddenly remembered that her grandmother had been to see him on Christmas Day and came back with a reference and ten pounds.

'Is that when you found out who my mother was?' she asked, her voice rising with anger. 'You've known I was your bastard for two years, but you said nothing, even when you knew Michael was still seeing me? What sort of a man are you?'

'Now look here, young lady,' he said in his more customary sharp manner. 'I only found out about this myself a few days ago, when Rose came to my chambers in London and told me.'

'She came to you when she's ignored me for years?' Adele's voice rose even higher and she jumped to her feet.

'She felt she had to do something when she read about your engagement,' he said quickly. 'She was right of course. We couldn't just ignore it.'

Adele's head was reeling. It was too big a shock to take in. She swallowed hard, gritted her teeth and took a big breath. 'How do we know she's telling the truth?'

'I, eh, knew she was pregnant when I left her,' he admitted hesitantly. 'Not very gallant of me I know, but there were good reasons.'

All at once, without any further details, Adele realized he was speaking the truth, however odious it was. She walked over to the window and stared out at the garden below. In its winter drabness it looked as cold and desolate as she felt. She remembered then how that night in London Michael had said he was sure her father came out of the top drawer.

What was he going to say when he discovered they shared that same 'top drawer' father?

'Have you told Michael yet?' she asked, not turning to look at him because her eyes were brimming with tears.

'I can't,' he said.

Adele turned to him, and saw his eyes were pleading with her. It was only then that she noticed with disgust that they were just like hers.

'You can't tell him!' she exploded. 'Whose bloody fault is it? Yours!'

'I know,' he agreed, making a plaintive gesture with his hands. 'But if I tell Michael it will start something I won't be able to stop. The whole family will be disgraced. Please don't ask me to upset so many people, Adele.'

She looked at him coldly. She had tried to imagine her real father so many times, but Myles Bailey was the last man on earth she would want it to be. He was a bully, a crashing snob, and now she knew he was a philanderer who abandoned pregnant women.

'I get it,' she said, putting her hands on her hips and glaring at him. 'You want me just to disappear out of Michael's life, that's it, isn't it? The easy way out for you, no one need ever know apart from you, me and my bloody mother.'

'If you tell Michael the truth it will damage him,' Myles pleaded. 'I know what he's like, he's sensitive like his mother and he'll just withdraw into himself. He has a career he loves, he couldn't fly if he knew the girl he wanted to marry and make love to was his sister.'

Adele knew that much was true. The thought of what they'd done made her feel sick now, and she was sure Michael would feel even worse.

'Get out of here,' she said, pointing to the door. 'I can't bear to be in the same room as you. You and Rose should have stayed together – my God, you'd make an ideal couple with your weakness and lies.'

'What are you going to do?' he asked in alarm.

'I'm going upstairs to be sick,' she shouted at him. 'Because I've just found out I was born to the worst parents in the world and I can't have the man I love. Are you satisfied?'

'Don't tell Michael, for pity's sake,' he pleaded.

'Get out,' she shouted again. 'I'll decide all by myself what I'm going to do. You aren't going to bully me.'

He had to go then. The door was half glass and the caretaker was outside, looking to see what all the noise was about.

Myles scuttled away like a frightened rabbit, leaving Adele red in the face and fit to burst with rage.

It was fortunate that Angela, her room-mate, had got a couple of days off and gone home to her family, for Adele was in no mood to speak to anyone, or to be seen. Once inside the room she locked the door, and collapsed on to her bed sobbing.

Michael was her everything, and if he was taken from her there was absolutely nothing left. But it was worse than that – even the beautiful memories of him were dirty now.

She was sick in the washbasin over and over again until there was nothing left but bile to come up. She pulled off her uniform, leaving it crumpled on the floor, and crawled into bed in her underwear. Beyond her door she could hear all the usual laughter and chatter, nurses borrowing one another's clothes to go out, others asking if the bathroom was free, and someone pleading for them to be quiet so she could study. They were her friends, girls she thought she could talk to about anything, but she couldn't tell them this. She couldn't tell anyone.

It was reminiscent of when she was a child going to school with bruising from the stick her mother had taken to her. She had to hide that away too because it was shameful. And then there was Mr Makepeace, she had to hide what he did too, and that her mother had been taken to an asylum. Why was it always she who had to hide other people's wrongdoing?

Yet she knew she must hide this. Not to save Myles Bailey any embarrassment – he could burn in hell along with her mother for all she cared. But she would hide it from Michael. This was something he wouldn't be able to deal with. It would destroy him.

But what should she do? She certainly couldn't see Michael face to face and lie to him, he'd know immediately that something was wrong. She couldn't even speak to him on the telephone as just the sound of his voice would make her break down. Yet if she simply hid away he'd keep coming down here and make a nuisance of himself. He would never let her go without a very good reason.

The following morning Adele made her way to Matron's office. She had dark circles under her eyes from a sleepless night, she still felt sick and she knew she was unable to work on the ward today. But she'd dressed in her uniform to stop any of the other girls questioning her.

'Come in,' Matron's voice boomed out at the tap on the door.

Adele slunk in and closed the door behind her. Matron was a formidable woman, around fifty, tall and thin with an aristocratic bearing and manner.

'Yes, Nurse Talbot,' she said.

'I can't work here any more,' Adele burst out. 'I have to leave.'

Matron looked at her sharply. 'Are you pregnant?' she asked.

'No, it's nothing like that,' Adele said. 'Please don't ask me questions as I can't answer them. I just have to go.'

'Has this got anything to do with the man who called to see you yesterday?'

Adele's heart sank. Matron always knew everything that

happened in both the hospital and the nurses' home, but she'd hoped that visit wouldn't have been noted.

'Yes, but I can't say anything more,' she said. 'It's personal.'

'Talbot, you have the makings of an excellent nurse, and I know you love it. I would hate to see you throw that away after nearly two years' training.'

'I don't want to stop nursing,' Adele said. 'I just can't do it here any more. Would it be possible for me to be transferred to another hospital?'

Matron frowned and peered at Adele over her glasses. 'That might be possible, but I couldn't arrange it without knowing the reason behind it. I can see you are very troubled, and I don't believe you are the kind of girl to get into anything criminal. So confide in me, Talbot, it will not go beyond this room.'

Adele knew Matron to be an honourable woman. She might be stern and very hard on nurses who she felt let the nursing profession down, but she was fair-minded and often surprisingly kind. Without her help, Adele knew she wouldn't stand a chance of finishing her training in another hospital. Perhaps she had to tell her the truth.

'The man who came yesterday told me he was my father,' she said. 'He's also the father of Michael, the airman I am engaged to.'

Even as she said it, Adele still couldn't really believe something like this could happen to her. Even Matron looked thunderstruck.

Adele explained the bare bones of how this had come about, and said that of course she had to stop seeing Michael. She began to cry at that point and Matron came round her desk and patted her shoulder.

'I see,' she said. 'That is an impossible situation to be in. I take it you are afraid that as Michael knows nothing of it he will keep coming here to see you?'

Adele nodded. 'I can't see him, I'd end up telling him and so it's best for everyone that I just disappear.'

Matron sat down at her desk again. She didn't speak for a while and appeared deep in thought.

'It would be very cruel to drop the young man without any explanation,' she said after a few minutes. 'And I don't agree with his father's opinion that it would be worse for him if he knew the truth. And what about your grandmother? Were you intending to light off without telling her where you are too?'

'I would have to for a while,' Adele said, wringing her hands together. 'She's the first person Michael would go to once he found I'd gone from here.'

'Adele, none of this is your fault,' Matron said, the use of the Christian name indicating she was entirely sympathetic. 'I am appalled that Michael's father should make you and those you love suffer so grievously while he gets off scot-free.'

'But it would hurt so many more people if the truth came out,' Adele insisted. 'Michael's mother, his brother and sister. And what would people say about me and my mother? It really is better if no one knows. I've thought about it all night and I know I'm right.'

'But your grandmother will be so worried about you. Don't put her through that agony,' Matron said.

'I can write a letter to her,' Adele said desperately. 'Say I've had second thoughts about Michael and I've gone away until he gets over it. I can keep sending her notes so she knows I'm all right.'

'Will Michael get a letter too?'

'Yes, of course. I'll say that I've realized he wasn't right for me.'

Matron sighed deeply and shook her head despairingly. 'It seems all wrong to me,' she said. 'But I can see that it wouldn't be practical to continue in this hospital under the circumstances. I do have a very good friend who is Matron at the London Hospital in Whitechapel, she is desperate for good nurses too. I could telephone her and see if she'll have you.'

'Oh thank you, Matron,' Adele said gratefully, tears rolling down her cheeks. 'But you won't tell her all this, will you?'

'Of course not, we are good enough friends for her to trust my judgement without explanations. Go back to your room now, I'll come and see you later once I've spoken to her.'

'I need to go today,' Adele said, sniffing back her tears.

Matron nodded. 'Leave it with me. I'll get someone to bring up some breakfast to your room. You must eat, even if you don't feel like it.'

At three that same afternoon Adele left the nurses' home with her suitcase and headed for Hastings station. Matron had fixed it with the London Hospital, and she had also promised that if Michael telephoned or called she would speak to him personally and say that Adele had left for personal reasons. The other nurses would be told the same story.

Adele had written to both Michael and her grandmother and she dropped the two letters in the first post box she came to. They were so difficult to write – she knew she couldn't allow them to think she was distraught, but neither could she sound uncaring about their feelings. To Michael she could only say that she had made a mistake, that she realized he wasn't right for her, or she for him. That she was going to another town to live and work, and that he must forget her.

She said much the same about Michael to her grandmother, but explained how she couldn't reveal where she was going until he had stopped trying to find her. She implored her not to worry, and that she would send other notes so she would know she was safe. She told her she loved her, and that all her best memories were of living with her on the marsh. Finally she said Honour mustn't think that this was history repeating itself, she was not like Rose and she'd be in touch soon.

As the train chugged out of the station Adele's eyes brimmed with tears again as she remembered the last time she had travelled to London. She had been so happy and excited that day, hardly able to sit still with it. But there would be no Michael to meet her at Charing Cross this time, no warm hug to greet her, no words of love. Her engagement ring was still on the chain around her neck, for it was against the hospital rules to wear a ring on duty. She knew she ought to have sent it back to him, but she needed the small comfort of it lying there warm between her breasts.

She was glad she was going somewhere horrible and overcrowded like Whitechapel. She believed that without the salt-tinged wind coming off the sea, no wide open spaces, grass, flowers and trees, she could forget.

Later she saw a plane in the sky. The pilot was practising acrobatics. He looped the loop, then swept down low and rose up again steeply. She saw the black and white under the wings and knew it was a Spitfire. It could well be Michael or someone else from his squadron, and she offered up a little prayer that he would forget her quickly, and that he'd stay safe when war came.

The only prayer she said for herself was to ask that she'd be a good nurse. She didn't believe she deserved happiness, or even safety.

Chapter Nineteen

September 1939

'Come and look at these little lambs being evacuated!' Staff Nurse Wilkins exclaimed from her position at the window of Women's Surgical. 'Some of them are so tiny.'

Adele and Joan Marlin joined Wilkins at the window, to see a long crocodile of children trudging along Whitechapel Road towards the station. Each one was carrying either a small case or bundle in their hands and a gas mask box slung across their chests. They all had a large label pinned to them, presumably marked with their name and age, and they were being shepherded by around half a dozen women who were most likely teachers.

'Poor loves, leaving their mums,' Joan said with an emotional break in her voice. 'Our Mickey and Janet are going today too. Mum was in a terrible state last night. She don't believe other people can be kind to kids who aren't their own.'

'It might turn out to be the best thing that's ever happened to some of them,' Adele said thoughtfully, remembering how it was for her when she got to her grandmother's. 'They'll be safe from any bombs and see a new way of life, find out about nature, birds, cows and sheep. And people can be really kind to kids in emergencies.'

'I can't think of anything worse than coming face to face with a cow,' Joan said with a sniff. She was a gregarious redhead from Bow, with freckles across her nose. The daughter of a docker and the eldest of seven children, she had become Adele's closest friend since coming to Whitechapel. Without Joan's ribald sense of humour, kind heart and jollity, Adele knew she couldn't have coped with the harshness of East End life.

'It doesn't seem possible that we're about to go to war,' Staff Nurse Wilkins said, looking up at the cloudless sky. 'I mean, the sun's shining, everyone's carrying on working, getting on buses and trains, even those kids think they're off on a big adventure. I keep expecting that it's all a mistake, that a week from now we'll see them take all those wretched sandbags away, tear down the blackouts and pull the strips off the windows. I really can't believe all our men are standing ready to kill people.'

Wilkins was very fond of questioning the meaning of life. She was twenty-five, skinny, mousy-haired and plain as a pike-staff, but a dedicated nurse and deeply religious. As a staff nurse she didn't have to live in the nurses' home, and a couple of months earlier she had taken Adele home with her for supper. As the senior nurse was so well spoken and educated Adele had expected her home to be a nice one. It had been something of a shock to be taken into a tiny, decaying terraced house in Bethnal Green. It was scrupulously clean, but devoid of any comforts. No rugs on the floor, only shabby oil cloth, no pictures, ornaments or even a wireless. A table and chairs, a sideboard, and beds upstairs, that was all. And the grace they said before a meagre supper of cold meat and potatoes lasted what seemed like ten minutes. Wilkins' parents and the two other daughters who still lived at home were all Evangelists, and they'd wasted no time in trying to get Adele to join them in what Joan laughingly called 'Holy Rollering'.

Adele's first impression of the East End had been complete horror. It wasn't as if she'd never seen the effects of poverty and unemployment, for parts of Hastings and Rye too were little more than slums. At worst she had expected it to be how she remembered Euston and King's Cross.

But the East End made King's Cross seem like paradise. Street after street of mean little houses, and a casual glance through open doors or broken windows revealed that the inhabitants owned little more than they stood up in. Ragged children with pinched, pale faces played listlessly in filthy alleys. Women with gaunt faces and hollow eyes, often with a baby in their arms, scoured the gutters as the markets closed for anything edible. Adele saw drunks and prostitutes, old soldiers with missing limbs, beggars and cripples sleeping wherever they could find a little shelter. And everywhere stank, a potent mixture of human and animal waste, rot, unwashed bodies and stale beer.

Day after day in the hospital she saw the end results of slum living. Severely malnourished children, women worn out with child-bearing, hideous wounds from drunken fights, lice, tuberculosis, rickets, and all manner of other complaints caused by poor diet, overcrowding and lack of basic hygiene.

Yet she soon came to see that however deprived these people were, they had spirit. They helped one another, were generous with what little they had, laughed at adversity, and they were colourful even if their surroundings were so dismal.

The pain of losing Michael was still almost as sharp as when she left Hastings, but Adele didn't think she could wallow in self-pity when all around her were such poverty and need. It was difficult not to laugh along with people who were so unfailingly optimistic and jolly. Everyone knew that London would be Germany's main target for bombs when the war began, yet there was no panic, no desperate fleeing the city.

When thoughts of Michael threatened to engulf her, Adele would look at the old man who stood outside the main door of the hospital selling newspapers. He was twisted and bent with rheumatism, clearly in pain, but he greeted everyone jovially and stood out there in all weathers, always with a smile on his face.

She vowed to be like him. No one liked a misery, and she knew now that most people had some problem in their lives. So she forced herself to smile, talked to people and found that it eventually became second nature. If she cried herself to sleep most nights, nobody but she knew.

It might not have been so bad if she'd only known how Michael and her grandmother had reacted to those letters she sent them. She had imagined all kinds of terrible things, like Michael not coming out of a dive in his plane purposely, or her grandmother slipping into the river and drowning. She went on sending a little card to her grandmother every week, always walking miles from Whitechapel to post it, so the postmark wouldn't give away where she was. Yet for all she knew, those cards could be piled up inside the door of Curlew Cottage, unseen and unread.

But then on her twentieth birthday in July she got a card from her grandmother. She couldn't believe it when she saw the familiar handwriting. How on earth had a woman who never went further than Rye found out where she was?

'I took the bus into Hastings and went to the Buchanan and demanded that the Matron told me where you'd gone. I always felt she'd had a hand in it,' Honour wrote in the accompanying letter.

She plays her cards close to her chest that one! But I eventually convinced her that I didn't want to know the reasons why, only an address. I will not of course pass it on to Michael should he call again. The poor boy came many times in the first few weeks, he flew over the cottage dozens of times too, always dipping his wing so I knew it was him. But I don't think he will call again now. He might not be over it, and as deeply puzzled as I am, but he has great dignity.

I thought you were cruel at first, but as spring came and I remembered special times here with you, I came to thinking that you have no cruelty in your nature. Maybe one day you'll be able to tell me about it. But I won't press you, I have secrets enough of my own I wouldn't share. And in my heart I know you didn't do it selfishly and must have had good reason.

I am very relieved that you stayed in nursing, for you were born for it. Write to me now, let me know my brave and caring granddaughter is, if not happy, making a new life for herself.

As for me, I'm well enough for an old biddy of sixty. I've got a dog now, an ugly-looking brute I call Towzer. Someone abandoned him, but he knew the right door to come and whine at. He's a good boy, doesn't try to get at the chickens or rabbits, and he's company. I've even got him to do a few tricks, but you will see those when you come home again.

We cannot fool ourselves that the war will be averted now. I won't ask that you move to a hospital in a safer place, a nurse must be where she is most needed. But don't take risks, my girl, and keep letters coming. This will always be your home and safe haven.

My love,
Granny

Adele marvelled at the cheerful and uncritical letter and cried over it too for she missed her grandmother so much and couldn't bear the thought of the torment she must have put her through. Yet more importantly, it gave her renewed strength. If a sixty-year-old woman without a soul in the world to turn to when she was hurting could not only survive, but show unfaltering love, then a girl with youth and good health on her side should be able to put this behind her.

'They've just painted a white cross on the bleedin' roof,' Joan informed Adele a little later that morning as they scrubbed down the two empty beds ready for new patients. 'Don't tell Staff or she'll be thinking this place is being turned into a church and she'll have us down on our prayer bones.'

Adele laughed. Joan was always making jokes about Staff Nurse Wilkins' religious fervour. 'Let's hope the German pilots don't think it's a runway and try to land on it!' she retorted. Yet as the words came out of her mouth, so an image of Michael shot into her mind. Last Christmas Eve when he came to the nurses' home in Hastings, he'd been wearing a sheepskin-lined leather flying jacket. He said all the fighter boys wore them, they not only kept them warm, but they felt they would be better protection if they were shot down by enemy fire. That hadn't meant that much to her then, but it did now. Once the war began he'd be up in the sky trying to shoot down German planes, but they might very well get him first.

All at once she felt sick and had to run to the lavatory. She only just got there in time.

'What's up?' Joan said from behind her. 'You were right as ninepence a minute ago. Want me to call Sister?'

'No, don't,' Adele said weakly. 'I'll be all right in a minute. Just go back on the ward and cover for me.'

She pulled herself together and went back to work. She felt Joan looking at her sharply every now and then, but with twenty-four patients on the ward there was no opportunity for conversation.

At six o'clock, however, when the night shift came on duty and Adele and Joan went back to the nurses' home, Joan questioned her friend. 'What was up today?' she asked.

'Nothing,' Adele said. 'I expect it was just something I ate which didn't agree with me.'

'If I didn't know you better I'd reckon you were up the spout,' Joan said.

'Don't be silly,' Adele said.

'I know something's wrong,' Joan said. 'You often go all quiet and broody. It's a bloke, ain't it?'

Adele gave a noncommittal shrug.

'I'm not daft,' Joan said. 'You got transferred 'ere from the coast. No one does that without some bloody good reason.'

Adele knew the other girl well enough to know she wouldn't give up easily.

'All right, it was a man, and talking about planes made me sick because he's a fighter pilot. But please don't ask me anything else, I came here to forget him.'

'Fair do's,' Joan said. 'But if you ever want to spill the beans, I'll be ready wif me lug-holes pinned back.'

When the day nurses got into the dining room for their supper, they were greeted by one of the orderlies with the news that Germany had invaded Poland earlier that day. It had been on the six o'clock news, and the wireless was still on, with people discussing what this would mean to England.

The treaty for the mutual protection of England and Poland had been drawn up after Germany invaded Czechoslovakia six months earlier in March, and a month later all young men between twenty and twenty-two were called up for active service. Neville Chamberlain would attempt now to get an undertaking from Hitler that he would withdraw his troops from Poland, but if that failed, England was duty-bound to declare war on Germany.

That night Adele lay in bed listening to the other nurses calling goodnight to one another all down the corridor. She had one of the few single rooms. It was tiny, with no room for anything more than a narrow bed, a chest of drawers and a desk which doubled as a dressing-table, but she was grateful for the privacy it gave her.

Back in Hastings she had always liked the noise and bustle of the nurses' home. She had never minded girls bursting into her room to chat, borrow things or share a joke. Yet she found it hard to cope with it here. She craved isolation and complete silence. She was irritated by the pettiness of the other nurses' rows and squabbles. Sometimes she even resented attempts to befriend her. Joan was the only other girl she had any real time for.

Yet the noise didn't bother her tonight. She felt soothed by the nurses' voices in just the way she used to like hearing her grandmother raking the stove at night, or moving her chair.

Perhaps she was recovering?

To test herself, she put her hand up to where her engagement ring lay nestling between her breasts, and made herself think of Michael's face the day he gave it to her. She could see him so clearly, his dark hair gleaming in the sunshine, the way the skin around his eyes crinkled a little as he smiled, and those dark blue eyes looking so intently at her.

No tears sprang to her eyes this time. Perhaps she had now cried them all. The sadness and the yearning for what she had once had was still there. She still had stabs of shame that she'd been to bed with her brother. Yet she felt more rational about it, after all they didn't know they were related, and she had done the right thing in going away when she found out.

All at once she knew it was time to go home and see her grandmother again. She had three days owing to her, and tomorrow she would ask Matron when she could take them.

'Walk, Towzer,' Honour said as she switched off the wireless. It was Sunday, 3 September and she had just heard the Prime Minister's speech. Germany had ignored the request to pull their troops out of Poland and consequently war was declared.

Honour hadn't expected that Germany would back down, not with that maniac Adolf Hitler at the helm. But she had hoped and prayed for a miracle.

She had woken early this morning to see clear blue skies, and a light mist hanging low over the river. Even before she had dressed she went outside and took Misty, Adele's rabbit, from its hutch and sat down on the bench to pet it, as she did every morning.

A flotilla of swans were on the river, wild geese flew overhead, and the branches on the elderberry tree were sagging with the weight of ripe berries. Everywhere she looked she saw beauty, from the long waving grass beyond her fence to the clump of vivid purple and mauve asters beneath the pink rambling rose, still in flower as it had been since June. She thought it was the kind of day when miracles could happen, but when the broadcast began her heart sank. She might have known that miracles were only a myth.

Honour could remember so clearly the day the previous war started. It was 4 August, she was thirty-five, Rose thirteen, and they were sitting in the garden shelling peas for dinner when a young boy whizzed down the lane on a bicycle and shouted the news to them. Frank got on his bicycle immediately and rode off into Rye. He reported back that there was great excitement everywhere and all the young men wanted to join up immediately.

Frank was excited too. But Honour remembered how she had first felt cross that he was behaving like a schoolboy, and later faintly sick. Perhaps it was a premonition that disaster was on its way.

She had the same feeling again today, so she would walk to Rye harbour with Towzer, and pick blackberries on the way.

'Come, Towzer,' she called, and smiled as he gambolled towards her. He was part collie, judging by his black and white curly coat, but she couldn't imagine what the other part was, for his head was large, he had only a stump instead of a tail and his legs were very long. He had been dreadfully thin, his coat coming out in clumps and riddled with fleas, when she found him outside her door four months ago. In a way it was very much like when Adele first arrived, Honour had to coax him to eat, dose him with medicine, and for a while it seemed as if he wouldn't survive.

But he did, and just as Adele's arrival had turned Honour's life around, Towzer's had done the same.

Honour was bereft after Adele disappeared. The brief letter of explanation told her nothing believable. She couldn't understand why Adele couldn't have come home first and confided in her about what was really wrong. Each time Michael came to the cottage looking for Adele, Honour was left feeling even more confused and upset because of his obvious pain. Sometimes he was full of anger, sometimes he just cried like a child, and she was very afraid that he might take his own life for that vital spark in him that had always been so attractive had gone out.

Then he suddenly stopped calling, and though Honour told herself that was good, for it meant he was accepting the situation, it also meant she was left with no one to share her grief and anxiety with. She began to let things slide. She hardly ate, she didn't clear up, or tend the garden. Sometimes she would merely feed the chickens and rabbits and crawl back into bed. A small voice kept telling her she was sliding down a slippery slope towards insanity, but why should she care, no one else did.

Then late one afternoon when it was pouring with rain, she heard the scratching at the door and curiosity got the better of her. She opened it, and there sat a dog, a pitiful, mangy-looking thing, looking up at her with pleading eyes.

Maybe she had gone a little mad, because she felt he had come to her for a special reason. She offered him some leftover rabbit stew and when he seemed unable to eat it, she fed him by hand, a tiny piece at a time, then made a bed for him in the shed, for he was too flea-ridden to bring inside.

He was still there the following morning, his stump of a tail trying to wag when he saw her. He ate a little more rabbit, then slumped down again as if exhausted, and her heart went out to him.

It took a long time to make him well again. Sometimes when she brought him food he'd just look at her with his big, sad eyes as if wondering why she was bothering because he wanted to die. But each day she got him to eat a little more, and she wormed him, treated his fleas, bathed and brushed him.

It was when she brought him into the cottage that he finally began to eat with enthusiasm. Honour thought now that they had healed each other: she fed him, he gave her adoration. They needed each other.

If she had known a dog could be such good company, she would have got one years before. To be woken in the morning by a cold nose pressing on her face made her smile. It was good to have him bounding by her side as she collected wood. And in the evenings when she listened to the wireless he lay with his chin on her feet and sighed with contentment. Maybe if Towzer hadn't bucked her up so much she would never have found the strength to go into Hastings and find out if the Matron at the hospital knew where Adele had gone.

There was no one out on the marsh despite it being such a beautiful day. Honour guessed that almost everyone in England had listened to the broadcast and would spend the rest of the day discussing it with neighbours, friends and family. She trudged across the shingle bank towards the sea, throwing sticks for Towzer to retrieve as she thought about Adele.

Now that war had come she would be right at the heart of any air raids as Honour guessed that Germany would target London's dockyards. The thought of her granddaughter in danger filled her with exactly the same kind of foreboding that she'd felt when Frank went off to war. She could remember standing on the beach, looking across to France and trying to will the war to end so he could come home. Now she couldn't even reach the sea because of the rolls of barbed wire intended to deter an invasion.

Michael would be in the thick of the fighting, and Honour wondered how he was now, and whether he had got over Adele. Somehow she doubted it. He might go through the motions of carousing with the other young airmen, but he was a sensitive, single-minded lad, and the anguish he'd suffered after Adele disappeared would have scarred him deeply.

'But why did she suddenly decide I was wrong for her?' he'd cried to Honour. 'It doesn't make sense.'

It did make some sense to Honour when Michael had eventually let it slip they'd spent a weekend in London together just prior to her disappearance. Honour had been so certain Adele had put that nasty incident at The Firs behind her, for she'd seemed so ecstatically happy with Michael. But maybe in an intimate moment it had all come back, and later Adele felt unable to proceed with an engagement and marriage when lovemaking revived such terrible memories.

Honour had been compelled to suggest this to Michael and his reply had made her weep.

'I'd thought of that too,' he said. 'I couldn't believe it was the reason, as she seemed as happy as me that weekend, but it's the only thing which makes any sense. I would have continued to love her just the same, though, even if she never slept with me again for the rest of our lives.'

Honour knew that however unrealistic that was, Michael believed it. He truly loved Adele, would walk on hot coals for her. And Honour doubted that he'd ever feel that way again about any other woman.

It was around three in the afternoon when Honour made her way back to the cottage. She'd deliberately walked herself to the point of exhaustion, for with so much on her mind she wanted to go home and sleep for hours.

Towzer seemed to understand how troubled she was, for he had not run off chasing birds like he usually did, but stayed close to her side, every now and then looking up at her with mournful eyes.

It was his bark that alerted her someone was coming towards them. The person was too far away for Honour to see who it was, but appeared to be waving at her.

She stopped in her tracks, her hands shielding her eyes

from the sun to see better. The person was running towards her, and suddenly she realized it had to be Adele.

Her heart began to thump with joy. She tried to run, but could only hobble.

'Granny!' she heard over the crunch of shingle under her feet and no sound had ever been sweeter.

She stood still and watched Adele come the last two hundred yards or so. She moved like a young deer, jumping over obstacles, hair flying out behind her on the breeze.

Honour involuntarily opened her arms, tears of joy coursing down her face. She was right after all, it was a day for a miracle.

Chapter Twenty

'Well done, Nurse Talbot,' Matron said as she handed Adele her SRN certificate and badge and the dark blue belt which signified she was now fully qualified. 'And please don't get any ideas about getting married. England needs her nurses now even more than ever.'

Adele smiled. Maybe other nurses were falling recklessly in love because of the war, but not her. She might have learned to live without Michael, but no other man she'd met even came close to making her forget him.

Matron moved on to Joan Marlin to give her a badge, belt and a similar warning about marriage. Later, all eight of the nurses who had passed their final exams would receive their new blue and white striped dresses and the more elaborate starched cap. They would have an increase in salary and move up to the second floor of the nurses' home to slightly larger rooms, but best of all they were no longer student nurses. They were fully qualified.

Adele grinned at Joan. Tonight they would go out to celebrate, a few drinks then off to a dance somewhere. It had been a long haul, but they'd made it. Adele knew now how Michael felt when he first got his flying wings.

It was 12 May. In two months' time Adele would be twenty-one, and so far the war had not affected civilian life very much. They called it the Phoney War. Sugar, butter and bacon had been rationed back in January, some goods were getting scarce in the shops and miles and miles of barbed wire and mines had been put along the beaches for fear of invasion. The main grouse was about the inconvenience of blackout. It annoyed everyone that they couldn't get around easily after dark, and they resented the ARP wardens who policed the streets looking for chinks of light coming through curtains. Absurdly, half the people brought into Casualty at night had suffered falls or banged into lamp-posts in the dark. And London hospitals were much less busy, dealing only with emergencies – anyone requiring an operation was sent to a hospital out of town.

Men and women in uniform everywhere were as much of a reminder of the real business of war as the casualty lists in the newspapers, but for most ordinary people it was still a distant danger which had not yet encroached on their lives.

Denmark and Norway had been invaded in April, then two days ago the German army entered Holland, Belgium and Luxembourg. On the same day Winston Churchill became head of the Coalition Government in place of Neville Chamberlain who had resigned a few days before.

Yet however peaceful it was at home right now, Churchill's stirring broadcasts on the wireless left no one in any doubt that everyone in the British Isles would be called upon very soon to face real war, in the air, the sea and on the ground. There was a sort of buzz in the air, anticipation and indeed excitement. Most people took the view that the sooner it came, the quicker it would be over.

'Cor! This is a bit of all right,' Joan said gleefully as she and Adele claimed their new room on the second floor after coming off duty. Adele had long since moved out of her single room and into a double with Joan, but it had been very cramped. This new one was at the back of the nurses' home, and though there was only a view of dismal rooftops and a few scrubby trees it was much quieter. It was also much larger, with its own washbasin and even room for two easy-chairs.

'The beds are just as hard,' Adele said, giving hers a test by bouncing on it. 'But it's super to have some space at last.

And you've got to be tidier. I'm sick of picking up your stuff.'

The two friends had begun sharing a room just after war was declared, following Adele's first trip home to see her grandmother. Going home again had been cathartic. While she was bombarded with poignant memories of Michael, the routine chores of stock-piling wood, feeding the chickens and rabbits, cooking and cleaning, helped to pull her together. She saw that she was strong, both physically and mentally, she had developed character and determination, and it was almost certainly the harshness of her early life that had made her such a good nurse. She resolved then to stop moping, to make new friends, to see new places. Giving up her single room was the first step when she returned to Whitechapel, and with noisy, fun-loving Joan as a room-mate she soon found she didn't get much time to brood on the past.

'I s'pose you think you're perfect,' Joan retorted. 'What about all the times you've woken me up with yer bleedin' nightmares?'

Adele blushed. In her waking hours she was fine, but she couldn't stop Michael invading her sleep. She told Joan she couldn't remember what the nightmares were about, but in fact it was always the same one, and so vivid she couldn't forget it.

In her dream she was walking out on the marshes, and she'd look up to see a plane overhead. She knew it was Michael as he'd tip his wing the way her grandmother had described. Round and round he'd go over her head, almost like a circus act, and she'd be laughing and waving her hands to him. Then suddenly there would be a bang, and his plane would go into a spiral. Flames would shoot out and she'd hear his voice above it screaming for help.

She'd had plenty of nightmares ever since she ran off from Hastings, but this one had started a few days after war was declared. She thought it was probably because she'd read in the papers that a young trainee pilot had been killed at Biggin Hill on taking a Spitfire up for the first time. Since then she'd heard of many more pilots being killed, both through enemy fire over France and accidents while still training. She used to scan the newspaper desperately every morning, her heart in her mouth. But she'd made herself stop it now for she knew very well that it wasn't healthy to be so obsessed.

'I expect I get nightmares because I'm sharing a room with you,' she shot back at her friend.

Joan laughed, and not for the first time Adele thought how lucky she was to have her as a friend. Cockney Joan was like sunshine, brightening even the dullest day. Her pretty, freckled face, her mop of unruly red hair and dancing green eyes, coupled with the ability to laugh at herself, made her popular with all the other nurses and patients. But what Adele valued most of all about her was her steadfast and uncomplicated personality. Once she'd decided someone was her friend, she accepted them entirely, warts and all. Time and again she'd got into Adele's bed with her after these nightmares and just held her tightly – she didn't pry, analyse or preach.

Adele knew very well that if she was to tell Joan about Michael, she would never tell another living soul. But she hadn't told her, that was one secret she intended to keep to the grave.

'So what we gonna wear tonight?' Joan asked, as always moving right on to what she saw as the really important things in life. 'Do you reckon I could get away with wearing the emerald-green frock again? Or will everyone think I've only got the one?'

'Well, I'll have to wear my striped one for the hundredth time as it's the only half-decent thing I've got,' Adele said. 'So you might as well wear yours too.'

They had no money for new clothes. Joan gave part of

her salary to her mother, and Adele sent money home to her grandmother.

'Let's try and lure a couple of steady blokes tonight,' Joan suggested. 'If we got ourselves taken to the pictures every week instead of paying for ourselves, we might be able to rise to buying a summer frock each from the market.'

Adele lay back on her new bed and laughed.

'Wot's so funny?' Joan asked.

'You, Joan,' Adele said through her laughter. She knew perfectly well that Joan was intent on fixing her up with a boyfriend, she had tried to get Adele interested in many direct and indirect ways in the past few months. But this one beat them all. 'Do you really think I'm cold-blooded enough to get a man to take me to the pictures every week just to save a couple of bob?'

'No, you bleedin' well wouldn't,' Joan said huffily. 'You'd probably pay for 'im and buy 'im fish and chips after, 'cos you'd think any bloke who wanted to go out with you couldn't be the full shilling.'

'Is that what you think I'm like?' Adele asked incredulously.

'I don't just think it, I know it,' Joan said. 'I watch yer, don't I? A bloke starts to chat to you and you don't flirt or nothin', you ask him questions, let 'im tell you 'is troubles. I dare say if 'e said 'e 'ad a boil on 'is backside you'd be wanting to lance it for 'im. That ain't the way to get a fella, Adele. You're too bleedin' nice.'

Adele didn't know what to say in reply. It was true she didn't flirt, for one thing she didn't know how to, and it seemed a pointless exercise anyway unless you really fancied someone. She had liked lots of the men she'd met with Joan, but not in that way. Why should she pretend otherwise?

'Does it cramp your style if I don't get fixed up with someone when we're out?' she asked.

'Course not,' Joan said vehemently. 'I'm proud you're my

pal, you've got class, and I ain't got much of that meself. I just worries about you, that's all. You could 'ave the pick of the fellas if you wanted, but I guess you've still got a thing about that airman?'

'Maybe,' Adele said, not able to commit herself to either a yes or a no. 'Or maybe I'm the sort who is just waiting for Mr Right to come along.'

Joan pulled a silly face. 'Well, can't we just play with a few Mr Wrongs for the time being?' she said.

Adele got up off the bed, and went over the pile of clothes they'd dumped on the chair. 'The striped dress will do for Mr Wrong,' she said with a grin. 'And you look so lovely in your emerald-green one that no other girl will get a look in.'

As if from a great distance, Michael heard Stan Brenner's voice telling him it was time to get up and that he'd brought him a cup of tea. He forced his eyes open to see his batman standing patiently beside his bed. Michael couldn't believe it was four already, he felt he'd only just closed his eyes.

'Okay,' he said. He felt unable to say more, his tongue felt thickly furred, and he could still taste the whisky he'd drunk the night before.

He pushed back the blankets and got out of bed rubbing his eyes, then drank the hot, sweet tea gratefully. Brenner left, satisfied he was fully awake.

Within ten minutes Michael was washed, shaved and on his way to the mess for breakfast. He didn't want any, as usual his stomach was churning, but he knew from experience that the fear would subside once he was in the cockpit and it might be hours before he got a chance to eat anything again.

The other chaps from the squadron were already in the mess, the air thick with cigarette smoke, but the only greetings were mere nods. No one talked at this early hour. Michael knew that like him, each man was bracing himself for the day ahead, trying not to think which of their number might be missing by tonight.

It was 28 May, and today would probably be a repeat of the previous one, flying over to France to try to intercept German bombers intent on massacring the British and French troops retreating towards Dunkirk.

Michael had shot down an ME 109 yesterday, but it had been the most terrifying, God awful day. It was bad enough seeing the straggling lines of soldiers trying to make it to the Dunkirk beaches, and transport home, but inland he had seen the vast hordes of refugees fleeing the Germans: women carrying babies in their arms, toddlers trying to keep hold of their skirts, men pushing carts piled with their belongings. They had to pick their way through mangled bodies, burnt-out vehicles, carts and dead animals, and Michael had felt murderous towards the German pilots who would open fire on innocent civilians.

A Spitfire only held enough fuel for an hour and a half at most. Twenty minutes to France, twenty minutes back, in theory leaving fifty minutes to attack German planes. But the only way to beat the bastards was to fly in at top speed of over 300 mph, get in close, fire everything you had, and then shoot off like a bat out of hell. But at top speed the Merlin engine guzzled fuel and Michael had to keep in mind he had to save enough for the trip back.

The fourth sortie of the day yesterday had been the worst. One minute the sky was clear, then suddenly the enemy was everywhere, like flying into a swarm of wasps. Michael went for one plane which was away from the main bunch, flying flat out and in for the kill. But suddenly he was surrounded, above, below and on both sides. He'd forgotten to put on his silk scarf and his neck was rubbed raw from his collar as he twisted and turned his head to keep lookout. He fired at the 109 beside him on his right, and at the one below, then went into a swift dive to evade them. He felt a bone-jerking judder as he was hit, and for a few moments thought that was it for him. But they'd only hit his left wing, and he managed to pull himself together to roll away and flee back to England. He only just made it, gliding the last few miles to conserve fuel, and the cockpit so hot with the sun on it that he could barely see for sweat running into his eyes. It had been a close shave.

After tea and a slice of toast, Michael joined the others to get on the transport to take them to the airfield, each carrying their parachute.

Cold, grey dawn on the airfield. Silent, but not deserted as the ground crews were there in readiness. Many of them would have worked through the night on repairs and adjustments to the planes.

Michael had seen the same scene many times, but it never ceased to move him. The row of sturdy little Spits with early-morning mist rising around them had the look of a pack of terriers braced for the hunt. Deathly quiet for now, but in minutes when the mighty engines roared into life, and the smell of petrol and engine oil filled the air, the airfield became a very different place.

Michael's plane was repaired, and he jumped up on the wing, put his parachute down, slid into the cockpit and started the engine. Once he was in his seat, his fear usually subsided, and today was no exception. He checked his instruments, radio, fuel and coolant gauges, and gave the thumbs up to the ground crew when he found everything fine. Then, switching off, he climbed out again and trudged back to the dispersal tent to wait with the other boys for the order to scramble.

This was the part Michael disliked most. He was keyed up to go, and didn't want to wait around with time to think. Some men read, some played chess, some lay down on the camp beds and slept, while others silently chain-smoked.

But Michael invariably found himself thinking about Adele. He had been on a roller-coaster of emotions since she turned him down. Disbelief, anger, pity, hate, and deep, deep sorrow. He had racked his mind for what he did wrong, and now and then told himself he was well rid of her. He'd tried to convince himself she'd been cheating on him, even tried to tell himself she was mad. But however he looked at it, he always came back to the same point. She must have been spooked that weekend in London by her experiences in that children's home. Nothing else made sense.

Yet if that was the case, Michael felt she needed love more than ever. And his feelings of abandonment were probably nothing compared with what was going on in her head.

He never went down to Winchelsea now, he couldn't bear to. If his mother wanted to see him she came up to London and he met her there. He had refused to see his father at first, holding him at least partially responsible because he hadn't approved of Adele. But when he turned up at Biggin Hill one day soon after war was declared, Michael couldn't refuse to see him without making it obvious to his fellow pilots that they were estranged.

To his surprise, his father was apologetic that he'd been so harsh about Adele. While he said all the things Michael had expected, that perhaps the break-up was for the best in the long run, he did concede that Adele had some very admirable qualities. He also showed unusual sensitivity. He actually hugged Michael and said that first love was invariably painful, and that he felt for him.

'Fancy a game of cards, Mike?'

Michael was startled out of his reverie by John Chapman's question. John was now his closest friend in the squadron, and though their backgrounds couldn't be more different, they'd quickly become soulmates when he arrived at Biggin Hill some seven months ago.

John was barely twenty, and looked even younger with his

chubby face, fair hair and innocent wide eyes. He was brought up on a farm in Shropshire, went to the local grammar school, and was working in a garage when he got his first taste of planes. He'd told Michael he was asked to drive out to an airfield ten miles from his work, to deliver some spare parts, and while he was there, he was offered a ride in a bi-plane. The pilot had taken him on a hair-raising ride, but scared as John had been, he knew flying was the only career for him, so he applied to join the RAF, quite prepared to be one of the ground crew if he couldn't make it as a pilot. But it seems the examining board liked what they saw, for he was selected for a short-term commission.

Michael agreed to play cards, it would take his mind off Adele and waiting for the order to scramble. John dealt the cards, but before picking his up he looked hard at Michael.

'If I don't make it today, will you get in touch with my folks?' he asked.

'Of course,' Michael replied. 'And you with mine?'

John nodded, and they began to play as if they had spoken of nothing more serious than where they would have a pint later in the day.

The order to scramble came at seven-thirty. 'Blast it.' John grinned as he hastily put on his Mae West lifejacket. 'I was hoping we'd get the second breakfast at eight o'clock.'

Michael fixed his silk scarf as he ran to his plane, jumped up on the wing, fixed his parachute in place on his seat, and started up the engine. His fear and trepidation left him then, for he knew that a relaxed pilot who flew by instinct stood a better chance of survival than one who thought too deeply about what he was about to face. He had only one thought in his mind as his plane waddled forward like an old goose towards the runway. To shoot at least one plane down and get back here safely.

As the squadron approached the Channel in tight formation,

Michael made a thumbs up to John flying on his right. It was perfect flying weather, with little wind and only a few puffy white clouds, and the visibility so good he could see a group of children on a road below, their little faces upturned, hands shielding the sun from their eyes as they watched the planes flying above them.

Within seconds he had passed over the cliffs, and there was only sea beneath him now. It looked so clear, blue and inviting in the sunshine, evoking happy memories of swimming with Adele. But the Channel was as much of an enemy to the pilots as the Germans. If you had to bail out over it your chances of survival were slim. He wondered if the pilot of the Hurricane he'd seen parachuting down yesterday had been picked up in time.

A warning came over his radio that at least a dozen ME 109s were heading for Dunkirk, and almost as soon as Michael got the message, he spotted them in the distance. He could see columns of black smoke rising on the French coast too, and braced himself for seeing more bomb damage as he got closer.

All at once the sky was full of enemy planes coming towards him, their silver crosses winking malevolently in the sunshine. He climbed to evade them and saw John do likewise to his right. But as he rose up through a bank of cloud he came upon two more fighters which had been hidden from view. He flew straight between them, firing his guns, and he thought he hit the one on the left, so went into a roll to catch it again and finish it off.

He couldn't see John now, and assumed he'd dived again. But as he came back to attack once more, he saw a flash of flame out of the corner of his eye. There was no time to check what it was, he was gaining on the fighter he'd hit and he had to concentrate to get himself in a good position for firing again. His quarry was trying to make a run for it, but the earlier hit had slowed it down. Michael came in so close he could see the German pilot clearly, and when he fired he caught the nose of the plane and saw a burst of coolant spray up over the cockpit glass. As he sped away he had the satisfaction of seeing it dropping like a stone, a trail of black smoke coming from it.

The sky was suddenly deserted, and looking at his fuel gauge Michael realized he'd flown further than he intended, away from the rest of the squadron. He wheeled round to head for home, and it was then that he saw John's Spitfire, upside down. The tail was ablaze – obviously the flash of flame he'd seen earlier – and though John was in the correct position for bailing out, it looked as if he couldn't get the cockpit open.

Sweat trickled down Michael's face and suddenly he was trembling. He had already lost four good friends in the squadron and heard that at least another dozen men he'd known had bought it. But although he'd felt badly about each and every one of them, and sympathized with their families, this was the first time he'd actually witnessed a fatality.

'Get the cockpit open!' he roared instinctively. But even as the words came out he was aware of the futility of it, for the only person who could hear him was the radio operator.

Michael cried all the way home. John was so innocent – only a couple of days earlier he had admitted that he'd never slept with a girl. His mother sent him a homemade cake almost every week, his father sent him weekly reports on the local football team's games. They had been so proud that their only son had been accepted as a pilot.

It wasn't bloody fair. John was a first-class pilot, he didn't have a mean bone in his body and everyone liked him. He'd got Michael out of the doldrums many a time with his jokes and sunny nature. He had so much to give. Why did it have to be him?

*

Honour stood in the garden shading her eyes as she looked up at the planes fighting in the sky. She was glad it was over Dungeness today, for at least if any of them crash-landed there were no houses out that way.

In the last six weeks, since the evacuation of Dunkirk, she had lost track of how many such dog-fights she'd seen. Winston Churchill had dubbed this battle in the air 'The Battle of Britain', and to Honour it seemed unbelievable that the average age of these young pilots who fought with such skill, courage and grim determination was only twenty.

Even when she couldn't see planes above her, she knew they were fighting somewhere, as the drone of the Spitfires and Hurricanes flying out woke her almost every morning. She would look out of the window and watch them flying off bravely towards the French coast in tight formation, only to see them coming back later in just twos and threes. At first she tried to keep a tally, to check if they all came back. But it made her too dejected when some were unaccounted for.

She'd seen two crash-land: one of the pilots came down on his parachute unhurt, but the other burned to death. What she'd seen was almost nothing, however, for there had been countless fatalities all over the South of England. Bombers slunk in unseen to drop their deadly cargo on air fields, killing ground-force crews and civilians. As for the bombers that couldn't make it to their intended target, they ruthlessly dropped their load anywhere, not caring if they hit hospitals, schools, villages and towns.

Six weeks earlier Honour had taken heart to see how ordinary people took to hundreds of little boats to rescue soldiers stranded in Dunkirk. She had believed that no one could conquer England when its subjects were so brave and determined. But now, seeing these fighter boys in action day after day, reading the casualty lists which grew longer each week, she was very afraid England hadn't got the manpower or weapons to win the war.

She went to sleep filled with anxiety, woke with it still there. At first her prayers were just to keep Adele and Michael safe, but now she felt it was wrong to think only of those she loved. Every single soldier, sailor or airman was someone's grandson, son, husband, sweetheart or brother. She felt for all of them.

'Watching the sky won't get the weeds pulled out,' Jim the postman called out jovially as he dropped his bike out in the lane to bring her some post.

'It certainly won't,' Honour said with a rueful smile, glad of a diversion from gloomy thoughts. She liked Jim. He was sixty-seven, with a shock of white hair and the bandiest legs she'd ever seen. He had fought in the first war, but although he wasn't in very good health, he'd taken over the post round from his son when he was called up. He said it made him feel useful and the exercise was good for him. 'But the weeds can wait a little longer if you'd like a cup of tea.'

'I hoped you'd offer one, I'm parched,' he said. 'And it's a red-letter day for you. Looks like this one's from your granddaughter. It's got a London postmark.'

Jim sat himself down on the bench by the door while Honour went in to make the tea. As she waited for the kettle to boil she had a quick read of the letter. '*Dear Granny,*' she read.

I haven't got much to report, everything is fairly quiet right now, only emergency cases to deal with as everyone else is being sent out of London. All the wards on the upper floors are closed and they've made new ones in the basement for safety in an air raid. I've taken up knitting on night duty, because there's so little to do, and nearly finished the back of a cardigan. It's awful that Paris has been taken by the Germans, isn't it? I sometimes wonder if our men can really stop them.

I wish I could come home for a holiday, London's so horrible in the summer, and the food here is terrible. I suppose it will get even worse before the war is over, there's shortages of almost everything now.

I've been to quite a few dances with Joan and some of the other nurses recently. It's funny how people seem set on enjoying themselves more now than they did in peacetime. You'd think they would all be scared and sombre. The West End is really jolly at night, despite the blackout, even if they have got Eros all boarded up. We stayed up there late one evening and you couldn't see a hand in front of your face out on the streets. But it makes people talk to each other more and help one another. I'm sick of carting my gas mask around though!

There's a great many more children back in London now, I do think their mothers are a bit foolhardy bringing them back, however much they miss them. I helped at my first caesarean birth the other night, the mother had been in labour at home for two days until a neighbour finally called an ambulance. It was an incredible thing to watch, and it made me much more interested in midwifery. The baby, a little boy, was fine, but his mother is still poorly. Her husband is in the army and she's got three other children to take care of. Some women have it so hard, don't they?

No other news I'm afraid. We're all a bit bored really with so few patients. How is Towzer? I'm really glad you have him, if a German drops out of the sky I'm sure he'll savage him for you!

Look after yourself and don't work too hard on growing vegetables. Just sweet talk the rabbits so they have more babies. Give Misty a cuddle, and Towzer a stroke from me. Keep safe.

Love,
Adele

Honour smiled, and tucked the letter into her apron pocket to read again later. She worried so much about Adele, but each time a letter came she could feel a little easier for a while.

At midday, as Honour was weeding her vegetable garden, Rose half sat up in her bed in London to reach for a cigarette.

'Damn,' she muttered on finding the packet empty, and slumped back on the pillows.

It was a year and five months since she got the thousand pounds from Myles Bailey, and at the time she thought she was set up for life. But then war broke out and her plans fell apart.

Everything was so good for a while, she didn't even want to drink much. Following advice from a businessman who used to eat in the restaurant where she worked, she bought a very cheap eight-room house in Hammersmith. He said she would make more money letting out rooms than she could earn anywhere else, and she'd still hold on to her capital. It sounded like good advice, and although she had difficulty finding a plumber to put in another kitchen and bathroom for the lodgers, she finally got it done and decorated too.

She toured the secondhand shops and haggled for furniture and other stuff she wanted, and once it all came together, for the first time in her life she really felt she was going somewhere.

It was bliss to have a real home of her own, a bathroom all to herself, a little garden, and enough money to splash out on clothes, perfume and getting her hair done. The first lodgers were perfect too. Two married couples in the two biggest rooms, and two older businessmen in the other two smaller ones. They all paid their rent every week without fail, the wives kept their own rooms and the kitchen and bathroom clean. The two businessmen went home to their wives at weekends, and they didn't even use the kitchen.

It was all so harmonious and peaceful – the most noise Rose ever heard was laughter and chatter between the two couples who had become friends. In her naivety Rose assumed they would all stay indefinitely – the two older men were past the age for call-up, one of the younger men was a fireman, and the other did something in the Civil Service which gave him an exemption. But Rose hadn't really considered that the start of war would affect civilians the way it did.

The man in the Civil Service got moved away from London and of course his wife went with him. The couple she replaced them with fell out with the fireman and his wife, and they used that as an excuse to move back home with her mother. Then the two businessmen left one after the other as they both felt they would rather commute to London each day and be home with their wives and children at night if bombing began.

Rose soon found she couldn't be so choosy about tenants as so many people were moving out of London that there were hundreds of flats and rooms to let. Before long she was letting the rooms to anyone who wanted them, and trouble quickly followed. She had Jewish refugees from Holland and Germany who couldn't speak English. Rough, noisy men who skipped off owing her rent. She had women with children who upset the other tenants. She had one man who used to smash things up when he was drunk, a woman who turned out to be a prostitute, and any number of fly-by-night characters who were in trouble with the police.

Still lying back on the pillows, Rose surveyed her bedroom with jaundiced eyes. She had been thrilled when the decorator put up the pink and white wallpaper – after what she'd been used to, it looked like a film star's bedroom.

The big window offered a view of leafy back gardens and the early morning sun made the walnut bed, wardrobe and dressing-table gleam with amber and gold lights. They suggested much-loved family heirlooms, as did the fringed pink and sage green carpet, but they were all secondhand. Rose had kept this room as if it were for royalty until quite recently, smoothing out the pink satin quilt, even putting a few flowers in a vase on the dressing-table. Sometimes she just sat in here, savouring how pretty it was, but she hadn't done that for some time now.

Clothes were dropped on the floor now, the sheets were none too clean, and a film of dust lay on the shiny furniture.

Rose was by no means destitute. She still had a couple of hundred pounds tucked away in the bank, and the rent she did get covered her living expenses. But she was demoralized. She had believed she knew every trick in the book that tenants could come up with. She thought she could recognize a shyster immediately, and she was also convinced she was tough enough to face up to anyone, but she was mistaken.

She felt like crying when she saw the damage some of the tenants did to their rooms and was revolted by how dirty some of them could be. But over and above all that, she was terribly lonely. She couldn't get friendly with people in her house or they would take her for a ride. Jobs like unblocking the sink or changing a washer in a tap were beyond her, and when she had to be ruthless and throw someone out she felt physically sick with nerves.

Yet worse in many ways was the guilt. Not about taking the money from Myles Bailey – she believed he owed her that – but about what she'd done to Adele.

It hadn't come to her straightaway, at first she was too cock-a-hoop about getting the house to care about anything. The guilt crept in almost unnoticed, just a little pang when she saw young airmen and their girls walking hand in hand, or if she saw a nurse from the local hospital. But she felt it more and more now, and however much she told herself she had to prevent her daughter marrying her brother, she knew Adele must see her as the most despicable woman in the world.

Rose was thirty-nine now, and when she looked in the mirror she could see for herself what time, drink, loveless affairs and selfishness had done to her. No amount of money would bring back her looks – money could buy company, but not real friends. It could buy material comfort, but not affection. Who would care if a bomb dropped on this house and killed her? There wasn't one person who would come forward to say something good about her.

She would lie awake at night remembering the holidays she'd spent as a child with her parents in Curlew Cottage. She could recall her parents' laughter as they made supper in the evenings, walking between them holding both their hands, sitting on her mother's lap by the fire while her father read to them. If Adele ever looked back on her childhood, Rose doubted she'd have even one good memory of her mother.

For so many years Rose had viewed those years of her own childhood on the marsh like some of her father's charcoal sketches, everything just shades of grey and black. Cold, gloomy and miserable. But maybe it was because she went back that day in bright sunshine that the charcoal sketch had gone, replaced by a picture in glorious Technicolor. In her mind's eye she saw waist-high meadowsweet swaying in the breeze, emerald-green grass studded with golden buttercups and purple clover. Darting kingfishers made brilliant flashes of turquoise along the river bank, and yellow wild iris grew in the boggy places.

She couldn't even see her mother as the hard-faced shrew she used to picture. Instead, she found herself remembering her telling her stories as they made gingerbread men together, picking wild flowers, or cuddling up together by the stove on cold evenings. It made her eyes smart when she imagined Adele in her place, the pair of them blanking out all memory of the mother and daughter who had cared so little for them.

Until quite recently Rose had never felt bad about running away from home the way she did. She could justify it completely, for she worked all the hours God sent at that hotel and had to hand over all her wages to a mother who didn't even appreciate how hard she had to work. Besides, Myles had seemed like her big chance in life. Then, when everything went wrong and she was alone with a baby on the way, she was too proud to write and admit she was in trouble.

She supposed she lost that pride somewhere along the road, and apathy took its place. Most of her adult life was now a mere blur, with only a few images sticking up like rocks through a mist. One was getting married to Jim in that horrible dirty register office in Ladbroke Grove. The registrar had smirked at her swollen belly and said something about 'they'd made it just in time'. There was Adele's birth too in a grim boarding house with bugs in the bed. She had hours and hours of white-hot pain, with only a sharp-tongued old biddy to help her. Was it any wonder she didn't feel loving towards a baby who had torn her apart, prevented her ever going home again, and forced her into marrying a dimwit like Jim Talbot?

Pamela's birth also stood out clearly in her mind, but a different experience entirely. It was quick and painless, and Jim had been so kind and loving that she almost fooled herself into believing she loved him. When she looked down at Pamela's sweet little face she felt such tenderness and pride, and she thought that at last her life had taken a turn for the better.

They moved into Charlton Street not long afterwards, and it seemed like paradise after the hideous places they'd lived in before.

Pamela was around eighteen months old when everything turned sour. Rose had had times before when she'd felt exhausted and morose, but it had always passed. This time, however, it was as if a cold grey fog was swirling around her, refusing to lift. She didn't want to get up in the morning – the thought of nappies to wash, meals to be cooked and the endless demands of the two children was just too much to bear. She wanted complete silence, to be alone, and just the sound of Jim or Adele's voice made her want to run out of the flat and keep running until she found the peace she craved.

It was Pamela who held her there. Hers was the only voice that didn't grate on her nerves. Her smiles were the only thing that lifted the fog a little. Rose wished she could feel the same way about Adele, but whenever she looked at her, she was reminded of Myles, and what he had put her through.

Once, when Pamela was three, she'd tried to leave with her while Adele was at school. She had managed to save a couple of pounds out of the housekeeping money, and she thought she'd catch a train out into the country and find somewhere to live. But as she began to pack up all the things they would need, she realized she hadn't got the strength to carry a heavy bag and a small child who couldn't walk far. She sat down on the floor and cried like a frustrated child.

She thought of leaving many more times after that, but she knew she couldn't work and look after Pamela. And the more trapped she felt, the worse it got.

Then Pamela was killed, and all at once there was nothing left in her life. Drinking dulled the pain a little, but as soon as she sobered up, it came back again. She had no real recollection of the events that led up to her being committed to the asylum. All she remembered was that after Pamela's funeral she felt as though someone was winding her up tighter and tighter like a mechanical toy, and she guessed that in the end the spring inside her broke and she lost control of her body and mind.

She did remember some of the treatments she had in the asylum. Being plunged into icy baths, being forced to swallow some terrible medicine which made her vomit. But what really brought her wits back was none of these things. It was being shut up in a room on her own.

To be left alone, no one trying to talk to her, asking her to do anything, to be able to sleep and sleep, that was what saved her. Once her mind and body were rested, she was able to think clearly again.

At the time she was informed her mother had become Adele's legal guardian, she was also told that she could not be discharged from the asylum without her husband's agreement. She knew that meant she'd be in there for life, as Jim wasn't likely to come forward.

Rose observed that the asylum staff were hardest on those who caused them any trouble. She had been beaten herself when she first arrived there for screaming abuse and fighting the staff. Fear of injury had made her become silent and obedient, and she saw that the only way she might stand a chance of escape was to stay that way.

So she gave up protesting that she wasn't mad, she didn't speak, cry or shout at all, just did exactly what she was told, and made no trouble for anyone. She thought if she kept up this docile silence they would begin to give her little jobs, and she could win their trust.

Her assumption was correct. Before long they gave her mending to do, washing floors, even work in the laundry, and finally they allowed her to walk in the grounds.

There were times when she even began to believe she really had lost the ability to speak, along with smiling, laughing and walking briskly. She got so used to keeping a blank expression, to shuffling along slowly with her head held down, just like the other patients, that she found she didn't even care when the staff talked about her in front of her as if she was a real imbecile. But she kept her eyes open, listened carefully and made mental notes of anything that could be useful to her.

She had told Johnny she escaped from there in a laundry van, and this was true. But what she would never admit to him or anyone else was that she used her feminine wiles on the simple-minded driver to get him to smuggle her out. She felt no real shame that she tempted him with the offer of sex so he would hide her in a basket of washing, that was fair game. But she was ashamed that once she was outside the gates she kept up the pretence of loving him so he would clothe, feed and keep her.

Poor simple Jack had never had a woman before and he had worshipped Rose. He didn't smoke or drink, he lived a frugal life in the same tiny, dilapidated cottage on the outskirts of Barnet that he'd been born in. His parents were both dead, he hadn't a real friend in the world, and his job as a van driver was the only thing he had to be proud of. It wasn't right that she stayed with him for over a year, gradually building up his belief that she was his woman, and all the time stealing from him until she had enough money to flee.

She read in the papers a few weeks after she'd left that he hanged himself in a wood. That made her feel really bad. He had willingly risked losing his job to help her. He might even have been sent to prison for harbouring her if he'd been found out. He was just thirty, a man who had spent most of his life as the butt of jokes, isolated and friendless. And she'd broken his heart.

Rose couldn't understand why she was suddenly dwelling on the past so much. She had always believed that once she had financial security and a decent place to live, happiness would come with it. But she wasn't happy. How could she be when she was for ever looking over her shoulder, tormenting herself with memories of people she'd used, shabby tricks she'd played, and remorse for what she'd done to her mother and Adele?

Sometimes, when she'd had a couple of drinks, she even tried to write to them and apologize, but she'd re-read the letters the following morning and tear them up. Whatever she said was never going to be enough to be forgiven.

Chapter Twenty-one

Honour paused at the kerb of Shepherd's Bush Road, making Towzer sit. Looking across to number 103, she felt a mixture of relief she'd finally found it, and trepidation at what was to come.

She had only been to London a few times in her life, and then only to art galleries or the West End shops, so she had little idea of what to expect of ordinary working-class areas. Instinct, and descriptions Adele had given her of the East End, told her that Hammersmith was a quite respectable area, but it looked hideous and squalid to her.

It was 23 August, yet another hot day, and the leaves on the trees hung down limply, covered in a film of dust and soot. Windows criss-crossed with sticking tape, and piles of sandbags were an inevitable and expected aspect of war, but the overflowing dustbins and the smell of drains repulsed her. She didn't think she could bear to live in a street where hordes of grubby children ran around yelling stridently all day. She thought the women in pinafores and turban-style headscarves gossiping on the front steps should get their backsides off and take their offspring to a park.

Yesterday, Honour had received a letter from Rose. Apart from the shock of a letter after all these years, she was greatly surprised by the uncharacteristic meek and apologetic tone to it. She had read and re-read it dozens of times in the course of the day, wondering at the real motive behind it. She began to reply to it last night but, defeated as to what she should say, early this morning she'd decided to come to London and see Rose face to face instead.

She wasn't merely curious to see how Rose lived now, or

even desperate to make the peace with her errant daughter. But she believed that it was time at least to attempt to draw a line under the past.

No one could predict what this war had in store for them, and there had been reports of bombs dropped around London very recently. One had landed in Wimbledon on 16 August when people were killed, and according to the map that wasn't so far from Hammersmith. Honour knew that if Rose was killed or badly hurt in an air raid she would always be sorry she hadn't at least attempted to see her. As it was a Saturday today she thought there was every chance Rose would be at home.

The train was slow, taking an hour longer than it should have, giving her far too much time to worry about what she was going to find at her journey's end. She had felt compelled to bring Towzer with her just in case something cropped up and she couldn't get back again tonight. While he seemed perfectly at home on the carriage floor, she wasn't sure what he would make of busy streets with buses and trams. Fortunately he seemed to be taking it all in his stride, and Honour felt quite proud of herself that she'd managed to find her way to Hammersmith unaided.

As Rose had said nothing about her personal circumstances, only that she let out rooms, Honour couldn't help but feel she must be in difficulties. Why else would she suddenly claim she was sorry for all the hurt in the past?

Honour was very hot, her best navy blue dress too thick for a summer's day. Her feet hurt, her eyes felt full of grit, and both she and Towzer desperately needed a drink. But on the plus side, number 103 was no better or worse than any other house in the street.

It was a soot-engrained terraced house that led straight on to the street, with no front garden. It had three floors and a basement, with a few steps up to the front door which was painted royal blue. Most of the windows were open, and she hoped that meant Rose would be in, and that her journey hadn't been wasted.

The bell rang loudly enough to wake the dead, but it was a while before Honour heard someone coming to answer it.

A young woman of about twenty-five, with bright red hair and conflicting lipstick, opened the door. 'Yes?' she inquired.

'I've come to see Mrs Talbot,' Honour said.

The girl shrugged. 'I dunno if she's in. Try knocking on that door.' She pointed to the second one down the hallway, then flounced off back up the stairs, leaving Honour to come in and close the front door behind her.

Honour knocked, then called out Rose's name. There was still no reply. Looking up the stairs, she could see an open door to a white-tiled room that looked like a bathroom. As she needed the lavatory and a drink for Towzer, she went up, taking the dog with her.

She used the lavatory, which she noted was none too clean, got Towzer's tin bowl from her bag and gave him a drink of water. As the window was open she put her head out to see what lay behind the house.

To her surprise, right down below at the basement level, there was Rose lying asleep in a deckchair. A lump came up in Honour's throat, as from so far away Rose looked young and vulnerable in a pink and white striped sundress, the skirt hitched up over her knees.

She leaned out of the window and called to her.

It was almost laughable that while Rose hadn't heard the loud door bell, the sound of her mother's voice made her jerk awake immediately, jump to her feet and look round in puzzlement.

'I'm upstairs, Rose,' Honour called out. 'I knocked on your door but couldn't make you hear.'

Five minutes later Honour was down in the back yard, with Rose sitting opposite her and Towzer between them panting and looking from one to the other, perhaps picking up on the tension between them.

'I shouldn't have sent that letter,' Rose said for the third time. 'I wasn't quite myself at the time.'

'You were drunk?' Honour said bluntly.

'No! Of course not,' Rose said, too quickly. 'I was just feeling a bit low.'

Honour was fairly certain Rose *had* been drunk and had no recollection of writing or posting it, for when she'd let her mother in she seemed completely dumbstruck at being found. That didn't bother Honour. While she didn't exactly like the thought that the letter was the rambling of a drunk who had forgotten it by morning, in her opinion people tended to speak from the heart at such times.

'I can't believe you came all this way on the train,' Rose said breathlessly, as if desperate to move the conversation on to a different tack. 'With a dog too! How did you find your way?'

'I might be sixty but my brain still works,' Honour said dryly. 'The travelling has made me very thirsty though. Are you going to offer me some tea?'

She had seen nothing of Rose's house but the bathroom and a fleeting glimpse of the kitchen, which Rose had quickly led her through to bring her out here. She had said something about it being cooler under the tree as she put up another deckchair, but having a suspicious mind, Honour doubted that was the real reason.

Rose blushed. 'Of course, I wasn't thinking.' She leaped to her feet. 'I'll go and make some.'

Honour stayed in her deckchair as she wanted to give her daughter time to gather herself. Stunned as Rose had been at her mother's arrival, she hadn't seemed horrified, nor had she been belligerent, the way she was when she'd called at Winchelsea. She also looked well, far less brassy than before, and the kitchen at least had been clean and tidy. It was only fair to give her a few minutes to get rid of anything in her living room which might embarrass her, and perhaps remember what she'd actually said in her letter.

The back yard was surprisingly pleasant – only a scrap of grass, but there was honeysuckle along the walls and a clump of Michaelmas daisies just coming into flower. It had been tended by someone, there were no weeds, and the concrete part by the steps up to the kitchen was well swept. Rose's letter had implied it was her house, and if this was so, Honour wondered how she'd got the money to buy it. But then there was so much she didn't know about Rose, and she knew if she was to get anywhere today, she had to curb her desire to ask too many questions.

Rose came back some ten minutes later with tea things on a tray. She had brushed her hair, put on a little lipstick, and she looked composed. The tea set gave Honour a bit of a jolt, for it was dainty bone china with a dark red band around the cups decorated with gold, and very like a set she had.

'How long have you had the dog?' Rose asked, putting the tea tray on a wooden crate between them. She reached out to stroke him, and it was clear to Honour that she was very unsure of herself and going to take refuge in neutral conversation.

Honour explained how Towzer had arrived, and why she had brought him with her today.

Over the tea they talked about the Battle of Britain. Rose appeared to be quite ignorant about it, but perhaps this was understandable as most of the air battles had been fought over Essex, Kent and Sussex. She complained about rationing, the blackout, and the many false alarms when the air-raid sirens frightened the life out of people.

'We don't take any notice of them now,' she said with a shrug. 'They won't bomb London. Some people just like to scaremonger. I wish they would stop it, it's hard enough to get good tenants as it is, without making out London will be flattened soon.'

369

From what Honour had seen of London today, there certainly didn't seem any cause for alarm. The transport was running smoothly, shops were open as usual, people meandering along in the sunshine looked carefree.

A woman she got into conversation with on the Tube had said that people were getting sick and tired of rushing into shelters when the sirens went off, only to find they'd wasted several hours for nothing as it was a false alarm. She said nothing would make her go into some filthy dirty shelter again. So maybe Rose was right. She lived here after all.

'Is it your house?' Honour asked after hearing a tirade against some of the people who had lodged here.

'Yes. I'd been saving for a very long time, and I got a little windfall. A friend said I should invest it in property.' She spoke defensively as if she'd rehearsed that explanation.

'Very sensible,' Honour said. She wanted to stop the chit-chat, and get back to why Rose had written to her. The tea set, so similar to her own at home, offered a possibility of getting on to a more personal level.

'Your tea set is almost identical to mine,' she said brightly, picking up the teapot to look at it.

'That's why I bought it,' Rose said somewhat sheepishly. 'I saw it in a secondhand shop and it was a reminder of home.'

'I wouldn't have thought you wanted any reminders,' Honour said, carefully keeping her tone light.

'You'd be surprised at how often I think about the past,' Rose retorted, and then hung her head a little as if she was aware she would have to follow up that statement with some kind of explanation. 'Okay, Mother,' she said, looking directly at Honour. 'I do regret a lot of things. If I could have my time over again, I would have done everything differently.'

Honour nodded. 'You said that in your letter, and that you hoped for forgiveness and a chance to try again. What made you suddenly want that?'

'It wasn't a sudden thought,' Rose said with a shrug. 'I've

wanted it for a very long time, but since the war began it's become more vital.'

'I've felt that way myself,' Honour said carefully. 'But pleased and relieved as I was to find out where you were, I can't promise forgiveness. That has to be earned.'

'How?' Rose frowned.

'Well, that's something you have to think about,' Honour said. 'You'll have to be honest with yourself about your motive for wanting it. Is it because you are lonely or troubled right now?'

'No, I'm fine,' Rose said indignantly. 'I've got this house, income from my tenants. I can show you round so you can see for yourself.'

'Material things don't impress me,' Honour rebuked her. 'They never have and never will. You and your father were once the axis my world turned on, now it's Adele. And just as I would have done anything to keep you and Frank safe and well, so I would with my granddaughter. So you have to convince me that your motives are pure before I'll allow you anywhere near her.'

'I don't know that I want to go anywhere near her,' Rose said in a sullen tone. 'We didn't get on when she was a child. I doubt it would be any different now.'

'If you're going to take that attitude then I might as well leave right now,' Honour snapped back. 'Adele and I are a package. If you want me somewhere in your life, you'll have to make amends to her.'

Rose said nothing for a little while, twisting her hands in her lap.

'I do want to make amends,' she said eventually. 'It's just that I don't believe she'll ever meet me halfway. I know I handled everything so badly that day I came to see you. There was so much I wanted to say, but I shouldn't have just turned up like that and been so—' She paused, clearly not knowing how to describe her attitude that day.

'Insolent?' Honour suggested. 'That's how you were, Rose. Ignorant, ungracious, unfeeling, all those things. I could see no trace left of the daughter I had nurtured so carefully. You must have lived with some very low sorts to get like that.'

Rose stiffened. 'Low sorts were the only ones to give me shelter,' she said defiantly. 'I wouldn't have married Jim Talbot if I hadn't been desperate.'

Honour looked hard at her daughter. She did look very much better than she had at their last meeting. Her blonde hair was shiny and fixed up in the latest style, a sort of thick roll along the back of her neck which puzzled Honour as to how it was achieved. She was suntanned, slimmer too now, and the pink and white sundress had a classy look. But there were lines on her face, and they weren't ones of laughter. She was still a very attractive woman, but she looked hard.

'Jim Talbot was in the distant past,' Honour said eventually. 'But have you dragged that past into the present?'

'What on earth do you mean by that?' Rose riled up. 'It seems to me you're the one who wants to drag the past up!'

Honour felt she had to be firm. 'Now don't start, Rose. Just listen to me for a moment. The way you left, and your father dying, made me bitter and reclusive. I remained that way right up till the day Adele turned up. So I do know why people drag the past with them and wallow in the misery of it. Now, once you got out of that asylum, did you make a concerted effort to change your way of life?'

'Yes, of course I did,' Rose snapped. 'Look at me now, am I living in a slum? Am I unkempt, dirty or barmy?'

'No, you aren't,' Honour agreed. 'But have you achieved what you have now by your own efforts and hard work?'

'I suppose you think I got it from a man.' Rose got up from her deckchair and glowered down at her mother. 'What do you think I am? A tart?'

Honour opened her mouth to reply, but she was stopped short by the sound of aircraft in the distance. A dull, droning sound that she knew from experience wasn't small fighter planes.

'Listen,' she said as she jumped up and caught hold of Rose's arm. 'Bombers!'

'So it may be, but they aren't going to drop any here.' Rose shook off her hand. 'It's bad enough you calling me a tart. I can't cope with hysterics too.'

Honour stood stock-still, her ears straining to hear the planes, and ignoring her daughter. There was a shrill whine, then a dull thud, quickly followed by others, and then the ear-piercing shriek of the air-raid warning siren which made Towzer howl.

'Where's the nearest shelter?' Honour asked, grabbing her bag and the lead for Towzer who continued to howl at full throttle.

'There's one down the road, but you can't take dogs into them,' Rose said tetchily. 'For goodness' sake, Mother, calm down and stop that damned beast making that horrible noise.'

'Then we must go inside, Rose,' Honour said, going over to Towzer and putting her arms around him protectively. 'Is there a cellar?'

'Yes, I use it for storing things,' Rose said, casually picking up the tray of tea things as if there was nothing to be concerned about. 'Don't panic, Mother. We'll go up to the top floor and look out, you can see for miles up there. Perhaps then you'll calm down.'

The room Rose spoke of did have a good view towards central London, but the sight that met their eyes robbed them both of speech. The sky was full of planes, so far away they looked no bigger than birds, but rising ominously up to meet them was a mushroom of black smoke.

All at once it was Rose who looked terrified, and she turned to Honour wringing her hands. 'Oh my God!' she exclaimed. 'They really are bombing! What shall we do?'

373

'We go and look at your cellar,' Honour said. 'I'm not going into a shelter without Towzer. How far away is that cloud would you say?'

'I don't know,' Rose gasped, her face suddenly white. 'The West End maybe, but it could be as far away as the East End. It's difficult to tell.'

'Whitechapel?' Honour asked, her legs suddenly feeling like jelly.

'Could be,' Rose said. 'Come on, let's get downstairs before they get here.'

Later, Honour was to realize that if the air-raid warning had not come when it did, she would not have discovered much about her now grown-up daughter. They probably would have ended up arguing, and Honour would almost certainly have travelled home later with as many unanswered questions as she arrived with.

It was four o'clock when the siren went off, but by seven that evening Honour had established that aside from the traits of selfishness and stubbornness that she already knew so well, Rose was easily panicked, averse to any kind of manual work, and had precious little humanity.

The noise was distant but incessant. Bombs dropped for two hours, and alongside this was the sound of ack-ack guns, ambulance and fire-engine bells. It was only when they listened to the six o'clock news that they had it confirmed that bombs had fallen only on the East End and docklands, not, as Honour had imagined, all over London.

She didn't know that then, though, and she felt it was imperative to create a place of safety as quickly as possible. But Rose dithered, chain-smoked and did no more than close the windows.

It was Honour who knocked on the tenants' doors to check who was in. It was she who cleared out the cellar, swept the floor, carried down chairs, blankets, pillows and other comforts. When Honour suggested Rose filled buckets with water to put out fires from incendiary bombs, she just looked blank as if she'd never heard of such a thing.

'This house might not be hit today,' Honour snapped at her eventually. 'But they almost certainly will get this far across London sometime. You've got to make preparations for that, Rose! And the safety of your lodgers might depend on you too.'

'Surely I haven't got to look after them?' Rose retorted in horror.

There hadn't been anyone in when Honour checked, but that was probably only because it was a warm day. Tonight, or any night, it might be different.

'Up to a point you must look out for them. Obviously as adults they can decide whether to go to an official shelter or not,' Honour said wearily. 'But in an emergency you must make this cellar available to them.'

The moment the all-clear went off, Rose rushed out of the front door without so much as an explanation, leaving Honour to continue making the storeroom comfortable. She was writing a list of things she felt Rose needed to buy to keep in there for emergencies, such as candles, tinned milk and foodstuffs, and a paraffin stove for heating in the winter, when her daughter came back with a bottle of brandy, saying someone had told her the docks were ablaze.

At seven-thirty, when the siren went off again, it was already dusk. If Honour hadn't already made corned beef sandwiches and a flask of tea and prepared Towzer's dinner with the food she'd brought with her, they would have gone hungry, for Rose rushed into the storeroom with her brandy, without a thought for anyone but herself.

As bombing began again, Honour went upstairs to check if any tenants had come in without her hearing them. There was no one there, but a look out of the top floor window shocked her. The night sky was a brilliant red over to the east, and clearly this was the dock fire Rose had spoken of.

Honour had not intended to tell Rose that Adele was nursing in London, at least not before she had established whether Rose deserved to be reunited with her daughter. But she was so afraid for Adele once she'd seen the flames that she couldn't help but blurt it out.

It was only then that Rose came out of the stupor she had been in. 'She's in the East End?' she said incredulously. 'I thought she was down in Sussex near you.'

Honour felt she had to explain how it came about. 'She was in Hastings nursing at the Buchanan until she broke off with her young man. The London Hospital, Whitechapel, is where she went to.'

Rose stopped drinking then and wanted to know the full story, and Honour felt a kind of release in sharing with her the details and the terrible anxiety she'd felt when she didn't know where Adele was. 'I still don't know the real reason why she broke it off with Michael, they were so happy together. But I can only suppose it was something to do with what happened in that children's home.'

Rose didn't say very much as Honour went on to tell her that full story too, but she supposed Rose felt too guilty to comment. As they were sitting in the two deckchairs in the gloomy light of just one weak bulb, she couldn't see her daughter clearly enough to note her expression, but Rose was wiping her eyes with a handkerchief, and when she finally spoke her voice was shaking.

'I'm so sorry, Mother, I had no idea. I got the idea she'd somehow gone straight from Euston to you. I didn't know she was sent first to a children's home. How could a man do something like that to a child?'

'There are a great many evil people in this world.' Honour shrugged. 'I know you won't thank me for reminding you of your failings as a mother, but it has to be said. If you had taken real care of your child, given her love and a feeling of being worth something, that man could never have sucked her into his nasty web.'

Rose cried openly then. 'How was I supposed to do that?' she sobbed. 'You've got no idea, Mother, what it was like for me. Living in hideous squalor with a man who had never known anything else, stuck with a baby I didn't even want. It was hell, and Adele was a constant reminder of everything I'd lost. I couldn't help but hold it against her. I loved Pamela though, I never felt that way about her. Then when she died, I couldn't bear to look at Adele. But I was sick in the mind. I couldn't help it.'

Honour listened patiently as Rose poured out the misery of her life with Jim, and of the black mood which she couldn't shift.

'I do sympathize,' she said when Rose had finished. 'I suspect I was in a similar place after Frank died. But you can't blame it all on some sickness, you have to admit to yourself that everything that happened to you was your choice, your fault. It's only once you do that, and really believe it, that you can find the way to make amends.'

'It's too late for that now,' Rose said brokenly.

'It's never too late for some things,' Honour insisted. 'Adele has a big heart. You find some way to make her proud of you and I'm sure she will forgive you. But maybe we ought to say a little prayer together for her safety tonight?'

'It's all right, you're safe now,' Adele said comfortingly to the elderly woman who had just been brought in with a bad leg wound. The woman was still whimpering with terror, and from what Adele had seen in her brief glimpses from the upper windows of the hospital, she was surprised that she wasn't screaming.

The air raid had caught everyone by surprise. It was a

beautiful warm Saturday afternoon, and people were happily strolling along Mile End Road anticipating the evening ahead, when suddenly the sky grew dark with bombers.

Adele hadn't been up more than an hour, for she was on night duty and not on again until six o'clock. She was just about to go out to buy some envelopes when the air-raid warning went off. There had been hundreds of false alarms in the past year, and many people now ignored the warning. Yet there had been a few bombs in south-east London recently, on 25 August some incendiary bombs in the City, and most recently, just two days earlier, the oil installations at Thameshaven and Shellhaven at the mouth of the Thames were set alight, so Adele wasn't so complacent.

Like most people, she believed the Germans were only interested in bombing airfields and ships, but she went out to see what everyone else was doing about this warning.

She got as far as Mile End Road when she heard the drone of aircraft and looked up to see what looked like hundreds of planes. As there was no anti-aircraft fire, for a second she thought they were English, until she saw Spitfires and Hurricanes speeding towards them. It seemed as if everyone suddenly realized this was the real thing, for all at once they began to scream and run for it.

Adele ran too, back to the nurses' home to put on her uniform. She was in her room when she heard the high-pitched scream of the first bomb, and she dived for cover as the windows shook with the blast.

She was so frightened she could hardly get her cap on straight, but she knew she must get to the hospital at once. A feeling in her gut told her this was going to prove the most demanding night of her nursing career.

Running down the corridor, other nurses joined her, but there was no time for any discussion about what was happening. Their frightened faces and caps askew said it all.

More bombs dropped as they ran full tilt to the hospital,

but they were behind them in the direction of Silvertown and the docks – a glance back showed a cloud of grey dust rising up into the sky. Above the air-raid warning sirens they could hear ambulance and fire-engine bells, and a truck screamed round the corner loaded with Civil Defence men.

In contrast to the noise and tumult outside, the hospital was eerily calm. Matron appeared as the night nurses flocked through the doors. 'Well done,' she said, with an approving nod of her head. 'I'm very glad you all had the sense to come immediately. I think we are going to need every available pair of hands tonight.'

To Adele's surprise she ordered them all to go downstairs to the canteen for food. On seeing the expression on their faces, she half smiled. 'The first casualties won't be here for a while. You might not get another chance to eat tonight.'

She was right of course, it was over an hour before they began to trickle in, and all that time the bombing was almost constant. Minor injuries were dealt with at first aid posts, so the first patients were mainly those beyond the scope of volunteer workers, those who had been knocked out by falling masonry and had serious lacerations or broken limbs.

At six, the time the night staff would normally have come on duty, the all-clear came, but though they had respite from the noise of the bombing then, it was short-lived. At seven-thirty the sirens went off again, and bombing recommenced.

Slowly, as the Civil Defence teams began to dig out people buried under rubble, the injuries grew even more serious and the trickle became a stream, quickly turning to a river of wounded.

The nurses and doctors had to work at great speed, hardly able to hear one another above the jangling of ambulance bells, the whine of bombs, and the sobs of hurt and shocked people. Every one of the wounded was covered from head to foot in brick dust, their eyes red-rimmed and wild-looking.

Many of them pleaded with nurses to get someone to find out if their children, husbands, wives or parents had been rescued.

From those still articulate enough to give an account of what had happened, the nurses learned that whole streets in Silvertown had been destroyed. They heard of dead bodies lying in the streets, and one woman had seen her own daughter's dismembered arm, which she recognized by a bracelet she'd given her. The rest of her daughter was probably buried beneath the rubble of their house, and it was believed many hundreds of others could be similarly entombed.

Each time a thud came close by, small pieces of plaster fell from the ceiling; Adele tried very hard not to think what would happen if the hospital got a direct hit. One nurse slipped upstairs and reported back that fire watchers were being ordered up on to the roof. She was told by one of them that the Surrey Docks were ablaze and fire engines from all over London had been sent there to help put it out. She said she thought the paint factory had gone up too for there were terribly acrid, choking fumes.

Time ceased to have any meaning for any of the nurses as they rushed from one casualty to the next. The floor was splattered with blood, and as fast as orderlies cleared it up, it became just as bad again. The most serious cases were operated on, then taken to a ward, but beds were filled in no time, so lesser injuries were dealt with and the patients then had to sit or lie down wherever they could out of the way of the medical staff.

Many of them were distraught because they feared for the rest of their families. In some cases there were children lost and feared dead. One woman with her arm almost completely severed was trying to get off the stretcher she'd been brought in on to go back and find her little boy.

Adele lost count of the different stories she heard of what these people had been doing when the raid began. 'I was just thinking about getting the tea.' 'I was out in the lavvy.' 'I'd just put the kettle on and the whole house shook and suddenly the roof was gone.'

Adele couldn't help thinking that if a raid like this had happened the previous September, right at the outbreak of war, everyone would have been ready for it. But the Phoney War had lulled them all into a false sense of security. People had given up carrying their gas masks and ignored the instructions of the air-raid wardens, because they felt they were bossy and self-important. Some people were barely aware of where the shelters were any longer. And Adele didn't expect that there was enough room in the shelters for the vast numbers who would need them tonight.

She and the other nurses weren't really competent to deal with injuries like these: whole legs smashed, backs full of broken shards of glass, crushed hands and feet. No amount of theory lessons had prepared them for such horrible, terrifying wounds.

Miles of bandages, tons of swabs, lint and sticking plaster, pints of antiseptic and gallons of water turned crimson with blood. Hastily preparing patients for theatre, rushing with kidney dishes to catch someone's vomit, applying pressure to a wound that pumped out blood at an alarming rate, and all the while trying to console and comfort the victims.

'Where will we go?' one poor woman with a bad head wound and a baby in her arms asked Adele pitifully. 'Our 'ouse is gone, with all our stuff, even me money. Where we gonna sleep? I ain't even got a dry nappy for the little 'un.'

It was two in the morning before Adele got a break for a cup of tea and a sandwich. Joan, who had been on duty all day, and stayed on as all the day staff had, joined her for a few moments. 'To think I had a date tonight with that fireman,' she said, drawing deeply on a cigarette. 'First bloke I've really fancied in over a year, and I might never get to see 'im again.'

Adele couldn't reassure her she would, for news had come in of how bad the blaze in the docks was. Everything was alight, and firemen were getting trapped as buildings on all sides went up in the blaze. Rotherhithe and Woolwich on the other side of the Thames had been badly hit too. One sixteen-year-old Fire Service messenger boy had been brought in with bad burns received as he cycled down a burning street with a message from one fire officer to another. He had bravely ridden on with his clothes alight to deliver his message before collapsing, and even as he lay on the stretcher he was worrying how the fire officers would manage without him.

Stratford Hospital had received a direct hit, but an ambulance driver had said the nursing staff were still working behind screens. There were many bombs dropped close to the London Hospital too, and still the bombers kept coming. With fires all along the riverside lighting up the whole of London, the Germans could easily pick out any target they fancied.

Again and again during the night, Adele heard people asking where the RAF had been in all this and why they hadn't stopped the bombers. She thought how easily people changed their allegiance. A few weeks ago in the Battle of Britain, fighter pilots were the most popular men in England; now they were being blamed for letting these German planes through.

But she had seen those bombers coming over. Three hundred of them, it was said. She'd also seen the Hurricanes and Spitfires tearing into them, and they were well outnumbered.

After the carnage of this day and night, she couldn't offer up a silent prayer for Michael. Not because she no longer cared, but it seemed wrong to pray for just one person when millions were in equal danger.

*

'Mother, it's madness to go there,' Rose said, trying to prevent Honour going out at eight the following morning. 'The bombers could come back at any time.'

'I have to see Adele,' Honour insisted stubbornly. 'You hold on to Towzer, because I'm not leaving him outside if I have to duck into a shelter.'

'But I doubt you'll get through,' Rose argued. 'There surely won't be any buses or Tubes.'

'Then I'll walk,' Honour said. 'Now, just you take good care of Towzer.'

They had heard on the early morning news that the East End had been hit, but presumably to save panic, or keep up morale, no details were given of how many casualties there were. Honour had heard bombs dropping all night, and at one point she'd gone up to the bedroom at the top of the house and stood for some time watching the red glow of the flames. She couldn't just wait to hear from Adele, she had to see for herself that she was unhurt. She couldn't possibly go home without knowing for certain.

Honour managed to get a Tube train as far as Aldgate. A ticket collector told her the section of line beyond that was being checked for bomb damage, but said it wasn't too far to walk to Whitechapel.

As soon as Honour came up on to the street her nostrils were assailed by the smell of burning, and the air was thick with dust. Everywhere looked as if it had been sprinkled with talcum powder or flour.

She hadn't gone far beyond the Tower of London before she saw bomb damage. The buildings were intact, but glass, lumps of masonry and roofing tiles lay in the road, and people were out with brooms sweeping it up.

But as she got further down Whitechapel High Street, the damage gradually grew more serious. Most shop windows were broken, sharp shards of glass dangling dangerously over the goods exposed inside. As she progressed further still, she saw her first bombed house, reduced to a pile of rubble. Grotesquely, the side wall was still intact, a picture of some swans on a lake still in place. A wizened old lady was standing in front of it crying, as two younger women desperately tried to find belongings amongst the rubble.

From that house onwards there were many similar sights. The direct hits were mainly on the side streets, whole terraces knocked down and white dust still swirling around in the breeze. Huge lumps of masonry blocked the gouged and pitted roads.

But it was the people who affected Honour the most, many with sticking plaster or dressings on stricken faces, staring at their former homes in bewilderment. One woman she saw with tears running down her face was pointlessly trying to sweep the street.

A group of Civil Defence men were clearing rubble from the Mile End Road, and Honour asked them what would become of these homeless people.

'They's letting 'em sleep in church halls and schools,' one burly yet ashen-faced man replied. 'But what you've seen 'ere, love, ain't nothin' to what went on down at Silvertown. They're still digging out folk trapped under the rubble. We'll be going on there soon as we've got this road cleared so more rescue trucks and mortuary vans can get through.'

'Is the London Hospital still standing?' Honour ventured.

'Yeah, that's okay. You got someone in there?'

'My granddaughter's a nurse there,' Honour said, her voice faltering. 'I was just going to check on her.'

'They've bin angels in there,' he said, giving Honour a comforting pat on the shoulder. 'I was in and out there half the night taking injured folk. It were like Bedlam, but they did us all proud.'

*

It was still like Bedlam in the hospital. Honour hadn't seen anything like it since the first war when she went to the hospital in Dover to find Frank. But then it was all wounded men, and mostly cleaned up and patched up ones at that, glad to be back in England for some respite from the hell they'd been through. Here there were women and children too, some with such shocking injuries she had to avert her eyes. Nurses with bloodstained aprons, fatigue showing in their young faces. Doctors in equally bloodstained jackets looking as if they were close to collapse, heads bent over their patients.

Honour stopped a nurse as she passed her. 'Can you tell me if Nurse Adele Talbot is here please?' she asked.

'She was until an hour ago,' the nurse replied. 'A few of them were sent off for a rest for a couple of hours.'

'Does that mean she'll be back later?'

'Oh yes, to relieve some of us. Are you a relative of hers?'

Honour nodded. 'She's my granddaughter. I just wanted to know she was all right.'

'She'll be fine after a bit of a rest.' The nurse smiled sympathetically. 'We all will be. You go on home. I'll tell her you asked after her.'

Honour left the hospital and began to walk back up the road towards Aldgate. But as she walked she felt she couldn't just get on the Tube, collect Towzer and go home. There had to be someone around here dealing with all the distraught homeless who could do with a helping hand for a few hours.

Seeing the Civil Defence man she'd spoken to earlier about to get back in his truck and drive away, she marched purposefully up to him.

'Find your granddaughter, did you?' he asked.

Honour explained that Adele had gone for a rest and that she thought perhaps she could make herself useful in the meantime.

'Hop in,' he said, opening the truck door. 'I know the very place.'

Honour could hardly believe what she was seeing as she was driven towards Silvertown, swerving round potholes and over debris. Whole streets were gone, rescue workers toiling away at the dust-covered rubble looking for both buried survivors and bodies. Beside the road lay bodies waiting for collection, some covered in sacks, others by blankets and old curtains. There were men and women digging desperately into the rubble with their bare hands, clearly searching for a family member who was missing. Honour saw what she thought was a mannequin from a shop window lying at the top of a staircase which was still intact but had come adrift from the wall which had once supported it. All at once she realized it was a dead woman.

The air was choking too, a mixture of powdered mortar and fumes from the fires still raging down in the docks.

The Civil Defence man, who said his name was Dan, tried to cheer her a little by telling her that a few hours earlier at first light they'd found both a baby and an old man still alive and unharmed.

'The wardrobe door had open and the whole thing fell over the old codger as the 'ouse come down. 'E thought he was in a coffin buried alive. The baby was still in its pram, under a door. 'E was yelling fit to bust, that's why we found 'im so quick.'

Dan and the other men with him had worked right through the night, helping out with anything they could. He said he was taking Honour to a church they were using as a rest centre. 'They'll be right glad of another pair of 'ands,' he said. 'That is, if you don't mind making sandwiches and tea, and 'elping take down folk's details to get them somewhere else to live.'

*

At four that afternoon Honour was as exhausted as most of the other people she'd been helping. Most of the day had been spent taking down homeless people's particulars, and the details of family members that still weren't accounted for, because it was soon noted by the other helpers that she was better educated and less emotionally involved than they were.

But as Honour heard one heartbreaking story after another, even her emotions began to get the better of her. She guessed these people had had very little before the raid, and now they had nothing and had lost family members too. She would never have imagined that she could take a dirty, hungry baby with a soiled nappy from its distraught mother, strip it and wash and feed it. The only baby she'd ever taken care of was Rose. But her sympathy proved much greater than revulsion, and she found herself doing it several times. She had cuddled and fed bigger children whose mother was not yet found, she had comforted old ladies and men, and questioned what seemed like hundreds of people and filed their particulars in alphabetical order, so their claims for temporary housing could be dealt with.

Even the people who still had a home had no gas or electricity, and they were all fearful of another raid. All day she'd heard that there weren't enough air-raid shelters for everyone, and many people complained that the Government weren't going to allow people down into the Underground stations.

But at five-thirty, despite so many people still needing help, Honour knew she must go, to see Adele and get back to Rose and Towzer. She no longer cared about going home to her cottage, she was determined to come to Silvertown again the following day to help out.

Her best dress was filthy, her eyes stung and her scalp itched from all the mortar dust, even her lungs seemed congested. Yet as she begged a lift in a truck going back in the direction of Whitechapel to see Adele, she thought how fortunate she was in comparison to the people she'd met that day.

The hospital was a little more orderly than it had been in the morning, and Honour found Adele very quickly.

She looked tired, her eyes red-rimmed, but when she saw her grandmother hovering nervously at the ward door, she rushed to her looking astonished.

'What on earth are you doing here?' she scolded. 'There could be another air raid any minute.'

Honour explained as quickly as she could that she had visited Rose, and how after the raid she'd felt compelled to come and see that Adele was all in one piece.

Adele's face had registered great shock at hearing about Rose. She flushed with anger and said Honour must be losing her grip leaving the safety of Winchelsea for someone so worthless. But when her grandmother reproved her for being so uncharitable, she shrugged, and began scolding her for risking her own life by coming to Whitechapel.

'Look, Granny,' she said, tutting over her filthy dress and shaking her head in disapproval, 'I really appreciate you thinking of me, but I'm quite safe, and doing what I've been trained for. Now, you get going right now. Collect Towzer and go home. Don't you dare stay a moment longer with Rose. London is no place for you.'

'I disagree,' Honour said defiantly, telling her what she had been doing all day. 'And I'm coming back tomorrow if Rose will mind Towzer. I can be of use here, more use than I am down by the coast.'

Adele looked really worried then. 'Granny, it's dangerous,' she said, edging her back to the door. 'Please, if you love me at all, just go home and stay safe. Now, before I get cross with you.'

Honour chuckled at the sudden reversal of roles. She had no intention of going back to Sussex, but she thought perhaps it was wisest not to tell Adele that now, not when she had so much else on her plate. She kissed her granddaughter and told her to get back to her patients.

The air-raid warning went off when Honour was halfway to Aldgate Station. She looked at all the people around her, but was confused as they were scattering in every direction. Someone had said during the day that they reckoned the Underground stations were the safest place to go, so breaking into a trot she went on.

She didn't look round when she heard the drone of the bombers, nor did she falter at the first whine of a bomb and the earth-shaking thud that followed it. She heard a man shout to her and the people running with her, but assumed he was only warning them to hurry.

Another whine, this time seemingly very close, and a woman screamed close by, Honour felt what seemed like a blast of hot air in her face, and all at once she was blinded by choking dust and something bowled into her, knocking her down.

Her last thought as a red-hot pain engulfed her was that she hadn't told Adele where Rose lived.

Chapter Twenty-two

'Don't you look at me like that! I don't know where she is,' Rose snapped at Towzer. When the air-raid siren had gone off half an hour earlier he'd become quite demented, barking furiously and running from room to room looking for Honour. He wouldn't come into the cellar with her, and Rose had been forced to drag him in by his collar.

Now as bombs were dropping he had his front paws on her lap, and the pleading eyes and sad whining noises were getting on her nerves.

'We'll be all right,' she said, relenting and stroking his head, guessing that he was picking up on her terror, for he'd been fine before the siren went off. They'd been down to Ravenscourt Park at midday for a walk, and then stopped in the pub at the end of the road for a drink on the way back, and everyone had made a fuss of him. Bob the landlord had even given him some scraps.

Everyone had been talking about the previous night's bombing in the East End and it was rumoured that hundreds of people had been killed. The general view was that the bombers had been targeting the docks and it was just an unfortunate mistake that civilians had been killed. Yet everyone was very jumpy. Most intended to go to a shelter that night, and several men said they were going to send their wives and children out of London.

Rose only stayed for a couple of drinks as she was expecting Honour back, but as the afternoon progressed and her mother didn't turn up, she began to feel cross and put upon that she'd been left with Towzer.

But now, listening to bombs dropping, with only him

for company, Rose couldn't help but think the worst had happened to Honour and possibly Adele too. She couldn't imagine her mother hanging around one minute longer than she needed to in Whitechapel. The only thing that would prevent her coming back for Towzer was not being able to find Adele.

As another thought popped into her head, a chill ran down her spine. What if Myles had told Adele the truth?

Rose had no recollection of either writing or posting the letter to her mother, so she'd obviously done it while she was drunk. She was absolutely stunned when Honour turned up, and her first thought was that she'd come to lay into Rose about the business of Myles and Adele.

Yet within minutes she realized this wasn't so, for Honour certainly wasn't angry with her. Rose relaxed then, believing Myles had found some other way to induce Adele to make the break with Michael, and hadn't admitted he was her father. Maybe he'd even offered her money, and that was why she hadn't told her grandmother.

Later in the evening, when Honour eventually told her Adele had come to London to get over Michael, Rose even smiled mentally. That's what she would have done herself, pocketed the money and disappeared off to the city. It seemed Adele wasn't the goody-two-shoes Honour liked to make out, but a chip off the old block.

But now, as Rose waited impatiently for Honour to return, she couldn't help but have a nagging feeling she might have misjudged Adele. What if Myles had told her the truth, and the girl had kept it from Honour to spare her feelings?

If that was the case, and Honour turned up at the hospital with the story she'd been with Rose, Adele might very well be furious. And if the two of them put their heads together, it wouldn't be long before they worked out how she got the money to buy the house.

Rose felt sick at the very thought of it. Was that why Honour hadn't come back? Because she couldn't bear to spend another night in the company of a Judas who took the proverbial thirty pieces of silver?

The whining shriek of a bomb, and then a thud, this time so close it made the light flicker, made Rose shake with fear. If the house was hit she could be buried under tons of bricks. She had never liked being alone – that was one of the reasons she'd wanted to have lodgers. But none of them were home tonight.

Margery and Sonia, the two young girls who shared the big front room on the first floor, had come back fleetingly this morning to get some clean clothes. They'd gone up West yesterday to do some shopping, and ended up spending the night in a public shelter. They said it was grim and they'd been scared out of their wits, and so they were going off to stay with Margery's parents just in case there was another raid.

Rose got out of the deckchair and lay down on the mattress, pulling a blanket over her and burying her head beneath the pillow in an effort to shut out the noise of the bombing. But the bombs, like her thoughts, couldn't be shut out.

In the pub she'd heard many of the people she drank with and classed as friends making arrangements to meet up in the local shelter if there was another air raid tonight. Yet no one had asked her to join them. Margery and Sonia hadn't asked if she'd be all right either.

She thought of how her mother had wanted to know about each of the lodgers last night – how old they were, where they came from, and what they did for a living. Rose hadn't been able to tell her, for she knew practically nothing about any of them. Today she hadn't even asked Margery where her parents lived.

Rose had never before thought it might be a failing to have so little interest in other people, but perhaps it was. Maybe Margery, Sonia and other tenants both past and present could only view her as a rent collector, not a woman on her own who might need company. Perhaps, too, all those people down at the pub saw her as an independent woman who had no room in her life for them?

All at once she realized she didn't have any real friends. She had dozens of acquaintances, she could walk into any one of half a dozen pubs in London and be greeted by someone she knew. But that wasn't real friendship, only the camaraderie of heavy drinkers. Who would mourn her if she were to die tonight?

If Adele had told Honour about Michael today, neither of them would give a damn if she was reported killed. And none of the many men in Rose's past life would either, for if they remembered her at all it would only be of how she used them.

'Mrs Harris! Can you hear me?'

Honour could hear a female voice, but there was a lot of other noise behind it, the way it was at a noisy party or in a railway station. She couldn't seem to open her eyes, and she hurt, though she couldn't quite make out where.

'Mrs Harris! You were hurt in the air raid, but you're safe now in hospital.'

Air raid! Hospital! Those words seemed to mean something but she couldn't quite grasp what. Was this a dream? Should she try to wake up and let Towzer out?

'Got to let Towzer out,' she managed to say, and forced her eyes open enough to see bright lights.

'That's better,' the voice said. 'We found your name on an envelope in your handbag, Mrs Harris. Do you live in London or is the address in Sussex your home?'

Slowly Honour's eyes began to focus and the blur in front of her became a face. A young, pretty face with dark brown eyes. She had a nurse's starched cap on her head, just like Adele.

'Is Adele here?' she managed to croak out though her mouth seemed to be full of dust.

'Adele who?' the nurse asked.

'Adele Talbot, my granddaughter. She's a nurse.'

'You're Adele's granny?' the nurse said incredulously. 'Oh my goodness.'

Honour was sure it was only a dream. She closed her eyes because the lights were too bright and slipped back to sleep.

'Granny!'

The sound of Adele's voice woke her immediately.

'Adele?'

She couldn't see her clearly, but the hand holding hers felt right. She didn't need to talk now Adele was here, it was safe to drift off again.

Adele rushed over to the Ward Sister's office when she left Honour's bedside. She had been nursing patients recovering from operations all evening, so she hadn't seen many of the casualties as they were brought into the hospital. It had been a terrible shock when Nurse Pople had come to her and broke the news that her grandmother was one of them. Adele had believed she was safely back in Hammersmith.

Yet it was even more frightening to see her lying there swaddled with bandages and to have the nurse tell her that they feared brain damage as she'd remained unconscious for so long.

Adele blurted out to Sister Jones that Mrs Harris was her grandmother. 'Nurse Pople said she might have brain damage,' she said. 'Is that right?'

'It's too soon to tell yet,' Sister said, and seeing the look of anguish on the young nurse's face, she patted her shoulder in sympathy. 'It's an excellent sign that she was able to ask about you, but the head wound is bad, she also has a broken leg and countless lacerations to her body and limbs.'

'She's very strong and healthy,' Adele said, her voice cracking with emotion. 'That will help her, won't it?'

'Yes, nurse, of course it will, and being here in the same hospital as you too. Now, does she have a husband?'

'No, she's a widow,' Adele said. 'She'd been visiting someone in London, and left her dog there. But I don't know the address.'

She couldn't bring herself to admit the someone was her mother. Since Honour had informed her she'd stayed the night with Rose, Adele had been seething with anger that she'd had the cheek to try to worm her way back into their lives.

The Sister explained how she'd been through Honour's handbag and found a letter. 'I didn't read it of course, but maybe you should, it might be from the person she stayed with. Now, how long have you been on duty, Talbot?'

'The same as everyone else really,' Adele said. 'Since yesterday's raid, and three hours off this morning. But I don't want to go off now Granny's here.'

Sister Jones looked at her sharply. 'I shall insist you go off for a few hours later,' she said. 'Exhausted nurses make mistakes. Besides, there isn't likely to be any change with Mrs Harris until at least tomorrow.'

When Adele went through Honour's handbag and found the plaintive letter from Rose, she felt even more furious with her mother. It beggared belief that she would have the nerve to ask for forgiveness after the misery she had caused.

Maybe she didn't expect Honour to jump on a train to London immediately, but to let her set off for the East End right after an air raid was criminal.

Adele knew what she'd like to do. Rush over to Hammersmith, snatch Towzer back and tell her mother in no uncertain terms that she never wanted to see or hear from her again. But she couldn't leave the hospital, or Granny, nor could she look after Towzer until her grandmother was better.

She supposed she would just have to ask the police to notify Rose about what had happened, and trust that she had enough remnants of decency to take good care of Towzer.

Rose was woken by the door bell at eleven the following morning. She had stayed in the cellar until the all-clear went soon after dawn, but she hadn't slept at all because she was so frightened. She took Towzer out for a short walk, and felt relieved to find there was no bomb damage to be seen around Hammersmith. She then went back to bed in her own room.

As she opened the front door and saw a uniformed policeman, she thought the worst and clutched her dressing-gown round her tightly.

'Mrs Talbot?' the policeman asked.

'Yes,' Rose said, her legs almost buckling under her.

'I'm sorry to bring bad news, but your mother was injured in an air raid last night.'

Rose didn't know what to say. She just stared at the policeman.

'She's in the London Hospital in Whitechapel. The message which we received early this morning was from your daughter who I understand is a nurse there. She reported that Mrs Harris has quite serious injuries but she is stable.'

'But I've got her dog here,' Rose said without thinking. 'What shall I do?'

The policeman looked askance at her. 'Take care of it until she's better?' he suggested with a touch of sarcasm.

'But how long will that be?' she asked.

'You could try calling or visiting the hospital to find out,' he said sharply.

Rose closed the door after the policeman had gone and walked slowly back into her flat. It took a few moments before what she'd just been told sank in, and several more moments before she realized that her reaction must have appeared callous. She stood at the back door, looking down the steps into her garden, and fumbled for her cigarettes in her dressing-gown pocket. Why had she said that about the dog? Now she'd given that policeman the impression that she cared more about getting shot of the animal than she did that her mother was hurt.

She lit the cigarette with shaking hands and drew deeply on it. All her life it had been the same, as if her mind didn't work in tandem with her vocal chords. So many different men had called her a bitch because she'd blurted out something deeply hurtful under stress. Even when she was really trying to be kind or sympathetic, somehow she always managed to sound unfeeling.

The time she was most ashamed of was that night back when she was seventeen and her mother gave her the new blue dress she'd made.

The terrible things she said that night weren't really about the dress, which was a sensible, serviceable one. But she was desperately in love with Myles, her whole being was crying out for romance, beauty and magic. The plain blue dress represented everything she despised about herself: being a waitress, living on the marsh, excluded from the glittering world she caught glimpses of at the hotel.

What she said that night to her mother and about her father was very nasty, but it was born out of frustration that she couldn't improve her lot in life, and envy of those who had so much more than she did.

Afterwards, running away seemed to be the only thing she could do. She took whatever she could find of value in desperation, for she certainly wasn't sure Myles would take her away with him, however much he wanted her. She had to tell him a pack of lies too, to make him agree. And she had to keep on lying even once she'd got to London with him.

Rose slumped down on the back steps and cried. She'd made such a mess of her life. All the way through it there had been crossroads, and at every single one she'd come to, she always took the route that looked easiest, the downhill way.

Two weeks passed before Rose went to the London Hospital to see Honour, leaving Towzer at home as she couldn't take him into the hospital. She had telephoned the hospital daily, and felt relieved to hear from the Ward Sister that Honour was improving with each day. It was Sister who advised Rose not to visit, as Honour would only fret about her dog if Rose was to leave him on his own.

Rose was only too happy to take the Sister's advice. She didn't like hospitals and the thought of coming face to face with Adele was terrifying. She knew she was hostile or she would have left a message with a number and a time when she could be reached. On top of this there were the air raids. The daytime ones had stopped, but as soon as night fell there was a constant barrage of bombing. The BBC and the newspapers didn't report on the extent of the damage and never mentioned the number of casualties, but everyone knew that the East End was devastated.

There had been enough bombs and incendiaries around Hammersmith for Rose to get the idea of what hell it must be in the East End. Each morning she saw new bomb damage close to her house, and as she queued to buy food she heard people talking about the worst-hit areas. It seemed that those who worked in the West End or the City often arrived at their office or shop to find the windows blown out or the roof caved in. They spoke of seeing huge holes in the street, piles of rubble, multicoloured telephone wires waving in the breeze, water and gas pipes fractured.

Rose was astounded that many people spent a sleepless

night in a shelter, and then walked miles to work. And that many café and shop owners still opened for business, even when their windows had been blown out. She thought they were mad – neither the King nor the Government was going to reward anyone for being so dutiful. She just went home after tracking down some cigarettes and food. No one was going to press gang *her* into working on a tea stall or handing out clothes to those who'd been bombed out.

By the time two weeks had passed, Rose was sick and tired of staying home alone every night with Towzer. Her lodgers all went down to the public shelters and they seemed to have a real laugh there. So when she rang the hospital and the Sister said Honour was well enough to be moved out of London, Rose's spirits lifted. She thought she might go up West once Towzer was gone, have a few drinks, and see if she could hook herself a new man. She was fed up with living like a nun, and by all accounts the West End was full of servicemen looking for a little fun.

As the Tube train sped along, Rose glanced disconsolately at her reflection in the train windows. Lack of sleep, anxiety and not eating properly had taken its toll, and though she'd taken great trouble with her appearance this morning, she looked her age. Yet looking around at her fellow passengers she was heartened to see they all looked far worse, grubby and shabby with gaunt faces.

'Good morning, Mrs Talbot,' Sister Jones said crisply as she came into the small waiting room Rose had been left in for over an hour.

Rose was in a state of shock at the scenes she'd witnessed since arriving at the hospital. Hundreds of people with every kind of gruesome injury took up every seat or floor area. One man still had shards of glass sticking out through his jacket, blood dripping on to the floor as he moved. A woman had been brought in on a stretcher, her features hidden by thick flourlike dust, and her leg partially severed. The sights were more than enough to turn Rose's stomach, but the noise was even worse – crying, screaming, shouting and wailing. She might have turned tail and run if a nurse hadn't ushered her into the relative quiet of this small room, but even that she was sharing with six other people in varying stages of distress.

'Mrs Harris has recovered enough to be moved now, and of course we desperately need her bed,' Sister said hurriedly without any preamble. 'She wants to go home, but she'll need someone to nurse her.'

'Don't look at me,' Rose said indignantly. 'I've got a boarding house to run.'

'Nurse Talbot expected that would be your response,' Sister retorted crisply. 'She is of course more than willing to nurse her grandmother, but I need her here, we are desperately short of nurses.'

'Where is she?' Rose asked. She didn't like the woman's snooty tone one bit.

'With a patient at present, but she knows you are here and will come to see you presently.'

'I can't wait here all day,' Rose said belligerently. She knew she was being unpleasant, but she couldn't help herself. Part of it was because she was scared stiff at the prospect of coming face to face with Adele.

The Sister gave her a searing look. 'Some of the injured out there have already waited eight hours or more,' she said with a wave of her hand towards the large waiting room beyond the small room. 'They are in pain, desperate for news of their relatives, and most have lost their homes too. I suggest you start counting your blessings.'

She turned and swept out of the room without another word, leaving Rose feeling as if she'd had her face slapped.

It was well over an hour before another nurse came into

the room. She was tall, slender and very attractive, even if her apron was splattered with blood. Rose jumped out of her seat. 'I've been waiting to see Nurse Talbot for ever,' she blurted out. 'Can you do something to hurry her up?'

'I am Nurse Talbot,' the young woman replied coldly. 'Hello, Mother! It's been a long time but I had expected that you'd recognize your own daughter.'

Rose was thrown into confusion and embarrassment as everyone in the waiting room was looking at her. She really couldn't believe that this very lovely young nurse with shiny hair the colour of autumn leaves and perfect teeth was Adele. She had built up a picture in her mind of a very plain, skinny young woman with a pasty face and dull brown hair. 'I-I-I,' she stuttered.

'You didn't anticipate I might have changed a little in nine years?' Adele said.

Rose sat down with a bump. 'You are so pretty,' she said weakly. 'I didn't expect that.'

'We haven't got time now for discussions on how we look,' Adele said with just a touch of acid. 'We have to make a decision about Granny. She wants to go home, and it's my opinion she'd recover quicker there, but I can only have a couple of days off to settle her. Will you stay with her?'

Rose was thrown. The Adele she remembered would never have dared to be so direct.

'I can't, I've got my lodgers,' she said quickly.

'Surely you could leave them to fend for themselves?'

'But there's the rent to collect, the stairs and bathroom to clean.'

'There's a war on, Mother,' Adele said sharply. 'People are dying in air raids. Does a bit of dirt on the stairs matter? You can get someone else to collect the rent. Besides, you'd be safer in Sussex too.'

Rose thought quickly. Much as she hated the idea of taking care of her mother, she knew if she refused she would be cut off for ever. Then there was Curlew Cottage itself. It would be very nice to sleep in peace, to have a bit of a holiday.

'How much nursing is Mother going to need?' she asked cautiously.

'Not a huge amount. She can walk a few steps with crutches. She'll need help with dressing, washing and things. Then there's cooking and cleaning.'

'I suppose I could give it a try,' Rose said weakly.

Adele fixed her with a fierce look and Rose was reminded of the many times she'd claimed her daughter's greenish-brown eyes were strange. There was nothing strange about them now, they were in fact very beautiful and framed by thick dark lashes. 'You could try and be a bit more enthusiastic when you see Granny,' she reproached her mother. 'You were the one who brought her to London, and now it's your chance to prove to her that you really meant what you said in that letter.'

Her tone was gentle, and there was a sweetness in her words that touched Rose. 'Of course I meant it,' she retorted. 'I'm just a bit harassed right now, what with the bombing every night and everything being so upside down.'

'Well, we'll go and see her now then,' Adele said. 'I'm sure she'll be very relieved and happy that you want to take care of her.'

The following afternoon as Rose packed a suitcase to take with her to Rye, she was a bag of nerves. A bomb had dropped just a street away during the night, and that and all the terrifying scenes she'd seen the previous day, not just in the hospital, but in the bombed houses all around it, had convinced her it was right to go. Mrs Arbroath, her next-door neighbour, had agreed to take care of the house, let rooms if necessary and collect the rents for her for a small consideration. She knew the woman could be trusted implicitly as she was very religious, so she wasn't frightened about what she might find on her return.

But she was frightened of Adele.

There was no trace left of the little girl who had accepted indifference and sometimes cruelty. The adult Adele was calm and very pleasant, she had said nothing to suggest she was harbouring a grudge, yet Rose had a sense of foreboding.

There was no reason for it. Everything Adele had said was rational, even kindly, and she was very practical. It transpired she had sent a telegram to the postman in Rye as soon as Honour was injured, and asked him to feed the rabbits and chickens. She had now sent another one to inform him they would be arriving sometime after midday tomorrow. She had organized someone to collect Rose and Towzer at nine in the morning, then to pick up herself and Honour and drive on down to Rye. In fact the way she spoke of the three of them being together almost sounded as if she relished them becoming a real family.

Maybe it was only a guilty conscience that made Rose feel so uneasy, for she couldn't quite rid herself of the idea that Adele was intending to extract her pound of flesh at some time.

Honour wasn't going to be a pushover either. Her broken leg might be in plaster, some of her wounds a long way from being healed, but there was no brain damage and she was as sharp as ever. She'd told Rose in no uncertain terms that she could forget packing 'glad rags' for she'd have no need of them, but to bring stout shoes and warm clothes. She reminded her about her ration book and to bring any stores of tinned food she had. She even ghoulishly asked if she could remember how to wring a chicken's neck.

Last night, as bombs dropped yet again, Rose had thought about the lack of bathroom and electricity at Curlew Cottage, and how far it was to the nearest shop. She regretted agreeing to go, and knew she'd hate being a slave to her mother, even if she would be pleased to get away from the bombs. But she couldn't wriggle out of it now – perhaps after a week she could invent some plausible reason for returning to London.

Chapter Twenty-three

'We'll go and collect some wood when you've finished that,' Adele said as Rose dried up the dinner plates in the scullery. 'I noticed this morning there's a couple of trees come down in the storm. We can hack off a few logs if we take the axe with us.'

Rose sighed. It was her second day at the cottage, and from the moment they'd arrived Adele had kept her busy; that was understandable as there were so many things to put straight, but Rose had hoped she could have a rest this afternoon.

They had been brought down here in a van, Honour in the back on a mattress, with Adele and Towzer beside her. Rose sat up in the front with the driver, an old, slightly deaf man who was prone to shouting questions as if it was they who were hard of hearing. All the way out through South London they had seen more terrible bomb damage. On two occasions the road had been impassable and they'd had to take a detour to get back on the main road.

Yet once they were out of London Rose's spirits rose at the autumn colours of the trees. Everywhere looked so sparkly and clean in the weak sunshine, even the nip in the air was invigorating, and as they passed through one serene and picturesque village after another, the Blitz began to seem like no more than a bad dream.

She even felt an unexpected surge of nostalgia and excitement at seeing the marshes again. The grass was so lush and green, bulrushes in the ditches waved in the wind, and the Old Man's Beard on the hedges glistened with dew-sprinkled cobwebs just the way Rose remembered as a child.

Jim the postman had been in to light the stove. There was a basket of eggs on the table, a quart of milk in a jug, an apple and blackberry pie, presumably made by Jim's wife, and a bunch of wild flowers in a vase to welcome Honour home. Rose laughed as Towzer ran around sniffing everything joyfully, for she felt just as gleeful as she used to when her parents brought her here for weekends and holidays all those years ago.

But the glee wore off very quickly when the sky darkened and it began to rain heavily and she had to run out to the lavatory to empty Honour's commode. To be fair to her mother, she had indignantly argued with Adele about the need for a commode, and would have braved the rain on crutches, but Adele wouldn't hear of it. She insisted that the crutches could only be used indoors, the ground outside was far too uneven and slippery. Rose heard her making Honour promise that she wouldn't backslide the moment she'd gone back to London. She even added darkly, 'However much Rose encourages you to believe it's safe.'

While Rose hated the thought of emptying commodes and dressing wounds for her mother, she didn't mind cooking and housekeeping for her so much. There was something very soothing about being back in her old home, with all the memories of her childhood, well away from the nightly terror in London. She even felt touched by seeing her indomitable mother so helpless.

Honour had always had such good posture. She had stood straight-backed, chest out and chin up, and she had been so strong and muscular. Rose remembered how as a child she'd watched her mother heave great buckets of stones around, dig the garden like a man and shin up on the roof with the agility of a monkey. She had never been one to give in to fatigue – she rose with the lark and worked till dusk.

Even when she'd arrived in Hammersmith it was clear she still had the same vigour. Her hair might be grey, and there were a few wrinkles on her face, but one sensed she would never bow to old age.

Yet she looked sixty now as she sat with her broken leg supported on a stool, and that huge dressing on her head. Her skin was yellow with bruising, noticeably crêpey and wrinkled. She had lost weight, and her eyes were rheumy – even her voice had lost its commanding note. Adele had put a colourful knitted blanket round her shoulders, and with her reading glasses resting low on her nose she was suddenly a picture-book frail grandmother.

The rain turned to a real storm later on, and they could barely hear the wireless for the howling wind and the rain drumming on the roof. But Rose found it infinitely preferable to bombs; the minute her head touched the pillow, she was asleep.

Adele slept on the couch in the living room. Rose suggested she share her bed, but Adele wouldn't hear of it. She laughingly said that she hadn't had more than three hours' sleep a night for over a fortnight, and if she slept in a comfortable bed she might never wake up again. But Rose had a feeling that her daughter just couldn't bear to be that close to her.

While she knew she couldn't expect Adele to clasp her long-lost mother to her bosom and forgive the past entirely, Rose wished she would say something that would give her hope for the future. She couldn't help but secretly marvel that Adele had turned out so well, not only beautiful, but clever, self-assured and very capable. She was the kind of daughter any mother would be extremely proud of, but it gave Rose a real pang of remorse to see she'd got that way despite her mother, not because of her.

Instinct told her Adele was not prepared to forgive or forget. She was watchful, her smiles were forced, and almost everything she said directly to Rose was thinly disguised sarcasm.

This morning, as she showed her mother how to change the dressings on Honour's head wound and a nasty one on her arm, Rose knew she was being scrutinized. Later, as they fed the rabbits and chickens, Adele didn't speak at all. It was as if she was boiling up for something, keeping a lid on her anger until the right time came to let it loose.

'The tree's down here,' Adele said as she marched on ahead with the old pram towards the Winchelsea road. She turned off at a gate, opened it and hauled the pram through. Two trees were lying on the ground, torn up by the roots.

While Adele began chopping at one of the trees with the axe, Rose gathered up all the smaller branches and twigs around the area, filling the pram in no time.

'Haven't we got enough now?' she asked as Adele continued to hack at the tree. She had already cut three big logs, and stripped off her coat and cardigan because she was so hot with the effort. Sweat poured down her face and she had wet patches all over the bodice of her dress.

'That stove takes a lot of wood,' Adele said, pausing to wipe her forehead. 'You'll need to come down here every day and chop off a bit more.'

'I can't do that,' Rose said in horror. 'I doubt if I can even lift the axe.' As the words came out of her mouth she knew she should have merely nodded agreement. Adele was giving her the coldest look, as though she thought her weak and pathetic.

'I'll try of course,' Rose said hurriedly. 'But I daresay there's a man around here somewhere to chop it up for me.'

Adele picked up the axe again and holding it in both hands, she gave a kind of mirthless chuckle. 'You haven't changed a scrap, have you?' she said. 'Always expecting a man to do things for you. I don't suppose you've ever done a hard day's work in your life, have you?'

'I've always taken care of myself,' Rose replied, but her

voice shook because she sensed this was the start of the showdown she'd half expected. 'At least since Jim abandoned me.'

'Oh really?' Adele's eyebrows shot up into inverted Vs of disbelief. 'And you somehow earned enough to buy a house?'

'Yes. Well, at least the deposit,' Rose retorted, and began to walk away because she was scared.

'Liar!' Adele shouted, and came after her, grabbing her arm. 'I can guess where you got that money. It was Myles Bailey, wasn't it? You blackmailed him!'

'I don't know what you're talking about,' Rose insisted defensively. 'Who's Myles Bailey?'

The crack across her face came so swiftly she didn't even see Adele's hand move. She staggered back, tripping on a fallen branch, and fell flat on her back. Adele stood over her and glowered down at her, the axe dangling from her left hand.

'You miserable, treacherous bitch,' she hissed at her. 'You are so stupid too, did you think he wouldn't tell me? He's a nasty piece of work too, but at least he had enough decency in him to try and protect his son! You, you're disgusting, you not only lacked the moral fibre to come and tell me yourself why I couldn't marry Michael, but you used it as a way to extort money.'

'I didn't,' Rose insisted wildly, knowing Adele couldn't have proof of that. 'I didn't take money. I only went to him because I couldn't come back into your life and tell you myself.'

'I'm grown-up now,' Adele snarled at her. 'I can look back at all the nasty things you did and said to me objectively, and work out why it was. I've probably spent more time thinking about you in one week than you've thought of me in twenty years. You treated me worse than a stray cat! You blamed me for Pamela's death, you allowed me to think your drinking was my fault, even my birth was something bad I did to you.

'After all that you can't fool me about anything. You're just a whore, a liar and a complete failure as a human being.'

Rose was astounded by the ferocity in Adele's voice, and she couldn't believe that anyone with so much venom stored inside them could have calmly controlled it for two days, waiting for the right opportunity to spit it out.

She lay petrified on the grass, her eyes on the axe in Adele's hand. She was sure she was going to attack her with it.

'I'm sorry, Adele,' she whimpered. 'I was sick, I had a mental illness, you know I did. Ask your gran. She knows.'

'I shan't be asking Granny anything,' Adele said, her eyes burning and voice rasping with emotion. 'She's had more than enough grief over you already. Wasn't it enough to break her heart? Did you have to come back and ruin my life and Michael's too?'

'I never meant to hurt Mother, I was young and silly,' Rose sobbed out. 'I didn't want to hurt you and Michael either, but I had to do something. If you'd married him and had children they might have been imbeciles.'

'I might have believed that if you'd come to me and told me the truth,' Adele roared at her. 'But you went to *him*, you saw it as a golden opportunity to make something for yourself.'

'If you think that little of me, why did you get me to come and look after Mother then?' Rose cried out.

'Maybe because I wanted to get you down here and kill you.'

To Rose's horror Adele took her axe in both hands, lifted it up, then brought it down swiftly, stopping only a few inches from Rose's head. 'You tried to kill me once, or have you forgotten that? And I'd done nothing to you.'

'I was sick and stricken with grief over Pamela,' Rose yelled, frantically trying to wriggle away, for Adele was making hacking movements with the axe now, and with each one she brought it closer to Rose's face. 'You've never heard my side of it. Myles abandoned me when I was carrying you. I worshipped him and he just left me to go to the workhouse. You can't know what I went through. Please, Adele, don't kill me.'

'How much money did you get from him?' Adele thundered, and she moved still closer to Rose, once again bringing the axe perilously close to her face. 'Tell me now, or you get this anyway!'

Rose knew there was no point in continuing to deny she'd taken money from Myles, she had a feeling Adele knew everything anyway. 'A thousand pounds,' she bleated out. 'But he owed that to me after what he'd done to me.'

Adele swung the axe again. Rose screamed and covered her face with her hands, involuntarily wetting herself. The blade came so close it almost brushed her cheek, and it landed in the grass right beside her ear.

'You disgust me,' Adele said scornfully. 'Look at you, completely terrified of the child you used to knock about! You deserve pain for what you've done to me, but I've got something more constructive in mind for you than death or disfigurement.'

'I'll do whatever you say,' Rose whimpered. She was so scared she didn't think she'd even be able to get up off the ground. 'Look, I'll sell the house, give the money to Mother.'

'Do you think she would want blood money?' Adele roared. 'Do you think I would ever let her know just how depraved her only daughter is?'

'What do you want then?' Rose cried.

'I want her to live to a ripe old age and be happy, that's all,' Adele replied, her voice cracking with emotion. 'I don't want her to have another day of anxiety. I want her to believe she and Frank brought a good, decent person into this world. Even if that isn't true.'

Rose could only shake with fear.

'Are you prepared to give her that, whatever it takes?' Adele hissed at her. 'Are you?'

Rose nodded. She knew she had no choice but to agree.

'Sit up then,' Adele barked at her. 'And listen carefully because I'm not going to repeat it.'

Rose sat up, and tried to wipe the tears from her face with her sleeve.

'Right!' Adele said. 'I'm going to give you just one chance to redeem yourself and it won't come easy.

'Somehow you are going to have to turn yourself into a cross between Florence Nightingale and Pollyanna. You will lavish care on Granny, empty her commode, bath her and feed her, and look after the cottage, the garden and the animals. You will become the kind of selfless daughter she deserves.'

'I'll do it,' Rose agreed desperately. 'I promise I will.'

'You'd better,' Adele said, and smirked. 'I know that within half an hour of me leaving you'll be working on some scheme to get out of here and back to your drinking and low life. But don't try it. Just one false move and I'll know about it. And I'll be after you. There won't be a second chance for you, I promise you that.'

Rose looked into her daughter's greenish-brown eyes and was reminded sharply of Myles. He had looked at her just the same way a short while before he left her. It was a kind of knowing look, as though he'd peered right down into her soul and hadn't liked what he saw there.

He must have discovered all her lies and trickery, just the way Adele had now. Perhaps it was as well Adele was more like him than her.

'There are things I should tell you about your father,' Rose started to say, for she had a sudden urge to unburden herself.

'I don't want to hear them. I dislike him as much as I do you,' Adele snapped. 'I've got this wood to get home. You compose yourself and then come in round the back of the cottage so you can wash your face before Granny sees you.'

Rose watched in stunned silence as Adele calmly went back to the wood-laden pram, slung the logs on the top and the axe in the side, then pushed it to the gate as if nothing had happened.

Rose got up, fumbled in her pocket for a cigarette, then slumped on the remains of the fallen tree, dragging deeply on the cigarette to try to banish her shakes.

Adele was wrong in thinking she had never thought about her all these years. She had. But she had never reproached herself for treating her badly. Even when Honour had taken her to task for being a bad mother, she hadn't really appreciated that she might have damaged Adele.

But she could see she had now. Coming face to face with such rage and hatred had stripped away all those defences she'd built around herself for so many years. She couldn't make any excuses for herself, she was what Adele had said – a liar, a whore and a cheat.

She began to cry, the sobs coming up from somewhere deep within her, bringing with them disgust at herself. She'd always used people, not consciously maybe, but now she thought about it she had always homed in on those who had something to give. Had she ever acted out of kindness, generosity or selflessness?

While she had often felt regret for deception, heartlessness, greed and manipulating people, she'd always found some way of justifying herself.

Rose covered her face with her hands, all at once so desperately ashamed of herself that she wished she could die and never have to face Adele or Honour again.

She stayed outside until dusk came, for she couldn't stop crying and it was a river of regret. She understood now what the old proverb 'As you sow, so shall you reap' really meant. How could she expect love, kindness or understanding when she'd never given any herself?

It was so tempting just to run from here, find a pub and drink herself into oblivion. That was what she usually did in a crisis. But this time she wouldn't. She would do exactly as Adele instructed. It would probably never be enough, not for her mother or her daughter. But she had to try.

A fortnight later Honour was sitting in her chair by the stove looking at her plaster-cast leg propped up on the stool in front of her. It was grubby now, the result of Towzer bounding in from outside and shaking his muddy coat near her. The grey sock pulled over her foot needed darning, revealing one purple-tinged toe, and her leg itched under the plaster. She was sick and tired of being unable to move around freely, bored to the point of desperation at being indoors, but she knew that she should count her blessings.

She was very lucky to be alive, and she should be glad all her other injuries had healed so quickly. Even the wound on her head was almost better, and within a few days she had been able to dispense with the dressing.

Rose was out in the scullery plucking a chicken, and every now and then she would sneeze as the feathers got up her nose. Each time it happened Honour couldn't help but smile.

Rose was not equipped for the country life. Her hands were too soft for rough work, she had no stamina and she was squeamish. If she had her way they'd be eating fish and chips every night, she'd buy bread and would probably choose to work in a munitions factory and pay someone else to look after her mother. But remarkably, she hadn't complained once since Adele left.

Honour knew the two of them had had some kind of fight before Adele went back to London, and that Rose had come off worst. They did their best to conceal it, but she sensed it by her daughter's cowed silence. Rose had listened attentively while Adele gave her instructions about Honour's medicine, how often her dressings needed changing and how to tell if there was any infection. She had meekly agreed to go up to the telephone box each week at an arranged time to ring Adele at the hospital with a report on how Honour was.

It was most surprising that Rose didn't snap at Adele when she harped on about keeping buckets of water filled, sand available, and the stirrup pump handy in case of incendiary bombs. After all, Rose had seen the aftermath of bombing, and read all the Government instructions on putting out fires.

But she had behaved as if she were just a servant, afraid to bite back with even a touch of sarcasm. And that, as Honour remembered, was very uncharacteristic, for Rose had always been feisty and sure of herself.

It was even more uncharacteristic for her to get up at six, rake the ashes in the stove and relight it, then bring Honour a cup of tea an hour later and ask if she was ready to use the commode.

Honour fully expected that such dutiful behaviour would fizzle out in a few days, but it hadn't. She fed the rabbits and chickens, she collected wood, did the washing and cooking. She was a surprisingly good cook too. It seemed she'd learned a few tricks of the trade while working in the restaurant, for the soup she made was much tastier than anything Honour could make. And she was very gentle when she changed dressings and helped Honour wash and dress herself.

She couldn't kill a chicken or rabbit, and Honour doubted she would ever be able to, but that didn't matter – Jim the postman was quite happy to oblige when necessary. Yet what surprised Honour most of all was what good company Rose could be. She liked the same programmes on the wireless, and they would both laugh their heads off at *ITMA*. She was good at card games and had taught Honour several new ones.

There had been many occasions when she'd been distant or looked very bored, and when she went into Rye on a message, she was gone longer than it warranted, which made Honour suspect she'd stopped off in a pub. But she was easy to be with, for she didn't prattle on about nothing like so many women Honour knew.

Life had settled into a pleasant routine, and although Honour felt irked by her incapacity, she had much to be grateful for, especially Rose coming back to her.

Once or twice she had almost told her how she felt, but it was far too soon, and she still had suspicions about her. Rose was something of an enigma; she still hadn't said anything about the years between running away from here as a girl and her time in the mental asylum. Or who Adele's father was. There were times when Honour thought it might be due to the treatment in the asylum. But if it was, it seemed odd that she could recall all kinds of incidents from her childhood, and seemed to enjoy talking about them.

She also asked a great many questions about Adele, especially about her time in The Firs, how she settled in here at the cottage and how and when she met Michael Bailey. Honour thought she imagined that by piecing together all the events in the years she'd been away from her child, she'd somehow gain Adele's forgiveness.

'I've finally finished the chicken,' Rose said from the doorway of the scullery, making Honour start.

'Well done,' Honour said, resisting the temptation to add, 'About time too.' 'Have you put all the feathers in the sack?'

'Yes, Mother,' Rose replied with the weariness of someone who had anticipated the question. 'And swept the floor too, before you ask. Shall we have a cup of tea?'

'I can make that,' Honour said, lifting her broken leg with both hands and putting it to the floor. 'It's about time I had a bit of exercise. You come and sit down, you've done quite enough for one day.'

Rose took off her apron before moving into the living

room. Honour hauled herself out of her chair and stood on her good leg, reaching for her crutch for support.

'I expect the muscles will have wasted away by the time the plaster comes off,' she said, moving closer to the stove to put the kettle on. 'I just hope I'm not left with a limp for the rest of my life.'

'Limping is better than hopping on one leg,' Rose said as she sat down.

That remark made Honour think of Frank. It was the kind of thing he used to say. She turned to look at her daughter and saw the same pensive expression he often wore.

'What's wrong, Rose?' she asked, as she opened the cupboard where she kept the tea things.

'Nothing really,' Rose said with a shrug. 'I was just thinking about Adele while I was plucking the chicken. I can't imagine how she can stand to see all that blood and guts, day after day. Ordinary nursing in peacetime is one thing, but she can't have any break from it now, can she? At her age she should be out dancing and having fun.'

'The war can't last for ever,' Honour said, hooking two cups on her finger and putting them on the table. 'There'll be time for dancing again when it's over. When we were her age we were both mothers.'

'Hmm,' Rose murmured. 'I was expecting Pamela then.'

Honour didn't dare to turn and look at her daughter, for it was the first time she had mentioned Pamela since she'd been here. 'How did you feel about having a second child?' she asked cautiously.

'I was horrified at first,' Rose said in a small voice. 'But Jim was so pleased, and I was kind of glad I'd made him happy. I wanted to be like other women, you know, the jolly smiling ones who dote on babies. It's normal to be like that, isn't it?'

'I don't know,' Honour said. 'I can't say I was. I wasn't one to want to cuddle other people's babies. I viewed them with great suspicion.'

'Did you?' Rose sounded astonished. 'I always got the idea you wanted lots of them.'

Honour chuckled. 'I certainly didn't. I liked you well enough, but I was always relieved each month when I found I hadn't fallen again.'

'Good heavens,' Rose exclaimed. 'I wish I'd known that.'

'What difference would it have made?'

'Well, maybe I wouldn't have felt so abnormal in not wanting children.'

The kettle boiled and Honour poured the water into the teapot. Leaving it on the side of the stove to brew, she sat down again.

'You had Adele under difficult circumstances,' she said. 'You were worried, frightened, and I suppose that could stop any woman seeing a baby as a joy.'

'I could never think of anyone but me,' Rose admitted. 'I blamed her that my body was stretched and torn, for the pain and the disturbed sleep. Other mothers don't do that.'

'Maybe they do, but don't admit it,' Honour said. 'My father-in-law got me a nursemaid. Without her helping out I might very well have found plenty to grumble about.'

'But you grew to love me, didn't you?' Rose asked.

Honour frowned. 'I loved you the moment you were put in my arms,' she said. 'You must know that?'

There was no reply and Honour turned to look at her daughter. Rose looked troubled, fiddling with the buttons on her cardigan.

'Surely you didn't think otherwise?' Honour asked.

'You don't think about such things when you're small,' Rose said. 'You just accept everything. But when Father went off to war I felt you had no time for me.'

'No time for you!' Honour said incredulously.

'Well, you were always shutting yourself in your room, going for walks on your own. It was horrible, like I was invisible,' Rose blurted out.

'I was upset. I missed him terribly and I was scared he'd be killed,' Honour said, but she felt a sudden stab of guilt as she remembered that she had isolated herself. She even sometimes resented Rose making demands on her.

'I felt all those things too,' Rose said. 'But you didn't seem to realize it.'

'Then I'm sorry. I suppose I must've been too wrapped up in myself,' Honour said sadly.

'I was only thirteen, Mother.' Rose's voice rose an octave. 'It felt like I'd lost both parents. You rarely spoke to me, you never asked how I was doing at school or if I had any friends, nothing. Perhaps it wasn't any wonder I couldn't love Adele?'

'Now, come on,' Honour said sharply, all at once afraid that Rose was trying to manipulate her. 'I might have gone through a bad patch but I didn't neglect you or harm you in any way.'

'Let's drop this subject,' Rose replied with a dismissive toss of her head. 'I don't want to rake over old coals.'

Honour looked at her daughter and saw she was now looking down at her feet, and she was reminded of how often Rose had behaved just like this as a girl. She would bring up some grievance, then suddenly grow silent, as if she were unable or afraid to continue. It used to irritate Honour then and it did now.

'For heaven's sake spit it out and be done with it,' Honour exclaimed. 'If you think I harmed you, tell me about it.'

'You didn't exactly harm me, even if you weren't very fair,' Rose said in a small voice. 'But it isn't what you did to me back then that hurts, it's more how you've presented me to Adele.'

'What do you mean?' Honour asked in exasperation. 'I haven't "presented" you in any way at all to her. Any ideas she has of you were formed by your own actions.'

'Did you ever tell her that from fourteen I was working my fingers to the bone in that hotel, bringing every penny I

419

earned home to you?' Rose asked. 'Did you tell her that I used to leave here before it was even light during the winter, and then returned home some fourteen hours later, through rain and snow?'

'I did say you worked at the hotel,' Honour said indignantly.

'And I bet she thought it was only for a few hours as a waitress,' Rose said bitterly. 'I laid fires, I emptied chamber pots, I cleaned silver and scrubbed floors. My hands were red raw, I ached all over long before I got to put on the black waitress dress and cap and went into the dining room to serve old men and women who treated me like dirt. After that I washed up. Only after everything was put away could I come home.'

'I don't understand where this is leading,' Honour said sternly. 'What is your point?'

'My point is that Adele believes that you were a perfect mother, and that I was all bad because I ran away and left you,' Rose said pointedly. 'She's never been told the reasons that led up to me leaving.'

'I don't know those myself,' Honour sighed. 'Suppose you tell me?'

'I was the breadwinner of the family at fourteen. When I got home so tired I could hardly drag myself into bed, you used to complain how lonely you'd been,' Rose retorted. 'Then eventually Father came home, and he was like a frightening stranger to me. You babied him but you never once thanked me for earning the money for his medicine and the extra food. You didn't even explain anything to me.'

Honour felt as if a curtain had been pulled back to reveal a part of her life she'd chosen not to look at before.

'I didn't think,' she said weakly.

'No, you didn't,' Rose snapped. 'The only day I got a chance for a lie-in was on Sundays, and one Sunday morning you woke me up at dawn to go out and get some wood for the stove. I

420

hadn't come home from work until after two. Father was sound asleep, you could have got the wood yourself, but no, you dragged me out of bed. Did you tell Adele that?'

'They were hard times for everyone,' Honour said defiantly.

'Yes, they were,' Rose agreed. 'And you were frantic about Father and probably not sleeping very well. But you treated me like a servant. I felt used.'

Honour had forgotten much of what went on during those years of war, but Rose's words were unlocking the memories. 'I'm sorry,' she said.

'Oh, I don't want apologies,' Rose said wearily. 'All I want is for you to recognize what lay behind me running away. I wasn't all bad, and I think Adele should know that too.'

Honour didn't speak for a moment or two. The things Rose had spoken of had created a beam of light into what had previously been a dark place. She was guilty as charged. She had presented the years between when Frank went off to war and Rose ran away only from her own perspective. She had failed to take account of the valuable role her daughter had played, indeed until now she hadn't considered that Rose had played one at all.

'You are right,' she said at length. 'I didn't show any appreciation, and I should have. I'm willing to admit it to Adele. But if you want to build bridges with her, you'll have to be honest with her about everything that came after. I can't help there.'

Rose got up and silently poured out the tea. She handed a cup to Honour and then sat down with hers. 'I didn't mean to launch into all that,' she said at length, and her voice was low and apologetic. 'It just came out.'

'Perhaps it's as well,' Honour said, and reached out to squeeze her daughter's arm. 'My mother used to use the expression, "You can't put new jam into dirty jars." Maybe we've cleaned them out now.'

Rose smiled weakly. 'I don't somehow think Adele will ever want to even try to understand me.'

Honour sighed. 'Don't judge her by your own standards. She's a clever girl with a big heart. Time and the sadness of this war might very well bring her round.'

Towzer came over to Rose and put his head on her lap. She scratched his head and stroked him. 'If only people were more like dogs,' she said. 'They don't hold grudges, or want explanations.'

'Maybe they don't,' Honour said with a smile. 'But the amount of care and affection they give to you is equal to the amount you give them. Humans are much the same in that respect. Towzer has grown to love you, and in time Adele will too if she thinks you are worthy of it.'

Michael shifted slightly in his seat to relieve the cramp in his left leg and glanced at the Lancaster bomber flying beside him, piloted by Joe Spiers, his Australian friend. Michael loathed flying at night, especially in January when it was freezing cold and cloud blocked out the moon, but it was some comfort to have Joe up alongside him.

As the cramp eased off, Michael smiled to himself. A few days earlier one of the WAAFs back at the base had called him Old Bailey because he was hobbling when he got out of the Spitfire. At twenty-three he felt like one too. Most of the boys in the squadron were nineteen or twenty, all new faces, his old chums practically all dead.

Sometimes, if he dared let the thought out, he wondered when he'd be shot down. It didn't seem possible that he who was no better or worse as a pilot than the others, should be spared. But then at other times he believed himself invincible, and that in its way was even more dangerous.

He was on his way to Germany now, on escort duty for the bombers. It was nowhere near as hairy as the days of the dog-fights in the Battle of Britain, but then night flying brought its own problems, and it didn't do to be complacent.

He thought that whatever the dangers, he'd sooner be up in the air than stuck in a desk job in London. The Blitz had been going on for three months now, the East End decimated by night after night of bombing. Those cockneys were a courageous bunch, though, they went down to the Tube station shelters at night and emerged next morning to find whole streets gone. Yet they went off to work regardless, often even without water for a quick wash or a cup of tea.

Michael had been forced into a shelter himself at New Year, having been daft enough to be persuaded by Joe that they should see the New Year in well away from the base. He nearly turned tail and ran when he got a whiff of the latrines. It was enough to make you sick, and he thought it was better to take a chance of being killed on the street than spend a night with that stench. But of course he stayed – as Joe said, discretion was the greater part of valour. And he even enjoyed himself, despite the smell and people packed as close as sardines. They made the best of it, each making their little space as comfortable as they could, looking out for one another. One old chap played the accordion, and everyone sang along with it.

They came from all walks of life that night. Ordinary locals who came every night and had the place organized, toffs in dinner jackets with ladies sparkling with jewels, and tarts from Soho who helped the women with babies and small children. Middle-aged suburban housewives, caught out by the siren before they could get home, wizened old people, bright young typists and shop girls, and a fair smattering of men in uniform too.

He and Joe met two girls from Yorkshire. They were both auxiliary nurses at a hospital in South London, and like Michael and Joe they'd come up to the West End to celebrate the New Year. Michael had really liked June, the pretty, dark-haired one. She was vivacious and funny, and he thought he might ring her and arrange to take her out as soon as he got some leave.

Joe kept saying that the best way to get over a 'Sheila' was to find a new one, and Michael was sure he was right. June didn't remind him of Adele in any way – she was petite, sweetly plump and chatted nineteen to the dozen. When he kissed her in the early hours of the morning she responded eagerly. That was what he wanted, an uncomplicated girl who didn't think too deeply. Someone who would never touch his soul as Adele had.

It began to snow and Michael cursed it. While it made it easier for them to arrive at their target unseen, it also made it harder to see enemy planes. Five more minutes and they'd be there, and with luck on their side in another ten they'd be on the way home.

A barrage of anti-aircraft fire and the accompanying flashes gave a glimpse of the airfield and hangars they were after. Michael and the other two Spitfires climbed to let the three Lancasters close in on their target, and as the first bomb was dropped, Michael heard a secondary bang, and looked down to see fire breaking out.

'Yes!' he yelled triumphantly, for it was clearly an ammunition dump or fuel tank.

His jubilation increased with each bomb, for he could see the airfield clearly now in the light of the fire, and they'd hit planes and flattened buildings.

The job done, all the planes rolled away to turn and go home, and Michael was cackling with glee, forgetting the cold and his cramp, and even to keep a watchful eye out for fighter planes.

The crack and judder on the right side of the plane made him start. His head jerked around, and he saw the Messerschmitt beside him and the red sparks of his guns. Michael fired automatically, but the German plane dived and evaded it, then before Michael could even think of climbing higher, it came up from beneath him in a flash and fired again, hitting the Spitfire on the nose.

Engine coolant sprayed up on to the windscreen, obliterating Michael's view, and it was only then that he saw his plane was on fire.

'Christ almighty,' he exclaimed, for this was the kind of end he had dreaded most. He could feel the sudden surge of warmth – a few seconds more and he knew he'd be burned alive. He could see nothing ahead – the coolant stuck to the screen and the snow saw to that. All he could see were orange and scarlet flames to his right side, and there was nothing for it but to flip over and eject.

He had trained for this. In theory the cockpit should open up at a touch and he should shoot out like a cork from a bottle. But he was belly side up now, flames all around him, and the cockpit wouldn't open.

He saw Adele's face for a brief second. She was running to him with her hair flowing out behind her like a banner.

'God help me,' he rasped out as he prepared to die.

Chapter Twenty-four

1941

Honour opened the front door as she saw Jim retreating back to the lane after delivering her letter.

'Come back here and warm up with a cup of tea,' she called out.

It was a bitterly cold February day with flurries of hail. The sky was black and Honour thought that by tonight there would be snow. She had had the plaster cast removed from her leg in time for Christmas, but to her disappointment she still needed to use a walking stick for support, for her broken leg had become weak through lack of use. Rose wouldn't let her do more than hobble around the garden for short periods, and not even that now it was icy, so Jim would be a pleasant diversion from her boredom.

Jim turned back, a broad smile proving her offer was welcome. 'I'm frozen solid, but I didn't knock because I thought you'd want time alone to read your letter.'

Honour laughed. 'You know perfectly well I've got more time alone than I know what to do with,' she said. 'Adele's letter can wait. Now, come on in.'

'Rose not here today?' Jim inquired as he stamped his boots on the doormat and closed the door behind him.

'She's just gone off to Rye to see if she can get oil for the lamps and some new library books,' Honour said. 'I wonder you didn't see her, she's only just gone.'

'I wasn't watching out for anyone,' he said, taking off his coat and sitting down. 'I was too busy thinking about poor Mrs Bailey.'

'What's the matter with her?' Honour asked.

Jim looked embarrassed. 'You haven't heard?'

'Heard what?'

'About Michael.'

'Don't tell me he's been killed!' Honour had to sit down quickly.

'Well, "missing, presumed dead", but that means much the same, doesn't it?' Jim said, then seeing Honour's stricken face he reached out and patted her arm. 'I'm sorry, Honour, I thought you'd have heard already. She got the telegram a week ago.'

'Not that lovely boy,' Honour sighed, and tears came to her eyes. 'How did it happen?'

'Shot down over Germany, they say,' Jim replied, peeling off his fingerless mittens and flexing his fingers. 'She's taking it very hard, well, you of all people know what she's like. Her neighbour told me this morning that she was out in the street last night in her nightclothes. Didn't know what she was doing!'

'He might have been taken prisoner,' Honour said. 'I've heard it can take weeks, even months, for the news to get through.'

Jim shrugged. 'That doesn't seem likely. Apparently she had a visit from one of Michael's squadron, he saw his plane on fire and didn't see him eject.'

'A real Job's comforter,' Honour said dourly. 'Couldn't he have given her some hope?'

She got up again to make the tea, but on seeing the tea caddy Michael had given her when he first met Adele, she began to cry.

'Now Honour, don't take on,' Jim said with concern. 'I wish I hadn't told you now.'

'Better that it came from you than gossip in the shop,' Honour said, sniffing back her tears. 'I was very fond of him. As you know, I always had hopes for him and Adele. I feel for his mother too, he was the only one of her children close to her. Whatever will she do now?'

427

Jim shook his head sadly. 'If she doesn't pull herself together her housekeeper will leave, that's for certain. I've heard she's been on the point of going dozens of times before this, and there's only so much a body can take.'

'Well, I hope she doesn't take off for a while,' Honour said indignantly. 'People do go off the rails a bit at times like this. They can't help it. I know how I felt when my Frank died.'

'Your bark is very much worse than your bite, Honour,' Jim said teasingly. 'You're a kind woman really.'

Honour gave a watery smile. 'Do children still think I'm a witch?'

He shook his head. 'That bit of nonsense died a long time ago, when Adele came here. Now you've got Rose too, and she's too comely to be the daughter of a witch.'

'I sometimes think all three of us are bewitched,' Honour said sadly. 'We've all had troubled lives.'

'Now, this isn't like you,' Jim said, his kindly face full of concern. 'I always think of you as invincible.'

Honour shook her head sadly. 'No, Jim, I'm not that. I'm just an old woman who does the best she can to get by.'

Jim stayed for a little while making small talk about rationing and how lucky they were that they weren't town folk without chickens and homegrown vegetables to fall back on. After he'd left, Honour lay down on the couch, pulled a shawl over herself and cried. She knew in her heart that Adele had never stopped loving Michael. She might go out with other young men, and no longer asked for news of him, but she wasn't fooling anyone. She was going to be devastated by his death, and Honour was sure Michael must be dead if his plane had caught fire.

But her tears were not only for her granddaughter, they were for Emily Bailey too. Honour had run into her once in Rye, during the time of the Battle of Britain, and she had asked after Michael. Emily had been transparently pleased to be able to talk about him to someone who knew him well. She had spoken of him with such pride, yet she had looked so tense and thin, and there were deep shadows around her eyes from sleepless nights.

Honour had come fully to understand that kind of anxiety and dread since she was caught up in the air raid. Yet she could remind herself that Adele was in an underground ward most of the time, that she could run to a shelter if she was outside when the siren went. Emily wouldn't have been able to reassure herself in that way. She knew as everyone did that when an aeroplane was hit, the chances of the pilot surviving were very small.

Honour knew too that if Adele were to be killed, she would be unable to bear the loss. She wouldn't even want to try. And she guessed that was just how Emily must feel right now. Her heart told her to put on her coat and boots and walk up to Winchelsea and see her. But she knew she wasn't able to walk that far – if she slipped on the icy road she might break her leg again. She would write a letter instead, it might be a small comfort for Emily to know that people felt for her.

It was half past three when Rose left Rye to go home, but already getting dark. There had been long queues in all the shops, and although she'd managed to get oil for the lamp, some cheese, butter and tea, no one had any sugar. She'd spent longer in the pub than she meant to, but it was fun having a flirt with two soldiers on leave. Her mother would not approve, but then if Rose couldn't have a couple of drinks and some male company now and then, she'd be climbing the walls and snapping her mother's head off.

After the pub shut she'd had to rush to the library, and now she was concerned that she'd left Honour alone for so long.

But it had been a good day, despite the bitter cold. Queuing might be time-consuming, but it hadn't been dull. Everyone had been chatting and laughing, and she'd seen a couple of women she'd been at school with, and both had been very pleased to see her. Her cynical nature told her that they only spoke because they hoped to get a few morsels of gossip to spread around, yet it had been nice to get re-acquainted. She was very touched to find they both believed Adele came to live with her grandmother when Rose became ill. She hadn't expected that her mother would resort to white lies to save Adele embarrassment or shame. Once she might have embellished her 'illness' further to gain sympathy, but she felt quite proud of herself that she'd passed it off with a shrug and said that Honour had been a better mother than she could have been.

Despite getting to the library so late, she managed to beat another woman to a copy of *Gone with the Wind*. She had been trying to get it for weeks now, but much as she wanted to bury herself in it tonight, she felt she owed it to Honour to allow her to read it first.

All in all, Rose felt pretty good about herself. For perhaps the first time in her adult life she was happy. To her utter surprise she didn't miss London at all, and once she'd learned to adjust to the chores at the cottage, she even found them enjoyable.

The day she spilled out all her old grievances to Honour had cleared the air. She found herself staggered that her mother was capable of admitting she'd been thoughtless. But then Rose had been agreeably surprised many times in the past months to find her mother was very different to the indifferent, prudish and bull-headed person she had created in her mind over the years.

Honour was in fact good company. She had a lively and often wicked sense of humour. She was earthy, straight-talking and very practical. There were of course days when they'd snarled at each other, but then it was difficult to get used to having someone else around all the time when you'd lived alone for so long. Rose had resented being at her mother's beck and call at first, and Honour had been deeply suspicious of anything Rose said or did. Not all the bitterness was entirely resolved for either of them yet, but as Honour was so fond of pointing out, 'Rome wasn't built in a day.'

Yet on balance there was far more laughter than rows, and Rose had experienced moments of extreme tenderness towards Honour, especially when she bore pain and immobility so stoically.

If it weren't for the situation with Adele, Rose felt she could live with her mother indefinitely, providing she could go out dancing or to the cinema every week. But she couldn't possibly forget the hatred and scorn her daughter had lashed her with. Or the threats, and she was certain that once Honour was fully recovered, Adele would expect Rose to clear off for good.

Each week when she walked up to Winchelsea at the arranged time to telephone her daughter, Rose felt sick with nerves. Adele wasn't insulting or even offhand, but there was no warmth in her voice, no suggestion she might be gradually softening, even though Rose knew Honour had told her in her letters that everything was working out well. As the London Blitz was still continuing, with bombing every night, Adele hadn't been able to get time off to come down here, not even at Christmas. Rose knew that until she did come home, and saw for herself that Rose had kept her part of the bargain and perhaps changed for the better, she was always going to despise and think the worst of her.

Rose and Honour were very aware that the news reports on the wireless were not giving the full picture of how it was in London or in the war at large. Adele's letters, information passed on by neighbours with family and friends in the city or on the front lines, revealed a very different one. People were being killed and injured in their thousands, the Germans were better equipped and had more manpower, and it didn't look possible that England could beat them. Nightly they heard bombers flying in, sometimes they heard bombs dropped well before the planes reached London. Refugees from both Europe and London arrived down here daily, having mostly lost everything in their flight. Sometimes Rose would stand at the window of the cottage looking towards the beach with its huge rolls of barbed wire, and wonder how long it would be before the Germans invaded Britain.

They would probably land along this stretch of coast, and she and Honour might very well be in graver danger than facing the bombs in London.

The daylight had gone completely by the time Rose drew near to the lane which led to the cottage. There was a full moon, but it flitted in and out of banks of clouds, giving only fleeting silhouettes of the rooftops in Winchelsea up on the hill and the black slick of river.

The blackout made night-time so scary. No welcoming light glowed at the cottage, or from the houses in Winchelsea. It was like being the only person left in the world, and very few cars came this way now as people saved their petrol for emergencies. The moon went behind the clouds again, and Rose cursed herself for not bringing her torch with her. It would be hell on the lane, stepping into unseen ice-covered puddles or stubbing her toes on big stones.

She hesitated where the lane began, looking up to where the moon had been moments before. 'Come on out, Mr Moon,' she said, and giggled at herself for being so childish.

A noise made her turn her head. It sounded like someone or something in the meadow by the river. Assuming it was a sheep, she stepped gingerly on to the lane. But on hearing the sound again, she stopped and listened.

The noise sheep made was the very fabric of life on the marsh, and this sound wasn't one of theirs. Sheep weren't given to walking about when it was as cold as this, they'd be far more likely to be huddled together under the hedge. She was sure this sound was human, for it was more than just feet scrunching on the frosty grass, but panting too.

The moon came out again, and to her astonishment she saw a woman in the meadow. The moon glinted on her fair or white flowing hair, and she appeared to be running towards the river.

The moon vanished again, but the sound of the panting was louder now, and it seemed to Rose that the woman was in distress. In a flash of intuition she suddenly realized she was intent on drowning herself.

There was no other explanation for her being in the meadow, not in the dark, or in such cold weather. Rose knew from her own experiences that people could do extraordinary things in moments of desperation, and she knew she must stop this woman.

Forgetting that seconds before she had been anxious about ice and stones, she dropped her shopping at the side of the lane, made for the hole in the hedge she often used when collecting wood and squeezed through. She couldn't see the woman now, but as she started over the meadow towards the river, she heard a splash.

Racing towards the spot where the sound had come from, she was just in time to see one very white hand flailing about in the dark water. The rest of the woman was submerged.

Rose looked desperately around her. The nearest house was her own, but Honour wouldn't be able to help with this. By the time she got help elsewhere the woman would be drowned. There was no choice but to deal with it herself.

She stripped off her coat and jumped, not daring to consider how cold it was, how deep the water or how strong the current might be. As she hit the icy water the shock was so great she felt her heart was going to stop, but she forced herself to tread water while she found the woman.

The moon came out again for just long enough for Rose

to make out something which wasn't weed floating on the surface. It took only four or five strokes to reach it, and as her hand met woollen fabric she realized it was the woman's coat or loose dress.

Still treading water, she grabbed it with one hand, the other feeling in the water beneath it. Her hand touched a limb, and she yanked it up.

It was a leg, with no stocking or shoe, and somehow that told her the woman had definitely lost her mind.

The water was so cold Rose felt almost paralysed, but still holding the leg so the woman wouldn't sweep off in the current, she reached down again, further this time, and upon reaching what seemed to be her waist, hooked her arm right round it and hauled her up. The weight pulled Rose under, and she had to let go of the leg to regain the surface, but she still held tightly around the woman's waist, and finally she managed to get her up to the surface.

The moon came out again, and to Rose's surprise the woman wasn't young, as she had supposed by the long hair, but middle-aged, and tied round her neck like some kind of bizarre necklace was a heavy chain. This was clearly the reason why she had been head down in the water.

Fear that the woman would pull her down too gave Rose new strength, and she wrenched off the chain. Suddenly the woman was very much lighter. She appeared lifeless, but Rose seemed to remember it took longer than just two or three minutes to drown.

She found it easy enough to get to the bank, swimming on her back and holding the woman's head up with her hands, but it was quite another thing to climb out while hauling someone else.

She tried holding on to the woman's coat, and had got halfway up the bank when it began to slip out of her grasp, weighted down by the body inside it.

'Damn you,' she shouted aloud. 'I'm bloody well not

leaving you in here, even if that is what you want. Help me, for God's sake.'

But the woman couldn't help, and there was no alternative but for Rose to slip back into the water. By now she was so cold she thought she might very well die of it too. Her hands were completely numb, but she got behind the woman, grasped her around the waist and with one almighty shove, got her halfway up the bank.

Scrabbling up beside her, Rose got on to the grass at the top of the bank, then reached down and caught hold of the woman under her arms. She hauled her up, then turned her on to her stomach on the grass.

Rose had only seen artificial respiration done a couple of times, and she wasn't sure she remembered how it was done, or even if it was far too late to attempt it. But she pressed down on the woman's back, then lifted her shoulders, and kept doing it.

'Breathe, for God's sake,' she yelled as she pumped. 'Do you think I want to die of cold out here with you?'

Darkness had never seemed so terrifying before. It wrapped round them like a thick blanket, and Rose was tempted to run for it now because she could do no more. Yet she still pumped despite the cold, tears pouring down her face, hot on her icy skin.

And then she heard a splutter.

'That's it,' she cried triumphantly. 'Come on, breathe, damn you! Breathe!'

She heard rather than saw water spurt out of the woman's mouth, and it sounded like gallons. Then more spluttering, and Rose put her head down by her face and heard faint, rasping breathing.

'Good girl,' she said, and left her for a second while she rushed to get the coat she'd dropped earlier. She wrapped it round the woman, holding her in a sitting position, and though her head was lolling, she really was breathing.

In Rose's mind there was only one thing to do, and that was to get herself and this would-be suicide back to the cottage. She didn't dare leave her as she might slip back into the river, and anyway she could die of cold before help got here. So she hauled her bodily to her feet, then bent over so the woman sagged across her shoulder, the way firemen lifted people. Stumbling under the weight, Rose made her way to the lane.

Water squelched out of her shoes, every part of her was so cold it hurt, and the woman was so heavy that Rose didn't think she could carry her more than a few yards. But she concentrated her mind on taking just one step at a time, each one getting her closer to the cottage.

She heard the woman vomit down her back, but at least that meant she was coming round. Still she plodded on, focusing only on reaching the front door.

'Mother!' she yelled as she reached the path. 'Open the door.'

Nothing had ever been more welcoming than to see the door flung wide and the golden glow of the lamp spilling out behind her mother's silhouette.

'What on earth have you got there?' Honour cried out. 'Is it an animal?'

'A drowned one,' Rose retorted, and she wanted to laugh then, for just to see her mother made her feel safe again.

'Oh my goodness,' Honour exclaimed as Rose laid her burden down on the hearthrug in front of the fire. 'It's Emily!'

She began stripping off the woman's sopping clothes and wrapping her in blankets. Rose told her briefly what had happened, but the combination of the sudden warmth of the room and the shock of the ordeal she'd been through was making her feel very peculiar and disoriented.

She recalled her mother ordering her to strip off her

clothes because she was dripping water everywhere. She supposed she must have gone into her bedroom to do it, for the next thing she was aware of was finding herself in her nightdress and dressing-gown, a towel wrapped round her wet hair. Honour was sitting on the floor cradling the woman in her arms and feeding her sips of brandy.

'I'm Honour Harris, dear,' her mother was saying to the woman, who was just looking at her with blank eyes. 'I'm going to take care of you, everything will be all right now.'

Rose was so terribly cold, she wanted to get over to the stove to warm herself, but she couldn't because her mother and the woman were in the way, and she felt somehow threatened. 'We can't take care of her, Mother,' she said. 'She needs to be in a hospital. She isn't a stray like Towzer, you can't mend her with a bowl of food and a warm by the fire. Once I've got warm I'll go and phone for an ambulance.'

'Shush!' Honour said, giving Rose one of her stern looks.

'Mother, she's gone mad! She jumped in the river, and if I hadn't heard her, she'd be washed down to the sluice gates by now.'

'She's only mad with grief,' Honour said with a shake of her head, still rocking the woman in her arms. 'Michael is missing, shot down over Germany.'

'Michael?' Rose said questioningly.

Honour looked up at her. 'Yes, Michael, the young man who was Adele's sweetheart. This is his mother, Emily Bailey.'

Rose reeled back like a drunk, her head suddenly feeling as though it was going to explode. *Emily*. It was too much for her to take in. Surely this woman she'd rescued couldn't be the same one who had once been some kind of she-devil in her eyes?

Emily Bailey, that shrew of a woman who didn't love her husband, but would never set him free to marry anyone else! Rose had never met her, never even seen a picture of her,

437

but when she was in love with Myles she had wished her and her damned children dead.

And now some twenty-two years later she had inadvertently saved her life.

'Rose dear, I think you are suffering from shock,' Honour exclaimed suddenly. 'You're as white as a piece of tripe, and quivering like a jelly. Wrap a blanket round yourself and get yourself some brandy.'

The clock struck six just a little later, making Rose realize that the dramatic events earlier which had seemed to go on for hours, had in fact all happened in about half an hour from start to finish. She was warmer now, thanks to the brandy, but she still felt very strange. Her mother was still sitting on the floor cradling Emily in her arms and murmuring soothing words, but Rose felt she was observing this from afar, unable to participate in any way.

'You can't stay there on the floor, Mother, you'll hurt your back,' she said irritably a while later. 'Let me lift her on to the couch. She's got to let go of you sometime.'

'If I believed my child was dead, I'd want someone to hold me,' Honour said stubbornly.

A lump came up in Rose's throat at her mother's words. 'You can hold her just as well on the couch,' she croaked. 'Come on, let me help you up and I'll make us some tea.'

It seemed odd that Rose had managed to carry Emily back to the cottage so easily, for just trying to lift her from the floor to the couch took every vestige of strength she had left. Perhaps Honour noticed this because once Rose had helped her up on to her feet, she hugged her daughter. 'It was such a brave thing to jump in there after her,' she said, her eyes swimming and her voice breaking. 'You could both have been drowned.'

Rose shrugged. 'It might have been brave if I'd thought before I did it,' she said. 'But I didn't, I just acted on impulse.'

'So lack of thought makes it less brave then?' Honour said with an attempt at a smile, perching beside Emily on the couch.

'Yes,' Rose replied. 'Now Emily, are you going to stop crying and have some tea?'

Rose didn't know if it was the sterner tone, but for the first time since she got into the cottage, Emily looked down at the blanket she was wrapped in, then around the room.

'Where am I?' she asked in a weak, strained voice, and she stopped crying.

'You jumped in the river, and my daughter pulled you out,' Honour said, and smoothed the still wet hair back from Emily's face. 'Do you know me? I'm Honour Harris, the grandmother of Adele who used to be your maid. And this is Rose, my daughter, she rescued you.'

Emily looked quizzically at Honour for a few seconds, her expression one of a child who had just woken from a bad dream. 'You came to my house once.'

'That's right,' Honour said patiently, glancing at Rose sitting in the chair opposite. 'I was a friend of your mother's. We talked in Rye once last year too, about Michael. I am so very sorry he's missing, I was very fond of him too.'

Emily's face crumpled and she began to cry again, but not almost silently like earlier, this time it was great heart-rending sobs, and she buried her face in Honour's shoulder and clung to her. 'It's not fair,' she sobbed out. 'He was so special to me, so kind and loving. I don't want to live without him.'

'But he may be in a prisoner-of-war camp,' Honour said gently. 'You can't give up yet. How would he feel if he came home after the war and found you'd taken your own life?'

'He won't come back, I know he's dead,' Emily insisted. 'His friend saw his plane in flames.'

'I'm sure he told you how many other pilots have parachuted out safely from burning planes,' Honour said. 'I've read dozens of such stories.'

'It's God's judgement on me,' Emily said woodenly. 'My punishment for wrongdoing.'

Honour glanced at Rose and half smiled. 'What wrong have you done?' she asked gently. 'Not much, I'll be bound!'

'I have, I have,' Emily insisted, wringing Honour's hand. 'I've been terrible to my family.'

'I don't think the blame was all yours,' Honour said evenly.

'It was. Myles was so kind and loving once, I changed him by being so impossible. That's why I'm being punished now.'

'I think we'd better have a nice cup of tea,' Honour said.

Later that evening Rose lay in bed, icy cold even though she had a hot water bottle. Emily was sharing her mother's bed, and the wind was howling around the cottage, making the windows rattle. She reached out for her dressing-gown and pulled that over her too, yet she knew no amount of bedcovers were going to warm her tonight, just as nothing Honour could say to Emily was going to ease her grief.

It was guilt and shame that was keeping her cold. Emily didn't want to live because she'd lost Michael, that was a normal reaction for a mother. But Rose had never wanted to live with Adele and had even wished it was she who had died instead of Pamela.

She could understand Emily's grief so well because of Pamela. And the madness which made her throw herself in the river. Yet Rose had never been a real mother to Adele. Never valued or loved her.

And how was Adele going to react to this news about Michael? Rose knew that she'd be just as devastated as his mother, but who could she pour that out to when everyone believed she'd jilted him? Only two people knew the truth about that, and Adele wasn't going to turn to either of them.

Rose had thought when Adele attacked her when they were collecting wood that it was one of the lowest moments in her life, but this was even worse. Living back here, getting to know her mother again and finding herself happy at last, had made her see how selfish, greedy and shallow she'd been. She had believed she was on the road to becoming a better person. At times she even liked herself.

But as Emily had tearfully poured out so much about her marriage and her family tonight, Rose had felt ashamed that she had probably been part of the reason why Emily's marriage had broken down. All these years Rose had told herself that she had been the innocent victim of a philanderer, who callously abandoned her when she was carrying his child, but tonight she could no longer cling on to that pretence.

It was true that she was a virgin when she met Myles while he was staying at The George, but she could hardly be described as innocent, for she set out to ensnare him cold-bloodedly. She wanted a life of comfort and gaiety in London, and sensing he was rich, lonely and vulnerable, she used her looks, youth and charm to get it. All he had done was kiss her a few times when she begged him to take her to London with him, wickedly claiming her father was ill-treating her.

Myles told her he was married with three children before they got on the train. He even made it quite clear that he could only help her find a job and somewhere to live. He was as good as his word, he found her lodgings and supported her, and if she hadn't used her feminine wiles on him, he would never have slept with her.

If only she'd used her wits to get a job instead of scheming and lying to try to force his hand to leave his wife and marry her! He told her dozens of times that he couldn't put his family through the disgrace of a divorce.

He was to blame for getting her pregnant, a sophisticated man of the world should have known how to prevent that. It was also heartless to leave her to fend for herself. But she had brought this on herself – if she hadn't lied to him constantly, he would have believed she was carrying his child and taken the responsibility. He was a snob, and often gutless, but he was soft-hearted and honourable. He certainly wasn't the brute she had portrayed him as.

Honour had a real down on Myles, but that was understandable in light of the way he treated Adele when she was working for his wife. Rose had seen the disbelief on her face when Emily insisted that he hadn't always been like that. But Emily was right, he'd once been a gentle, loving man, and Rose felt more than partially responsible for the change in him.

Now he'd lost his younger son, and Rose was reminded of how jealous she used to get when Myles smiled tenderly at the mere mention of Michael, who was just a toddler then. She had always claimed she loved Myles, but perhaps the truth was that she'd never loved anyone but herself.

Chapter Twenty-five

'You won't tell anyone what I tried to do?' Emily begged Rose as they walked together back to Winchelsea.

'No, of course not,' Rose replied. 'Not if you promise me you'll never do such a thing again.'

It was three days since Emily had tried to drown herself. The morning after, Honour had got Jim to go and see her housekeeper and tell her that Emily had been taken ill while visiting and she'd be home as soon as she felt stronger. She had slept much of the first day, then became very tearful again, but she appeared to be much calmer now, and Rose was taking her home.

'I promise,' Emily said in a small voice. She looked very pale and drawn, and her coat, which Honour had dried out, had shrunk. In a borrowed pair of Rose's shoes, which were too big for her, her appearance was more like that of a refugee than of a woman from the upper classes. 'You were very brave, Rose, you make me feel so ashamed.'

Rose gulped. Emily had said this several times in the last couple of days, and though it was nice to be thought courageous, Rose was still battling with her guilt.

As the two women walked up the hill to Winchelsea, Emily slipped her arm through Rose's. 'You've done me a power of good, Rose,' she said. 'I don't just mean by saving my life, but by getting me to talk. I feel different today. Sort of stronger.'

Rose couldn't help but smile at Emily. There was something so girlish and sweet about her even if she was fifty-four, fourteen years older than Rose. Over the last couple of days they talked a great deal, and Rose had found a great deal to like about her.

'You might hear good news about Michael yet,' she said. 'So just try to stay calm and hopeful. You don't want to end up in a place like the one they sent me to.'

Emily nodded. 'No, I don't. Maybe I ought to try again with Ralph and Diana. They've always been against me, but I suppose that's my fault, what with my drinking, funny turns and things. You don't know how lucky you are having a daughter like Adele. She must be a great comfort to you.'

Rose smiled, but with sadness. Last night she had told Emily what a bad mother she'd been, but clearly Emily hadn't listened. She was still the way Rose used to be, so wrapped up in herself that other people's lives and problems had no impact on her.

Adele was feeling exhausted as she came off night duty, but when she saw a letter for her in her pigeonhole at the nurses' home addressed in her grandmother's familiar copperplate handwriting, she perked up.

It had been another night of very heavy bombing, with an even greater flood of casualties than usual. She couldn't understand why so many people, particularly the older ones, ignored the public shelters and stayed in their homes. Surely they ought to know the dangers by now?

She went into the dining room and helped herself to some porridge. One of the real bug-bears about night duty was getting meals the wrong way round. She couldn't eat a dinner of meat and vegetables when she'd just got up, then after a long night on the wards she was starving and had to make do with just porridge or congealed scrambled egg and toast.

She sat down at the same table as Joan and a new nurse from Birmingham called Annie. She opened the letter as she ate, and after reading only two lines she dropped her spoon with a clatter.

444

'What's up?' Joan asked in concern.

'It's Michael. He's missing,' Adele gasped out in horror. 'His plane was shot down.'

She had to rush off to her room then because she couldn't hold back her tears.

It was some time later that Joan peeped cautiously around the door.

'Can I come in?' she asked. 'Or do you want to be alone?'

'No, I'd like you with me,' Adele said, sniffing back her tears and wiping her eyes. 'It was such a shock, Joan. I loved Michael so much, I can't bear the thought of him being gone for good.'

Joan was her usual comforting self, hugging Adele tightly and pointing out that he might very well be a prisoner of war.

'I doubt that,' Adele sniffed.

'You've got to 'ave 'ope,' Joan said. 'Remember your grandfather in the last war. 'E were wounded and left for dead, weren't 'e? But 'e made it 'ome.'

Adele had been having bad dreams of Michael being shot down in his plane since the start of the war, so now it had happened, she felt his death was an absolute certainty. But she nodded anyway, as if in agreement with her friend.

The two girls got into bed a little later and Joan fell asleep immediately. Adele lay awake, holding on to the ring around her neck as she remembered all the things she loved about Michael and realized that time hadn't diminished her feelings for him at all. The pain she felt now was just as sharp as it had been when she left Hastings. Yet then at least she'd been able to imagine Michael walking, talking and laughing. She could even hope that one day they'd meet up again and she could have him back again as her friend and brother. Now everything was wiped out.

She would never be able to feel proud when he was decorated for valour. Or feel some joy for him when she heard he'd married. There wouldn't even be a grave she could visit to put some flowers on.

She wondered too how her grandmother was, for her grief was apparent in her letter, and no doubt she was remembering how Frank went off to war and returned a very different man. Perhaps she could ask Matron if she could have some leave to go home and check things out for herself?

It was the end of March before Adele got leave, and then only because she was ill. She had carried on working through a series of colds, an outbreak of boils on her neck and a stomach upset. But it was only when Joan went to Matron and pointed out that Adele was losing weight, not sleeping or eating properly, that she was ordered to see a doctor.

Adele guessed that her condition had been brought on by hearing about Michael. She was afraid to close her eyes at night because of the nightmare in which she watched him burning to death. She thought about him constantly, and it had robbed her of any appetite. But she couldn't tell the doctor that, and protested that she was only in the same state as everyone else as a result of overwork. But the doctor thought differently and said she must have at least two weeks' rest.

Although relieved to be able to go home, Adele found the journey exhausting. By the time she reached the cottage door late in the afternoon, after the long walk from the station, she was close to collapse.

'Adele!' her grandmother exclaimed in surprise as she staggered into the living room, for she hadn't sent a telegram saying she was coming. 'What's the matter? You look ill.'

'I'll be all right now I'm here,' Adele said, allowing herself to be enveloped in her grandmother's arms. 'I've got leave to have a rest.'

She was vaguely aware of Rose coming forward to peel off her hat, coat and shoes, and making her lie down on the couch. She wanted to brush her off, but she had no energy left to do or say anything. She must have fallen asleep immediately, and awoke later when it was nearly dark outside, to see Rose stirring something on the stove.

'What are you doing?' she asked, bewildered because the stove was a place she associated only with her grandmother. 'Where's Granny?'

'I'm here, dear,' Honour said from Adele's left, where she was sitting in the armchair. 'Rose is chief cook these days, she doesn't let me near the stove.'

For the next three days Adele slept most of the time. She was vaguely aware of going out to the lavatory now and then, of meals being brought to her, and Honour sitting beside her on the bed asking her questions. But Adele had nothing to say, for in five months of the Blitz she'd seen little outside the hospital except destruction, and within it there was nothing but pain and suffering.

She would have liked to be able to tell her grandmother how she felt about Michael. But that was impossible. Granny would completely share her sorrow at losing a dear friend, for she had loved Michael too. But she wouldn't understand why Adele should feel as if she'd had her heart pulled out, not when she'd given him up because he was wrong for her.

Ever since she got her grandmother's letter she had been in a kind of bubble, aware of what was going on around her, but unable to feel anything but her own pain. Michael was both her love and her brother. People would give boundless sympathy if they knew he was either of those. But an ex-fiancé, or a friend, didn't rate more than a brief 'I'm sorry', and a hasty shift on to another subject. So she'd had to hold it all inside her, putting on a brave face and listening to other people's problems, and all the time getting pulled lower and lower.

Before she arrived home, her intention was to see that

Honour had fully recovered, and check that Rose was looking after everything. All that was forgotten when she fell ill – she hadn't noticed anything, not the state of the cottage and garden, or if Honour looked well. She certainly hadn't been up to checking whether Rose was taking advantage of the situation. The only thing which had any impact on her was the absence of noise from bombs and being allowed to sleep.

It was the smell of frying bacon that finally brought her out of her torpid state, and it was only later that she discovered it was her fourth day at the cottage. She was still in bed, partially awake when the smell reached her, and for the first time since she got the news about Michael, she felt hungry.

She got up, went to the door of her room and saw Rose standing at the stove happily humming 'White Cliffs of Dover' as she flipped the bacon in the frying pan.

For a second Adele wanted to retreat. She had thought a great deal about Rose in the past few months, and mostly with pure hatred. Each time she spoke to her on the telephone she had a struggle to be civil, despite the fact that Granny had reported in her letters that she looked after her well.

Adele had no desire to try to forgive Rose – the idea of finding something to even like about her was laughable. The image she'd kept in her mind was of a brassy, over-madeup woman wearing tight clothes, teetering on high heels, with a cigarette dangling from scarlet-tipped fingers.

Yet she didn't look that way now in a shabby pair of khaki slacks and a blue jumper with darned holes in the sleeves. Her blonde hair was tied back in one thick plait, and her face was free of makeup.

As a child, Adele had gauged her mother's mood by whether she'd put her makeup on or not. Without it she had to be approached with extreme caution. And even though there was nothing threatening about her mother's stance, for she looked relaxed and happy, the old memories were enough to make her freeze with nervousness.

All at once Rose must have sensed Adele standing there, and she turned and smiled. 'I was just cooking you this for a treat,' she said.

Bacon *was* a treat. Adele couldn't remember when she last had some, and the delicious smell was making her mouth water.

'We never get bacon in London,' she blurted out, caught off guard by the extraordinary idea of her mother giving her a treat.

'We don't often get it here either,' Rose said evenly. 'I queued for over an hour for this yesterday. But it will be worth it if it bucks you up. It's been awful to see you so poorly.'

It crossed Adele's mind that this could be some kind of wild flight of fancy brought on by illness, for as a child she had often fantasized about waking up one day to find her mother had suddenly changed into a loving, smiling, happy person.

Everything looked too good to be true. The sun was shining in through the windows, there was a vase of daffodils on the sideboard, and even more astounding was that her mother's face was pink and white, glowing with rude health, and her eyes had lost the coldness she remembered.

'We had our breakfast ages ago,' Rose continued, seemingly unconcerned by Adele standing there as if she were in a trance. 'Mother's out feeding the rabbits, but it will give her a real boost if she comes in and sees you tucking into this. You know what she's like!'

'You look different,' Adele said weakly.

'I expect I do,' Rose said, and chuckled. 'More like a land girl now than the bar fly I used to be. But you look a lot different too, too thin, pale and anxious. Sit down at the table, this is nearly ready. How do you feel today?'

'I'm not sure yet,' Adele said, for her legs suddenly felt weak and she reached out for the back of a chair to steady herself.

Rose sped to her side, tucking her hand under Adele's arm to help her. 'You're still weak,' she said, and her voice was soft with sympathy. 'Oh, Adele,' she sighed. 'Your gran may think this was brought on by too much work. But I know the truth. It must have been hell keeping all that grief inside you.'

Adele turned to look at her mother, a sarcastic retort on her lips, but was stopped short by her expression. It was one of complete understanding. Adele was well used to reading expressions in her nursing and she knew Rose wasn't faking it. Her words had definitely come from her heart.

'Yes, it was,' she replied. 'It still is.'

She fully expected Rose to start gushing, but she didn't. 'If you want to talk later when we can be alone, just say,' she said simply, then turned away to the stove.

The bacon and eggs, toast and tea were put on the table with no more said. Adele began to eat, and at the almost forgotten taste of bacon she grinned. 'Umm,' she said appreciatively. 'This is marvellous.'

Honour came in then with Towzer, and when she saw Adele at the table, her face broke into a smile of pure delight. 'Well, look at you!' she exclaimed. 'Rose said you might be tempted out by the smell of bacon, but I didn't believe her. I've just been telling Misty it would be a few more days before you went out to see her.'

Towzer went straight up to the table and looked at Adele with begging eyes. She was just going to cut him off a bit of bacon when Rose wiggled a disapproving finger at her.

'Don't you dare waste it on him, the dog is a glutton. You eat every scrap. You need building up.'

There was something so completely maternal about that reproach that Adele's eyes filled with tears and she had to look away.

Rose and Honour went out into the garden together, perhaps feeling they might put Adele off eating by hanging around her. But after nurses' home breakfasts of powdered egg and cold burnt toast, nothing would put Adele off this feast.

The time alone was valuable. She could look around at all the old familiar things, enjoy the silence, and make observations.

Honour looked like her old robust self, and the way she and Rose had gone out together so companionably suggested they were getting on. The cottage also looked cleaner and tidier than Adele had ever known it before.

She knew she wasn't able to be objective about Rose yet. That telling little aside she made about being more like a land girl now than a bar fly, had all the hallmarks of someone who had looked at herself critically and appreciated she must change. Her understanding of how Adele felt showed she had given thought to the wider effects of Michael's disappearance.

It was going to take time to find whether Rose's new image was the real thing, or if it was just a little window-dressing. Yet right now, rested, away from the constant drama of the hospital, with the sun shining, Adele was prepared to be optimistic.

By the end of her first week home Adele felt a hundred times better. She was eating well and sleeping like a log, the colour had come back to her cheeks and the dark lines beneath her eyes had faded. Yet Rose wouldn't hear of her doing any chores.

'You need complete rest before you go back to White-chapel,' she insisted, backed up by Honour. 'So read a book, go for a walk, you are not to attempt anything else.'

Adele had done as she was told, for after the pressure and trauma at the hospital it was bliss to do absolutely nothing. She would wander on the marsh for hours, sometimes finding a spot where there was shelter from the cold wind, and just sit and listen to the wild birds and the sea pounding on the shingle, trying to sort out her feelings about her mother, and Michael.

Now she was here, in the place where she had met him, she couldn't believe he was dead. If he was, surely his spirit would return here and she would sense it, the way the smell of gorse flowers wafted on the wind, or she could taste the salt from the sea on her lips. She could picture him so clearly, the way he was that first day they met. It was the same time of year, with the same cold wind and hundreds of new lambs frolicking in the fields. She imagined him balancing on the fallen tree over one of the streams, arms outstretched, laughing a little nervously as his feet slipped on the mossy surface. She knew he was going to be important in her life even then.

With hindsight, of course, it might just have been the blood tie which drew them together, and if so, she thought that his spirit was even more likely to come here and release her from the torture of false hope.

But if it was bittersweet coming back here to find hope for Michael again, Adele was discovering even more conflicting emotions about Rose. All her previously held convictions about the lazy, cruel, moody woman without a heart had been challenged by what she observed in the cottage.

Rose was rarely idle. She kneaded the dough for the bread with energy, raked a seed bed for planting with enthusiasm, and prepared meals with great care. She had learned to chop wood, pluck chickens and even skin rabbits, and was always browsing through books on gardening in an effort to learn more about growing vegetables. She smiled readily, with great warmth, she had a sense of fun, and a youthfulness that was very attractive.

There had been times when Adele had found herself laughing at something funny her mother said, forgetting for a moment or two that she must keep up her guard. There were times too when she was tempted to ask Rose searching questions, not with malice, but to try to bridge the gap between this present-day woman she was in danger of liking, and the woman from the past whom she hated.

The previous afternoon Rose had cycled into Rye, and although Adele had welcomed the opportunity to be alone with Honour, she found herself silent and thoughtful.

It was as if Honour was reading her thoughts, because she suddenly spoke about Rose.

'I think you must accept, Adele, that your mother wasn't well for much of your childhood. I know I didn't see her then, but she's told me a great deal about it, and the way she treated you. I believe she had a mental disorder, and that is far worse for a body than a physical disease. But then as a nurse you'd know that.'

'Am I supposed to forgive everything then?' Adele replied sharply.

'If Towzer bit me while I was trying to examine an injury he'd got, would you want me to abandon him?' Honour retorted, equally sharply.

Adele looked down at the dog lying with his chin on her grandmother's feet, gazing adoringly up at her. 'That would be different,' she said. 'A dog can't explain that he's in pain.'

'Maybe Rose couldn't either,' Honour said with a shrug. 'The one thing all three of us have in common is an inability to express our true feelings. We all rely on our deeds to show affection and care.'

'You know as well as I do she never showed me anything but resentment,' Adele said heatedly. In that second she had an overwhelming desire to tell her grandmother everything, including how Rose demanded money from Myles, knowing that Honour could never condone that. But she bit it back. She had told Rose that day on the marsh that her new role was to make Honour feel happy and secure, and she had, so Adele couldn't possibly damage that.

'By taking care of me when I needed it, she was trying to

show us both that she regrets the past,' Honour said with a sigh. 'Surely you have seen the care she's taken of you too since you came home?'

'Yes, but I can't help thinking she has an ulterior motive.'

'Have you thought that motive might just be she wants to be loved by us both?'

'Pigs might fly, I can never love her,' Adele snapped.

Thinking over yesterday's bitter remarks, Adele felt a twinge of remorse. Was she perhaps a bit afraid that Rose was taking her place in Granny's affections? Or was it just that she needed Rose as a kind of whipping boy, someone to blame for anything in her life she didn't like?

Adele didn't want to return to London as the end of her two weeks' leave drew nearer. She had heard there had been no raids for two nights, and some were saying that the Blitz was now over. But even if that was foolish optimism, she knew her reluctance to return wasn't the thought of the hordes of injured, or the tumult and filth that accompanied raids. It was more that she felt she had left something undone here, though she couldn't think what it was.

Two days before she was to return to London, she walked up to Winchelsea to buy some candles and matches. The cold wind had dropped, the sun was shining, and as she got up to the Landgate and looked down across the marsh towards Rye in the distance, it looked so lovely she felt a lump come up in her throat.

Michael had taken a photograph of the same view before he went up to Oxford. He said he would pin it on the wall as a reminder of happy days. It was thinking of that which made her suddenly decide to go and call on Mrs Bailey.

Her grandmother had said Emily had called on them at the cottage a couple of times since she got the news about Michael. Adele had found that surprising, but as Granny said, she was just desperate to talk about her son to someone who had known him well and shared her sorrow.

Adele wasn't quite sure Emily would view her in the same light, but she felt she had to call anyway.

The housekeeper answered the door, asked Adele into the hall, then went upstairs to tell Mrs Bailey. As Adele waited, memories of her time working here came flooding back, how she'd scrubbed out the dusty hall, hung up all her mistress's clothes, and struggled to cook meals which were much fancier than anything she'd cooked at home.

Yet these thoughts weren't bitter ones, for it occurred to her that if it were not for the experience gained in this house, good and bad, she probably wouldn't have coped with the discipline of nursing training.

Mrs Bailey came down the stairs slowly as if her legs were stiff. She had aged since the day Adele was invited here for tea to talk about the engagement. Her skin had a yellowish tinge, and her hair was more grey than gold. She was wearing a tweed skirt and pink twin set, but it didn't give her that elegant look she once had. The defeated stoop to her shoulders and the deep lines around her mouth gave away her heartbreak.

'I hope you won't see this as an intrusion,' Adele blurted out. 'But I felt I had to call and say how terribly sorry I am about Michael.'

'That is so kind of you, Adele,' Mrs Bailey said graciously. 'Do come into the drawing room, the fire's alight in there.'

'Have you had any further news?' Adele asked once they'd sat down.

'No, nothing. I have of course contacted the Red Cross and they tell me they are still checking POW camps, but I cannot be hopeful.'

Adele wanted to tell her of her feelings while out on the marsh, but as Mrs Bailey believed she dropped Michael through a change of heart, that didn't seem appropriate.

'You must try to keep your hope,' Adele said. 'If you'd seen the sights I've seen in London you would soon believe in miracles. People believe their relatives have been killed all the time, and then they turn up unhurt.'

'Honour tells me you have become a very good nurse,' Mrs Bailey said. 'She is very proud of you.'

Adele was just about to say that the continuing bombing in London made her and most of her fellow nurses feel ineffectual, when suddenly the door opened and to her consternation in came Myles Bailey.

Every memory she had of this man was an unpleasant one, and the last, of the day he told her he was her father, was by far and away the worst of all. She couldn't say she hated him for that, she had always been aware that he'd had no choice but to tell her the devastating news. She even remembered that he'd been quite gentle about it. Yet whenever he came into her mind she pictured him here, the bully of a man who had slapped her face and told her to get out of the house on Christmas Eve. And it was for that that she despised him.

He looked much the same, as ruddy-faced and plump as the last time she saw him. He was dressed in a formal dark suit with a stiff-collared shirt, and his face drained of colour when he saw Adele.

'I'm sorry,' he said, backing away. 'I didn't realize you had a visitor, Emily. I had to come and see someone near here and I just dropped in to see how you are.'

'Do come on in, Myles,' Emily said, and she smiled as if pleased to see him. 'You remember Adele, of course, she just called to offer her condolences about Michael. I'll ring for some tea.'

'I should be going now,' Adele said hurriedly, getting to her feet.

'Please don't rush off, Adele,' Emily said, putting a restraining hand on her arm. 'Honour and Rose often tell me things you've written in letters about the hospital in London and the Blitz, and I'd love to hear more.'

Just the mention of Rose's name in front of Myles made Adele squirm. 'I feel I am intruding now Mr Bailey is here,' she said nervously, hardly daring to look at him.

'Nonsense, Adele,' Myles spoke out. Clearly he'd gained his composure. 'I'd like to hear about your nursing too. And Emily has so much to say to you, she has been so grateful to your mother and grandmother for rescuing her, as I am too.'

Adele looked at him in bewilderment. 'Rescuing her?' she said.

'You don't know about that?' he asked, and looked concerned. 'Now, there's discretion for you! I fully expected they would have told you. Emily fell in the river and your mother jumped in and hauled her out. A very brave deed on a cold January night.'

Adele couldn't have been more surprised if Myles had said Rose rode on an elephant through Rye, for she'd been told nothing. 'Really!' she exclaimed. 'I knew Mrs Bailey had visited them, but Granny didn't say anything about a fall in the river.'

Emily got up, her face pink with embarrassment. 'I'll just go into the kitchen and see about the tea myself,' she said.

Adele felt that someone could perhaps fall in the river during the summer while walking along the bank, but they wouldn't be likely to go anywhere near it during the winter months.

The moment Emily rushed out, she looked sharply at Myles. 'Did she fall or jump?'

'She claims she slipped on the mud, but we can both draw our own conclusions, as it was just a few days after we had the telegram about Michael,' he said in a curiously gruff voice. 'Your mother could easily have drowned too while rescuing her, the river was swollen and very fast-flowing. I would have called to thank her myself, but because of our past connection, that didn't seem appropriate.'

Adele was surprised that he was being so open, especially here in his wife's home. 'No, it certainly wouldn't have been. But I rather wish you hadn't said anything about the river. Mrs Bailey must have been beside herself with grief at the time, and now she'll be so embarrassed that I know about it.'

'It never occurred to me that your family wouldn't tell you,' he said thoughtfully.

'My grandmother has never been a gossip, and she's a very big-hearted woman,' Adele said proudly. 'She was very fond of Michael, and so of course she felt for his mother and wouldn't want such a thing to get about. As for my mother, well, maybe she has some saving graces after all.'

Emily came back then with a tray of tea and the three of them made small talk about the war, Honour's injuries in the air raid, and nursing air-raid victims.

It seemed to Adele that Emily was coping. She had seen her in far worse states when she worked for her. Losing Michael had clearly opened her eyes to the plight of others, and she showed real concern for all those who had been made homeless by the bombing and for the widows and orphans.

Myles was much less caustic and opinionated than Adele remembered, softened perhaps by grief. His eyes glistened with unshed tears when he spoke of both his older son and son-in-law who were about to be posted overseas, and clearly he was afraid he might lose them too. He didn't belittle Emily in any way, and when he mentioned his grandchildren it was with great affection.

Adele stayed just long enough to be polite, then using the candles she had to buy as an excuse, she said she must go.

'Bless you for coming,' Emily said, kissing her cheek. 'Do

ask Honour and Rose to call on me sometime. Tell them I'm doing some voluntary work now, and I'm fine, thanks to them.'

Myles shook Adele's hand and wished her well, then escorted her to the door to see her out.

As she stepped out on to the pavement, Myles suddenly stopped her. 'I'm so very sorry,' he said.

Adele looked him right in the eyes. 'What for?'

'For causing you so much unhappiness,' he said.

'So you want me to see you in a better light, do you?' she said mockingly. 'I think the biggest shock to me was discovering my father was a bully, a snob and a man that strikes servants.'

'*Touché*,' he said, and winced. 'You may not think much of me, Adele, and who can blame you for that? But I've seen a great deal in you to like and respect. Since Michael went missing I have had to evaluate everything about my character and life. I found much of it lacking in substance.'

'That doesn't mean anything to me,' she said, irritated that he could bring everything back to how he felt. 'I've had to live with heartache since the day you told me who you were, and it grew even worse when I heard Michael was missing. I hope and pray he is in a POW camp somewhere and comes home safe at the end of the war. You'll be fine then, so will your wife. But I'll still be in the same situation, unable to greet him with joy as a sister, or as his sweetheart.'

'I'm so sorry,' he said, and took her two hands in his. 'Truly sorry. If you should ever need any help, in any way, come to me, Adele. I can't change the past, but maybe I could do something for you in the future.'

Adele wanted to say something cutting, but no clever words would form in her mind. All she could see was those eyes so incredibly like hers, hear the sincerity in his voice, and feel the warmth of his hands on hers.

He took a card from his pocket and put it in her hand, closing her fingers round it.

'Call on me. Whatever you think of me, whatever hurt being your father has caused, a big part of me feels proud to know my child grew up to be such a good, strong woman.'

Adele backed away. She knew that as a lawyer he was experienced in making moving speeches, which almost certainly were mostly lies. Yet what he'd said had moved her. She felt as if he'd suddenly filled an empty place inside her. She knew she must flee before she cried.

Chapter Twenty-six

1942

'I'm bored stiff,' Joan yawned as she poured a cup of tea for herself and Adele. 'I've a good mind to crawl into one of them empty beds and 'ave a kip.'

It was just on midnight, the few patients they had on their ward were fast asleep, and they had slipped into Sister's room for tea and a chat.

'To think we once complained about being too busy,' Adele laughed.

During the previous April while she was down in Rye, the nightly bombing in London had stopped. By the time she arrived back in London people had more or less slipped back to normal living patterns, optimistically believing the Blitz was over for good. But on 10 May there was a terrible raid, the worst so far, and by morning it was rumoured 3,000 people were dead. The Law Courts, the Tower of London and the Mint were all hit. Every bridge between the Tower and Lambeth was impassable, and hundreds of gas mains were severed. Westminster Abbey was badly damaged, even Big Ben had its face pock-marked, and there wasn't enough water available to put out the fires, particularly over in the Elephant and Castle area.

That night and for two further days and nights, Adele and all the other medical staff worked flat out dealing with casualties. While no one expressed their fears openly at the time, Adele could see the same question on every face, 'How can we stand any more of this?'

But after the injured were patched up and sent home, the dead buried and the roads cleared, there were no further raids like that one. While there was spasmodic bombing in

London and in other cities too, it seemed the Blitz really had come to an end, and the hospital returned to relative calm.

The previous December the Japanese had bombed Pearl Harbor, and as a result the Americans had now declared war on Germany and Italy, and joined forces with England.

The two girls saw the New Year of 1942 in at a dance at The Empire in Leicester Square, and two days later the news broke that Japan had taken the Philippines and was invading the East Indies. Towards the end of January American troops began to arrive in England, creating great excitement amongst the nurses. Even Adele, who had remained fairly impervious to men until now, couldn't help but find these fun-loving, well-mannered and generous men attractive.

Since February she'd been out dancing at least once a week, and had been taken to the pictures or for a drink by five different men. She really liked fair-haired, blue-eyed Lieutenant Robert Onslow from Ohio, whom she had met at Rainbow Corner, a club for other ranks in the old Del Monico's restaurant at the corner of Shaftesbury Avenue and Piccadilly. He took her to see Noël Coward's *Blithe Spirit* at the theatre, and they saw *Rebecca* and *Goodbye Mr Chips* at the cinema. But he had been posted to a base in Suffolk in May, and his letters had gradually fizzled out.

Adele wasn't unduly saddened by the budding romance dying – as Joan so rightly pointed out, there were plenty more fish in the sea. She had been happy enough just to find she was capable of fancying a man again. It was good to become like all her friends, living for the next night out, enjoying herself and not taking anything too seriously.

She realized now that the day she came face to face with Myles again in Winchelsea had been a turning-point in her life. Her present serenity had almost certainly come about by finally managing to deal with the bitterness she felt for her mother.

After talking to Myles that day she had returned home to

ask Honour and Rose to tell her about Emily's near-drowning. Rose had little to say on the subject, shrugged off her involvement, and went out for a walk, but Honour was far more voluble. She not only described in graphic terms the events of that night, but said that Emily did indeed owe her life to Rose's courage, stamina and complete disregard for her own safety. She mentioned too that certain things which Emily had said while she was distraught had made Honour confront her own failings as a mother.

With her eyes full of tears, she told Adele how she had treated Rose when Frank came home from the war. She explained that she felt angry that he'd returned a broken shell of the man she loved, and that sometimes she even wished he'd died in France. She took her guilt at thinking such things out on Rose.

It wasn't the first time her grandmother had tried to make Adele see it was time she forgave her mother. But this time, perhaps because Adele was moved by Rose's courage in saving Emily, she felt as if a door had opened on to the past. All at once, all the past information she'd gathered and observations she'd made recently gelled together, and she could see the whole picture. And Rose in a very much more sympathetic light.

That evening Adele had felt very much more comfortable around Rose. At one point as they were sitting on either end of the couch, listening to the wireless, Adele put her feet up on the couch, and Rose took them and placed them across her lap. Just a little thing, but it felt affectionate and companionable.

The following morning Adele accidentally let one of the rabbits escape from its hutch while she was giving it clean straw, and Rose came to help her catch it. The rabbit was intent on evading them, and as they both blundered around trying to capture it, they laughed their heads off.

Rose offered to go with her to see her off at the station when she had to go back to London, and as they walked into Rye, Adele told her what Myles had said to her up in Winchelsea.

Rose didn't comment for a little while and Adele got the idea she was brewing up to say something nasty about him. But she wasn't, she was just thinking it over. 'I wish I'd had just an ounce of your common sense and humanity when I was your age,' she said with a sigh. 'I think you take after him far more than me, Adele.'

Adele changed the subject then and asked Rose whether she would like to go back to her house in London now Honour was fit again. 'You can, you know,' Adele said. 'Neither Granny nor I would feel you'd let us down, we both know it isn't much of a life for you here.'

Rose smiled then. 'It's a better life than in London,' she said. 'A far better one. And I like being with Mother.'

Adele had returned to London with a great deal to think about. Nothing was in black and white any longer. No one was wholly bad, and no one was perfect either, least of all herself. She knew then that she had to learn to live with what had been doled out to her.

By thinking of Rose as just Rose, rather than as a failure of a mother, she found she was able to see her differently. She became intriguing rather than suspect, amusing rather than hurtful. When they spoke on the telephone they found a great deal to laugh about. There was warmth where once there had been stiffness and lack of trust.

Each visit home had brought more understanding as they shared a bed and the chores, went to the pictures together, and sometimes to a pub for a few drinks. They argued, often their views were totally opposing, but a year on Adele could honestly say they had become friends. Rose was the only one who knew her real feelings for Michael, and she understood.

Adele could also confide in her about other men she met. Rose reciprocated by telling her about men in her past, including Myles. She had once joked that they couldn't have a normal mother-and-daughter relationship, because neither of them really knew what that meant. Adele thought that was very true. But in some ways what they had was better, for they could be more honest with each other.

'I wonder what would 'appen if Sister caught me kipping?' Joan giggled.

'She'd hang, draw and quarter you,' Adele said, quickly giving their cups a wash. 'And she'll be back any minute, so we'd better find something to do.'

As she spoke the telephone rang.

'Bloody 'ell!' Joan exclaimed as she went to answer it. 'So much for a peaceful night. That'll be some inconsiderate bugger wanting a bed.'

'Women's Surgical,' she said brightly as she picked up the phone. She frowned as she listened to the voice on the other end. 'Just one moment,' she said, and held out the receiver to Adele. 'It's for you,' she said. 'It's your mum.'

Adele's heart lurched as she snatched the phone from her friend. Rose would only call here at night in an emergency.

'What's happened, Mum?' she asked, her heart in her mouth. 'Is it Granny?'

'No love, nothing nasty,' Rose replied. 'It's good news. I know it's the middle of the night and I'm probably the wrong person to be passing it on to you. But I knew you'd want to know immediately. Michael's been found!'

Adele gasped, her legs went to jelly and she had to catch hold of the back of a chair to support herself as she listened to her mother. Rose was staying over at Winchelsea because Emily Bailey had twisted her ankle in a fall and her house-keeper was away visiting relatives. Rose was just helping Emily up the stairs to bed, when a call came from the Red

Cross. They said they'd just got notification that Michael was in a POW camp.

'Are they sure?' Adele asked cautiously, unable to believe it could be true.

'Yes, it's definite, they don't tell relatives until they've checked properly,' Rose said, her voice unnaturally shrill with excitement. 'It seems he was badly injured and taken to a hospital, then moved from pillar to post afterwards, that's why Emily hadn't heard anything.'

'Is he all in one piece?' Adele asked, her heart sinking at the thought of Michael disfigured by burns and with missing limbs.

'They could only say he was well, and that letters from him should soon arrive. But he's alive, Adele! To Emily that's enough. You should've seen her, laughing and crying all at once. Such joy! I couldn't let you know until I'd got her into bed.'

'Tell her how glad I am, and thank you too for ringing me immediately, but I'll have to go now, Sister's coming,' Adele said quickly as she heard heels tapping on the corridor outside. 'Try and phone me again tomorrow morning, about nine at the nurses' home.'

Throughout the remainder of the night Adele glowed with happiness, whispering to Joan how miraculous it was, and how happy her grandmother was going to be when she got the news.

Joan gave her a couple of odd looks, clearly wondering why Adele had given this man up if she cared so much. She also asked curiously why her mother should be with Michael's mother, when as she understood it, the romance had failed because of family disapproval.

In her joy Adele would have blurted out the entire story if they hadn't been working, for she knew Joan could be trusted to keep it to herself. But Sister kept coming in and out, and such a long and complicated story couldn't be easily told in whispers.

If she'd been able, Adele would have danced the polka around the ward, woken everyone up and rattled bedpans to celebrate. She wished she could catch a train home right now for by morning everyone in Winchelsea would be talking about the wonderful news. Michael was alive, and that was the most wonderful news she'd ever had.

In the last hour before it was time to wake the patients, while Joan laid up the early-morning tea trolley out in the corridor, Adele sat at the ward desk writing up the patients' notes. But she stopped suddenly, thinking of Myles.

Two months after she'd met him again in Winchelsea, Adele got out the card he had given her and telephoned him. She wasn't sure why, just a vague feeling they had some unfinished business. She fully expected that he'd have thought better of wanting to see her, and that he'd make some excuse. But she was wrong, he was very pleased to hear from her.

He took her to lunch at a French restaurant in Mayfair, a place he said had been very grand before the war. It wasn't that grand any more because it had been damaged by bombs a couple of times and they'd been unable to redecorate it. Most of the diners were servicemen with their wives or girlfriends, and an old accordion player was attempting to create a romantic atmosphere.

Almost straight away Adele realized Myles wasn't the ogre she'd come to think of him as. He was opinionated and in-clined to be brusque, but he was also attentive and disarmingly truthful.

Over the simple but well-cooked meal he gave her his version of his relationship with Rose.

Rose had told Adele a great deal about it already, even as far as admitting the lies she had told him to persuade him to take her to London. In almost every detail Myles's story was the same as Rose's, except he was gallant enough to blame himself for encouraging her interest in him in the first place.

'I should have known better,' he said, sorrowfully shaking his head. 'But I was lonely, Emily had been impossible since Michael was born, wild hysterics one minute, cold as ice the next, and Rose was so very lovely, and interested in me. That's a huge draw to a man.'

He spoke about the first few weeks in London with Rose with obvious nostalgia. She had never been to London before and found even the most ordinary things like tram rides thrilling, and he clearly enjoyed taking a pretty and excited girl to see the sights. Adele got the idea that it was the first time in his life he'd really had any fun, yet at the same time he was terrified of the scandal which would ensue if he was found out. Adele had mixed feelings about his excuse that he finally became nervous when he realized Rose had no intention of standing on her own feet, despite all her claims that she expected nothing of him when they first left Rye.

'I didn't expect her to go into service, even though that looked like the best solution at the time,' he said, his brow furrowed with a frown. 'I knew she hadn't the right mentality, she was too sparky and untamed. But she turned her nose up at every other kind of work, even a position in a select gown shop where they were offering a good salary and accommodation too.'

Rose had told Adele that she used to pretend that she'd been turned down for positions when she hadn't even applied for them. She said she had no intention of getting any job because she thought that if Myles continued to support her, before long he would divorce his wife and marry her. Maybe that was wrong of her, but Adele supposed that in those days most women expected their man to keep them.

In her opinion, Myles had been something of a cad. Maybe Rose did use every trick in the book on him, especially sex, but the fact remained that he was a married man in his thirties, playing around with a seventeen-year-old who was still a virgin when he met her.

'So did you know she was expecting me when you left her?' Adele asked bluntly.

'She claimed she was,' he admitted candidly. 'I chose not to believe her. When she didn't come after me later to ask for money, I took that as confirmation I was right.'

Adele bristled at that. 'You could have checked to see she was all right,' she said accusingly. 'Anything could have happened to her. You said you loved her! How could you be so callous?'

'My wife and children were my priority,' he said in that arrogant tone she remembered from the past.

'But they weren't a priority when you skipped off to London with Rose,' Adele reminded him tartly. 'I think you behaved very badly.'

'I did,' he said. 'But I was in an impossible situation.'

Adele could see there was no point in arguing with him. He was typical of his class, believing that anyone further down the social scale didn't really matter.

'So what did you think when Rose turned up twenty years later and told you about me?' she asked, wanting to move on to more recent events.

His face turned an even ruddier hue. 'I was absolutely floored. It was bad enough to hear she had in fact had a child, but to find you were the girl I'd met at Emily's, and Michael's intended, was absolutely horrific. I panicked – you see, I didn't imagine Rose intended to keep it to herself.'

'So you paid her off? Weren't you afraid if you paid her once, she'd keep coming back for more?'

His eyes flashed with anger then, reminding her of the night he'd slapped her. She thought it quite surprising he hadn't attacked Rose.

'Yes, I was. But I was more afraid of what she'd do if I didn't pay up. How did you find out about the money though? Surely she didn't admit that to you?'

All at once Adele felt an unexpected tug of loyalty for her mother. 'Yes, she did,' she said airily. 'When we got together again after my grandmother was hurt in an air raid, she told me everything. I don't approve of blackmail, but then I don't approve of men who abandon a woman carrying their child either. And she had to get you to stop the marriage, didn't she?'

Myles looked at Adele thoughtfully for some time before replying.

'Yes. And I have to be completely frank with you about this, even if there had been no blood tie, at that time I would have done almost anything to stop Michael marrying you.'

Adele riled up at that. 'The common girl from the marshes marrying a barrister's son,' she jeered. 'Oh Mr Bailey, how terrible that would have been!'

Myles grimaced. 'Right now I'd happily see Michael married to a street-walker rather than "missing, presumed dead",' he said sorrowfully. 'But back then I wanted my son to have a wife out of the top drawer.'

'What a bigot you were!' Adele could not resist goading him. 'After I'd run off up to London I used to try and comfort myself for losing Michael by telling myself I'd had a lucky escape not having you as a father-in-law.'

Adele didn't want to see Myles ever again after that lunch. He'd told his side of the story with honesty, and she even felt that the nastier side of him she'd seen in Harrington House was a result of years of Emily's impossible behaviour, but she thought he was what her grandmother called a 'stuffed shirt'. He didn't appear to feel any guilt at abandoning Rose. Nor had he lost any of his snobbishness.

But a few weeks passed and when he called her up and

invited her out again, she thought she needed to get to know him better. This time she found him more mellow, far more interested in her than trying to impress on her that he was an important man. By the time they'd met for the fourth time a whole new picture of him was forming. His stern, cold and humourless manner was only a facade. Adele felt he'd been conditioned to form it by his domineering parents, a disastrous marriage, and his career. When he dropped it, she saw the real Myles Bailey, a kind and gentle man who loved his children and grandchildren, a man who hadn't had much fun or laughter in his life, and precious little love.

It was during the fourth lunch that Adele found herself really liking him. He told her about some of the more amusing court cases he'd been involved with, and his dry humour and ability to re-create for her some of the more absurd characters he'd either defended or prosecuted had her almost crying with laughter.

'No wonder Michael was so taken with you,' he said with a smile. 'You are such good company.'

Adele just laughed, she couldn't think of any witty retort.

'I look back at that day at the nurses' home in Hastings as one of the lowest things I have ever done,' he said, reaching out across the table and taking her hand. 'I came expecting abuse, threats and goodness knows what else, I was prepared for an ugly scene. Yet you took my news with such quiet dignity, it took the wind right out of my sails.'

'Don't let's talk about that,' she said, embarrassed by the intensity in his voice.

'But we have to talk about it, Adele,' he insisted. 'We can't sweep it under the table. I have to admit I was relieved you made it so easy for me. But afterwards I felt such an absolute heel.'

'Serves you right,' she said, attempting humour to side-track him.

'I got my comeuppance in a way I would never have

expected,' he said. 'You see, even though I had to tell you I was your father, I didn't have any paternal thoughts, not then. Those only came afterwards, when I thought how brave, selfless and gutsy you were, especially when I learned you'd cut yourself off from your grandmother too, and had never told her the real reason. That's when it hit me. You were the sort of girl any father could be proud of. But how could I be proud? I'd had no influence on your character or upbringing, and I'd been so cruel to you! Do you understand what I mean?'

'I think so,' she said.

'I wish I knew what to do,' he said sorrowfully. 'I was weighing it up this morning before we met, but I still don't know what is right.'

Adele frowned, not knowing what he meant. 'Do? You don't have to do anything!'

Myles shook his head. 'I think I do. I haven't had anything to do with your last twenty-three years, but I'd like to have a part in your future.'

'We can meet up from time to time,' she said with a smile.

'But I suspect that each time I see you I'll want more than a casual lunch or dinner,' he said.

Adele took her hands away from his and laughed to cover her sudden nervousness. 'If we had anything more, people would talk,' she said.

'That's my quandary,' he admitted. 'I want more and I think I ought to publicly admit you are my daughter.'

'You mustn't do that!' she said in alarm. 'Imagine what a can of worms that would open up! Aside from your children and Emily's feelings, there's my grandmother's too. She would work out immediately how Rose got her house, and that would just about finish her off.'

'But it's you who should count,' he insisted. 'Not them. I failed to do the right thing years ago. I think I should do it now.'

'No. Let it be,' she said firmly. 'I'm really touched you feel you want to do that. But just hearing you say so in private is enough. There's been too much hurt in our families already.'

'You are right in that respect,' he sighed. 'But if Michael is found to be alive, I will surely have to reveal it to him. After what he must have been through, don't you think we owe him the truth about why you dropped him?'

Adele had not thought about what Myles had said that day until now. Maybe that was mostly because it seemed all hope of Michael being found alive was gone, but also because her life had become so full. She was no longer a recluse in her off-duty time, she had dozens of friends apart from Joan and often went home with them to meet their families.

She often visited old patients at home too to see how they were getting on, and she was studying as well because she intended to get a midwifery diploma. Dances, going to the pictures or the theatre, and visits back to Rye when she got a couple of days off, all left very little free time to brood about words or deeds in the past.

She still wore Michael's ring about her neck, he'd never left her heart. But because she thought he was gone for good, she'd tucked memories of him away and had got on with her life.

But sitting here in the quiet ward, watching the first rays of daylight trying to filter through the blackout, all those feelings she had for Michael were struggling through too. She could see his face before her, those dark blue eyes, the long lashes and his lips curling up at the corners as if permanently smiling.

She could also hear Myles insisting that if Michael was alive, he must tell him that she was his sister.

Adele remembered only too clearly the sheer horror she'd felt when Myles had told her that shocking news. She had had three years to get used to it, yet even now it still made her feel tainted. She had no doubt Michael would feel exactly the same.

Things had been further complicated by Emily, Rose and Honour becoming such good friends. In the past year they'd spent a lot of time together. What would be more natural than for the two families to want to join forces to celebrate when Michael came home?

Yet Emily and Honour would be secretly hoping that he and Adele could patch up whatever their differences were. On the other side, Adele, Myles and Rose would all be trying to stand aloof and hide their destructive secret.

Michael would be right in the middle of the two camps, and he'd be completely confused by conflicting signals unless he was told the truth.

Yet even if by some miracle he could accept it, how would the pair of them know how to behave with each other? Adele couldn't imagine ever being able to hug him the way a real sister would. Surely just an innocent brush against him would make her feel guilty? They'd be nervous of each other and the fact that their secret had the power to hurt so many other people.

Presumably Myles would've been told about his son at the same time Emily was, and Adele thought perhaps she should ring him later and arrange to meet again so they could discuss all this.

'But he's alive,' she reminded herself, for surely nothing should detract from that fantastic miracle. 'We should just celebrate that for now, and not ponder on what to do when he gets home.'

As Adele sat at the ward desk, Myles was in the stable yard at The Grange, his home in Alton. He was filling his car up with the last of the petrol he'd stored in case of an emergency. He had woken at five, too thrilled by the news about Michael he'd received the previous evening to sleep any longer. He hadn't telephoned Emily then because of the late hour, and so he decided that today, instead of taking the train to London to work, he would drive over to Winchelsea so they could celebrate together.

He was somewhat surprised that his first thought was to rush to her. Over all the years of rows and bitterness, he had grown used to disregarding Emily and thinking of all three children as his, alone. If he did sometimes concede they had traits from their mother, it was always the negative ones. In the past, if there was anything to celebrate, he wouldn't for one moment have asked Emily to join him.

It was only when Michael was reported missing that he saw Emily as an ally. Until then she'd been a nuisance, an embarrassment, someone he would gladly have cut right out of his life and done his best to forget. It was only a sense of duty and responsibility which made him visit her.

But once he believed Michael was dead, Emily was the only person who he knew would share his grief. The only one he could reminisce with. And he rushed to her and she gave him solace.

Then she told him of her close shave with death, and how Rose rescued her. He found it absurdly ironic that it was Rose and her mother's influence that was helping Emily hold herself together so well, and in turn supporting him. On some of the darkest days he felt God was playing some terrible joke on him. Why should it be that he could only gain comfort from an estranged wife who had never given him any before, and feel indebted to another woman who had brought him great heartache?

Yet by recognizing that Emily was still important to him, Myles found it harder to decide what to do about Adele. He wanted her in his life, up in the forefront of it, visiting his home, meeting his friends and colleagues. He wanted to treat her as a daughter, not meeting her in secret as if he were ashamed of her.

Until last night, 80 per cent of him believed that he must tell his whole family about her. He didn't expect Diana and Ralph to be very happy about it, but he'd thought that if Michael was found alive he would prefer to know the truth about why Adele ran out on him. But now Myles was afraid his desires were selfish and that the truth would bring nothing more than hurt.

Myles arrived at Harrington House shortly after nine, having stopped a couple of times en route so he wouldn't arrive too early. He was so keyed up now that he could barely stand still and wait for the door to open.

The door opened, but it wasn't the housekeeper or Emily standing there as he expected. It was Rose.

A cold chill ran down his spine and he moved back. He knew of course that Rose spent a lot of time with Emily, but he hadn't run into her before, and hadn't for one moment anticipated she might be at the house today. She looked so very different too to the way she'd been when he last saw her in his chambers.

'Don't look so stricken,' she said in a low voice. 'I'll behave perfectly.'

He assumed that meant she intended to act as if they'd never met before, but only a complete fool would trust a one-time blackmailer.

Yet this Rose had nothing in common with the brazen, over-madeup harpy who had stormed into his chambers. She looked pretty and fresh-faced in a simple print dress, with bare legs. Gone was the elaborate hair-style – now her blonde hair hung down her back in one neat plait. She might be in her forties now, but she looked closer to thirty.

'I am not your enemy,' she said in a low voice, then quickly explained why she was there. She said she was just about to go up and help Emily down the stairs, and then telephone Adele at the hospital. The respectful way she spoke and acted was as if she were a younger sister of Emily's, meeting her brother-in-law.

'Come on in,' she said more loudly, switching on a bright smile. 'I'll just make you both some breakfast, then I'll clear off and go and tell my mother the wonderful news. You two have a great deal to talk about today.'

Myles's fear abated as she flew up the stairs. Adele had claimed she'd changed for the better, and he supposed that if she was going to tell Emily anything, she would have done it a long time ago.

'Oh Myles, isn't it wonderful news?' Emily said rapturously as she came hobbling down the stairs on Rose's arm. 'I'm so glad you've come. No one else could possibly know how I feel today.'

Myles involuntarily went to hug her once she was down in the hall, something he hadn't done for years, and she responded with great warmth. She giggled and caught hold of his cheeks, pinching them affectionately between her fingers. 'I think we must be the happiest people on this earth today. I feel about eighteen again.'

Myles thought she looked lovely. Her cheeks were flushed, her eyes shining, and he was reminded of how much he had loved her once.

Rose laughed too, and it was the sound of someone who shared their joy. 'I'm off to cook the breakfast,' she said. 'You'll want to be alone.'

Myles and Emily went into the drawing room. 'I hope Adele and Michael will get back together eventually,' Emily said as she sat down. 'Adele must still love him, Rose said she was thrilled at the news when she rang her last night. One good thing that's come out of this wretched war is the breakdown of class barriers. That's what split them up in the first place.'

477

'And my disapproval,' said Myles, suddenly feeling uncomfortable.

'But you don't disapprove of her any more, do you?' Emily said. 'You said you were mistaken about her that time you called when she was here.'

'No, I don't disapprove of her. She's a sweet and kind girl,' Myles said, wondering what Emily would make of it if she found out they often met in London. 'But the fact she cares that Michael is alive doesn't mean she loves our son still. I suspect her feelings are only friendship.'

'Honour doesn't think that,' Emily said with a pout. 'She thinks they were made for each other.'

'Now, Emily,' Myles sighed. 'It's enough that Michael's alive, without planning his future for him. The war is still raging on, we can't count on anything. Let's just live for the day, shall we?'

Emily couldn't remember when she last had such a perfect day, and she didn't want Myles to go home. They had talked and talked, about Michael, happy times in the past and where they wanted to be in the future. Myles hadn't been critical about anything, in fact he'd been so kind and helpful, washing the breakfast things and tidying up – he'd even gone along to the shop to try to get her some sugar. He couldn't get any, but brought back some saccharine instead. When he tried it in a cup of tea he pulled a face and said he'd rather go without sugar than be poisoned.

'I suppose the war is a great leveller,' he said thoughtfully as he peered into the pantry to look for something they could have for supper. 'Here we are, rich by most people's standards. But money alone can't get you sugar, bacon or a fillet steak. It's odd to think that even the King and the Prime Minister have exactly the same rations as us and those who live in slums.'

Emily was sitting at the kitchen table peeling a few potatoes.

478

'Rose and Honour eat well,' she said. 'But then they grow stuff and keep chickens and rabbits. Those eggs we had for breakfast were from them.'

Myles closed the pantry door, a tin of Spam in his hands. 'You talk about them a great deal,' he said with a trace of sarcasm. 'Why is that?'

'Because I admire them,' Emily said evenly. 'They may live in a primitive cottage, wear shabby old clothes and have to work very hard, but they've got something special about them.'

'Such as?'

'Honour is very wise, she understands things about people without ever asking questions. As for Rose, she cheers me. She's so honest, she admits she spent most of her life being a real witch to everyone who cared about her. Yet I really like her, she's practical, a bit bossy, and she doesn't allow me to wallow in self-pity. I do so hope it works out with Michael and Adele when the war's over.'

Myles sat down beside her then and took her hands, making her drop the potato and the peeler. 'You've got to stop this, Emily,' he said.

She laughed because his tone was gentle, not a bit like the brusque way he used to speak to her.

'I'm serious,' he reproved her. 'I don't believe it will work out for them, and you'll only be disappointed if you keep this up.'

'I know my son,' she said with a shrug. 'He still loved Adele the last time I saw him, just a week before his last flight. He told me so.'

'Maybe he did, but a lot has happened to him since. Affairs between real people aren't like the ones in fairy tales. Love can die when it isn't nurtured.'

'Like it did for us?' she said, and her eyes filled up with tears.

'Yes, just like that,' he said.

*

479

Myles suddenly felt unbearably sad. He could remember how his heart had been bursting with love and pride as he turned to watch Emily coming up the aisle on her father's arm on their wedding day. Just sixteen, and the white silk gown, golden hair, flowers and her veil made her look like a beautiful angel. He remembered feeling quite sick with nerves about their wedding night, for he was sure someone so ethereal would be disgusted by carnal desires. Yet she hadn't been. Once alone in the bedroom at The Grange, which had been newly decorated for them, she'd been as passionate as he was.

'I wish I had understood you better, and been less selfish,' she said softly. 'You deserved better.'

Myles was astounded. She had never held herself in any way responsible for the failure of their marriage before. 'I should have been more tolerant when Michael was born,' he replied. 'I've heard it's quite common for women to lapse into melancholia after giving birth.'

She nodded. 'Rose told me she suffered from it too when Adele was born. We were both bad mothers.'

'Michael turned out fine though,' Myles said, wanting to distract her from talking about Rose again.

'And so did Adele. Perhaps it was partly because of the way Rose and I were with them that they were attracted to one another.'

'I expect it did give them a bit of extra understanding about people,' he said. 'But you look tired, Emily, after supper I'd better go home.'

'No, don't go,' she said. 'Stay the night.'

'I can't,' he said. 'I have to go to London tomorrow too, I have a big case to prepare for. But I'll come back at the weekend if you want me to.'

'I do,' she said, and smiled. 'And try to get some champagne so we can really celebrate.'

Chapter Twenty-seven

Adele smiled as she watched Myles studying the menu. They had met for dinner at a restaurant in Greek Street, Soho, but although the menu was very long, nothing Myles had ordered so far had been available.

She wondered why he didn't just ask the waiter what he *had* got. But she supposed Myles thought that would mean he'd be fobbed off with whatever dish the restaurant had most of.

It was November now, and though the threat of invasion seemed to have passed since the Americans joined the Allies, bringing with them their Flying Fortresses, bombers capable of flying much longer distances without refuelling, the Navy had taken a terrible thrashing this year. The public weren't supposed to know, but over a thousand British warships had been torpedoed by German U-boats.

Yet there was optimism too. The RAF now had Lancasters and Stirlings, planes which could also carry bombs for long distances, and with the Americans' help they were giving Germany a taste of their own medicine. News had just come in that Britain had recaptured Tobruk in North Africa, and with an alliance between Britain and Russia there were plenty who now believed the Germans could be beaten.

'You looked tired,' Adele said. Myles's face wasn't as ruddy as usual and there were shadows under his eyes. 'Have you been out on the tiles?'

'No, I haven't,' he said, but grinned boyishly. 'As a matter of fact I've been very busy trying to help get some Jewish people out of Germany. You do know what's going on there, don't you?'

Adele nodded. With so many Jewish people living in the East End and coming into the hospital, she was very aware of their plight, both here and in Europe. There was some very strong anti-Jewish feeling amongst Londoners, who tended to blame Jews for everything. Much of this was ridiculous and contradictory. One minute they were saying Jews took up all the room in the shelters, the next they were saying they were so rich they all went out of London in air raids. They were accused of running the black market and of looting bombed houses, but true cockney girls like Joan who knew all the local villains said it was they who were the black marketeers, and the Civil Defence workers who cleared the bombed houses were the looters.

Adele had got to know a lot of people in the Jewish community, and she was inclined to believe their stories of how badly their relatives in Germany and Poland were being treated. They said they were being rounded up and herded into ghettos, packed off on trains to camps, and shot outright if they tried to escape.

'Is it all true?' she asked Myles, for there were plenty of people claiming that such stories were mere propaganda. 'The camps and stuff?'

'Yes, Adele, I'm afraid it is,' he said, and sighed deeply. 'I've just managed to help a Jewish friend, who was a lawyer in Berlin, to get to England. He and his family are now staying with me at The Grange and they have lost everything, their home, money, valuables, to the Nazis. He has told me things that would seem impossible if they'd come from anyone else. My friend fears that Hitler intends to eradicate all Jewish people.'

'But he can't do that. Can he?'

'I believe he's already part of the way there. Reuben

tells me he had already built camps with gas chambers and crematoria to burn the bodies afterwards. He says that when Jews are sent off on trains to be "resettled", that's where they are bound. Women and children too.'

'No!' Adele exclaimed. 'That's monstrous. Surely ordinary German people wouldn't go along with something as barbaric as that?'

Myles shrugged. 'People are too afraid of losing their own lives to speak out, I suppose. And it is difficult to believe such a fantastically evil plan. But let's not dwell on horror tonight. Emily and I received another letter from Michael, and he sounds quite chipper, all things considered.'

Adele leaned forward eagerly. In the first two letters, or rather just brief notes from Michael, the content was frustratingly vague, parts of it blacked out by the censor. They only knew he was in POW Camp Stalag 8b, but where that was, how he got there, and the extent of his injuries, they could only guess at.

He obviously didn't know that they had believed him to be dead, and mentioned that his leg was 'playing him up'. He said the food wasn't too good, he wished he had some books, and that they played football and cards. He appeared to be more concerned as to how they were.

Myles said he'd probably been told by the Germans that most of England had been flattened.

'He was clearly thrilled to get our first letter,' he remarked, pausing to apologize that he hadn't brought Michael's letters with him as Emily couldn't be parted from them. 'He's delighted Emily and I are friends now, and grateful for all the news I'd managed to get about his chums in his squadron. He said a few books and parcels had come through from the Red Cross, he was reading an Agatha Christie, and he'd got quite good at sewing because he had to patch up his uniform. The rest was all questions about the family, his nieces and nephews, and about how we were all coping with the war.' Myles paused. 'He asked to be remembered to you and your grandmother too.'

Adele felt her eyes prickle. At their first meeting after the news that Michael was in Germany, she had insisted that Myles should not mention her in letters to his son. Emily could hardly be stopped entirely from doing this as she had regular contact with Rose and Honour, and would naturally want to inform him that they were relieved to hear he was safe. Adele would have loved to have written to him herself, but she was afraid that might give him the idea she still held a torch for him. Yet whatever she'd said, however much she knew she was doing the right thing by keeping her distance, her heart still stubbornly wanted more.

The waiter brought their meal then and Adele was glad of the distraction. Sometimes she wished she'd never got to know Myles this well, because the closer she grew to him, the more impossible the situation became.

They talked about many different things during the meal. The Siege of Stalingrad, which Myles thought would end very soon as the German army were losing so many men, Montgomery's victories in North Africa, and the fall of Mussolini in Italy. Myles conceded that England had desperately needed America's help with troops, tanks and planes, but he suspected that when the war was finally won, America would take all the credit for the victory as if our men had been sitting on their hands for the last three years.

'I don't like Yanks,' he said viciously. 'They act so damned superior, but where were they in the Blitz? How many of their pilots could have done what our boys did in the Battle of Britain? They swank around England in their smart uniforms, bribing the gullible with their cigarettes, chewing gum and nylon stockings. Not a real hero amongst them.'

Adele could only smile at that, for she was guilty of

accepting a few pairs of nylons and bars of chocolate herself. She was tempted to tell Myles that Rose had an American admirer too, a military policeman from Arkansas called Russell. Apparently he'd stopped her in Rye to ask the way to Hastings, and had later taken her to a dance. According to her grandmother, he was a good man, but then he had brought her some tinned peaches and oil for her lamps and fixed a fence that had fallen down in a gale.

'They aren't so bad,' she said, and laughed because she could see that Myles was about to launch another tirade. 'Their men are getting killed too, and if they hadn't come in when they did, we might have been invaded. So stop being such a bigot. The Yanks I've met have been charming.'

He opened his mouth to say something, then shut it again. 'Just don't marry one and go to live over there,' he said with a wry smile.

'No one has asked me yet,' she grinned. 'But I could be tempted. Imagine having any amount of butter, cheese and meat. Living in a properly heated house and not having to make do and mend. My clothes are all so shabby now, I'd give anything for a new dress.'

He looked thoughtfully at her, perhaps noticing that she had on the same dark brown dress she'd worn at all of their meetings since the summer ended, the only difference being that she'd draped a cream and brown scarf around the neckline this time.

'You've had a tough life, haven't you?' he said with a break in his voice. 'When I think what Diana had as a young girl! Dancing and music lessons, scores of pretty dresses and shoes. It makes me feel very sad that you had so little.'

'It didn't make her the happiest girl in the world though, did it?' Adele said tartly. She didn't like him feeling sorry for her, and she remembered Diana being sour-faced and mean-spirited.

Myles sighed. 'No. She's still not happy, and I often think

that's my fault. I was preoccupied with my career when the children were young, and I didn't spend much time with them. They saw so much strife between Emily and me too. I don't think I've ever talked to Diana the way I do to you.'

Adele didn't know what to say to that. As a young girl she'd always imagined that wealthy people lived enchanted lives, but she knew now through talking to Myles that this wasn't necessarily so. He sometimes said how big and empty his home in Hampshire felt, and she guessed his two older children and their families didn't visit him very often. She thought he was a man who had many regrets, and this was yet another reason why she felt unable to distance herself from him.

Myles went back to the hotel in Bloomsbury where he was staying after he had dropped Adele off at the nurses' home. Instead of getting into bed, he sat in the chair by the fire the maid had lit for him and thought about Adele. He wondered why he hadn't looked ahead after their first couple of meetings and realized he was digging his own grave.

It had never occurred to him that he might grow to love her as much, if not more, than his other children. For that was what he felt for her now. Not simply affection because she was bright and warm-hearted. Nor guilt because she'd had a miserable childhood. It wasn't just pride either, though sometimes he felt so full of it he was tempted to boast about her.

It was love.

He had always considered himself such an intelligent man, and his fellow lawyers considered him honourable. Yet here he was caught up in a clandestine relationship which, if it was discovered, might very well turn Emily and his other children against him. Yet it seemed so wrong to keep it secret.

As Myles stared into the fire, he remembered how Michael had always loved the big one they always had in the dining room at The Grange in winter. Was he imagining it right now? Seeing the table set for dinner with crystal glasses and the family silver shining in the candlelight? Did he picture his mother looking beautiful in the deep blue sequinned evening dress that he had always urged her to wear for family parties? And how would he picture Myles? Would he be dressed for the City in his dark suit and bowler hat? In tweeds and riding boots? Or in wig and gown, as in the picture which stood on the sideboard in the dining room?

Myles sighed deeply, for whatever the mental picture the boy had of his parents, Myles doubted he ever thought of his father having such a troublesome dilemma.

Michael had always been so honest. Myles couldn't ever remember him lying about anything. So he supposed that if he was to ask him what to do about all this, Michael would urge him to tell the truth and let the cards fall where they may.

But Michael was one of the cards, Emily yet another, Ralph, Diana and his grandchildren too. What if he lost them all?

Michael was hungry and cold, huddled under one scratchy, worn blanket, on a lumpy, damp mattress. Hut C was about twenty-five feet long by fourteen feet wide, with twelve rough, three-tier wooden bunks around the walls. The floor was just planks. In the centre of the hut were a stove, a table and a couple of benches. Michael had a lower bunk and he was nearest to the stove, in deference to his disabilities. But the stove hadn't been lit for two days now as they'd run out of fuel. Tomorrow the men were going to badger for more, but in all likelihood it would be several more days before they got any.

By day Michael could keep cheerful. He had made some good friends here, they could chat, play cards, write letters, read, and there was always 'Goon Baiting', the sport of annoying or tricking the guards to pass the time. With twelve English, three Americans, one Canadian, two Australians, four Poles and two Frenchmen sharing the hut, it was an interesting mix and there was rarely a dull moment. Michael found he could cope by day with not being able to join the others running around the perimeter fence, playing football, or even practising gymnastics because of his bad legs. But he dreaded the nights.

Tonight like every night he was trying to blot out the disturbing sounds of his fellow prisoners snoring, the pain in his legs and the howling wind outside, by listing all his favourite memories of England.

Playing cricket at school, the sun warm on the back of his neck, grass soft and springy beneath his feet. Freewheeling down a hill on his bike, his shirt billowing out behind him like a parachute. Rowing down the river at Oxford, the sun sparkling on the water and the ducks scuttling away in fright under the overhanging trees. His first solo flight, going up above the clouds and looking down at the awe-inspiring expanse of billowy whiteness beneath him.

He had grown adept at not dwelling on the horror of his last flight, when the plane was on fire, spinning out of control and he couldn't get the cockpit open. He couldn't remember it finally opening, he must have lost consciousness by then, for the next thing he knew he was on the ground tangled in his parachute. All he remembered after that was pain, searing, white-hot agony that was only halted temporarily by passing out again.

He had vague recollections of nuns, an all-white room in which the only decoration was a large wooden crucifix. Later he was to learn that the villagers had carried him to the convent on a stretcher, and but for those nuns he would have died. Both his legs and one arm were broken, his hands and face were burnt. They had worked a real miracle on the burns, for new skin was growing again. Harry Phillpot, one of the men in Hut G who had interrupted his medical studies to enlist in the RAF, said he would only be left with slight puckering around his eyes and mouth, nothing worse than a few wrinkles.

It was his legs that bothered Michael most, for they had been broken in two places, and the nuns hadn't had enough medical knowledge to set the limbs correctly. He limped very badly and was in constant pain, especially now the weather had turned so cold. Every day he did the exercises Harry recommended, always hopeful that one day soon he'd recover completely.

Many of his fellow prisoners talked of little else but escape. Michael was with them in spirit, but he knew he couldn't be included in their plans, he was too much of a liability. Dreaming was a form of escape, though, and he'd become an expert at that. Sun-drenched dreams were good for forgetting how cold he was, past sporting triumphs helped the pain. Yet oddly it was the ones of memorable cold or wet days with Adele that really transported him home.

Tramping over the marsh, cycling in the rain, and best of all the freezing cold day in London, the first time they made love.

He could smell her skin and her hair, feel the silkiness of her warm skin, and hear her whispering that she'd love him for ever. There had been other women since then, but no one had ever touched him inside the way she did.

His mother had written at length about what a good friend Rose, Adele's mother, had become to her. According to his mother, Rose had helped her achieve what no doctor had ever managed: she no longer had bad days when she had to stay in bed, and she hardly drank at all any more.

Michael fervently hoped that was true, and he was glad she had a good friend as well. Yet it was very difficult to imagine Rose Talbot, the woman who had been so uncaring about her daughter, being a friend to anyone.

He also wondered how Rose had managed to worm her way back into Mrs Harris's life. But he supposed the only person who could tell him that was Adele. He'd like to ask her too why she went to see his mother when she first heard he was missing. It didn't make any sense for Adele to offer her concern and sympathy to someone who had treated her so badly. Unless, of course, she did still love him.

It was that faint hope which kept up his spirits when things looked blackest.

Chapter Twenty-eight

1944

'Do get a move on, we'll be late,' Honour snapped at Rose, who was scraping around the edge of her compact with a nail file, trying to utilize the last remains of her face powder. 'You don't need that muck on your face just to see Emily.'

They had been invited to Harrington House for supper, to celebrate the success of the Normandy landings which had begun a week earlier, on 6 June. But they both felt that the true purpose of the supper-party was because Emily and Myles wanted to show what good friends they had become. Perhaps they even hoped that in time they could live as husband and wife again.

Honour was delighted that they were friends again – she'd already packed two bottles of her gorse wine into a string bag to take with them for a toast. It was from a batch she'd laid down at the start of the war with the intention it should be drunk when it was over. They had opened a bottle after Michael was reported to be alive, and found it to be like nectar, and as Emily said Myles was always grumbling about the difficulty in getting any wine now, and whisky and brandy were almost extinct, Honour hoped he'd be impressed.

'Is this dress too tight?' Rose asked, putting away her compact and standing up. She smoothed the pale blue crêpe down over her hips and looked at her mother nervously.

The dress was at least eight years old and one she'd brought back from Hammersmith on her last trip to London.

'No, it's not too tight,' Honour said honestly. 'You only think that because it's so long since you dressed up. I should think Emily will be quite envious, it's very pretty.'

Honour privately thought her daughter looked a picture. Five years of war, shortages of food, lack of new clothes and permanent anxiety had made many women look dowdy and drained, but not Rose. Fresh air, exercise and little alcohol had done wonders. Her blonde hair shone as it did when she was a young girl, her skin glowed and her figure was taut and svelte. She'd gone to bed last night in curlers, and now her hair fell in luxuriant waves to her shoulders. Maybe the dress was a little dated – the utility clothes on sale now were very plain and sparing with material, whereas Rose's old dress had embroidery on the bodice, and the skirt was cut on the cross so it clung seductively to her hips. But no woman on earth would not prefer it to the dull, cheaply made ones most had to wear.

'Now, for goodness' sake let's go,' Honour said irritably.

Rose silently picked up her handbag, and the torch in case it was dark when they returned home. She didn't want to go. The idea of having to sit across a table from Myles filled her with dread.

She was very pleased that he and Emily had settled their differences. She had grown extremely fond of Emily and took pride in the fact that her present happiness was partly due to Rose helping her to pull herself together. But to be forced to spend an evening with Myles, whom she hadn't spoken to for more than a couple of minutes since the day they came face to face at the front door when Michael was found, was frightening. He must be still very angry that she'd blackmailed him, just as she was still creased up with embarrassment about it. Then there was Honour and Emily blithely believing Michael and Adele would fall into each other's arms the moment he returned. The four of them sitting round a table with so many secrets between them was just a recipe for disaster.

They locked the front door and walked quickly up the lane. It was just before five, the sun still very warm, and the evening so peaceful. Until the previous day they'd been able to hear the constant rumble of heavy guns across the Channel. Honour had said it sounded the way it did twenty-eight years earlier in the Battle of the Somme.

'What did you say she was cooking for us?' she asked as they walked up the hill towards Winchelsea.

Rose smiled. Her mother had been preoccupied with food for months now. She brought the subject round to it at every opportunity. Rose wondered how she'd survive if she lived in a city and had to manage purely on rations. She didn't seem to appreciate how lucky they were having items like eggs, chicken and rabbit, and to her it was the end of the world when they ran out of sugar.

'She said she'd managed to get some lamb,' Rose said. 'I just hope she's followed my instructions on how to cook it.'

Emily's housekeeper had left some time ago, and she couldn't find a replacement. She still had Mrs Thomas who came in to clean a couple of times a week, and Rose had given Emily cooking lessons. To everyone's surprise she had picked it up quickly and enjoyed it. In fact she'd become a good housewife, taking pride in her home and garden. She often said that the day she heard Michael was alive had made her realize she had been blessed, and she became determined that by the time he came home, he'd have a mother he could be proud of.

'These shoes are killing me,' Honour said, pausing under the Landgate and looking down at her feet which were swelling over the shiny brown court shoes. 'I shouldn't have listened to you, and worn my old ones.'

Rose sighed. A while ago she had persuaded Honour to make a new dress for herself with some fabric she'd had for years. Just this week she'd finished it, and it looked lovely, a button-through style with short sleeves in pale green cotton with small white daisies. She still had a good figure, and with her hair put up in a bun, for once she looked almost elegant.

But getting her to put on stockings, and smart shoes too, had been a battle.

'After a glass or two of your wine you'll forget about your feet,' Rose said. 'You couldn't have worn those old boots, what would Emily and Myles have thought of you?'

'People have to take me as I am,' Honour said tartly. 'I'm too old to attempt being a fashion plate.'

Honour did forget her shoes were too tight once she'd had a couple of glasses of wine. It was a real treat to be sitting at a table beautifully laid with polished silver, snowy napkins and sparkling glasses, to say nothing of the delicious lamb, slow-cooked until the meat fell off the bone, just the way she liked it. She hadn't realized that she missed the sophistication of elegant dining until now. But then it had been well over thirty years ago, back in Tunbridge Wells, that she last ate this way.

Emily sparkled as brightly as the glasses, clearly thrilled she had managed to get everything just right. She looked pretty and girlish in a rose-pink chiffon dress, with her hair piled up in loose curls on the top of her head. She had said she had bought the dress back in 1929 when Michael was twelve, and hadn't worn it since as the fashion had changed and skirts had become much longer.

Myles was very attentive, and if he was a little anxious at finding himself the only man amongst three women, it didn't show. Honour found herself warming to him considerably, for he wasn't as stuffy and pompous as she had thought when she first met him. She thought that making the peace with Emily, and the work he was doing helping Jewish refugees settle in England, had brought a new dimension to his somewhat staid character.

He also adored her gorse wine, ignoring the claret he had brought with him to drink it, and he kept saying that he could sell all she could make in London.

Conversation flowed effortlessly, and they laughed a great deal as Rose told amusing stories about her tenants in London, and some of the problems she'd encountered since coming back to live on the marsh. Honour just sat back and listened, feeling proud that Rose could be so entertaining. Since she'd come here to live she'd completely lost that hard, rather common image she'd had previously, yet she had retained enough of the insight into the lower levels of society to give her a fascinating edge.

'What are you planning to do when the war ends, Rose?' Myles asked. 'Will you stay here, or go back to London?'

'I'd like to stay here and run a caravan site,' she said.

'A caravan site!' Honour exclaimed. 'Where on earth did you get that idea from?'

'People will be desperate for holidays by the sea and if I could sell my house I could buy five or six caravans, and build a washing and toilet block,' Rose replied, seemingly undaunted by her mother's surprise.

'Where were you thinking of putting these caravans?' Honour asked indignantly. 'I hope it's not on our land!'

'No, Mother,' Rose laughed. 'I know you wouldn't want a horde of noisy holidaymakers on the doorstep. Mr Green has some land by his place, I suggested I rented it off him, and he could open a little shop. He was all for it.'

Honour immediately realized it wasn't such a crazy idea after all. Oswald Green owned a couple of acres between her place and Pett Level. It was rough, pebbly ground close to the sea, and not suitable for sheep to graze on. Oswald had some business interests in Hastings, and he had once told her that he was always on the lookout for schemes that would produce an income without him needing to oversee them. She also suspected he had a soft spot for Rose too as he was a lonely widower in his mid-fifties.

'It might work,' she said with pretended indifference. 'If you were prepared to put your back into it.'

'Sounds a good idea to me,' Myles said, slurring his words just slightly for he'd drunk a lot tonight. 'I personally couldn't imagine anything worse than a holiday in a caravan, but I dare say it would appeal to people who can't afford hotels. Honour could sell them her eggs and wine too.'

'Maybe Adele could be persuaded to come back down here and help as well,' Emily said brightly.

At this remark Honour suddenly took Rose's idea completely seriously. She missed Adele so much, and she had often tried to think of something which would lure her away from London. 'Now, that's a smart idea,' she said, beaming at Emily. 'She loves an outdoor life, I can imagine her getting really excited by painting up caravans and putting in a few flower beds.'

'And maybe she'd get back with Michael too,' Emily said excitedly.

Honour hadn't had more than a couple of glasses of wine, and perhaps that was why she noticed both Rose and Myles stiffen at Emily's remark. Assuming Myles still held some reservations about the suitability of her granddaughter and his son, she looked at Rose.

'And what have you got against that?' she asked.

Rose blushed. 'Oh, mother,' she said a little brusquely. 'Adele wouldn't like us to match-make.'

'She still loves him, as well you know,' Honour said tartly. 'And Emily tells me Michael asks after her in every single letter. Now, if Myles was to just get off his high horse and accept it, there would be nothing to hold them back.'

'Honour's quite right, Myles,' Emily said, reaching out to pat her husband's hand affectionately. 'We all know Adele dropped Michael because of our disapproval, and we were very wrong to think that way. Adele is a wonderful girl, we've all been thrown together in adversity and found we really like one another, so let's all drink to Michael and Adele's possible future together.'

Emily held up her glass, and Honour followed, but she noticed that Rose and Myles were looking at each other in a stricken manner and had not picked up their glasses.

'What is it?' Honour asked, looking from one face to another. 'Do you know something I don't? Myles! Is there something wrong with Michael that you haven't revealed?'

Emily giggled. 'Oh, he's just being silly. Michael's fine, even if he does have a limp now. He can get a job in aviation when he comes home, the world will be his oyster.'

'Adele doesn't want to marry Michael.'

At that firm statement from Myles Honour looked at him sharply. She sensed hurt in his voice and something akin to panic in his eyes. 'How do you know that?' she asked.

'Because she told me,' he replied.

'When, darling?' Emily asked. She was tipsy but clearly trying to act as if she were entirely sober.

Myles looked very embarrassed. 'I took her out to lunch in London,' he said. 'I wanted to apologize for treating her so badly when she was working here.'

Honour immediately realized that something fishy was going on. Adele would've told her if she'd been asked out to lunch by Myles, unless of course the pair of them had something to hide.

'Let it be, mother,' Rose piped up, and she had a curiously hard expression in her eyes. 'You and Emily are clinging on to a foolish dream. Myles is right, as far as Adele is concerned Michael is just a family friend.'

Honour looked from Myles's face to her daughter's, and saw the same fear in both their eyes. They shared a secret, that much was obvious, and then she remembered how reluctant Rose had been to come this evening.

'You two hatched up something to split them up, didn't you?' she said wildly. 'What did you do? What did you say to them?'

'Did you, Myles?' Emily asked, her voice taking on a shrill

edge. 'But how could you plot it with Rose? She didn't even live here then.'

Honour realized this was so, but she had come for that visit ages before, and Honour had told her Adele had a young man. But why would she want to split them up? It didn't make sense.

Yet when she thought back, Adele's hostility to her mother was above and beyond what Honour would have expected. She had despaired of them ever making it up. And Adele was such a forgiving person normally.

'You will tell me what you two did,' Honour said harshly. She got up from her chair and looked menacingly at them. 'I want the truth, the whole truth. Right now!'

There was complete silence. Myles and Rose were looking furtively at each other, Emily was staring at Honour open-mouthed.

'I may be getting old but I am not senile yet,' Honour thundered, and waggled a warning finger at Myles. 'I am certain you and Rose hatched up a plan together to make Adele drop Michael and run away to London, and if you won't tell me what that was, I can find out.' She paused for a moment to give her words more impact. 'The Matron at the Buchanan Hospital will tell me. She knows, for it was she who told me that Adele had moved to the London Hospital. She wouldn't have arranged that move without good reason. So have I got to go and ask her? Or are you going to tell me?'

There was deathly silence, both Myles and Rose looking as if they wanted to run from the room.

Myles broke the silence. 'I'll tell you,' he said in a small voice. 'I promised Adele I wouldn't, but I can see now that I must.' He paused, shot a look at Rose who was grimacing at him, and then cleared his throat. 'The truth is that Adele is my daughter.'

Honour thought it was a weak joke, at least for a second

or two. She looked at Emily and saw her mouth was gaping open in shock. 'Don't be ridiculous, Myles,' she said in a shrill little voice. 'How can she be?'

'I had an affair with Rose,' he said.

Honour was just about to ask him to repeat that, assuming she'd misheard, but he was hanging his head and Rose clapped her hands over her face.

'It was when I was sent down here to wind up an estate during the last war,' he went on after a brief pause. 'I stayed at The George in Rye, and Rose worked there. But when Adele worked here, I didn't know that she was Rose's daughter. I didn't know until Rose came to see me at my chambers after she'd seen the engagement notice in *The Times*.'

Honour sat down with a thump, completely winded by the news. 'But that makes Michael her half-brother,' she said weakly.

Emily jumped off her chair, rounding on Rose. 'You had an affair with Myles? How could you? I thought you were my friend.'

Honour's head was reeling from the shock. She wished she'd never forced this out, but however shattering the news was, it made sense of many things which had hitherto puzzled her.

'Sit down and shut up, Emily,' she said firmly. 'Let them explain first.'

It was Myles who did most of the explaining, and considering his extreme embarrassment and Emily's frequent gasps of outrage, he did it well.

Honour felt every kind of emotion as the story unfolded. First and foremost there was tremendous anger that Adele's happiness had been destroyed by her own mother's actions, and that she'd been forced to cope with such a bombshell, alone.

She didn't know whether it was rage or sympathy she felt for Rose and Myles, it seemed to be a mixture of both, for whatever the rights and wrongs were of them having an affair, they could never have known that it would have such far-reaching results.

As for Emily, for her she had profound pity. She'd managed to pull herself together in the past year, and this looked certain to make her fall apart again.

Rose only found her voice when Myles began to falter as he described how he went to the hospital in Hastings to break the news to Adele.

'Maybe I should have come to you and asked your advice about how to deal with this, rather than let Myles go to Adele,' she said plaintively to Honour, her eyes filling with tears. 'But I didn't know what reception I'd get from you.' She paused to wipe her eyes and then looked at Emily. 'I had never met you until the night I pulled you from the river. When I discovered who you were I couldn't believe that fate could take such an ironic twist. And I haven't been faking my friendship with you. It's entirely genuine, though I doubt you can believe that now.'

Emily wanted to know exactly when the affair took place, how long it lasted, and whether Rose knew Myles had three children. Myles hung his head as he told her, then told them all about his meetings with Adele in London. 'I've come to love her,' he said simply. 'She urged me never to divulge any of this, she had always been afraid of it hurting Emily, Michael and my other children.' He turned to Emily then and tentatively took her hand. 'I've always been tempted to tell you. It might have seemed kinder to everyone else involved to keep it under my hat, but it never seemed right to do so.'

'What have you got to say Emily?' Honour asked gently, for she was now leaning her elbows on the table, her hands covering her face and her slim shoulders heaving as she sobbed.

'Nothing.' Emily uncovered her face and sniffed back her

tears. 'I'm as much to blame for this as Myles. I was awful to him at the time it happened. Just as I continued to be awful right up till we split up and I came here.'

'That's a very honest and generous attitude to take,' Honour said, and she moved her chair nearer to Emily and put her arm around her. 'Perhaps we should think now whether Michael should be told the truth.'

'I don't know,' Emily said. 'What do you all think?'

'It would stop him believing there was hope for him and Adele,' Myles said.

'But maybe that hope is keeping him going right now,' Rose said.

Emily suddenly slumped forward on to the table, knocking a glass of wine over on the tablecloth. 'Emily!' Honour exclaimed. 'Are you all right? Would you rather Rose and I left now to let you and Myles sort things out between yourselves?'

She lifted Emily up and cradled her head against her breast, for the woman was sobbing again and seemed distraught. 'This must have been a terrible shock to you,' Honour said soothingly, stroking her hair. 'We both were guilty of dreaming dreams of a wedding and our two families becoming one. We can't have that of course, not now, but maybe we can reconcile ourselves to a deeper friendship based on true understanding.'

Rose got up from her chair and came nearer to Emily, putting a hand on her shoulder. 'I wish I could turn the clock back,' she said sorrowfully. 'Do you know, Emily, that you are the only true friend I've ever had? I can't bear that I've hurt you so much. Please forgive me!'

'And me too,' Myles said. 'I should have understood that your nervous problems were related to the birth of Michael, and got you help. I became so hard on you. I'm so sorry.'

Emily lifted her head from Honour's shoulder, looked at the concerned faces all focused on her, then got up, moving round the table. She picked up a glass of wine and downed it in one gulp. 'None of you need to apologize to me,' she said, wiping away her tears with a napkin. 'I deserved everything I got, and more besides. But looking at all three of you, so full of concern, makes me very ashamed of myself, and I know I must tell you something I thought wild horses wouldn't drag from me. For Adele and Michael's sake.'

She leaned forward and filled her glass again with shaking hands.

Honour was frightened now. There was a dangerous look in the woman's eyes, she had already had more drink than was good for her, and her apparent calm was almost certainly a lull before a storm.

'Let me help you up to bed,' Honour suggested. 'We've all had enough shocks and distress for one night.'

'And I'm going to give you more,' Emily said, picking up her glass and glugging down the wine. When it was empty she continued to hold it in her hand, and looked at all three intent faces before her.

'Michael isn't Myles's son. He's the child of the gardener at The Grange.'

There was complete silence for a moment. Honour could only stare at Emily, thinking she'd misheard. Myles and Rose were doing the same.

A loud crash brought them out of it. Emily hurled her empty glass at the fireplace where it shattered into pieces.

'It's true,' she shouted defiantly, her hands fluttering. 'I fell in love with him, he begged me to run off with him, but I couldn't.'

'Jasper?' Myles exclaimed. 'Was it him?'

'That's right,' she said. 'You called him Jasper. His name was actually William Jasper, I called him Billy. Michael looks just like him.'

Honour turned to look at Myles. He was ashen-faced, stunned by the news, and for a moment Honour thought it was just Emily's cruel way of getting her revenge.

'I-I-I,' he stuttered. 'I sometimes wondered why you spent so much time with him in the garden. But I couldn't believe that of you.'

'Men are so foolish sometimes.' Emily gave a tight little laugh. 'They think it's fine for men to stray, but women are supposed to sit at home with their embroidery and wait for them to come home. I was so alone at The Grange, Myles. You left early in the morning and came home late, often you were away for days on end. All I had was your blessed parents preaching to me about how the young mistress should conduct herself. They didn't even let me play with Ralph and Diana, they had to be brought up by the nursemaids. Billy made me feel wanted and loved, he made me feel alive.'

'Why didn't you tell me?' Myles said.

'What, that I was having an affair with the gardener and was expecting his child?' Emily cackled drunkenly. 'You would have thrown me out on my ear. I'd have ended up in the same plight Rose found herself in.'

'I meant about how unhappy you were, before you began the affair,' Myles rebuked her.

'What would you have done?' she tossed back. 'Given me a lecture on how long The Grange had been in the family? Your parents were getting frail, someone had to be there with them. Even when the first war broke out, I wasn't allowed to do anything more than sit and knit balaclavas. Billy had wanted to enlist, do you remember that?'

Myles nodded. 'I persuaded him against it because I said we couldn't manage without him.'

'Yes, that's what you said. But he was in love with me even then and wanted to leave because he was afraid of where it would lead, and we hadn't even so much as kissed then. You should have let him go. He went in the end and died in the trenches. I don't think he even tried to survive.'

Honour could hear the raw pain in Emily's voice and knew then why she had been such a troubled soul for so many years. She remembered too how she felt about Frank, and knew in her heart that any woman feeling that strongly for a man would do what Emily did, right or wrong.

Rose was crying too, whether it was because she also understood Emily, or because she felt responsible for bringing further grief into this house, Honour couldn't tell.

Myles was looking at Emily who was now sitting at the table again with her head in her hands. He looked as if his whole world had crumbled.

Honour wanted to cry too. She had been looking forward to tonight for days because she thought it was on the cards that Emily and Miles might become husband and wife again. Now that was wiped out.

'I think we should go home, Rose,' she said quietly.

Rose and Honour left then, creeping out without saying a word. It was dark now, and the night air warm on their bare arms. They didn't speak, but linked arms and walked quickly away from Harrington House.

It was the start of August before Rose and Honour saw Emily again. They had both written her a letter after the supper-party, but neither of them received a reply. They were told by Jim the postman that she'd gone away but they had no idea if she was with Myles or alone.

Honour and Rose had discussed when Adele should be told, the morning after the supper-party. It would of course be wonderful news for her, for there was nothing now to stand in the way of her and Michael marrying when he came home. But they couldn't just tell her without consulting Myles and Emily first. It was their family secret, after all, and they might want to explain it to Adele themselves, once they'd decided whether or not they were going to tell Michael.

But talking further about what had happened that night was like a minefield. Honour got angry and said Rose should have told her the truth a long time ago and saved both families such grief. She said she would never have accepted the invitation for supper had she known Rose had once had an affair with Myles. She guessed too that Rose had blackmailed Myles, and she was so disgusted she didn't speak to her for days. At times the atmosphere was so tense between them that Rose was tempted to go back to London.

It didn't help that it rained almost continually, forcing them to be indoors a great deal. They went about their usual tasks by day, at night they listened to the wireless or read, but not in the easy, companionable way they had before. It was when they heard that a new pilotless plane known as the V1 was being launched from Germany to drop bombs on London again that Honour showed her real anxiety.

'What on earth are Emily and Myles up to? Why don't they contact us?' she raged. 'I want to get this over and done with, it's playing hell with my nerves.'

Rose knew that in reality she was afraid Adele was in danger again, as these new bombs meant she wouldn't get any leave for a while.

People called the new threat 'doodlebugs' or 'buzz bombs', and it was said that they were Hitler's revenge for the Normandy landings as they began soon afterwards. They could be heard flying overhead, but the only news on the wireless or in the newspapers was quite casual; reports of attacks on the south, but no detail. Adele's weekly letters reported that the hospital was very busy again with casualties, but she didn't say much more than that the doodlebugs were an infernal nuisance, because there was no warning of their arrival.

'She'll be all right, Mother,' Rose said soothingly. 'And Emily and Myles will surface again soon. They've got to make a really important decision, they can't rush it. I know you are dying to tell Adele, but she's believed Michael was her brother for three years, another couple of weeks of thinking that won't make any difference to her.'

'It's not just Adele I'm fretting about,' Honour admitted. 'I keep worrying about Michael too. How's he going to feel when he hears that the gardener was his father?'

Then, on the first dry day they'd had in some time, Emily came visiting at Curlew Cottage. She looked well, having been away in Devon with Myles for several weeks. She apologized for not contacting them, but said she and Myles had felt they needed time and distance from everyone to think things through.

'It might seem strange to you both, but I'm glad it's all come out now,' she said, her eyes brimming with tears. 'Myles and I have a chance to maybe start again, all fresh and new. And there won't be anything to hold Adele and Michael back now either.'

She went on to say they had decided that they would tell Michael when he came home, but it should be his decision whether Diana and Ralph were also informed. She said that Myles thought they should tell Adele next time she came home on leave, and he would come down so they could all tell her together.

'He thinks I should be there too,' she said. 'To show I'm happy that's she's now part of our family.'

Despite Emily's understandable anxiety about how Michael would take the news that Myles wasn't his natural father, she seemed relaxed and happy. She said that her secret had caused her great misery over the years, and that now it was out, she felt a huge burden had been taken from her shoulders. Myles had said it didn't change his feelings for Michael in any way, and he was also very happy that he no longer had to hide his meetings with Adele.

'I hope you two are still my friends?' Emily said, looking from Honour to Rose. 'It has, if nothing else, made us real family too.'

They had always thought of Emily as charming, but weak

and self-centred, yet they suddenly realized how brave and unselfish it had been for her to admit her infidelity and deception that night. She could have raged at Myles, taking the moral high ground and gaining everyone's sympathy, but she didn't.

All she'd seen was the obstacle between her beloved son and the woman he loved. Knowing she had the power to remove that obstacle, however much it cost her, she had been prepared to pay the price.

'Of course we'll always be friends,' Honour said, her voice thick with emotion. 'You, Emily Bailey, are a brave and very honest woman.'

Emily stayed all afternoon, and the three of them found a great deal to laugh about as they exchanged gossip, and news about what had gone on since they last met.

'You two should have a day out together,' Honour suggested as they had yet another pot of tea. 'There's probably things you need to say to one another without me there. And you could do with a bit of fun for a change.'

'We could go to London,' Emily said immediately. 'I need some new things and there's nothing in the shops in Rye.'

'Is that a good idea with these doodlebugs?' Honour asked.

'Adele said in her last letter that they are mainly south of the river,' Rose replied. 'Besides, I need to check on my place in Hammersmith. And London's more fun than anywhere else.'

Honour smiled at that, for she was glad to see the clouds had rolled back for both Rose and Emily. 'On your heads be it,' she said. 'Just don't grumble to me afterwards if all the trains are delayed.'

It was on a Thursday, almost at the end of August, that Rose and Emily caught the eight o'clock train from Rye to London. The entire summer had been very wet and chilly, but that morning was bright with sunshine. Emily looked very elegant in a pale blue costume and a cream, broad-brimmed felt hat. Rose joked that she looked like the poor relation in a striped summer dress and a rather battered straw hat trimmed with a new ribbon.

'We could look at wedding hats,' Emily said dreamily as she looked out of the train window.

Rose half smiled. She thought her friend was such a child sometimes. It was almost as if she believed in fairy godmothers, and that with a wave of a wand, Michael and Adele would just waft down the aisle without even a glance backwards. For all they knew, Adele could be seeing someone new, she might never feel the same way about Michael as she once did. As for Michael, they didn't know the full extent of his injuries, and they certainly couldn't even guess at the impact the news that his real father was buried somewhere in the fields of Flanders was going to have on him.

'Don't tempt fate,' Rose rebuked her. 'Anyway, as it's almost impossible to buy a lipstick or face powder now, do you really think we'd find a shop with decent hats?'

'Let's buy something extravagant for Honour then,' Emily suggested. 'What about some pretty pyjamas?'

Rose laughed. She found the thought of her mother slinking around in fetching pyjamas hilarious. 'That would be a waste of money and coupons. She'd appreciate the thought but she wouldn't wear them, she likes a flannel nightie. She'd much prefer a pair of slacks or some knitting wool to make herself a jumper. Or even chocolate.'

'My mother said she was very beautiful as a young woman. She said she wore the most lovely hats when she first moved into Curlew Cottage. Your father was a handsome man too, Rose. Mother said all the ladies used to admire him.'

Rose smiled. She could recall her parents dressed for dinner when they lived in Tunbridge Wells, Honour wearing midnight-blue velvet, with sparkly combs in her hair, and smelling divine. Frank was tall and slender, and his fair hair was thick and curly. She remembered him in a maroon waistcoat with mother-of-pearl buttons, and she'd made him laugh when she said he looked like a prince.

'They were a handsome couple,' Rose agreed. 'But I don't think either of them really cared for dressing up in finery. They had everything they wanted with each other, they were happy with a simple life.'

'I wonder if I would have been like that if I had run off with Billy?' Emily said thoughtfully.

'I couldn't see you living in a gardener's cottage,' Rose said. 'You weren't really born to rough it.'

'Neither was Honour, or you,' Emily said.

Rose was quite shocked to see how shabby London looked. She had come up on several flying visits in the last couple of years, but as she was alone and going straight to Hammersmith, she hadn't noticed any significant changes. But as she and Emily strolled in the sunshine up the Haymarket, through Piccadilly and on to Regent Street, she felt saddened by the boarded-up windows, the soot-stained facades, and the general dreariness of everything. It was true that the West End had had its share of damage during the Blitz, but she had expected it all to have been put right again. The rubble might have gone, but there were parts of buildings missing, weeds growing in gaps in the bricks.

This part of London had always been synonymous with glamour to Rose. Elegant women wearing the latest fashions stepping out of taxis. Flower stalls that boasted blooms never seen away from the West End. Jewellers' windows displaying fabulous gems, and gown shops stuffed with beautiful clothes.

There were no smartly dressed women window-shopping now. Everyone looked shabby and down at heel. There was little to excite Rose and Emily in the shop windows either, just dull utility clothing, nothing frivolous or glamorous. Nor were there many men in uniform around. Clearly they had all gone off to Normandy for the landings.

In a coffee shop, which in fact did not serve coffee, only tea, they overheard a couple of women on the next table talking about the doodlebugs. It seemed they had caused a great deal more destruction than Rose and Emily had imagined. 'If the engine cuts, that's it for you,' one woman said to the other. 'No point in running, you can't escape.'

'Still, we're safe enough around here,' her friend replied. 'It's Croydon way and the East End that gets them. I've got a neighbour who knows about them and he says they can't fly further than that.'

'Do you think Adele is all right?' Emily whispered nervously. 'Should we go over there?'

'Don't be silly,' Rose snapped. 'Look what happened to Honour when she went there! Besides, Adele would've told us not to come to London if it was dangerous. We'll be all right up here, that woman said the rockets can't reach the West End. And we can telephone the hospital later to speak to Adele.'

The two women forgot about the threat of doodlebugs when they went into Swan and Edgar's at Piccadilly Circus and Rose found some nice scented soap, and a pair of navy blue linen slacks that were her mother's size. Emily bought a pretty blouse, then, cheered that there were actually some goods worth buying in London shops, they decided to go up to Selfridges in Oxford Street, and go over to Hammersmith after lunch.

The two women stopped just before reaching Selfridges' doors because there was an old-fashioned hurdy-gurdy organ playing. The owner was wearing a battered top hat and bedraggled tails, and he had a little monkey dancing on top of the organ.

For both women it was evocative of their childhood, when such sights were commonplace, and they went into raptures over the cute little monkey in its red coat and fez. Since war broke out, pets had become rarer because of food rationing. Most people had hung on to ones they already had, of course, but they weren't replaced if they died. As for a monkey, it was the first one they'd seen in years.

The monkey's owner let Rose hold it, and it clambered up on to her shoulder and perched there silently. Emily wanted to hold it too, but she was nervous of it, and she giggled like a schoolgirl.

Suddenly they heard a plane overhead. They looked up, as everyone else did, and the monkey on Rose's shoulder suddenly began to chatter and show its teeth. The hurdy-gurdy man snatched the monkey back. 'Doodlebug,' he informed them, and caught hold of his machine and began wheeling it away, down a side street.

Rose looked around her, and saw everyone around them on the pavement was just standing looking up, or ignoring it completely and walking on and into Selfridges. No one was rushing for shelter, and although she wanted to flee, she was afraid of looking foolish.

She reached out for Emily's hand as the droning noise came closer. 'Oh Rose, I'm frightened,' Emily exclaimed, holding her hand very tightly.

'It's all right,' Rose said, although she was frightened too. 'It'll pass over us, you'll see.'

All at once they appeared to be isolated from all the other shoppers who had moved into shop doorways, or disappeared down into Bond Street Tube station. Instinctively they moved towards a shop with a striped sun awning. Then suddenly the droning noise stopped.

Remembering what they'd overheard in the café, Rose dropped her shopping bag, flung her arms around Emily and held her tightly. She heard a kind of whistling buzz, and the ground vibrating beneath their feet. Dust flew up like a snowstorm, and as they bent their heads into each other's shoulders, Rose felt rather than saw the awning falling down above them, for it was like a black shadow engulfing them. Something else hit them too, knocking them to the pavement, still locked in each other's arms. The last thing Rose thought as she felt the pounding of rubble burying them, was that they should have followed the man with the monkey.

It was Myles who first received the news of Rose and Emily's death. He had spent all day in the courts and had gone back to his chambers at around half past four. He was collecting up some files to take home with him, when his secretary came in and said a policeman wanted to see him.

Myles was in a jovial mood. He'd had a good day in court, the case he had been prosecuting had been wound up a day early. As he had no real need to be in London tomorrow and the weather was so beautiful, he thought he would go down to Winchelsea tonight for a long weekend and surprise Emily.

'Honest, guv, I didn't do it, whatever it was,' he joked as the tall, thin policeman with a rather hangdog face came into his office.

When the policeman didn't smile, Myles immediately realized he'd come to report something unpleasant.

'I'm very sorry, sir,' the policeman said. 'There was a bomb in Oxford Street earlier today. We have reason to believe that one of the victims might be your wife. Was she in London today?'

Myles went hot, then cold. He'd heard earlier in the day about a doodlebug in Oxford Street, but paid very little attention. In the first few weeks of the V1 attacks there had been panic. The lack of warning, the very nature of a pilotless rocket, was terrifying. But like during the Blitz, people got used to them, even blasé. Although at first cinemas and theatres closed through lack of audiences, that soon changed and everyone carried on with their lives regardless.

He hadn't even asked if there had been any loss of life at this attack today.

'I don't know,' he said, trying to control himself. 'She did say she was planning a day out with a friend. But she didn't say what day, or where she was going. Why do you think it was her?'

'We found your business card in with her ration book, sir,' the policeman said. 'Was her friend a blonde, with the surname of Talbot?'

'Yes,' Myles whispered, and slumped down into his chair. 'Are they badly hurt? Which hospital are they at?'

'I'm sorry, sir,' the policeman said, bowing his head. 'They were both fatally injured.'

'They're dead?' Myles looked at the uniformed man before him in horror. 'They can't be. It must be a mistake.'

'No sir, no mistake. There were several people killed today, and more injured. Is it possible for you to come with me now to identify them? And can you let me know the next of kin of the other woman, Mrs Talbot?'

'Her daughter is a nurse here in London,' Myles said brokenly, and tears sprang to his eyes. 'Oh God, I can't bear this! Why pick them?'

That same question ran through Myles's head throughout the procedure of identifying the bodies and taking a taxi afterwards to see Adele. Rose and Emily had been taken to the mortuary just as they had been found, their arms wrapped tightly around each other. Although their bodies had been crushed by falling masonry, their faces were unmarked. In a strange sort of way that was comforting to Myles, for they were both beautiful and somewhat vain women. And he'd loved them both.

Chapter Twenty-nine

'Funerals are always so harrowing, but at least it didn't rain. Sad her elder son couldn't get leave though.'

'I don't think they got on. He hardly ever came to visit his mother. But I think that's his wife over there talking to the daughter.'

Adele moved away out of earshot of Mrs Grace and Mrs Mackenzie. They both lived in Winchelsea and were well-known gossips. Adele guessed that by the time they'd had a second sherry they wouldn't even bother to keep their voices down as they were now.

It felt strange enough to be back in Harrington House with all the memories it evoked, let alone having to cope with so many people. Both the dining and drawing rooms was crowded, and many more had gone out into the garden. Most Adele knew by sight if not by name, but there were a fair few total strangers too.

She would have felt a little more comfortable if she could have gone out into the kitchen and helped there, but Myles had hired four women to serve the refreshments, and she knew neither he nor her grandmother would approve if they saw her handing out cakes and sandwiches.

Myles and Honour were together in the corner of the drawing room, their heads bent together in earnest conversation, and even though Adele knew she could and should join them, she felt unable to do so.

Sidling out into the hall, she took a quick look round to make sure no one was watching, then, opening the front door, she let herself out.

*

From the night nine days ago when Myles had come to the nurses' home to tell her Rose and Emily were dead, she hadn't been able to sleep or eat. She had been chatting to some of her friends when he arrived, and she'd barely taken in the devastating news before he bundled her into a taxi to catch the last train from Charing Cross back to Rye.

There was no taxi at the station and so they walked to Curlew Cottage. As they got to the end of the lane, they saw Honour waiting, torch in hand. It transpired that she had expected Emily and Rose back around eight, and when they hadn't turned up she had assumed that they'd stopped to see a show or a film and would catch the last train. Afraid that they might trip in the dark without a torch, she'd come out to meet them.

'Where are the girls?' she called out, while they were still some distance from her. 'Have they stopped off in Rye?'

Adele remembered how Myles gripped her hand. He didn't know how to respond. Then all at once Honour must have realized it wasn't some sort of wild coincidence that they'd also been on the last train, and she began to wail.

Adele thought she had witnessed every kind of grief while nursing in London, yet she had never seen or heard anything so tragic as her grandmother's reaction.

It wasn't a sob, or a scream, but the sound of pure heartbreak. A dirge-like howl that came from deep within her. The light from her torch was moving every which way, and Adele ran to her blindly, Myles following close behind her.

Since that first terrible long night when Honour sat hunched in a chair, rocking and wailing like a madwoman, Adele had watched her closely, for she was afraid that in her grief, Honour might attempt to take her own life.

In the days that followed she became completely silent. While she was able to wash, dress, feed the animals, and even chop wood, she was locked into a world of her own. She didn't even seem to be aware Adele was with her.

Adele knew all about shock, she saw it daily in the hospital and was aware that it took many forms. But she was equally shocked herself, and she needed to talk about her mother, to express how she felt about her, both alive and now in death. She couldn't deal with a wall of silence, or the way her grandmother looked at her as if she were an intruder.

The vicar from the church in Winchelsea called at Myles's request, for he had felt Emily and Rose should be buried, as they died, together. But it was as if he was invisible to Honour. She stalked around the room as he was asking her about hymns she liked, and even when he got up and took both her hands, there was no light of recognition in her eyes.

It was only yesterday, the day before the funeral, that Adele finally broke through to her.

'You've got to listen to me,' she shouted at her angrily. 'Mum wouldn't have wanted this, and you know it. She'd be telling you to pull yourself together.'

Honour was kneading some dough on the table. They didn't need any bread, Jim the postman had brought them a loaf the day before. But Honour had always made bread on Fridays, and Adele hadn't tried to stop her, thinking it might help her out of her darkness naturally. But as she banged and kneaded, making the table judder on the floor, it began to get on Adele's nerves, and that was when she shouted for her to stop and listen to her.

She got no response, so Adele snatched the dough away and slapped her grandmother's face. 'I'm talking to you, that bloody bread isn't important. This is! Rose is going to be buried tomorrow. You've got to be there at the church with me and Myles. You can't act like a madwoman, not even if your heart is broken.'

Still getting no response, Adele grew furious. 'What about me?' she screamed at her. 'How do you think I feel? Rose was an appalling mother to me. All the worst things that ever happened to me were her fault, and you were all I had. Are you going to turn away from me now because she's dead? Don't I mean anything to you?'

Honour turned to her slowly. 'No one can know how I feel,' she said in a toneless voice. 'I've been through all this before. I can't do it again.'

Adele had to assume she was referring to the time when Rose disappeared as a young girl. 'She hasn't left you because she wanted to,' she shouted. 'She's dead, killed by a bomb. It can happen to anyone. It's not right that she should go before you do, but she has, and there's nothing that can change that.'

'I was always on at her for something,' Honour said, her voice still flat. 'After that supper-party I said some very cruel things.'

Adele sighed. On the train ride back from London Myles had told her about what came out at the supper-party. It was astounding, almost unbelievable, but it had lost much of its impact coming on top of hearing her mother and Emily were both dead.

'It doesn't matter what you did or said to Rose in the past,' she said tersely. 'It was over before she and Emily went to London. And whatever came out at that supper-party, it was for the best. They became friends again. They died together in each other's arms.'

'It was me who suggested they had a day out together,' Honour said brokenly.

'So maybe you did, but that doesn't make it your fault they died,' Adele said in exasperation. 'Blame Hitler. Blame the Government for not shooting down the rocket. Blame anyone you like. But not yourself. They were enjoying themselves when they died. They probably didn't even know what happened. That's a better way to go than most get.'

'You don't care, do you?' Honour said, her voice suddenly returning to normal. 'You still hated Rose!'

'Don't be ridiculous,' Adele snapped. 'Of course I care. I

didn't hate her. Maybe I wasn't always capable of forgetting some of the nastier things she did to me. But I'd forgiven her. I liked her. I could even say I grew to love her. That's what I bloody well wanted to talk to you about. Hasn't it occurred to you that I might be feeling guilty? You haven't got the monopoly on guilt, you know.'

She had stomped out of the cottage then, too angry to deal with anything more.

She did feel guilty, and very sorry that she hadn't actually told Rose how glad she was that she'd come back into her life, and how much she had come to mean to her. She felt bitterly ashamed, too, that even as she was crying for Rose and Emily, she could barely contain her joy that Michael wasn't her brother after all. What sort of a person was she that she could only think of herself at such a time?

For a couple of hours she walked and walked, crying most of the time. When she finally returned home, Honour was more like her old self. Sad, a little bewildered, but not mad or withdrawn.

Honour dressed herself this morning in the same black dress and cloche hat she'd worn for Frank's funeral over twenty years earlier. Adele hadn't known she still had them, for they'd been packed away in a box beneath her bed. Adele guessed, but didn't dare ask for confirmation, that Honour had made the dress especially for Frank's homecoming from France, for it had elaborate pin-tucks down the bodice and handmade lace collar and cuffs. It had been dyed black, but she guessed it was originally pale blue, and the miracle was that it still fitted her.

Myles had brought Adele down a dress and hat of Emily's, for she had nothing suitable to wear. Ironically, she could remember admiring the dress when she once pressed it for Emily. It was the height of fashion at the time, linen with drawn thread-work details, mid-calf length, with padded shoulders, a boat neckline and a wide belt around the waist. The hat was small and veiled, and Emily had always worn it with an artificial rose pinned to one side.

'Rose would have liked to have seen you wearing that,' Honour said with a break in her voice as Adele came out of the bedroom wearing it. 'She would've said you looked like a film star.'

Adele's eyes prickled with tears, for she remembered only too well that Rose had always taken a great deal of interest in what film stars wore. Even moving to the marsh hadn't entirely ended her love of glamour. It seemed appropriate then that she should be dressing the way her mother would have liked.

It was a beautiful, moving service, and the church was packed. To Adele's surprise there were a great many more people there for Rose than there were for Emily. Honour had often said in her letters that Rose had become well liked, that when they went into Rye together they could hardly get up the High Street for people stopping to chat to her. Adele had always been cynical about it, imagining they were just gossips hoping to get some titbit of information, but like so many hard-held ideas she had about her mother, once again she was mistaken.

Several women had come up to Adele in the churchyard and spoken of Rose with affection, clearly genuinely upset that she was gone. Their little stories all had a similar tone, that she'd been a memorable woman, gay and lively, funny and warm. They said too how proud she'd been of Adele, and how excited she always was when she was coming home for a holiday.

Maybe if those friends and acquaintances had taken up Myles's invitation to come back to Harrington House, Adele might have felt able to stay, but they'd obviously felt the class and social gulf when they saw Emily's old friends and family flocking into the big house.

Adele certainly felt it. Emily's closest friends would know that Rose had played an important role in her recent life, and might want to talk to Adele and her grandmother. But Ralph's wife and his sister Diana had looked at her with contempt. To them she was just the girl from the marshes, an ex-servant who had got above herself.

Adele was weeping by the time she got down to the river. For Michael, who would soon get the letter telling him his mother was dead. For Myles, who'd finally found a friend in Emily, only to have her snatched away, and for Honour, who held herself responsible for everything and everyone.

But over and above the tears for those she cared about, she was crying for her mother. If only there had been more time!

Why didn't she ever tell Rose that she'd become proud of her, that she looked forward to seeing her? That her letters made her laugh, that she felt warm inside knowing Granny was being taken care of, and that the past didn't matter any more?

She felt ashamed of herself that she'd never prompted Rose to talk about her memories of Pamela, how she felt about Jim Talbot, or where she was during those missing years after she was sent to the asylum. Adele had always wanted to, not to lay blame or stand in judgement, but just so she could see the whole picture of her mother.

It would've helped Rose to know her daughter cared, and Adele had no doubt Rose would have told the more disturbing parts with her customary self-deprecating humour. That, Adele realized now, was one of the most attractive aspects of her mother's character. She wasn't afraid to admit her mistakes, and when she told a story she could paint the characters in such a vivid manner that they became as clear to the listener as they were to her. She had always claimed to be entirely self-centred, yet her understanding of her own and others' failings suggested this wasn't entirely true.

Maybe she was deeply flawed, no saint – that much was certain. But she had proved she was capable of honesty, kindness, loyalty and bravery. Adele just wished she'd been big enough herself to step back from her old grievances and see all the good in Rose. Before it was too late.

Letting herself into the cottage, she went into the bedroom. She had always thought of it as being her own room, but today she was very much aware that it had been Rose's first, and last. She opened the wardrobe, and sniffed. It smelled of lavender, and she remembered that Granny had said Rose had always loved that smell right from a young girl when she would stuff little pillows with the dried heads of the flowers.

Adele ran her hands over the clothes. Most of them were pre-war ones, bright pinks, reds and emerald-green, confirmation that Rose had always liked to be noticed.

Granny had once said that she was exactly the same as a young woman, that she'd never liked conventions or rules. She had joked at the time that Adele's father must have been quite a sober man, for Adele didn't appear to have inherited Honour and Rose's wild side.

'I would have loved to have been a little wilder,' she murmured wistfully to herself. It had never been possible, for poverty, the Depression and then the war had moulded her into a cautious, sober role. 'When the war ends, then I'll cut loose,' she promised herself. She didn't dare voice the hope that she and Michael might be reunited, for even though there was no real obstacle any more, she might have hurt him so badly that his love had died.

*

In the late afternoon of 8 May 1945, Adele stood at the window of Men's Surgical, gazing thoughtfully out on to Whitechapel Road. Last night they had been told the news on the wireless that this would be a public holiday to mark the end of the war in Europe, yet the news had been met with surprisingly little excitement. Adele supposed this was because everyone had been virtually holding their breath since the news broke on the 2nd that Hitler had been found dead in his bunker.

But at midnight, every single ship in the docks and on the river let off their sirens, and church bells began to ring joyously. In the nurses' home, all the girls had clambered out on to the roof, to see fireworks being let off all over London. It was so thrilling – from the same spot they'd seen the fires of the Blitz, the doodlebugs and V2s, but now the noise and light were all for peace.

Permission had not yet been given for blackout curtains to be removed, but many people weren't prepared to wait for it. From the roof the girls could hear people shrieking with delight as they stripped their windows of the hated black fabric and light flooded into the streets again.

But Adele woke this morning to a thunderstorm, and as she and the other nurses took over from the night shift, the mood seemed very subdued. The heavy rain stopped, and there were longer queues than ever outside the bakers and fish shops, but people were wandering aimlessly, as if they were waiting for a signal to begin to celebrate.

It wasn't until three o'clock, when Winston Churchill's promised speech was broadcast from Downing Street to the nation on the wireless, officially announcing that the war in Europe was now over, that people suddenly began to look as if they truly believed it.

Now, at five, Whitechapel Road was filled with people waving flags, blowing on hooters, and many of them sporting paper hats in red, white and blue. Bunting had appeared as if by magic in the last couple of hours, festooned across every shop, from lamp-post to lamp-post. Adele expected that many women were at home busy preparing for street parties, perhaps finally deciding that this was the day to get out any currants, sugar and other foodstuffs they had managed to hoard away. She could see men hurrying along the road with crates of beer, and she guessed that by midnight most adults would be as drunk as lords.

She turned away from the window and smiled at the number of empty beds in the ward, for the promise that the war was soon to end had had a remarkably rejuvenating effect on patients. Those who hadn't been thought to be fit to go home a few days ago had suddenly taken a turn for the better and been discharged. Others expected in for operations had cancelled, and even the men left were in a highly excitable state – she and Joan had both been asked for kisses, cigarettes and beer today. If Sister was to hear such requests she'd have a blue fit.

Yet even more pleasing than the joyful evening ahead was the knowledge that next week she was going home for two whole weeks. The past eight months since Rose's death had seemed interminable. She was worried about her grandmother being alone, afraid she might retreat into herself again, or fall in the garden and lie there for hours before she was found. Was she eating properly? Was she warm enough at nights? What if she ran out of wood, or oil for her lamps? And Myles worried her too, for although she could telephone him, both at home and at his chambers, he wasn't likely to admit to her that he was unhappy or troubled.

It had been a long, bitterly cold winter, and for some of the old people around here living in bomb-damaged houses, open to the elements, on a meagre diet, it had proved fatal. Coal was rationed and hard to come by – each day children were brought in with injuries sustained as they tried to collect wood to burn from bomb sites. The we-can-take-it spirit which had been so remarkable during the Blitz had disappeared. People were bone-weary of hardship, they looked gaunt and grey-faced, and as if the doodlebugs hadn't been enough of a menace, then along came the V2s, which were even more deadly.

The destruction they caused was unbelievable. Huge craters appeared in the ground, and clouds of sooty black smoke, plaster and brick dust left rescuers choking. There had been one at Smithfield Market before Christmas, killing and maiming over a hundred people, then in January one struck a block of flats just across the road from the hospital in Valence Road, and demolished the one next to it. Adele had seen sights that day which for the first time in her nursing career had made her want to strip off her apron and cap and run. The dead and injured were mainly women and children, as the bomb had struck in the morning after most of the men had left for work.

The war in Europe might be finally over, but long after the servicemen came home, flats and houses rebuilt and repaired, there would be children with missing limbs still hobbling around. What of all those orphaned? The widows and those left homeless? Would the remaining slums and tenements be replaced with decent housing? Would there be new schools, hospitals, and work for all? Adele wanted to be optimistic today, but somehow she suspected it would be years before England returned to anything approaching normality.

'Penny for 'em?' Joan said, creeping up behind Adele and making her jump. 'Wondering if 'e's bin released and is on 'is way back right now?'

Adele smiled. She had finally told her friend the whole story when she returned to the hospital after Rose and Emily's funeral. She had to, for the misery she felt was too great to keep to herself any longer.

Joan acted like a safety valve. She held her, let her pour it all out – her guilt, her sadness and her fears – and without that she might have crumbled. It was Joan who finally persuaded her to write to Michael. As she pointed out, it wasn't a question of just offering him condolences and sympathy, he could get that from any one of his relatives. Their mothers had been friends and had died together, and as such her letter would mean so much more. She also added that she had to start the ball rolling if she wanted Michael back.

Once Adele had recovered from the shock and devastation of her mother's death, there was great joy and hope to be found in knowing Michael wasn't her brother. She did want him back as her sweetheart, she wanted it more than anything in the whole world. For such a long time she'd been forced to squash any memories of intimate moments, but now she could think of nothing else. She had only to imagine kissing him, holding him in her arms or running her hands over his bare skin, and she was aroused. Often she couldn't sleep at night because of it.

It was frustrating that Michael was limited to writing only one short letter a month, that they took such an age to arrive, and that the censor prevented him saying anything meaningful. But at least she knew he appreciated hers, for in the reply to Myles he'd said, *'Tell Adele her letter was beautiful. One day soon we'll sit in Camber Castle and talk it all through.'*

'I wasn't actually thinking of him, not then, more about whether or not England will become a better place now,' she said. 'The men who came back from the first war didn't find a land fit for heroes, did they?'

'Only you could be gloomy on such a day,' Joan laughed. 'I reckon's we'll all get what we deserve. In my case that should be a wedding ring from Bill, and a ticket off to America to live the rest of my bleedin' life in luxury in Philadelphia.'

Joan had met Bill Oatley, an American marine, back at the

beginning of the previous year. It had been a serious love affair from the very start and Joan had been in a state of terror that he would be killed when he went off to Normandy. Fortunately he'd been spared, and was still somewhere over in Germany. He had written and asked her to marry him a few months ago.

'So what do I deserve?' Adele asked.

'Better than being stuck 'ere in this poxy place,' Joan said firmly. 'Go on back 'ome to yer granny, you know that's what you want to do. Start up that caravan camp your mum 'ad in mind, that's a winner if ever I 'eard of one. Me and Bill will be yer first customers for our 'oneymoon.'

'I haven't got any money to do it,' Adele said with a smile.

'You 'ave. Yer mum's old 'ouse is yourn now.'

Adele shrugged. 'I can't sell it till everything's settled.'

'You don't need to,' Joan said firmly. 'You just go up a bank and get 'em to lend you some on it.'

Adele said she hadn't thought of that.

'Well, don't think about it today, me old cock,' Joan laughed. 'What yer got to get yer 'ead round now is what yer gonna wear tonight and where we'll go. Nothin' else.'

A call from one of the patients had Joan scuttling away, and Adele realized she was right. Today wasn't a day for thinking deep thoughts, it was a day for happiness and frivolity.

She would wear that gorgeous blue dress of her mother's that Granny had altered for her, drink a lot and be wild. Next week would be soon enough to decide what to do with the rest of her life. She would even stop thinking about what she was going to say to Michael when he got home. Like the song said, 'I'm gonna get lit up when the lights go up in London.'

Chapter Thirty

Adele perched on an upturned crate and surveyed the land around her with excitement and delight. It was very stony, little more than shingle, but she thought that was all to the good – at least it wouldn't be waterlogged when it rained.

It was the end of June, a hot day without a cloud in the sky, and she intended to spend the whole of this long weekend away from the hospital out in the sun. Dressed in shorts, an old sleeveless blouse and a pair of plimsolls, she felt rejuvenated already.

The war might still be dragging on in the Far East, rationing was as desperate as ever, and it was still well nigh impossible to get timber, paint or any other building materials. But every day troop ships were bringing men home from Europe, and soon Michael would be back too. They'd even started to remove the rolls of barbed wire along the beach. She was sublimely happy.

She had recently applied for nursing jobs in both Hastings and Ashford, but she'd heard nothing back yet. But even if she was turned down, she had decided to come back here in August for good, to put Rose's idea for a caravan site into practice.

It was not going to be some sort of memorial to her mother, that wasn't her style. It was a brilliant idea, and one that really appealed to Adele for many reasons, not least that she could earn a living while looking after her grandmother. Last time she was home, in May, she'd met Mr Green, who owned the land, for a chat about it. He'd said he'd be prepared to let her have the land rent free in exchange for a small percentage of the profits. She had talked to Myles about it, and he'd offered not only to lend her the money to start up, until the house in Hammersmith could be sold, but also to sort out all the red tape with the local council for her.

Maybe she might call it 'Rose Beach Caravan Park', or some such name to remind her where the idea came from. She certainly intended to plant a few rose bushes, the most vibrant-coloured, heavily perfumed ones she could find. She had no doubt that Rose's spirit would be flitting around here anyway, for she had already felt something warm and friendly around here the first time she'd come to look.

Adele could barely close her eyes at night for thinking about it. She would need water pipes to be brought in, a cess pit, and a toilet and wash-room block. She thought she'd start with six caravans, but there was room for at least twelve. Mr Green said that the hotels and guest houses in Hastings were all fully booked for the whole summer, and she knew herself that by next summer, when she'd got the site ready to open, every family in London would be burning for a holiday by the sea.

As for the caravans themselves, Joan had an uncle in Southend who could supply them. They would be old ones of course, but sound – all they'd need was a coat of paint and some tidying up inside, and she'd have all winter to do that, ready to open at Easter.

Getting up, she walked over to the fence that ran alongside a small stream. There were some straggly bushes and trees growing there, and through them she could just see the roof and chimney of Curlew Cottage. Granny had been talking this morning about getting electricity put on and building a bathroom. It seemed the end of the war had galvanized her into wanting a bit more comfort. Adele hoped that whoever she got to do the work on the caravan site would do that at the same time.

As she stood there thinking how exciting all these new developments were, she saw a flash of light by the cottage, as if someone was signalling with a mirror in the sunshine. Realizing it had to be a car windscreen, she thought Myles might have called to say he'd had further news of Michael, so she set off for home at a fast trot.

News had come from the Red Cross that his POW camp had been liberated back in early May, but they couldn't say how long it would take for him to get home as the whole of Europe was in turmoil. Power supplies had failed, telephone lines were down, and many of the railway lines had been damaged by bombs and tanks. Tens of thousands of refugees, displaced people and prisoners of war were adding to the problems.

As Adele got closer to the cottage and saw that it really was Myles's car, she ran even faster. He had become even more important to her since Rose's death, for she could talk frankly to him about her feelings for her mother, knowing he had experienced that same potent mixture of love, anger, amusement and distrust. Even if she couldn't publicly announce that he was her father, the knowledge that he was gave her a feeling of security she'd never known before.

Adele burst through the door of the cottage. 'Myles,' she panted, rushing over to where he was sitting on the couch, to hug him. 'I saw your car and ran all the way. Any news yet of Michael?'

He returned her hug, but said nothing, and when she looked at his face found he was grinning from ear to ear.

'I look such a mess,' she said, assuming that was what he found amusing, for her hair was tangled and her old shorts had been patched so often they wouldn't even do for cleaning rags. 'I've been at the caravan site, checking it out again. Have you been here long?'

'About twenty minutes,' he said, still grinning.

Adele turned her head to look at her grandmother, who was laying some cups on the table, and that was when she saw him.

Michael was sitting in the chair over in the far corner of the room.

Adele gasped, clapping her hands over her mouth. 'I don't believe it!' she exclaimed. 'I never thought . . .' She stopped short, suddenly shy and very daunted by how he looked.

He was terribly thin, the skin on his face scarred and puckered, and a walking stick was propped up against the wall beside the chair. Yet his grin was the same as the day she first met him, lips curling up at the corners in the way she'd always found so irresistible, a flash of white teeth, and his eyes as blue as the sky.

'Michael! Oh my goodness,' she murmured, and her heart began to pound.

For a brief moment the shock was too great. The last time she'd seen him was as he tenderly kissed her goodbye at Charing Cross station after they had spent the weekend together. She had held that image of the dashing young man in uniform, his shiny dark hair and skin as smooth as an apple, for six whole years, tucked away with the tears and heartache. But this wasn't the Michael she'd held in her heart, it was a thin stranger in civilian flannel trousers with hair cut too short and a scarred face, and she wanted to run and hide.

'You never thought you'd see me again? Or never thought I could change so much?' he prompted, one eyebrow raised quizzically.

It was his voice that stopped the desire to run. It was just the same, deep and resonant, so very different to the cockney voices she heard daily at the hospital, or the Sussex brogue down here.

'I don't know what I was going to say,' she said, and moved closer to him. 'I'm lost for words because this is so unexpected. It's so good to see you again. I just wish I'd known you were coming, I look such a mess.'

'You don't look so different to the way you were when I first met you here on the marsh,' he said. 'I expected in six years you'd have become sophisticated, your hair all rolled up the way most women seem to wear it now.'

Adele blushed. She'd left her hair loose this morning, in fact she'd hardly bothered to comb it. It probably looked like a haystack.

'Tea's ready,' Honour said from behind them. 'Would you like it there, Michael, or at the table?'

'I'll get up,' Michael said, and pressing down his hands on the arms of the chair, lifted himself to his feet.

Adele watched as he walked to the table. Both his legs were stiff, reminding her of artificial limbs, but to her relief they clearly weren't, for he turned on his heels easily and looked back at her. 'You see, I can walk without the stick. It's only a kind of security to have it with me. And I'm told there's a small operation which will put things right.'

Adele could see by her grandmother's fond expression as she looked at Michael that she believed all the hurts of the past were wiped out just by him being here. Adele was very aware that wasn't so. Explanations would have to be given, and even if he did still care for her, he would need to learn to trust her again.

Over tea and fish-paste sandwiches Myles explained how he had driven to Dover the day before to meet the ship Michael had been brought home on. He'd only got the message that morning that he was coming, and they'd stayed the night in a hotel in Dover because it was almost dark when the ship got in.

'I was like a child waiting for Christmas,' Myles said, his voice shaking with emotion. 'One of hundreds of people waiting for their sons, husbands and fathers. I was scared too, afraid I'd been told the wrong day, the wrong ship, and even that I wouldn't know him. There were so many men on stretchers, so much noise and confusion. Then at last there he came walking down the gang-plank. My boy, back home safe and sound.'

Honour somewhat pointedly told Adele that Michael had asked to come to Harrington House first before going on to Hampshire to see his brother and sister and their families.

'I needed to adjust before that,' Michael said, looking at Honour and half smiling as if rather amused by her view on his decision. 'In the camp we all thought of nothing but those at home, but the reality of getting back is a bit overwhelming. I know everyone will be asking questions, and there is so much I want to say. But at the same time I've got nothing to say.'

Honour looked puzzled, but Adele knew exactly what Michael meant. When she had come back here during the Blitz she had felt just the same way. Right now, she too had a million questions for Michael, but found she couldn't ask even one.

She knew she was staring at him, her heart was still beating too fast, and she wished they could be alone together so she could say all the things she needed to.

Myles explained for Michael that the camp, Stalag 8b, was in Silesia, in Poland, not Germany as they'd imagined. It had been liberated by Americans, and Michael and a few other men not able to march were put into trucks and moved from pillar to post before eventually getting back to England.

'It was like the world gone mad,' Michael said pensively. 'Thousands of people trudging along with bundles of belongings, little children trailing behind them crying with hunger. Whole villages razed to the ground, bodies still lying in ditches, burnt-out tanks and bomb holes. I saw a glimpse of some of the survivors from one of the concentration camps too. They were like living skeletons. I'm still finding it hard to believe what was going on in those places. They say millions were killed.'

After the tea and sandwiches they went outside to sit in the sunshine. Michael lay down on the grass in the shade of the

apple tree, with Towzer beside him, and Adele could see
that he was not up to talking. His eyes showed complete
exhaustion, and she thought that it was because he'd seen so
much horror in the past weeks that he hadn't yet said anything
about his mother's death.

He fell asleep suddenly, and Honour suggested that she
and Myles should go up to Harrington House to open the
windows and make up beds for them, and that Adele should
stay here with Michael.

After they'd driven off, Adele fetched a book to read, but
she found herself unable to tear her eyes away from Michael
fast asleep on the grass. She saw that the burn scar on his
cheek wasn't anywhere near as serious or disfiguring as she'd
first thought. It had healed well, and once he put on some
weight, and his hair grew long enough for a decent cut, it
would hardly show. She found herself focusing on his lips,
wanting to lie down beside him, hold him in her arms and
kiss him. All the feelings that had lain dormant for so long
were bubbling up inside her.

While it was good to find she hadn't imagined she was
still in love with him, it hurt too. She didn't know whether
she could bear it if he didn't return her feelings.

His grey flannels and white shirt, clearly pre-war ones that
Myles had taken down to Dover, were far too big now, and
only his belt was preventing them from sliding down over
his bony hips. It was so strange to watch him sleeping, his
dark lashes like little brushes on his cheeks, so relaxed and
peaceful. She hoped that meant he felt safe and at home
here, but maybe after the horrors of the camp, he'd find
almost anywhere quiet, equally soothing.

Time wasn't on her side. She had only this weekend to
make everything right between them. Once she went back
to London and he began looking up old friends and family,
their influence might be stronger than hers.

Without talking to Myles alone, she had no idea what had

already passed between them. She doubted Myles would have been so insensitive as to launch into the real explanation as to why she dropped Michael all those years ago, not when he was so exhausted.

So what should she say when Michael brought up the subject? More lies?

Michael woke after about an hour, opened his eyes and looked startled to see a tree above him. He turned his head, saw Adele in her chair looking down at him, and smiled.

'I thought for one horrible moment I'd only dreamt I was back here,' he said. 'Whatever must you think of me dropping off like that?'

'I think you are a man who is exhausted,' she said. 'It's going to take time, lots of sleep and good food before you recover completely.'

'Said just like a nurse,' he retorted. 'What I want is a few pints, to swim in the sea and to eat fish and chips out of the paper.'

'Fish is very hard to get,' she laughed. 'But swimming might be good for your legs, and Myles will be happy to take you for a few pints.'

'I rather hoped you might want to do that?'

That sounded so much like an invitation to be alone together, but Adele wasn't sure of anything now. She felt awkward, uneasy and very shaky.

'I would, but you need rest first,' she said, and even to her own ears it sounded like the way she spoke to patients, not an old, dear friend.

'You've become even more beautiful,' he said. 'Do all your patients and admirers tell you that?'

Adele blushed. He was looking at her so intently, and she wanted to retort with something that would show him his were the only compliments she valued.

'I don't nurse anyone long enough for them to notice if

I'm improving,' she said, and once again she was afraid she sounded starchy. 'But it's nice you think so,' she added.

'It's nice too that you've become such good friends with Father,' he said, taking her by surprise by deftly changing the subject. 'I can't quite see how it came about though. Just one of the many slightly mysterious things I'll have to delve into.'

'So you want to delve into things, do you?' she said, in what she hoped was a more flirtatious manner. 'Mind you, so much has happened, I won't know where to start. It will be a bit like trying to start a new jigsaw.'

He moved to sit up and massaged his right leg.

'Is it hurting?' she asked. 'Can I get anything for it for you?'

'No, it's okay with a rub,' he said, and gave her a long, penetrating look. 'Let's get back to the jigsaw. I always used to pick out the edge pieces first. Once I had the frame I found them easier. The frame in this case seems to be that my mother and yours became friends. Now, that's a puzzle on its own.'

'Not really,' she said nervously.

'Well, all I know of Rose was what you told me years ago,' he said 'And she didn't sound like a woman who'd have anything in common with my mother.'

'Exactly what I thought when I first heard about their friendship,' Adele said carefully. 'But in reality they had a great deal in common. Both on their own, estranged from their children, damaged women really. It was you being reported missing that brought us all together. Granny and Rose got to know Emily first, they comforted her. Later, I went to see her, met up with Myles, and so it went on from there.'

'Yes, but why did you go to Mother in the first place?'

'Because I knew how devastated she would be.'

'Weren't you afraid she would tell you to push off?'

Adele didn't know whether he meant because of bad

feeling when she worked for his mother, or because Adele had hurt her son. 'Yes, I suppose I was, but I was upset about you and that overcame my fear.'

'Ahh!' he said, and chuckled. 'Well, we've got one side of the jigsaw done now. Only three more and the whole of the middle to go.'

'You may find many things puzzling now, as the war has changed everyone to some extent,' she said. 'It's broken down the class structure, made people more equal. I think it's also made most of us realize what's important and what isn't.'

'What's important now to you?' he asked, squinting up at her.

'This,' she said, waving her hand to include the cottage and the surrounding marsh. 'There was a time when I thought it might be trampled under German jackboots. Seeing Granny's cared for, my friends, Myles, and you.'

'Me!' he exclaimed. 'I can sort of see why my father might become important in your life, despite how he was to you in the past, because he told me it was him who broke the news to you about Rose and my mother. I suppose that would create a bond. But what importance do I have?'

'Because I never stopped caring about you,' she said simply, and blushed furiously because he was looking at her so intently.

'First love and all that?' he said.

'First and only love,' she said, and bent over to retie the laces on her plimsolls to hide her embarrassment.

'Are you saying there's never been anyone else?'

'I've been out with a few men,' she said, still keeping her head down. 'But none of them were special or important.'

'What's that around your neck?' he asked.

Adele instinctively put her hand over the ring which hung on a chain around her neck. It had come out of her blouse as she bent over.

'Come on, what is it?' he asked.

'Our ring,' she said in a small voice.

'You've still got it?' He sounded incredulous.

Adele sat up and looked him in the eye. 'Of course. I've never taken it off,' she admitted.

'Dare I hope that was because you had regrets about running out on me?'

Adele suddenly felt very hot, she could feel sweat breaking out all over her. She looked away. 'Of course I did. I never stopped loving you.'

'Look at me,' he said sternly.

She did as he asked, but his eyes looked too big now for his thin face, and they had a slightly scornful expression. 'Don't play games with me, Adele,' he said. 'I was thrilled when I got your first letter, I desperately needed something good and hopeful to think about. But I'm not in that damn camp now, I'm back in the real world, about to pick my life up again. I don't want anyone feeling sorry for me.'

'Why would you assume I feel sorry for you?' she asked. 'You made it home, that's more than some of the men did. I didn't say anything in my letters I didn't mean.'

Adele didn't know whether to be relieved or sorry when Myles and Honour suddenly arrived back. She was afraid things were getting a bit intense, but at the same time she would have liked more time to have made her feelings plainer.

As it was, Michael got up to greet them, and Honour launched into one of her disapproving tirades about the dust in Harrington House, and how she wished she'd had some warning Michael was coming so she could have gone up there and cleaned it.

'If you'd seen how I've lived for the past couple of years you wouldn't worry about that,' Michael laughed. 'Sheets and hot water are sheer luxury to me.'

'But there's no food there,' Honour protested. 'Myles got a few bits and pieces from the shop but not enough to make a proper meal, especially for a lad who needs building up again. You must stay here for supper, I've got a pot of rabbit stew.'

Adele thought her grandmother was pushing too hard. 'Michael needs rest,' she said firmly. 'He's dead on his feet, and we could give them some of that rabbit stew to take back with them, they'd only have to warm it up.'

'The indomitable Nurse Talbot strikes again,' Michael said, grinning at his father. 'But I suppose she's right, and I can fit another few pieces in tonight with your help.'

'Pieces?' Honour asked.

'Of the big jigsaw. What's gone on while he's been away,' Adele explained, and she looked pointedly at Myles, hoping that he'd take that as a warning to be cautious.

Honour berated Adele after they'd left. She seemed unable to grasp that everything couldn't be put right immediately. 'You weren't even very welcoming,' she said plaintively. 'What's wrong with you?'

'How am I supposed to behave?' Adele retorted in exasperation. 'I can't throw myself at him. He really did look all in. And he's going back to his dead mother's house, where he may very well find out that the man he calls Father isn't. So with all that in the back of my mind, do you really think I could sit here tonight batting my eyelashes at him, with what amounts to a UXB in the next room!'

'But did you tell him you still care?'

'Yes I did, Granny,' Adele sighed. 'But there's a whole lot more got to come out before he'll trust me again. It's difficult enough dealing with this myself without you getting on at me.'

Myles called round briefly the following morning to say that Michael was still sound asleep, and he was going to leave him to wake up of his own accord. He left before Adele got a chance to ask him whether Michael had asked any difficult

538

questions the previous night. And how Myles had answered them.

Presumably nothing had arisen for he came back later in the afternoon with Michael and suggested they all took a drive down to Camber Sands and had a meal in a restaurant in Rye later.

Michael seemed very distant, but Adele put that down to Myles having just taken him to see his mother's grave. The few questions he asked were all about her, he appeared a little bewildered by everything he was told, and though he said how good it was to see Rye again, Adele got the feeling he wished he was anywhere but there.

Myles dropped them back at the cottage and said he and Michael were going to the pub for a few pints. Adele mentioned that she was going back to London on the seven o'clock train the following day, but she didn't get the expected response that they would see her before she went.

That night Adele decided that Michael did only think of her as an old friend, nothing more. If he had still loved her, surely he would have questioned why she left him?

Looking back at what had passed between them, she felt he had been embarrassed to find she still had his ring, and even more so by her claiming he was her first and only love. She cried then, for her stupidity in thinking there was hope for the future for them.

The following morning Adele got up early and went out for a walk. When she got back she put on her newest dress, a green and white polka dot sun-dress, just on the off-chance Michael would call.

She was out in the garden petting Misty when she heard Myles's car coming down the lane. To her surprise Michael was in it alone.

'Hello,' she said as he came into the garden. 'How did the pints go down last night?'

'Quickly,' he said. 'Two and I was pie-eyed.'

'And Myles?'

'That's what I came to see you about,' Michael said, his brow furrowed with a frown. 'He seemed troubled about something last night. Like there was something he had to tell me, but couldn't. I wondered if you knew what it was?'

Adele's stomach churned. If Myles couldn't tell Michael, she certainly couldn't.

'I expect he's feeling much like you,' she said quickly. 'So much he wants to ask and tell you, but he can't find the words. I'm the same.'

'He said Mother had left me Harrington House in her will,' Michael said. 'He wouldn't, or couldn't, say why. It seemed very odd to me that it wasn't to be shared between Ralph, Diana and me.'

'Ralph and Diana didn't come to visit her much,' Adele said, though she guessed Emily had made this provision for Michael just in case he was blocked from inheriting anything from Myles. 'Besides, she knew you loved it around here. It was her family home, remember, I expect she wanted to ensure it didn't get sold to someone else.'

He smiled then. 'I hadn't thought of that,' he said. 'Let's go over to Camber Castle,' he said, glancing towards the house as if daunted by Honour's presence.

'Can you walk that far?' she asked.

'I'm not a cripple,' he said defensively.

'I can see that,' she retorted. 'But it's rough ground and you mustn't overdo it.'

'I feel more normal today,' Michael said after they'd walked in virtual silence for at least ten minutes. 'It's been weird ever since I got off that ship. Almost like I was someone who was trying to pass himself off as Michael Bailey. Can you understand what I mean? Like I'd learned all the background stuff about this chap, but once I was confronted with all the people from his past life, I didn't know how he would respond.'

'You look and sound like the real Michael to me,' she said. 'But if you like I'll test you.'

'Go on then!'

Adele giggled. 'What was I wearing the first time you saw me?'

'Baggy trousers tucked into Wellington boots, and a navy jumper with holes in it.'

'You have passed the first question,' she said. 'What was the first present you gave my gran?'

'A tea caddy,' he said.

'Top marks. I'd say you are definitely the real Michael Bailey,' she laughed.

'I have one for you,' he said. 'What was it like when you first met up with your mother after all those years?'

Adele thought for a bit. 'Difficult. I felt nothing but contempt for her, but I had to force myself to be pleasant because of Granny's feelings. I suppose you could say I seethed with resentment for a very long time.'

'What changed that?'

Adele looked sideways at him, feeling this line of questioning had something behind it. 'Why do you ask that?'

He shrugged. 'I'm still trying to fit pieces into the puzzle.'

She explained how Honour was hurt in the air raid, and that she asked Rose to come here and look after her. 'I suppose that's when things changed. Mum looked after Granny so well, she made her happy. I didn't expect that, so she kind of proved herself to me. She became a very different woman to the one I spent my childhood with, she was lively, funny and very hard-working. I grew to like her. And I had forgiven her well before she died.'

They were approaching Camber Castle now and a few

sheep darted out on hearing them coming. Adele took Michael's arm to steady him as they walked through an area with a lot of half-buried boulders.

'Have you forgiven me?' he asked as they got inside the castle.

They were very close to the spot where they had been sitting the day he tried to fondle her breasts when they were kissing, and she thought it was that he was referring to.

'There's nothing to forgive you for,' she said.

'There is. I shouldn't have taken you to London that weekend. You weren't ready for it. I should have known.'

Adele was puzzled by what he meant. She sat down on the grassy hillock they'd sat on so often in the past and looked up questioningly at him.

'I thought about it all a great deal in the camp,' he said, looking down at her as he leaned on his walking stick. 'You'd been through so much as a child, especially that incident in the orphanage. You didn't have any close friends, no father around, just your grandmother. Stuck out here away from the real world. Then I came along.'

'That was the best thing that ever happened to me.'

'I wasn't fair to you though. I had another life that you couldn't enter into, and I made things worse by getting you to work for my mother. You had no life of your own, and they were so beastly to you. You went from that into nursing, cloistered away with other women, rules and regulations stopping you from any exploring of your own. Was that why you broke away?'

'No, of course not,' she said hastily.

'But that's what you implied in that letter,' he said sharply. 'So how about telling me the truth now? If it wasn't that, what was it? It had to be something pretty dramatic to up sticks and run away from your gran too. Tell me!'

Adele felt queasy. His eyes were boring into her, and she knew he was too intelligent to be fobbed off with a lie. Yet she couldn't bring herself to tell him the truth. Not now, it was all too soon.

'It was a combination of lots of things,' she said weakly. 'Things I couldn't explain to you.'

'You mean me rushing you into going away for that weekend?' he said, and he lowered himself down on to the ground beside her. 'You weren't ready for that, but you couldn't tell me.'

Adele began to cry. She wanted to tell him that wasn't so, but she couldn't.

'I thought as much,' he said. 'You knew your mother had been abandoned by your real father after she'd gone to bed with him, your stepfather walked out, and a man you trusted interfered with you. And I was so stupid and callow that I didn't stop to think that I might bring back the nightmares you'd tried so hard to overcome,' he said, and his voice shook with emotion. 'So you bolted because you thought I would leave you too.'

Adele was about to protest that this wasn't so, but Michael prevented her by carrying on.

'I suppose I always knew that was the real reason. But things you said on Friday, and talking to my father last night, confirmed it for me. He was saying something about how stuff in the past messes up the present. He wasn't exactly coherent, we'd both had a bit too much to drink, and I think he was trying to tell me how he felt he'd failed me and Mother. He's grown so fond of you too, Adele, he kept saying that you were very special and that he was ashamed of the past. Then all at once it all kind of gelled together, and I understood. I even asked him if he thought there was any hope for me to start again with you.'

'And what did he say?' Adele asked, hardly daring to breathe as she wiped her eyes.

'He said I'd have to ask you that. So that's what I'm trying to do. Is there?'

Adele cautiously took hold of one of Michael's hands in both of hers. 'Maybe,' she whispered.

His hand between hers felt so right, the electricity flowing between them making her tingle from head to foot. She couldn't talk any more, all she wanted was to be kissed and held until words were no longer necessary. He was so close she could feel his breath warm on her cheek, and she turned to meet his mouth with hers.

There was no resistance. As her lips met his, his arms came around her and they sank back on to the grass, kissing as though their very lives depended on it.

Adele had been kissed by other men in the last six years, but never like this. It was like rockets going off, swept away by huge waves, or freewheeling down a steep hill. It had been the same that night in London, but they had been innocents then, with nothing to compare it to. They were both worldly adults now, and Adele knew that if just one kiss could wipe out all the heartbreak, then it had to mean they had something worth fighting for.

'Can I change my mind to "definitely"?' she said as they finally paused for breath.

He smiled and stroked her cheek with one hand, looking right into her eyes.

'Even when I was angry with you after you disappeared, I never stopped loving you or wanting you,' he whispered. 'In the camp, even before you wrote to me, I used to dream of being here with you again. But now we are here, it's really weird, I can't quite believe it's for real.'

'But it is,' she said. 'I'm just so sorry I put you through all that, you see . . .' She was just about to try to start an explanation when he silenced her with another kiss.

'It's twelve years since you first brought me here,' he said as he finally tore himself away from her lips. 'And after six years of war and all the stuff both of us have been through, I don't want to hear you apologizing for anything. I think we deserve a brand-new start, without looking back. That is, if you think you still love me?'

Adele ran her finger lightly over his scarred face, and tears of joy prickled behind her eyes. 'I already told you I never stopped,' she said truthfully. 'In fact, I love you more now because of all the things I've been through.'

'Have you really worn my ring all this time?' he asked.

She nodded. 'I don't even take it off in the bath,' she said. 'I think I believed as long as it was touching my skin there was hope for us.'

'Why didn't you write again then, in that first year, and tell me how you felt?' he asked, a look of puzzlement in his eyes. 'I would've understood. What I hated most was you leaving me high and dry without a real explanation.'

Adele paused before answering, looking for truthful words without apportioning blame on anyone. 'What explanation could I have given you?' she said. 'I couldn't even explain it to myself, and I thought you'd be better off without me.'

'My father said something last night about you not appreciating your own value,' Michael said. 'I got a bit nasty with him and said that was rich coming from him, the man who'd been so unpleasant to you.'

'And what did he say to that?' she asked.

'"I got my comeuppance,"' Michael said, and chuckled. 'I took it that meant you got your own back at some point?'

'We had a few words,' Adele said, and laughed.

'One of these days when we've got nothing better to talk about I want you to tell me everything you two said to one another,' he said. 'But not now, all I want to do is kiss you again and again.'

He kissed her again then with even more passion, leaning over her as she lay on her back, his fingers running through her hair.

Adele knew he had no more questions or he wouldn't be as relaxed as he was. He was home, he was happy, it had all come right. But before she could relax and make love there was something she had to do.

'I love you so much,' she said with a sigh, 'But we could be much more comfy with a blanket to lie on, and a picnic. Then we could stay here all day.'

He lifted his head and grinned down at her with the same boyish wickedness she remembered so well. 'We could go back to your gran's and get both.'

'It's too far for you to walk there and back again,' she said.

'Look, Nurse Talbot,' he said indignantly, 'I've dragged myself around half of Europe, I can make it to the cottage.'

'You could, but you're not going to,' she said wriggling out from under him. 'You save your energy for later. Have a snooze in the sun. I can be back in twenty minutes.'

She ran off before he could argue, laughing as she went.

As she had expected, Myles had turned up, and he was sitting in the garden with Honour. They looked up at her questioningly as she came haring in.

'I came back for a picnic,' she said breathlessly. 'I made Michael wait there.'

'I couldn't tell him last night,' Myles said, frowning with anxiety. 'I tried to, but I simply couldn't. I was just telling Honour, it was too hard.'

'Much too hard,' Adele nodded. 'And unnecessary now. He doesn't need to know any of it.'

'Adele!' Honour exclaimed, frowning up at her. 'What on earth do you mean?'

'He has his own ideas about why I left him, and they are far kinder to everyone than the truth,' Adele replied. 'Let him believe them.'

'But surely I have to tell him you are my daughter?' Myles said in surprise.

'Why?' Adele asked.

'Because I've come to love you,' he said, his eyes welling.

'Surely being your daughter-in-law would do just as well?' she said, and leaned down to kiss him on the forehead. 'I could call you Father then without anyone finding it odd.'

For a moment they just looked at each other, then Adele leaned forward and wiped away a tear that was rolling down Myles's cheek. 'Emily would like it this way,' she said. 'She would never have wanted Michael to feel different to Ralph and Diana. And I think Michael would if you told him the truth.'

She waited as Myles and Honour looked at each other.

'I think Rose would agree with that too,' Honour said after a moment's thought. 'I saw her distress the night all this came out. She wouldn't want anyone to suffer further for her past mistakes, or for Michael to feel less for his mother.'

Myles sighed. 'You are just making it so easy for me to take the coward's way out,' he said.

Adele knelt down in front of him and picking up one of his hands, she held it to her cheek. 'There's nothing cowardly about a man who can forgive an unfaithful wife, and continue to give protection and love to her child. Let Michael remain in blissful ignorance. Please?'

'But what if it was to come out at a later date?' he said, light coming back into his eyes.

'Who's to tell?' Adele said with a grin. 'Only us three know. Well, aside from my friend Joan, but she's going off to America soon and she isn't the kind to blab. And us three left, we're the best secret-keepers of all time.'

He gave a little chuckle and smoothed back Adele's hair from her forehead.

'Go and have your picnic. And by the time you come back I want to see that ring back on your finger.'

'And pack a bottle of the elderberry wine,' Honour said, a wide smile spreading from her lips up to her eyes. 'Frank always used to call it my love potion.'

*

547

Ten minutes later, Myles and Honour watched Adele running like a gazelle towards the castle with a basket in one hand and a blanket under her arm. Her hair was flowing out behind her like a banner, and even from such a distance they could sense her joy.

'Oh, to feel that way again,' Honour said softly.

'We may not have any passion to look forward to,' Myles said with a little catch in his voice. 'But we'll have excitement enough with a wedding and maybe grandchildren too.'

'I'll be a great-grandmother,' Honour said reflectively. 'Hmm. Not so sure I like that!'

Myles began to laugh.

'What's so funny?' she said indignantly.

'You were always a "great" grandmother,' he said. 'I'm sure that's what Adele would say.'

Lesley Pearse

Lesley Pearse is one of the UK's best-loved novelists, with fans across the globe and book sales of over 2 million copies to date.

A true storyteller and a master of gripping storylines that keep the reader hooked from beginning to end, Lesley introduces you to characters that it is impossible not to care about or forget. There is no formula to her books or easily defined genre. Whether crime, as in *Till We Meet Again*, historical adventure like *Never Look Back*, or the passionately emotive *Trust Me*, based on the true-life scandal of British child migrants sent to Australia in the post war period, she engages the reader completely.

Lesley's life has been as packed with drama as her books

Truth is often stranger than fiction and

read more

Lesley's life has been as packed with drama as her books. She was three when her mother died under tragic circumstances. Her father was away at sea and it was only when a neighbour saw Lesley and her brother playing outside without coats that suspicion was aroused – their mother

She was three when her mother died under tragic circumstances

had been dead for some time. With her father in the Royal Marines, Lesley and her older brother spent three years in grim orphanages before her father remarried (a veritable dragon of an ex army nurse) and Lesley and her older brother were brought home again, to be joined by two other children who were later adopted by her father and stepmother, and a continuing stream of foster children. The impact of constant change and uncertainty in

Lesley's early years is reflected in one of the recurring themes in her books: what happens to those who are emotionally damaged as children. It was an extraordinary childhood and, in all her books, Lesley has skilfully married the pain and unhappiness of her early experiences with a unique gift for storytelling.

Lesley's desperate need for love and affection as a young girl was almost certainly the reason she kept making bad choices in men in her youth. A party girl during the swinging sixties, Lesley did it all – from nanny to bunny girl to designing clothes. She lived in damp bedsits while

Lesley did it all – from nanny to bunny girl to designing clothes

burning the candle at both ends as a 'Dolly Bird' with twelve-inch mini-skirts. She

read more

married her first husband, fleetingly, at twenty and met her second, John Pritchard, a trumpet player in a rock band soon after. Her debut novel *Georgia* was inspired by her life with John, the London clubs, crooked managers and the many

Lesley met her third husband, Nigel, while on her way to Bristol for an interview

musicians she met during that time, including David Bowie and Steve Marriott of the Small Faces. Lesley's first child, Lucy, was born in this period but with John's erratic lifestyle and a small child in the house, the marriage was doomed to failure. They parted when Lucy was four.

It was a real turning point in Lesley's life – she was young and alone with a small child, but in another twist of fate, Lesley met her third husband, Nigel, while on her way to

Bristol for an interview. They married a few years later and had two more daughters, Sammy and Jo. The following years were the happiest of her life – she ran a playgroup, started writing short stories and then opened a card and gift shop in Bristol's Clifton area. Writing by night, running the shop by day, and fitting in all the other household chores along with the needs of her husband and children for seven years was tough.

Some strange compulsion kept me writing, even when it seemed hopeless

'Some strange compulsion kept me writing, even when it seemed hopeless,' she says. 'I wrote three books before *Georgia*, then along came Darley Anderson, who offered to be my agent. Even so, a further six years of disappointments and massive re-writes followed before we finally found a publisher'.

read more

There was more turmoil to follow, however, when Lesley's shop failed in the 90's recession, leaving her with a mountain of debts and bruised pride. Her eighteen-year marriage broke down, and at fifty she hit rock bottom – it seemed she was back where she had started in a grim flat with barely enough money for her youngest daughter's bus fares to school.

Her eighteen-year marriage broke down, and at fifty she hit rock bottom

'I wrote my way out of it,' she says. 'My second book *Tara* was shortlisted for the Romantic Novel of the Year, and I knew I was on my way.'

Lesley's own life is a rich source of material for her books; whether she is writing about the pain of first love, an unwanted abused child, adoption, rejection, fear, poverty or revenge, she knows about it first hand. She's a fighter, and with her long fight for success has come security. She now owns a

> ## She's a fighter, and with her long fight for success has come security

cottage in a pretty village between Bristol and Bath, which she is renovating, and a creek-side retreat in Cornwall. Her three daughters, grandson, friends, dogs and gardening have brought her great happiness. She is president of the Bath and West Wiltshire branch of the NSPCC – the charity closest to her heart.

read more

the books

GEORGIA
Raped by her foster-father, fifteen-year-old Georgia runs away from home to the seedy backstreets of sixties Soho …

TARA
Anne changes her name to Tara to forget a shocking past – but can she really be someone else?

CHARITY
Charity Stratton's bleak life is changed forever when her parents die in a fire. Alone and pregnant, she runs away to London …

ELLIE
Eastender Ellie and spoilt Bonny set off to make a living on the stage. Can their friendship survive sacrifice and ambition?

CAMELLIA
Orphaned Camellia discovers that the past she has always been so sure of has been built on lies. Can she bear to uncover the truth about herself?

ROSIE
Rosie is a girl without a mother and a past full of trouble. But could the man who ruined her family also save Rosie?

CHARLIE
Charlie helplessly watches her mother being senselessly attacked. What secrets have her parents kept from her?

NEVER LOOK BACK
An act of charity sends flower girl Matilda on a trip to the New World – and a new life …

the books

TRUST ME
Dulcie Taylor and her sister are sent to an orphanage and then to Australia. Is love strong enough to keep them together?

FATHER UNKNOWN
Daisy Buchan is left a scrapbook with details about her real mother. But should she go and find her?

TILL WE MEET AGAIN
Susan and Beth were childhood friends. Now Susan is accused of murder, and Beth finds that she must defend her …

REMEMBER ME
Mary Broad is transported to Australia as a convict and encounters both cruelty and passion. Can she make a life for herself so far from home?

SECRETS
Adele Talbot escapes a children's home to find her grandmother – but soon her unhappy mother is on her trail …

'AMONGST FRIENDS'
THE LESLEY PEARSE NEWSLETTER

A fantastic new way to keep up-to-date with your favourite author. **Amongst Friends** is a quarterly email with all the latest news and views from Lesley, plus information on her forthcoming titles and a chance to win exclusive prizes.

Just go to **www.penguin.co.uk** and type your email address in the 'Join our newsletter' panel and tick the box marked 'Lesley Pearse'. Then fill in your details and you will be added to Lesley's list.

---

read more

WHAT ARE YOUR FAVOURITE BOOKS?

My all time favourite is *Gone With the Wind*, but I also loved *The Thornbirds*, *Destiny* by Sally Beauman and *The Divine Secrets of the Ya Ya Sisterhood* by Rebecca Wells. But I also love thrillers, especially Lee Child.

AND YOUR FAVOURITE FILM?

I love *Babe*, the film taken from Dick King Smith's book, and another favourite is *Pretty Woman*.

WHAT IS A TYPICAL DAY LIKE FOR LESLEY PEARSE?

I walk the dogs until about ten. If it's a nice day I do some gardening, if not I write. Both are equal passions so it's not a hard choice. Or shop! I love that too, but not grocery shopping, only clothes, shoes, or trips to garden centres. I don't eat at lunchtime unless I'm out with friends. I don't do housework unless anyone is expected. I often have a snooze at around four, or read a book for research, depending on my state of mind. Then I walk the dogs again and feed them. If some household chores really have to be done, this is the time.

I eat my dinner watching *Emmerdale*, about the only TV I do watch, and then write often till one or two in the morning, by which time the dogs start pestering. Even when they have persuaded me to go to bed, I often read for a couple of hours. I don't seem to need much sleep.

WHAT IS THE BEST THING ABOUT BEING A WRITER – AND THE WORST?

The best time of all is when I've written the whole book, then I go back over it to polish it up. By then I know all the characters as well as I know myself, the agony of sorting out the plot is over, I've done the research. It's a bit like arranging your stuff in a newly decorated room. A tweak here, something added there, and a

read more

few bits taken away too. I could go on doing it forever.

But I also love meeting my readers either at book signings or some functions when I'm giving a talk. It's wonderful to hear how they feel about my work. And curious how they often imagine me quite different to how I really am. In the flesh I suppose I come across as a bold outspoken person, but they are expecting someone much quieter and softer. I think this is because I have almost a dual personality, and the thoughtful side, which comes across in the books, doesn't manifest very often in public.

The worst moments are the absolute panic that I'm becoming boring. Writing is such a solitary pursuit, you know there isn't anyone who can do it for you, unlike decorating or ironing. It's also an outpouring of the inner self, and you could be accused of being self indulgent. When you tell a story in public you get an instant response, whether that be laughter or a few wet eyes, or the audience falling asleep. But sitting alone at your desk, you have no such response. I would sooner give up writing altogether than plod on producing books that weren't entertaining.

WHEN DID YOU START WRITING?

I first started writing when I sent a letter to *Woman's Own* on the contents of my fridge. It held little more than a piece of grey pastry, a curling up slice of ham and one egg. I wondered why it wasn't like ones in magazines with a golden cooked chicken, glossy veg, a juicy ham and a bottle or two of champers. They picked it as their star letter of the week and paid me the princely sum of £25. I was hooked. But it took many years from that first letter to my first published book.

read more

HAVE YOU BECOME FRIENDS WITH OTHER WRITERS?

I know many writers who I count as friends, like Martina Cole, Dee Williams, Jojo Moyes, Jilly Johnson, Jill Mansell and Katie Fforde. I love reading their books, all so different but equally enthralling. We email or chat on the phone, but we don't meet up often, as we all have busy lives. It's great to be able to talk, laugh and grumble with people in the same business, but I have found recently that this need is lessening. I spend most of my time thinking about the book I'm working on, and when I do get out and about, I want to forget about it. So the older I get, the more I fall back on the old friends I've had for donkey's years. They see me as just Lesley, they know me inside out, and they certainly don't want to talk about the publishing industry.

WHERE DID THE INSPIRATION FOR SECRETS COME FROM?

Secrets touches on subjects which were taboo in the period the book was set in. The NSPCC was of course there in the forefront for helping abused children from as far back as 1886. In the 30s and 40s, if a complaint of cruelty to a child was made, 'The Cruelty Man', as their uniformed officers were commonly known, would have called to take the child to a place of safety. Now we have the Child Protection Line. If anybody has concerns about a child being ill-treated, they can call 0808 800 5000 at any time.

Sixty or seventy years ago, any kind of mental illness had a stigma attached to it, and at best it would be alluded to as 'Nervous Trouble' and was virtually ignored – at worst considered madness which led to being put in an asylum. But Rose's problems began with what we'd now call Post Natal Depression, which can

read more

happen to all kinds of women, from all walks of life, regardless of their personal circumstances. It is of course treatable, as is any kind of depression, and if any of my readers feels the way Rose did, or has someone close to them who they feel may be suffering from it, my advice is get medical help quickly.

Likewise, domestic violence is something no one should have to put up with. Women's Aid (www.womensaid.org.uk 0808 2000 247) will offer advice and help to any woman who needs it. The Child Protection Line mentioned earlier will also help with many other domestic problems by passing on the names and telephone numbers of appropriate agencies.

LESLEY PEARSE

If you enjoyed this book, there are several ways you can read more by the same author and make sure you get the inside track on all Penguin books.

Order any of the following titles direct:

0141016965 SECRETS	£6.99
0141006498 REMEMBER ME	£6.99
014100648X TILL WE MEET AGAIN	£6.99
0141006471 FATHER UNKNOWN	£6.99
01410293353 TRUST ME	£6.99
0140282270 NEVER LOOK BACK	£6.99
0140272232 CHARLIE	£6.99
0140272224 ROSIE	£6.99

Simply call Penguin c/o Bookpost on **01624 677237** and have your credit/debit card ready. Alternatively e-mail your order to **bookshop@enterprise.net**. Postage and package is free in mainland UK. Overseas customers must add £2 per book. Prices and availability subject to change without notice.

Visit www.penguin.com and find out first about forthcoming titles, read exclusive material and author interviews, and enter exciting competitions. You can also browse through thousands of Penguin books and buy online.

IT'S NEVER BEEN EASIER TO READ MORE WITH PENGUIN

Frustrated by the quality of books available at Exeter station for his journey back to London one day in 1935, Allen Lane decided to do something about it. The Penguin paperback was born that day, and with it first-class writing became available to a mass audience for the very first time. This book is a direct descendant of those original Penguins and Lane's momentous vision. What will you read next?